W9-BXP-453

Titles by Sara Desai

THE MARRIAGE GAME
THE DATING PLAN
THE SINGLES TABLE

R0202730297

11/2021

PRAIS...

The Marriage Game

"This novel has all the funny banter and sexy feels you could want in a romantic comedy—and, of course, a terrific grand gesture before the happy ending."
—NPR.org

"[An] enticing debut."
—She Reads

"*The Marriage Game* is a hilarious blend of humor, romance, and family."
—The Nerd Daily

"Desai has done a wonderful job showcasing Indian culture—it informs every aspect of the book and makes for a complex and entertaining story. The humor and banter in this book are superb—they had me in stitches in parts."
—Frolic Media

"Desai's delightful debut is a playful take on enemies-to-lovers and arranged marriage tropes starring two headstrong Desi American protagonists. Rom-com fans should take note of this fresh, fun offering."
—*Publishers Weekly* (starred review)

"This witty and delightful story about family, forgiveness, and letting go is utterly satisfying. Desai's first book will be a hit with fans of Sonya Lalli's *The Matchmaker's List*."
—*Library Journal*

"I fell hard for *The Marriage Game* from the moment I read Layla and Sam's dynamite meet-cute. It's a hilarious, heartfelt, and steamy enemies-to-lovers romance."
—Sarah Smith, author of *Faker*

"A writer to watch."
—Bustle

**PALM BEACH COUNTY
LIBRARY SYSTEM**
3650 Summit Boulevard
West Palm Beach, FL 33406-4198

PRAISE FOR

The Dating Plan

"I can't wait for more from Sara Desai!"

—Alexa Martin, author of *Snapped*

"Outrageously funny, meltingly hot and tender, and wrapped up in heartwarming community, this book will warm you in the best ways. Daisy and Liam are just the kind of sexy, joyful magic we need in the world right now."

—Sonali Dev, author of *Recipe for Persuasion*

"A smart, sexy read. If you haven't done so already, prepare to mark Sara Desai as your new fave author!"

—Sajni Patel, author of *The Trouble with Hating You*

"Geek-chic Daisy makes an endearing heroine, and the dysfunctional Murphy family provides believable tension. Desai's fans will be thrilled to reconnect with the eccentric Patels, and new readers will be hooked. This is a gem."　　　—*Publishers Weekly* (starred review)

"Desai returns with another thoughtful, goofy, and sexy enemies-to-lovers plot that explores first crushes, second chances, and familial love."　　　　　　　　　　　　　　　—*USA Today*

"This book is funny, adorably outrageous, and just purely delightful."

—BuzzFeed

"A hilarious, heartfelt romance."　　　　　　　　—Frolic Media

"An incredibly sweet and charming story."　　　　—HelloGiggles

THE
Singles Table

· SARA DESAI ·

JOVE
NEW YORK

A JOVE BOOK
Published by Berkley
An imprint of Penguin Random House LLC
penguinrandomhouse.com

Copyright © 2021 by Sara Desai
Penguin Random House supports copyright. Copyright fuels creativity,
encourages diverse voices, promotes free speech, and creates a vibrant culture.
Thank you for buying an authorized edition of this book and for complying with
copyright laws by not reproducing, scanning, or distributing any part of it in
any form without permission. You are supporting writers and allowing
Penguin Random House to continue to publish books for every reader.

A JOVE BOOK, BERKLEY, and the BERKLEY & B colophon are
registered trademarks of Penguin Random House LLC.

Library of Congress Cataloging-in-Publication Data

Names: Desai, Sara, author.
Title: The singles table / Sara Desai.
Description: First edition. | New York: Jove, 2021.
Identifiers: LCCN 2021018176 (print) | LCCN 2021018177 (ebook) |
ISBN 9780593100608 (trade paperback) | ISBN 9780593100615 (ebook)
Subjects: GSAFD: Love stories. | Humorous fiction.
Classification: LCC PR9199.4.D486 S56 2021 (print) |
LCC PR9199.4.D486 (ebook) | DDC 813/.6—dc23
LC record available at https://lccn.loc.gov/2021018176
LC ebook record available at https://lccn.loc.gov/2021018177

First Edition: November 2021

Printed in the United States of America
1st Printing

Book design by Kristin del Rosario

This is a work of fiction. Names, characters, places, and incidents either
are the product of the author's imagination or are used fictitiously,
and any resemblance to actual persons living or dead, business
establishments, events, or locales is entirely coincidental.

To Kaia, Sapphira, and Alysha
for listening to my stories.

WHEN Zara Patel, hopeful girlfriend of an A-list movie star, entered Peter Patterson's Extreme Paintball Adventure for her cousin's bachelor-bachelorette party, there was a spring in her step, a song on her lips, a cake in her hands, and a celebrity autograph on her arm. Nothing could spoil her good mood, not even the high-pitched shriek of Parvati Chopra, her roommate and long-suffering best friend.

"What happened to your dress? Stacy is going to kill you!"

On a scale of disasters, a stained dress was hardly cause for alarm even if Stacy Jones, the bride's Maid of Horror, did tend to overreact. In the last six months alone, Zara had lost two jobs, three boyfriends, and four tires—stolen off her Caribbean Blue Chevy Spark when she'd been arguing a case in court. She'd also been rejected five times from the Hamilton app, which meant it would be at least another year before she could even try to get discount tickets to see her favorite Broadway musical of all time.

"Chad Wandsworth signed my arm!" Zara turned to the side to better display the bold strokes of the movie star's name etched in black Sharpie on her biceps. "I'm never going to wash again."

"I'm more interested in that stain." An ER doctor at San Francisco General Hospital, Parvati liked to drill down to the facts as quickly as possible. "I didn't think the dress could get any worse."

Her gaze fixed on the bodice of Zara's hot pink '80s-style explosion of a dress adorned with taffeta, tulle, bows, sequins, ruffles, and sleeves puffed so high they obscured Zara's peripheral vision. "It'll be awesome," Stacy had said when she'd informed the bride's friends that they would be wearing secondhand bridesmaid's dresses for the paintball game. Zara wasn't convinced that a cleavage-baring minidress was the best attire for playing paintball in the middle of a forest, but she adored her cousin Tarun and his bride-to-be, Maria Gonzales, so she'd said "yes" to the dress and handed over her five dollars for the thrift store special.

"I was in an ice cream shop. You know I have no self-control when it comes to anything ice cream." She gave a resigned shrug. "I had a milkshake in one hand and the cake in the other when Chad— we're on a first-name basis now—walked in. He's in entertainment. I want to get into the business. I figured I should give him my card in case he ever finds himself in need of an attorney. I put the milkshake on the cake box, reached into my purse, and . . ."

"I can see what happened." Parvati sighed so loudly she startled a couple walking past. "I should have known the temptation would be too much. You couldn't just go in and buy the cake."

"Thank goodness for that," Zara retorted. "And for the fact my dress is standout hideous. Chad would have walked right past me. Instead, being a gentleman, he stopped to help me." She shot an envious gaze at Parvati's sky blue gown. With seven tiers of ruffles, puffed sleeves, and a hoop skirt, she was missing only a pair of glass slippers and cartoon birds fluttering around her sleek dark hair. It wasn't fair. Parvati didn't care for musicals. If anyone should have had the *Enchanted*-style princess dress, it was Zara. Instead, Stacy had punished her with the worst '80s fashion had to offer simply because Zara had accidentally spilled a glass of wine on her at the engagement party when she thought she'd seen Lin-Manuel Miranda at the bar.

"We'd better get the cake to Stacy," Parvati said. "She's already upset that we have to have mixed teams. When she sees your dress she's going to lose it."

Zara followed Parvati through the log building that was the beating heart of the paintball experience. Men in full camo and tactical gear stalked past them, ammo belts strapped across chests, weapons slung over backs, faces masked or painted like they were about to go full commando in the bush. "I thought this was supposed to be a fun, family-friendly activity," Zara muttered. "They look like they're about to go to war."

"Some people are very serious about paintball," Parvati said. "They buy their own custom gear and get an annual park pass so they can come here every weekend. You don't want to be on the field with those guys. They play to win. No mercy."

Zara shuddered as a monster of a man lumbered past, combat boots thudding on the plank floor, his body so heavy with gear he could barely walk. "I'm really rethinking the dress idea. I have a feeling we're going to wind up with a lot of bruises. Maybe even dead."

Parvati looked over her shoulder as the dude walked away. "Or we might find a Prince Charming in need of rescuing. If you see a hot guy with a broken arm or leg, a branch through his eye, a perforated gut, or even just a twisted ankle, text me."

"You're such a romantic." Zara couldn't keep the sarcasm from her tone.

"Romance is overrated," Parvati said. "I work eighty or ninety hours a week. I don't have time for flirting and long dinners. I don't want to waste valuable hours gnawing on an overcooked, overpriced steak in a dimly lit restaurant when all I really want is to get down and dirty."

"Even if he's injured? His performance might be impaired if he's in pain."

"I'll save him, heal him, and then I'll take him to bed." Parvati opened the door to the party room. "The grateful ones are the best. So eager, compliant, and willing to please."

"Cake is here." Zara smiled at the twenty women seated around a long table covered with a white plastic *Be My Bachelorette* tablecloth.

"I thought you'd never get here." Stacy gave a dramatic sigh and took the box from Zara. By some incredible twist of fate, Stacy had managed to "find" a brand-new perfectly sized pomegranate chiffon dress at the thrift store. With a waist-cinching bodice and elegant plunging neckline, the "secondhand" dress accentuated her slim figure and set off her beautiful auburn hair.

Zara gave Maria a quick hug before joining Stacy at the refreshments table where oblivion was waiting in the form of a five-gallon Box-o-Chardoneigh garishly decorated with pictures of galloping horses. She filled two glasses and gave one to Parvati before drinking hers in one gulp, shuddering at the bitter, acrid taste. Maybe the pictures of horses on the box were a hint that the liquid inside wasn't actually wine.

"Oh. My. God. Your dress!" Stacy slapped a hand over her chest like the shock of a stained dress that was imminently going to be splattered with paint pellets might actually stop her heart. "You're all wet."

"I hear that a lot," Zara said dryly. "And never as a complaint."

Parvati choked on her Chardoneigh. Maria laughed out loud. Half-Portuguese and half-Spanish, Maria had gone from street kid to award-winning food-truck chef and was one of the most hardworking people Zara knew. After meeting Maria at her food truck one sunny afternoon, Zara had hooked her up with Tarun. Six months later they were engaged and Zara added another win to her matchmaking scorecard.

Not to be outdone, Stacy grimaced. "What's on your arm?"

"I met Chad Wandsworth at the ice cream shop when I was picking up the cake . . ." She paused, waiting for the information to sink in. Timing was everything both onstage and in court. "He autographed me."

"Well." Stacy huffed. "It's a good thing you're not a bridesmaid. You'd have to wash it off."

Zara mentally marked Stacy as her first target once she got the paintball gun in her hand. "This autograph is forever. I'll be going strapless at the wedding reception so everyone can see it."

"Say good-bye to your chance of meeting someone." A woman in a formfitting strapless green dress with a delicate chiffon skirt and nary a frill or puffed sleeve in sight gave her a tight smile. With big blue eyes, her blond hair pulled up in a perfect bun, she looked like a fairy, all ready to flutter her way into somebody's heart. "No guy will want to compete with Chad Wandsworth."

"Maybe not, but our aunties will be there." Parvati sipped her wine, smiling as if the vile liquid hadn't just scorched its way down her throat. "Nothing can put them off pairing up all the young South Asian singles at a wedding. They have a competition every wedding season to see who can make the most matches. The only way to escape is to secure a quick hookup at the singles table or show up with a plus-one."

"You make it sound like it's easy to find someone." Stacy expertly sliced the slightly melted cake into even pieces. "I mean, really . . ."

"When you've got five hundred or a thousand guests it's easy to find someone—or even a dozen someones—you've never met before."

Zara finished her wine and followed it with a spring roll chaser. "Multiply that by at least five or six weddings during the summer season plus the same number of prewedding parties. Add the lovey-dovey atmosphere of single people all dressed up and eager to get out there and have some hot sex, and the hookup possibilities are endless."

Zara instantly regretted her outburst, but Stacy had a way of getting under her skin. She reminded Zara of her mother.

"Well . . ." Stacy cleared her throat. "I would think most brides and grooms would be upset at the thought of people trolling their wedding for a hookup."

"I'm not talking about me," Zara protested. "I enjoy weddings for the opportunity to match people up. It's just a hobby. I don't get involved in the auntie competition."

"Zara is an excellent matchmaker." Maria beamed. "She set up Tarun and me."

"If you're so good, why are you still single?" Stacy shared a snide look with the woman in green.

Zara opened the spigot to pour herself another glass of wine. "I'm not interested in getting involved in a relationship." Her parents' devastating divorce had taken care of that. One minute she was part of a happy family; the next her world was ripped apart.

Stacy handed her a slice of cake. "That's what people say when they can't find a man."

"I can find men," Zara said. "I just don't need one forever."

JAY Dayal checked his paintball gun and slid it safely into the holster on his tactical vest. Although he'd left his career as a combat search-and-rescue pilot flying helicopters for the air force almost ten years ago, old habits died hard. A holstered weapon was a safe weapon. But once the game began, the blue team would be going down in flames. Whether he was in a boardroom pitching for funding to expand his security company, shooting hoops with his friends, or taking down enemy combatants in a bachelor-bachelorette paintball game, Jay played to win.

"I've split Maria's friends between our two teams." Tarun joined him at the weapons shed where Paintball Pete was explaining gun safety to three women in frilly dresses and heels. Along with Avi Kapoor and Rishi Dev, Tarun had been one of Jay's closest high school friends, as dedicated to his goal of becoming a doctor as Jay had been to pulling himself out of poverty and making a success of his life. They had lost touch after high school when they went their separate ways, but a fellowship opportunity and a new fiancée had brought Tarun back to San Francisco, and they had reconnected, as tight now as they had been fifteen years ago.

"Why not just put them all on one team and we can be on the other?" Jay suggested. "They're just going to slow us down in those clothes." He gave a disdainful sniff when a woman in a barely-there green dress tiptoed across the field, struggling to keep her heels from sinking into the grass. A season pass holder, he visited the park at least twice a month with his business partner, Elias, and had little time for people who didn't take the game seriously.

"It wouldn't be fair," Tarun said. "We'd destroy the other team in five minutes."

Jay suspected that first-time paintballer Tarun would have little part in crushing their opponents, but it was Tarun's day so he just nodded in agreement.

"I know that look," Tarun said with a grin. "Just for that I'm putting Avi and Rishi on my team. You can have a few extra newbs to even things out."

"Tell them not to get in my way. I'm here to win." Jay patted his holster. This season, he'd splurged for the Planet Eclipse CS2 Pro paintball marker, a Ninja compressed-air tank, a Spire III hopper, and a strapless harness pod pack. His mask had a reflecting DY-Etanium lens that shielded him from UV rays and completely hid his face. He preferred anonymity on the field. Better the other team didn't know who hit them.

"I'm here to make sure Maria has a good time," Tarun said. "Go easy on her if you see her in the field. She's here for the game, not your *Mission: Impossible* level of intensity. If you had a girl of your own you'd understand."

"Not interested in getting tied down right now." Jay tightened his harness. "Work takes up all my time, and then you, Rishi, and Avi all decided to get married this summer. You couldn't have given a dude a break? Maybe spaced things out?"

"It should have been four weddings," Tarun teased. "We always did things together."

"Are you kidding?" Jay had always put work over relationships, and his eight years of service in the air force had been the perfect excuse to avoid getting involved. When he'd transitioned to civilian life and opened his security company with Elias, he'd put his drive and focus into making J-Tech Security a success. Achievement was his top priority. Everything else was a distraction.

Tarun grabbed a rental helmet. "Your perspective changes when you meet the one."

Jay's mother had thought she'd met her "one" at the age of sixteen and look how that had turned out. His dad—an exchange student—had returned to England a few months after Jay was born, and his mom's strict Indian parents had disowned her, leaving her penniless and alone with a newborn baby. If he did marry—which was doubtful given the all-consuming nature of his work—it would be after he had taken his company to the top. His future wife—classy, sophisticated, and elegant—would be a reflection of that success.

A shout echoed across the field. Moments later, a woman in a ridiculous froth of pink ruffles came racing toward them, long tanned legs moving so fast her sneakers barely touched the ground. "I'm heeeeere!"

Jay grabbed Tarun and yanked him out of the way. Without even an acknowledgment of the near miss, she barreled past them and into the weapons shed, pulling up inches short of hitting Pete in a full-on body slam.

"That's my cousin Zara Patel," Tarun said, following his gaze. "She introduced me to Maria. Life is never dull when she's around."

"Indeed." With her dark hair in a messy tangle down her back, breasts straining against the tight bodice of her stained dress, Tarun's cousin was everything Jay avoided in a woman—loud, unruly, wild, and totally out of control.

He helped Tarun choose his gear and suit up for the game. They had just pulled on their helmets when the bachelorette party walked past them on their way to the field. Jay sucked in a sharp breath when he saw Zara's weapon.

"Did Pete seriously give your cousin his Tiberius Arms T9.1 Elite?" With a weapon as close to an actual rifle as a paintball gun could get, even an unskilled player could be a formidable opponent. "He wouldn't even let me handle it."

"I'm the groom and he wouldn't let me handle it, either," Tarun grumbled.

Zara pointed her gun at the nearest hay bale and pulled the trigger, missing her target by a good two feet.

"What a waste of a good weapon," Jay muttered under his breath. "Please tell me she's on your team."

"Sorry, dude." Tarun clapped his hand on Jay's shoulder. "She's all yours."

2

"I'VE got the feel of it now. I'm ready to kick some blue team ass." Zara jogged back to her team, joining Parvati and a handful of women wearing various shades of bridesmaid pastel. The remaining members of her red team—all wearing army fatigues, their faces hidden in protective helmets—were practicing on the other side of the range.

"I had a good look at the dudes before they put on their face shields," Parvati said. "Three of them have beards. Two are under five feet eight. One has long hair. That leaves four maybes and six solid contenders, one of whom has been keeping to the shadows under the tree." She raised her hand. "I call the hipster with the hair."

"I thought Stacy didn't want us trolling for hookups."

"She might as well ask me not to breathe." Parvati gave a dismissive snort. "Look where we are. It's alpha central. I'm not going home alone tonight."

"Don't you get enough at the hospital?" Zara protested. "Every day you text me about some intern you've dragged into the break room for a little 'R and R.' It's very inconsiderate. Who do I have at work for an afternoon quickie? A partner who wears Yoda ski hats and carries a custom lightsaber? Another partner who wears bike shorts and Rollerblades around the office? A delusional investigator who pretends he was in the CIA? Or Mole Boy, who only ever leaves his cubicle in the dark of night?"

Parvati shrugged. "You chose to work there."

"It wasn't really a choice. I was desperate. No one else would hire me." After dozens of rejections and an offer from her mother's friend that she was loath to accept, she'd almost given up any hope of finding a firm where she truly belonged until she'd seen an opening for a personal injury lawyer at a small boutique firm. Tony Cruz and Lewis Lovitt didn't care that she'd been let go from two big-city law firms. They were looking for associates who didn't fit the traditional mold, people who could think outside the box and were willing to take risks. By the end of the interview, she knew she'd found her place.

"How about I just check the hipster out for you?" Parvati said. "That's what good friends do."

"I don't want your sloppy seconds. The last time you checked out a guy for me, he couldn't walk for days. Besides, I need to focus on the game." She eyed her camo-clad teammates. "Some of these dudes look pretty serious. I have a feeling they aren't planning to just run around and have a few laughs . . ." She trailed off when a dark shadow blocked out the sun.

"Time to change, ladies."

The stranger's deep, penetrating voice rumbled through Zara's body. Rich and full, it was the kind of voice that made lawyers spill milkshakes and babble incoherently as they thrust sticky business cards into celebrity hands.

"Is there a problem?" Parvati made a show of inspecting her weapon while Zara tried to untie her tongue. Although she couldn't see the dude's face, he was tall—at least six-two—and powerfully built, the top of his coveralls unzipped and tied around his narrow waist. His black T-shirt clung to his broad shoulders and magnificent pecs as if it had been painted on his muscular body. One thick, deeply tanned forearm bunched and flexed as he unholstered his weapon in one smooth practiced motion.

He waved vaguely in their direction. "Not if you want to be covered in painful bruises."

"I've been kicked by horses, bullies, and even by my piano teacher," Zara said. "I've also been stung by a wasp, pecked by a goose, and swarmed by ants. I've broken an arm, a finger, and a toe, and I dislocated my shoulder on a trampoline. A little pain isn't going to slow me down."

Seemingly satisfied by Zara's commitment to winning at all costs, the dude angled his head in Parvati's direction, dipping it ever so slightly, as if inviting a similar assurance.

Parvati fixed him with a stare. "I don't bruise easily."

"Unlike me," Zara interjected. "My ex gave me a small love bite one night, and I had to wear two scarves to work because it looked like someone had been chewing on my neck."

Silence.

"We're not together anymore," she said quickly, assuming he was appalled by her ex's behavior. "Although it had nothing to do with the hickey. Who doesn't like a reminder of a great night?"

Clearly not Mystery Man, because he shook his head. "Not only will your dress leave you vulnerable to weapons' fire, it will hamper your ability to run and hide, thereby lowering our chances of success."

Well, that was one less potential hookup she had to worry about. He was probably one of those uptight alpha CEOs who had made his first billion by the time he was thirty and owned a jet, a fleet of sports cars, a fancy penthouse, and maybe even a red room of pain.

"Have you considered that my dress might be an asset? I could strip down in the forest and distract the opposing team." She checked her paintball pod, opening and closing it with a loud click. "Just so we're clear . . . the bride wants the dresses so we're wearing the dresses."

"Actually, the dresses were Stacy's idea," Parvati said.

Zara poured the paintballs into the hopper and turned away from the officious bastard with the bedroom voice. "Then I'll shoot her first and him second."

If Mystery Man had any further comments, he was forced to keep them to himself when a middle-aged man in a military-style camo vest called the two teams together to go over the rules. *Keep your mask on. No climbing trees. No shooting at the head. It's all about teamwork. No physical contact.* After a few quick pointers, he sent them into the forest for their first game, capture the flag.

"Everyone, pair up." Mystery Man, seeping alpha maleness, quickly took charge when everyone started talking at once. He pointed at people in pairs. "You and you. You and you . . ." He pointed to Parvati and a frail twiglike woman in a yellow satin dress, who gave a betraying blush. "And you and you, sweetheart." He paired off the rest of the team with a few more condescending terms of endearment for anyone in a dress.

What a jerk. Zara didn't need to see his face to know him. He was every cocky bastard who had charmed a woman into his bed and strung her along with promises of a future that was never going to happen. A hunter in his natural habitat. Well, she wasn't prey.

Mystery Man split the pairs into three groups, leaving Zara standing alone. "The front-runners are in charge of scoping out the flag and our opponents' ambushes," he said. "The middle group will cover the front and try to eliminate a majority of our opponents. The back defends our flag and territory. One third of the pairs will run up the middle while the other two thirds flank on the sides. We'll communicate with whistles. Once you step onto the field, I expect you to be focused. We're here to win." He allocated the positions to the teams. "Any questions?"

Zara held her hand up in the air. "What about me?"

"You're on your own."

"Why can't I go with you? You don't have a partner."

"I prefer to work alone." He strode into the forest while the rest of the team spread out and disappeared into the bushes.

"I thought this was all about teamwork," she called out, following behind him. "There are no lone wolves in a team. And just so you know, I used to play capture the flag on the school playground and I always won."

"This isn't school." His deep voice was as clear as if he were facing her.

"It isn't a real war," she pointed out. "It's a game. We're at a paintball field in San Jose that gives a ten percent discount if you buy your paintballs in bulk and charges an extra five dollars to cover laundry fees. Maybe you should lighten up."

He glanced over his shoulder. "Maybe you should stop talking."

"Why?"

"Because I'm not listening."

Zara waited until he'd walked a good twenty feet away before she shot him in the ass.

"What the f—?" He whirled around to face her, his hand gripping the injured area.

"I was helping you on your way." She turned and walked through the bush, using her weapon to clear a path.

"You won't last five minutes," he called out.

"Watch me."

. . .

FROM the safety of her leaf-filled ditch, Zara could see the blue team's flag fluttering in the breeze no more than one hundred feet away. As far as she could tell, most of the blues had been tagged out. She had no idea how many reds were left, but the whistle hadn't blown so the game was still on. Hopefully, someone had shot Mystery Man and put him out of his arrogant, supercilious, alpha male misery.

Inching forward, she grabbed a black tree stump covered in leaves. Shock gripped her when the stump moved. She jerked back, scrambling to her knees for a better look. Not a stump. A boot.

With a bark of irritation, the owner of the boot flipped onto his back and raised his weapon.

Zara's heart pounded in her chest. She reached for her gun in a desperate attempt to stave off the inevitable. Once he pulled that trigger, it would all be over.

"Don't even think about it." Low and menacing, his deep voice froze her in place.

Mystery Man. She should have recognized the cocky tilt of his head and the thick biceps protruding from beneath the sleeves of his shirt. "Down, boy. We're on the same team."

He gave a disappointed snort. "I was hoping you'd been shot long ago."

"Delighted to disappoint. I found a nice cozy ditch, and I've been hiding out while everyone shoots everyone else around me. Now I'm going to grab the flag and take it home for the win." She held her hands up in a mock cheer and whispered, "Zara! Zara! Zara!"

He gave a snort of derision. "It's not your name they'll be calling out."

Difficult, stubborn, and obstreperous. Why couldn't she have found someone fun to hide out with? "Well, it won't be yours. You never introduced yourself. What is your . . ." She trailed off when she heard the sound of branches snapping underfoot, leaves rustling.

He froze, instantly alert. "This isn't the time for small talk."

"Names make communication much easier," she protested. "Instead of yelling, *Hey, you in the black shirt and black boots with the arms like steel pistons, cover me while I go for the flag,* I can just say, *Cover me, whatever your name is.*"

A paintball whizzed past her head, and she flattened herself in the ditch. "I was here first." She waved him away. "Go hide somewhere else."

"I'm not hiding," he snapped. "This is a tactical maneuver. I'm going to ambush the guy behind the tree and take the flag."

"Unfortunately for you, I have dibs on the flag," she said, just because she knew it would annoy him. She wanted to win but not if it meant putting herself in the path of a speeding paintball. With three weddings to attend over the next eight weeks, and a celebrity autograph to show off, she couldn't afford any bruises.

"The person with the best chance of bringing it home should grab it, and that's not you." His head dipped, gaze skimming over her leaf-covered dress. "You'd be a clear target, whereas I can move quickly and covertly through the bush because I'm dressed to blend in."

"I've survived as long as you in my pink dress," she countered. "I plan to take the flag just for the thrill of running through the bush in a blaze of glory with the blue team hot on my heels."

"It's not about having fun." He flipped to his front and inched forward, his heavy body crushing the leaves and sticks beneath him. "It's about winning the game."

"I didn't realize they were mutually exclusive."

"Now you do."

Zara lifted her weapon and aimed it at the unmarked side of his ass. If anybody deserved a second shot it was him.

"I wouldn't advise it," he said without turning around. "Your ammo is better served taking out the enemy."

"That's exactly what I was thinking."

He huffed out an irritated breath and moved forward another few inches. "Follow me. I have a plan."

Amused by his overly serious nature, Zara mirrored his movements. When he moved his left hand two inches, she moved her left hand two inches. When he crawled, she crawled. When his ass—and it was a magnificent ass—wiggled, she wiggled, too. She was almost on top of him when she noticed he had turned his head to watch her.

"Are you *mocking* me?" His voice rose, incredulous.

"Mocking means 'tease or laugh at in a scornful or contemptuous manner,'" she retorted. "I haven't said a word, but I am following you, just as you ordered."

She had been so right about him. He was exactly the type of man she went to great pains to avoid. Arrogant, egotistical, sucking the joy out of life like a black hole.

He held up a hand and pointed forward. "Enemy ahead. Seventeen degrees northeast."

She looked up and laughed when she saw her friend Kamal leaning against a tree, helmet off, his focus on his phone instead of the blue flag tied to a nearby bush. "Why didn't you just say *behind the big tree*?"

"I like to be accurate."

Of course. "If we're being accurate, then he's not an enemy. That's Kamal Chandra. He's the brother of one of my college friends. He's a graphic designer and plays the ukulele, aka a huge disappointment to his desi family. He won't shoot me, so if he's the only one left guarding the flag, then it makes sense for me to get it."

"How do you know he won't shoot you?"

"Parvati said so. She thinks he has a crush on me."

"Who's Parvati?"

"My roommate. She was wearing the blue dress. You paired her up with one of your sweethearts." On impulse, she pushed to stand. "I'm getting the flag. Cover me."

Ignoring his bark of protest, she raced toward the blue flag, leaves falling off her dress as she pounded through the bushes. A paintball whizzed past her. Mystery Man swore. She heard the crack of a paintball gun. The rapid exchange of gunfire. Kamal jumped out from behind his tree, weapon at the ready.

Zara lifted her visor as she ran past him. "It's me!"

"Damn." Kamal lowered his gun. "Pretend I didn't see you. The others will kill me if they knew I let you get away."

"I'll buy you a thank-you drink at the sangeet next Thursday." She grabbed the flag from the bush and turned to assess the forest ahead. One drink at the big dance party that preceded Tarun and Maria's wedding day was a small price to pay to stick it to Mystery Man.

"Two drinks and a dance," Kamal called out when she took off through the forest.

"Done." She heard more swearing, the crunching of leaves, heavy footsteps, and then Mystery Man appeared in front of her, cutting her off, his gun pointed at her middle.

Zara's breath caught in her throat. "Are you covering me? Or are you going to snatch the flag away like a petulant schoolchild and go for the win? If so, I'll warn you that I have martial arts training. I can have your sorry ass on the ground before you know what happened."

"Give me the flag." He held out his hand. "You'll never make it. A straight run is suicide."

"Or what? You're going to shoot me? Your own teammate?" Her heart pounded even though the gun was only loaded with paint pellets, and at most she'd get a little sting. She wasn't a competitive person, but today she wanted to take the flag home, not for her team, but just so Mystery Man didn't get all the glory. His ego was big enough.

Taking a chance, she held out her arms. "Go ahead. Shoot me. Snatch the flag away. If it really is all about the win, you'll do what it takes."

For a long moment they just stared at each other. She could see her visor reflected in his and wondered what she would have read on his face at that moment. His weapon dropped an inch and then another, but before she could be sure he was giving her a pass, a gun cracked the silence and blue paint splattered across his shoulder.

"I got him," Kamal yelled from deep in the forest. "Go, Zara. Don't forget you owe me."

Without hesitating, Zara took off, sprinting through the bush, the blue flag clutched in her hand. It was only when she reached home base to the cheers of her team that she realized her victory wasn't as sweet without the snarl of the man she'd left behind.

3

JAY pushed open the door to the sports bar where the post-paintball party was already in full swing. He'd stayed behind with one of the groomsmen to shoot a few rounds at the practice range, but even that hadn't been enough to release his pent-up frustration. He'd had to put up with Zara's high-spirited energy for the entire afternoon. She had broken formation, sneaked across enemy lines, taunted the blue team with catcalls and dances, and reduced their team to laughing tears with her antics. He couldn't understand why she couldn't take the game seriously. After all, what was the point of playing if you weren't trying to win?

The drive for success defined Jay's life. He never lost sight of the ultimate objective. His experience growing up with a single mom had shaped how he approached any challenge. He crushed obstacles in his way. And yet for some unfathomable reason, he'd let Zara walk—no, run—all over him.

As he looked for Tarun, his gaze fell on a group of women at the bar shouting encouragement while the bartender poured beer down someone's throat with a funnel.

Jay made a derisive sound. He prided himself on his self-control and that meant never getting drunk the way he had in the past. High school had been a difficult time. He'd been angry at his father for not being there, angry with a world that gave little support to hardworking single moms, and angry with his mother's family for abandoning them. He'd gone through a rebellious stage, causing his mother endless heartache and worry. If not for a sympathetic school counselor who had suggested that he enlist to focus his anger on something that mattered, he would have destroyed his life.

One of the women shuffled to the side, slowly revealing the subject of everyone's attention. He caught a glimpse of long, toned legs, pink Converse sneakers, a ruffled dress, and the barely concealed bosom of the woman who had thrown him off his game. Was Tarun aware that his fiancée had such questionable taste in friends? Maybe Jay should warn him before he said *I do*.

Pushing herself up on one elbow, Zara wiped her mouth with the back of her hand and lifted her arms in victory. It was the paintball field all over again. No doubt within the hour someone would have to call a cab to take her home. There was nothing Jay liked less than a person who lacked discipline. He'd fired employees for overindulging at the office Christmas party and covering his desk with photocopies of someone's ass.

So why was he still looking her way?

He searched the crowd for a distraction and spotted Avi at the far end of the bar. His closest friend of the group, Avi had been the first person to stand up for him when he'd been bullied at school. They shared a love of video games, fantasy football, and high-end sports cars.

"Congrats on the big win," Jay said. Avi greeted him with a slap on the back. Shorter than the rest of their friend group and slightly built, he wore his dark curly hair extra thick for the illusion of height.

"I'm surprised you and Zara managed to get through the day without killing each other." Avi grinned. "Tarun said he put you two together to see the sparks fly."

"I'm glad to have amused him," Jay said dryly. "I've never played with anyone so determined not to follow the rules." He could still see Zara at the other end of the bar. She'd survived the beer funnel and was now giving high fives to her entourage. He'd caught only a few brief glimpses of her without the mask over the course of the day, but he could see her clearly now, an outrageously beautiful woman who vibrated with energy. With her dark hair now an unbound mass of curls falling softly around her shoulders, full mouth curved in a smile, dark eyes sparkling, she was the kind of woman who stirred a man's blood. He couldn't tear his gaze away.

"We could use another dancer for the groom squad dance at the sangeet," Avi said, drawing Jay's attention back to their conversation.

"I have two left feet and no sense of rhythm. I don't think I'd be an asset to the group." Jay's mother loved Bollywood dancing. She'd taught him the basic steps when he was young, and they'd danced together at home, often collapsing in laughter when they tripped over each other's feet. Those days had ended when he hit his teens and turned his focus to the man he wanted to become. Successful. Respected. A man who didn't dance or subject himself to activities that would affect his carefully cultivated image.

"You might surprise yourself. Sometimes if you open yourself up to new experiences, you discover skills you never had." Avi followed Jay's gaze to the bar, where Zara's friend was pulling her away from the bartender, who had procured an even longer funnel. "Are you planning to do a funnel? Please say yes."

"Of course not." Jay shook his head. "It's a disaster waiting to happen. No one can metabolize a second pint of beer that quickly. Where's Rishi? He's Tarun's best man. It's his job to make sure no one winds up in the hospital tonight."

"Zara can look after herself." Avi chuckled. "But if it makes you feel better, I'll go ask him to keep an eye on her. I think he's playing beer pong, so no promises."

After Avi left, Jay watched Zara get into position, laughing and chatting with everyone around her. She reminded him of his former copilot JD Hobbs. He'd been a full-throttle kind of guy, performing unimaginable feats of strength and endurance until he crashed spectacularly, putting himself and sometimes the entire squadron at risk. Jay had always had his back until the one time JD really needed him. Now JD was gone and a dozen good men with him. Someone had to look out for Zara. Since Rishi wasn't around, he would have to step in.

ZARA twisted her hand through Stacy's hair, holding it back while the maid of honor threw up in the toilet.

"Beer funnels aren't for everyone." Zara rubbed Stacy's back with her free hand. "You can't expect to get it on your first go."

"You made it look easy." Stacy sobbed into the bowl.

"I've had a lot of practice. My older brother, Hari, used to bring his friends over to our house to do funnels when my dad was out. I hid in the broom closet so I could learn all their tricks." A little white lie. By the time she was sixteen, she was doing the funnels with Hari and his friends, not just watching them.

Stacy retched into the toilet. Zara gathered up the folds of Stacy's dress, holding the torn, paint-splattered chiffon off the floor. She was perversely pleased to see it had not survived the rigors of the paintball game.

"Why are you being so nice?" Stacy drew in a shuddering breath. "I gave you the worst dress. On purpose."

Zara glanced down at her stained, ripped, and paint-covered dress and tried to think of something positive to say. "I think it's a lucky dress," she assured Stacy. "I met Chad Wandsworth in this dress. My team won all the paintball games. And you and I have sort of become friends. Who knows what other lucky things will happen while I'm wearing it tonight?"

"I'm feeling a lot better now." Stacy sat back, resting her head against the wall. "You don't have to stay. I'll freshen up and call a cab to take me home. Could you let Maria know? I don't think she saw my text."

"Of course. But I'll come back and keep you company until the cab gets here." After fixing herself up, Zara ran a quick hand through her hair, trying to smooth down the unruly curls. Unbound and out of control, her hair had frizzed from the heat and humidity of the bar. Even a quick finger-comb and a firm pat-down with a damp paper towel weren't enough to tame it.

A wave of exhaustion hit her, sucking the air from her lungs before she made it to the door. The day was catching up with her. Thank God Parvati had stopped her from doing that second funnel. Bracing herself on the sink, she pulled her emergency energy supply from her purse. No way was she crashing now.

Two handfuls of gummy bears and a stern talking-to later, she pushed open the door. A stranger leaned against the wall across from her, a scowl creasing his breathtakingly handsome face.

"I'll call a cab to take you home."

His voice, vaguely familiar, slid across her skin like dark velvet. Tall and brooding, with a strong, sexy jawline, and the barest hint of a five-o'clock shadow, he wore a black dress shirt that had to have been custom-tailored for his muscular body, hugging the broad expanse of his chest like a glove.

"Do I know you?" And how did he know she had crashed? She hadn't even realized she'd run out of energy until she'd felt the familiar heaviness in her chest. It wasn't a medical condition. Just a physiological quirk that allowed her to push past her physical limits until her body decided it had had enough.

He raised one thick eyebrow in what appeared to be disbelief. Delicious shivers slid down her spine as she assessed his cool, sensual face. His eyes were the deepest shade of brown, dark like the forest floor she'd hidden on before she'd taken a chance to claim victory for her team. A hint of a cleft in his chin and full lips in a beautifully shaped mouth softened what might have otherwise been a severe expression. As his gaze raked up and down her body, her nipples tightened and she crossed her arms over her chest, silently thanking the '80s for her massive puffball sleeves.

"Are you kidding me? We were on the same team today."

She studied him, trying to place his deep voice. Something niggled at the back of her mind, but after a few hours of drinking, her memories were a little fuzzy. "Sorry. Don't recognize you. I'm good with faces. Not so good with masks. Excellent with beer funnels, though, so you can cancel that cab. I've been doing them for years. I've got a special trick where I relax all the muscles in my throat so the beer can slide right down. I could get a fire hose down there and not choke."

"I . . ." He cleared his throat. "Didn't need to know that."

"If you think I need a cab, then you did need to know that." She gestured toward the bar. "I need to find Maria and let her know she's down a bridesmaid."

He lifted his chin in the direction of the restroom door. "Does she need a hand?"

Despite his abrupt manner, the dude had a good heart to go with his looks, Zara decided. He was the whole package. "Thanks, but I've got it under control." She walked down the hallway, acutely aware of the gorgeous man following slightly behind her. "Your concern is a refreshing change from the douchebag I was paired up with on the field this afternoon. Talk about bossy. He thought he knew everything about paintball."

She stopped as they emerged into the bar, hoping he would continue on his way. He was too attractive, oozing power and confidence with every step. For a woman who had sworn off men, he was a dangerous temptation.

"Maybe he did know everything about paintball." He frowned again, his voice clipped and hard.

"I doubt it," Zara said. "Even if he was a pro, I can't stand guys like that. I'll bet he's one of those wannabe military types who spends his weekends playing paintball with his geek friends, pretending he's the real deal. It was sad, really. He clearly wasn't good with strategy. You can't win by doing what everyone else is doing, but he wasn't interested in hearing what anyone else had to say."

"'Wannabe military'?" He gritted out the words like they were a personal offense.

Zara felt a prickle of unease when his brow creased, but it was too late to backtrack now. "You know who I'm talking about. The guys who love the idea of serving our country but don't have the balls to enlist . . ." She trailed off when his scowl deepened. "Is he a friend of yours?"

"Not exactly." He walked slightly ahead of her, clearing a path through the crowd with a calm competence that made her feel curiously safe.

"I've been looking all over for you." Parvati intercepted them a few steps away from the bar. "Maria's going to try the funnel. You have to come and cheer her on."

"I can't." Zara watched Parvati's attention focus on the man beside her. "I have to look after Stacy. She's all partied out for the night."

Parvati held out her hand to Zara's companion. "Parvati Chopra. Currently single."

"Jay Dayal . . ." He shook her hand, his gaze sliding to Zara, lips curling in a smirk. "Otherwise known as the douchebag."

Zara sucked in a sharp breath. Why had she not recognized him? It was all right there staring her in the face. The height. The muscular chest. The thick biceps. And that voice. She'd definitely had too much to drink. "My apologies." She swallowed hard. "If I'd known it was you, I would have kept my opinions to myself."

"I think that's highly unlikely," he said bluntly. "In the short time we've known each other, you haven't kept your opinions about anything to yourself."

Ah. For a moment there, she thought she'd misjudged him. "How's the injury?" Her lips quivered at the corners. "I've never shot anyone in the ass before. Does it hurt?"

His brow lifted. "I don't feel anything."

"How apropos."

Was that the ghost of a smile she saw on his lips? Or the start of another frown? She had never seen him smile, she realized. It was probably a good thing. He was already far too attractive. A smile might force her to overlook his prickly personality and lure him into her bed.

"We've ordered a few bottles of champagne to celebrate Zara's big run to the finish," Parvati said, misunderstanding the situation. "Do you want to join us?"

"Thank you, but I've got other plans." His gaze flicked to Zara, his eyes lingering on her mouth.

Desire, unwanted and unbidden, smoldered inside her. Gritting her teeth, she spoke with a calm that she didn't feel in the least. "None of them even half as interesting as what I'm going to do tonight."

Determined to get away before she lost all self-control, she turned for the bar only to see her aunt standing in the doorway beside a tall, skinny dude with a lollipop head.

"Oh my God." She grabbed Parvati's arm. "Bushra Auntie is here. Someone must have told her about the after-party. I need to hide."

"It's too late," Parvati said. "She saw you. She's walking this way."

An amused smile tugged at Jay's lips. "I'm glad to see I'm not the only one who suffers the attention of matchmaking aunties during the wedding season. Fortunately, I'm only half-desi so they consider me a second-rate candidate."

On impulse, Zara grabbed his wrist. "You can't go. We need you to run interference."

He stiffened and she realized that she'd pulled him close. Too close. She could feel the heat of his body against her skin, draw in his scent of cool dark forests and fresh mountain air. His pulse beat strong and steady beneath her fingertips, sending a current of electricity arcing through her veins.

"You need me." A knowing smirk curved his lips.

Nothing annoyed Zara more than that look of smug male arrogance. She took a deep breath, expelling it softly as she released his wrist. The fog of desire lifted and her mind cleared.

"Actually, I don't," she said in a firm voice. "I had an uncharacteristic moment of panic but I'm over it now. I should have expected my aunts to find me. I'm used to dealing with them during the wedding season. They have a competition each year to see who can make the most matches. No holds barred."

"My mother mentioned their competition." He shook his head. "I never imagined . . ."

"Yes, well . . . Welcome to my life." Tilting her head, she forced a smile. "Thank you for the offer to call me a cab. As you can see,

I'm quite well. Now, if you'll excuse me, I have a potential suitor to meet." Bracing herself for the oncoming storm, she left him by the bar and walked toward Bushra Auntie and the poor man who had no doubt been dragged to the party with the promise of a bride.

"You never told me your mystery man was so gorgeous," Parvati whispered as they wound their way through the tables.

"I didn't know what he looked like when we first met. He was wearing camo and a face mask. Not that it would have made any difference. His difficult personality shone right through." She shot a curious glance at her friend. "Do you want me to set you guys up? You could be my first match of the season. I'm planning to outdo the aunties without letting them know I'm in the matchmaking competition. I wouldn't wish him on my worst enemy, but if you want him . . ."

"He'd be too much for me," Parvati said. "Too brooding and intense. I think I'd be constantly depressed if we were together."

"Who said anything about a relationship? Take him home for a night. See what you think."

Parvati laughed. "He's not a car that I'm taking for a test drive."

"If he was a car he'd be a Lamborghini Huracán Evo," Zara mused. "Pure combustive drama, traffic-stopping looks, and a wild, unfettered soul hidden beneath sensational styling." Zara loved sports cars, not only for their mouthwatering designs but also for the speeds that could take her breath away. "I think he has hidden depths. If he wasn't so grumpy, he'd be intriguing."

"Are you trying to sell me on the car or the man?" Parvati said, looking back over her shoulder. "Because it's not me he's watching right now."

· 4 ·

JAY'S ass was on fire.

Who knew that a direct hit with a paintball pellet on the most padded area of his body could cause so much pain? Not that the investment banker across the boardroom table or his daughter seated beside him would ever guess he was suffering. Jay had been through hell during his years in the air force, enduring every bullet wound, broken bone, cut, burn, fight, and fall without even a whimper. But Christ. Not even the enemy had shot him in the ass. Three days later, the bruise was only getting worse.

He shifted slightly in his seat as his business partner, Elias Woods, wrapped up his presentation on J-Tech Security's financials. Six feet five inches of solid muscle, with a body honed by hauling injured soldiers into airplanes and lifting heavy crates of medical supplies, Elias stood out among the suits no matter how hard he tried to slouch. Jay and Elias had met at a VA clinic shortly after Jay had left the service. Ex-army, Elias had been discharged after he'd been severely injured in a mortar attack. He needed work. Jay needed a partner to help him realize his dream of starting a security company staffed by veterans. By the end of the week, they had a name, a business plan, and seed capital from a generous investor.

Over the years they had expanded state- and then nationwide. With plans for an international expansion in place, they had come to investment banking firm Westwood Morgan Financial to pitch for funding. Jay had handled the sales and logistics part of the presentation, leaving Elias to handle the financials and wrap-up.

Jay checked his watch. A few more minutes and he would finally be able to stand, but dancing at Tarun's upcoming sangeet was going to be out of the question. Would Zara be there? His mind had drifted to his gun-toting nemesis time and again over the last few days. It made no sense. He had no trouble finding women to date. So why did he keep wondering how it would feel to sink his hands into the soft curls of her hair, or to press his lips against her full, lush mouth? Was it because she had defied him at every turn? Or was it the challenge? He was used to being in control—getting what he wanted. Zara was very much her own woman, and she didn't want him.

"Jay? Do you have anything else to add?" Thomas pulled him back to the present. Jay closed the door on thoughts of a beautiful woman racing through the forest in a barely there dress, screaming as she waved the enemy's flag in the air.

"I think Elias summarized it well," he said. "The global market for personal guarding services is projected to reach two hundred twenty-eight point six billion U.S. dollars by 2025, driven by growing crime rates, and the increasing security needs of high-networth individuals and businesses. With a solid national presence, J-Tech is well placed for international expansion with Westwood Morgan's assistance."

"Brittany? Any questions?" Thomas smiled at his daughter, a recent MBA grad who was now interning with her father's bank. Tall and slim, and dressed in a black suit and white shirt, her auburn hair sleek and cut just above her shoulders, she was a female version of Thomas right down to the wide cheekbones and hazel eyes.

"What about the Triplogix lawsuit?" She'd clearly done her research and wasn't pulling any punches.

"It's nothing." Jay waved a dismissive hand. "Our client Triplogix suffered a data breach. They believe someone got past our security guards and entered the building to upload a virus into their servers. We're confident the virus came from outside the building and the people responsible hacked through their computer firewalls. We've got a court hearing next week. Our attorney assures us it will be dismissed before it even gets to trial."

"That's good to hear." Thomas scrawled something on his notepad. "Keep us updated."

"Of course." He shared a quick glance with Elias, who'd spent the last few days at the client's facility working to sort out the mess. They'd been trying to find a bank to fund their global expansion for the last six months and the damn lawsuit was making investors wary. No one wanted to hire a security company that couldn't keep a building secure.

"So, can we count on your support?" Elias's chair gave a relieved creak when he stood.

"It's not just up to me." Thomas walked them to the door with Brittany following behind. "I have to take your proposal to the board. With a strong recommendation from me, however, there shouldn't be any resistance."

Jay heard the message loud and clear. "Are there any other assurances you need? We're open to suggestions. Debt refinancing . . ."

"We don't just look at the financials of the companies we consider for investment," Thomas said. "We look at their leaders. Stability is important. Family. A connection to the community. If your head office weren't here in San Francisco, to be honest, we wouldn't be having this conversation. We're still small enough that personal ties matter."

Jay had no idea what to do with that. He'd always kept his work separate from his personal life. J-Tech's early investors didn't care whether he was married or not and weren't interested in where he lived or how he spent his spare time. They wanted to see the bottom dollar, and if the company could turn a profit then they were happy to provide the cash.

"We are one hundred and ten percent committed to the global success of J-Tech and we'll do what it takes to make this deal happen." Jay clasped the older man's hand, giving it a firm shake.

Even as a child, Jay had understood that hard work and determination could unlock opportunities that could make even the poorest man wealthy. He'd devoured autobiographies of self-made men who had come from nothing and now ran multinational businesses. He'd dreamed of giving his mother the kind of life she deserved—one without the stress of wondering how the bills would be paid or skipping meals so her son could eat the next day. Nothing had made him happier than the day he'd enlisted, knowing he'd finally be able to make some of those dreams come true.

"That's good to hear." Brittany shook his hand just a fraction too long, her gaze holding his until he understood her interest wasn't just business-related. In any other circumstance, Jay might have given her hand a squeeze, met that gaze with a smile. Brittany was the kind of woman he pictured himself with in a far distant future when he'd reached his goal of taking his company to the top. But right now he had no interest in mixing business and pleasure. Not when they were about to take the company global. Not when Zara kept intruding on his thoughts.

"If we do go ahead with the investment, Brittany will stay involved." Thomas opened the door to let them out. "I want her to get to know our clients so she can take over for me when I retire." He put an arm around Brittany and gave her a squeeze. "There isn't anything I wouldn't do for my girl."

"I DON'T trust that dude. He wants something." Elias walked beside Jay through the vast marble-and-glass lobby of Westwood Morgan's office building. Everything from the modern designer furnishings to the Chihuly glass sculptures proclaimed the bank's success. One day, Jay thought, J-Tech would have offices like this.

"He probably wants an equity share in our company or something else he knows we're not likely to give." Thomas was no pushover, Jay reflected. He could see the value in the international expansion and would want to share in the benefits of J-Tech's future success.

"Brittany was checking you out during the meeting," Elias said. "She's totally your type. Sophisticated. Professional. Classy. Smart. She couldn't take her eyes off you."

With a laugh, Jay opened the front door. "Maybe it's you she wanted and she knew you were staring so she had to look at me."

Elias shook his head as he followed Jay out. "Women like that don't go for guys like me. I wouldn't know what to do at a ball or banquet or charity dinner. I've never been to the opera, and my idea of fine dining is all-you-can-eat wings at the bar around the corner."

"You're making assumptions," Jay warned him. "Maybe she spends her weekends backcountry camping and she's the wing-eating champion of the Bay Area."

"No way. Her nails were too perfect. If you're a backcountry camper you keep them short so they don't get in the way." Elias slowed his steps as they approached Jay's vehicle. "You gonna ask her out?"

"I don't have time to get involved in a relationship and I'm definitely not hooking up with the daughter of the man who holds the key to our global expansion. That's just asking for trouble." He unlocked his vehicle. Like everything he bought, he'd chosen the Audi R8 not because he loved it, but because of what it represented. Wealth. Power. Success. Growing up in poverty had made him very aware of appearances. No one bullied kids who wore the right clothes and the right shoes and didn't have to rely on the school to feed them every day.

"He's not gonna turn us down if you're dating his daughter," Elias persisted. "He said he'd do anything for her. You two would make a good couple."

Jay shot Elias a curious look. Elias was clearly attracted to her. So why was he pushing Jay in her direction? "If you want to ask her out, then ask her out. I won't stand in your way. Just wait until after we have a decision about the funding and the documents are signed."

"No way." Elias shook his head. "I'm too messed up for a woman like her. Two years of therapy for my PTSD and I still have nightmares."

Jay had nightmares, too, but he didn't talk about them. Talking made them real and he didn't want his past intruding on his present or affecting his future. He kept the trauma of his last deployment locked away and under control. If that meant he had to keep a tight handle on his emotions, then it was a small price to pay. Nothing was going to stop him from achieving his goal.

"You want to go grab a couple of cold ones and talk through the other investors on our list?" Elias nodded in the direction of the sports bar across the street.

"I'm going to pick my mom up at the daycare and take her for our usual Friday dinner. Another time."

"It's nice that you and your mom are close, but you gotta get out more." Elias pulled out his phone, no doubt to find a drinking buddy for the evening. "The last time I saw you cut loose was when we took that trip to Vegas."

That had been the day Jay's mother had been declared cancer-free. They'd had a quiet celebration at home, but the next morning, overwhelmed with emotion, he hadn't been able to go into the office. Somehow Elias had known what he was going through, and within a few hours they were on a plane to Vegas for a weekend of pure debauchery.

"Vegas was one hell of a good time," Elias said.

"I wish I remembered it."

"I wish you did, too."

JAY'S mood lifted the moment he walked into the Sunny Days Childcare Center. Four-year-old twins Mia and Eve ran to take his hands, and five-year-old Adrian—a born acrobat—climbed on his back.

"How are my little monsters?" he asked.

"We're not monsters," Eve protested. "We're kids."

"I'm a monster." Adrian lifted his head and bellowed a roar.

"Indoor voices, please." Annalise Abbott, the daycare manager, greeted Jay with a smile. "Take Jay into the other room. Miss Padma is reading a story. And keep an eye on him. I recall he had a loud monster voice when he used to come here as a boy."

Worried that Annalise might share some less-than-flattering stories about his years in the daycare center when he'd been young, Jay led his entourage past the brightly painted bookshelves and toy bins to the preschool room.

He spotted his mother in the reading circle with ten toddlers in various stages of attentiveness. Her dark hair, cut into an easy bob, was liberally threaded with gray and fell softly around her face. But her eyes, a deep brown flecked with gold, sparkled with youth despite the first lines of age fanning out at the corners. Exercise and chasing after toddlers had kept her trim over the years, and when she smiled, she looked no different to Jay than she had when he'd been a boy. She wore a red polo shirt with the daycare logo on the back, sturdy running shoes, and a pair of well-worn jeans that had survived everything from runny noses to spilled paint.

Jay hunkered down, letting Adrian scramble off his back before he took a seat on a tiny red chair at the edge of the reading circle. "What story are we reading today?"

His mother grinned. "*The Cat in the Hat.*"

Jay bit back a groan. He had never enjoyed the nightmarish story of an impulse-driven cat who barged into a home determined to have fun without thinking of the consequences of his actions. The only sensible creature in the story was the fish, the voice of reason and order who stayed safely in his bowl and insisted that the house be tidied before the mother got back home.

After story time, Jay watched spaceship battles and car races. He held dolls for their "mommies," fixed broken airplanes, and lent his body to the advancement of children's climbing skills. As always, he was a passive participant, rarely leaving his little red chair, but the children never seemed to mind.

Many sticky kisses and good-byes later, he helped his mother and the rest of the staff tidy away the toys.

"I've invited a friend to join us for dinner tonight." His mother wiped down the kitchen counter. "His name is Rick Sanchez. I met him at a bar after my book club meeting. We've been out a few times and I thought it might be nice for you to meet him."

The skin on the back of Jay's neck prickled in warning. His

mother sprung these surprise boyfriends on him only if she knew Jay wouldn't approve. "What's wrong with him?"

"Oh, darling. You worry too much." She left him to finish up and returned shortly after in a soft black sweater, her hair freshly combed and her lips glistening red.

Jay followed her out the door. "Just tell me he's not a criminal."

"He's a biker." She shrugged on a leather jacket he hadn't seen before and turned to show him the back. "His club is called the Diablos . . ."

Jay's heart skipped a beat when he saw the Diablos patch on the back. "Jesus, Mom! They're a motorcycle club."

With a chuckle, she zipped up her jacket. "They aren't an outlaw club, if that's what you're thinking. They're just regular guys who own Harleys and get together for weekend rides."

"You're not . . ." Jay sucked in a sharp breath, bracing himself on the nearest wall. "Going to ride on his bike?"

Jay had just completed his term of service when his mother was first diagnosed with breast cancer. He had returned home to look after her, determined to ensure she had the best possible care. Until this moment, he'd thought he was over the fear of losing her. But the frantic pounding of his heart said he was wrong.

"I've been on his bike several times already. He can't stand being in a 'cage.' That's what he calls a car."

It took several deep breaths before Jay could speak again. "What happened to that nice accountant who drove a Honda Civic and bowled on Tuesdays?"

His mother shrugged. "He didn't make me feel alive."

"I want you to feel alive and be safe," Jay grumbled. "How am I going to sleep at night if you're riding through the streets on the back of a biker's motorcycle?"

"You don't need to look after me, Jay." Her face softened. "Not anymore."

"It's who I am." He had completed multiple combat deployments in Iraq and Afghanistan as a decorated combat search-and-rescue pilot and tactical officer and then channeled that desire to serve and protect into providing security nationwide. He couldn't just turn it off, especially when it came to the only person he loved.

"It's you I'm worried about." She leaned against the railing that kept the children from running out into the parking lot. "It's Friday night. You should be out on a date, or going to clubs or bars with your friends, not having dinner with your mother. You need to find someone to share your life. What if something happens to me?"

"Nothing's going to happen," he said abruptly. "You got your five-year all clear." His pulse kicked up a notch. "Or are you trying to tell me something?"

"I just need to know you won't be alone," she said softly. "I got through my treatment because I kept thinking, *who is going to love my boy if I'm gone?*"

"Christ, Mom." He swallowed past the lump in his throat. "Don't do this to me five minutes before I have to meet your biker boyfriend."

"I want you to promise me you'll try to find a partner," she said. "Someone who loves you for who you are. Someone who will be there for you. Someone you can love in return." She held up her hand when he opened his mouth to protest. "I know what you're going to say. You're busy with work. It isn't the right time. But I've found something with Rick I didn't even know was missing, and I want that for you, too. Promise me you'll be open to the idea, that you'll make an effort to find someone. No more Friday nights with your mom."

"What about Sunday dinner?" They'd always had Sunday dinner together. Even when she'd been too sick to eat, they'd spent the evening drinking sports drinks and watching old movies on TV.

"We'll still have dinner on Sundays. That's our time. I wouldn't miss it for the world."

Even without the worried niggle at the back of his mind, Jay couldn't deny his mother anything, and she knew it. "Fine." He sighed. "I promise."

The rumble of an engine echoed through the small parking lot, and a heavyset biker drove up to them on a massive Harley-Davidson touring bike complete with sixteen-inch ape-hanger handlebars.

"Seriously?" His stomach knotted with tension. "You're going to ride on that?"

"Stop scowling," his mother said. "I like Rick so I expect you to be polite. One day you'll meet someone who makes your heart sing and you'll realize that life isn't meant to be lived alone."

Annoyed at the concession he'd been forced to give, he folded his arms across his chest. "I like to be alone."

"He has a daughter . . ."

"Mom . . ." Thirty-four years old, CEO of his own company, and his mother was still trying to set him up. "I'm busy building something great. The last thing I'm interested in right now is a relationship, and especially not with the daughter of a man who can't even sit in a car."

His mother didn't understand that being at the top meant he could finally breathe. It meant that when the time finally came to have a family, his children would never have to wonder where their next meal would come from or where they would be sleeping at night. It meant that if someone got sick, he could pay for the best medical care. It meant security, and that was all he'd ever wanted.

"It's not just about a relationship," she said softly. "It's about love."

"I don't need love."

"Everyone needs love." She leaned up to kiss his cheek. "Especially you."

· 5 ·

COMPARED to Zara's previous law firms, Cruz & Lovitt was barely a blip on the Bay Area legal scene. With only two partners, three associates, and a handful of staff, the boutique personal injury firm couldn't afford financial district rents. Instead, the partners had converted the loft of a historical residence in Lower Potrero into a unique modern office space. Zara loved the exposed brick walls and wide-plank wood floors that ran through the reception and kitchen area. Bright, airy meeting rooms had been converted from former bedrooms, and her spacious office had once been a dining room. Furnished with a large black leather couch, reclaimed-wood shelving, and a wide live-edge desk beside a huge casement window, her office would have been the envy of the city associates she'd left behind. Except for her unexpected visitor.

"Why are you sleeping on my couch?" She nudged Faroz Jalal awake. The firm's private investigator had made himself cozy with the yellow throw and pillows she'd bought to match the *Lion King* musical print on her wall.

"It's more comfortable than a cardboard box." He yawned and rubbed a hand through hair cut military short. A former CIA operative—or so he claimed—Faroz wore combat boots buffed to a perfect shine, camo pants, and a tight gray T-shirt that clung to the planes and angles of his lean frame. He was in his late thirties and had been working with the firm for the last three years. "How did it go?"

Zara dropped her laptop case on her desk. She'd spent the morning on a movie set, and the afternoon in a tiny boardroom with her stuntman client and four sweaty insurance lawyers who didn't seem to have heard of deodorant.

"We couldn't come to a settlement so it looks like we're heading for trial." Zara grinned. There was nothing she enjoyed more than litigating a case in court. "I thought taking the insurer's legal team to visit the movie set would make a difference. It's one thing to read about someone jumping out of a burning helicopter; something else to see exactly how far our client fell when his safety harness snapped. But they still weren't prepared to give us what we wanted."

"Did I just hear you didn't settle the case?" Tony "the Tiger" Cruz walked into the office, his lanky six-foot frame hidden beneath a slightly oversized suit, thick blond curls escaping from beneath his green Yoda beanie. A former stuntman, Tony had suffered a career-ending back injury after an accident on a movie set. A bad settlement with the studio's insurers had led him to pursue a career as an attorney. After a few years working for the public defender's office, he'd opened the firm with his friend Lewis Lovitt. Their clients came through Tony's connections to the movie industry, a network of paid informants, and aggressive advertising based on a branding platform that was second to none.

"Looks like we're going to court." Her smile faded when Tony frowned. "Or not?"

"Not." He turned to Faroz and lifted a brow. "Don't you have work to do? I thought you were chasing down a lead for that banana peel slip-and-fall."

"Report is on your desk. The plaintiff is a serial banana peel planter. Five grocery stores this month." Faroz stood and stretched.

"I guess I'll go chase a few ambulances since a man can't even relax for five minutes in this sweatshop."

With a short laugh, Tony waved him out the door. "I heard there was an accident on Central Freeway. You might want to stop by." He enjoyed playing the role of slimy PI lawyer, but he and Lewis operated an ethical firm—no ambulance chasing, crash site visiting, or trawling emergency wards. They were good employers, savvy businessmen, sharp negotiators, legal aid supporters, and fierce advocates for their clients. Zara had no qualms about recommending the firm to her friends and family.

"You don't seem happy about taking the case to court," Zara said after Faroz had gone.

"Trials are long, expensive, and stressful for clients." Tony leaned against the doorframe, one foot crossed over the other. "They're also not cost-effective if we're working on a contingency basis, and there is always a risk that the client walks away with nothing. We hired you for your court experience, but we hoped you wouldn't have to use it."

"So back to the settlement table?" She swallowed the fear that Tony would use this as a reason to let her go at the end of her one-year contract. After leaving her two previous positions by mutual agreement, she'd never get hired by another firm if this job didn't work out.

"Tell Janice to book one of the meeting rooms for tomorrow morning and we'll go over it together," he said. "I've dealt with that insurance company before. They have no interest in going to court. We just need to find the right pressure points." He adjusted the custom-designed lightsaber holstered at his side. A big *Star Wars* fan, he claimed the Force helped him with his most difficult cases, and with his track rate of success, his clients were inclined to agree.

"Thanks, Tony. I won't let you down."

"Lewis and I are taking Daniel for a drink to celebrate his recent settlement. Do you want to join us?" He checked his watch. "He should be here soon."

Daniel King, aka Mole Boy, worked at night and slept during the day as a result of a sleep disorder that he had struggled with since he was young. Whereas other law firms had been unwilling to accommodate an associate who couldn't work regular office hours, Lewis and Tony had jumped at the opportunity to provide twenty-four-hour service to their clients.

"I would love to, but my dad is coming to pick me up for my cousin's sangeet in Carmel Valley." She was grateful for the excuse. Mole Boy's nocturnal existence meant he was socially awkward at best, and the few times they'd been out for drinks together she'd been forced to carry the conversation for both of them.

"Weddings are the best place to find clients." Tony started for the door. "Keep a stack of cards handy in case someone falls on the dance floor or chokes on an oyster. Don't forget to tuck one under the windshield of every car in the parking lot. Who knows what misfortune might befall someone on the way home?"

When he'd gone, she tidied her desk and sent her meeting notes to Janice to put in the file. This was so not the life she'd imagined when she'd graduated from law school with visions of meeting celebrities and doing meaningful work promoting diversity in the entertainment industry. But that path had taken her to two big-city firms that were rife with competitiveness and backstabbing. Cruz & Lovitt had offered her an alternative. Firm believers in work-life balance, and accepting of people who didn't fit the corporate mold, Tony and Lewis had given her a chance to forge her own path in an atmosphere of mutual cooperation.

"*Beta*, all ready to go?" Zara's father walked into her office, a smile on his face. Taller than her by five inches and on the lean side because he often forgot to eat when he was painting, her dad had thick dark hair with only a hint of gray and a beard and mustache that he usually forgot to trim.

"Your receptionist, Janice, told me to come on in," he continued without waiting for her answer. "She was busy playing Candy Crush. I told her to play the fish candy last because they will go for any remaining jellies."

"I'm almost ready." She tossed a few boxes of business cards in her purse, each one bearing a picture of the firm mascot, a growling tiger. Although she had some reservations about handing them out—tigers didn't scream *professional*—she was prepared to do what it took to make herself invaluable to her new firm.

"What do you think of my new outfit?" He held his arms wide, showing off a burgundy Nehru vest over a yellow, floral-printed jacket and matching pants. Zara blinked rapidly, trying to figure out who had sold him such a fabulous kurta pajama and where she could buy a pair of the Kolhapuri chappals he wore on his slim feet.

"It's fantastic. Very you."

"You think the ladies will like it?" He turned once so she could see the colorful embroidered flowers from all angles. "I got it from that new store on El Camino Real. The one between the garden center and the tire shop. The saleslady said it was classy, masculine, but simple at the same time."

He was so delighted with his new purchase, she had to smile. "There's nothing simple about that outfit."

"Simply the best." Her father loved to quote commercial jingles when he wasn't slaying chocolates and licorice whips in Candy Crush, banging on his drum, or painting up a storm in his canvas-strewn loft. "And look." He turned his arms. "She said if I want to grab female attention at the sangeet, I need to roll up the sleeves of the kurta to my elbows. Show a portion of the forearms to look manlier. Women love that."

This time she laughed. Her dad loved the company of women—all except her mom. "The outfit is perfect but this particular woman would like her dad to appear more dad-like. Maybe don't show so much skin. Is that too much to ask?"

"Yes, because look . . ." He held out his foot. "One inch off the cuff. She said the ladies like a turn of ankle, too."

Zara grabbed her travel bag and her lehenga choli from the cupboard. She planned to change at the venue so she didn't arrive all creased. "What happened to that sculptor who was renting in your building? I thought you and she . . ."

Her father waved a dismissive hand. "She took up metalwork. You know what a light sleeper I am, and the loft is open to downstairs. I couldn't sleep with the blowtorch hissing all night, so I ended it. Just in time. I heard she set her last boyfriend's curtains on fire. Now I'm free to mix and mingle as a single, and there's no better place to meet a special someone than at a wedding."

"We'd better get going." She handed him the bag. "Your lucky lady might be waiting for you."

Weddings weren't just a good place to find happily-ever-afters; they were also the best place to find clients. This afternoon's sangeet was about making connections as well as doing a little recon to identify singles for the matching. She only hoped that Tarun's irritating friend wouldn't be there to spoil her fun. Who did he think he was, strutting around in his tight T-shirts and sexy low-riding jeans? Smug, arrogant, and entirely too cocky, he needed more than a paintball in the ass to dent that supersize ego.

She gave a snort of irritation as she followed her father out to his minivan. She preferred the company of men who were open to suggestions instead of just barking orders. Men who would ask questions instead of assuming answers. She wanted a man who could open himself up to possibilities and new experiences—a man who could understand her family's brand of crazy . . .

Except she didn't want a man, she reminded herself. And she especially didn't want Jay.

· 6 ·

JAY had never truly understood the concept of "running the gauntlet" until he walked into the courtyard of the Tuscan winery where Tarun's sangeet was in full swing. Dozens of *rishta* aunties stood between him and the bar, heads swiveling in his direction, noses scenting his single status. To the middle-aged matchmakers, he was fresh meat, and he hadn't taken more than a few steps before the frenzy began.

"What are your intentions?"

"Have you met my niece? She was former Miss Pakistan."

"What are you looking for? Tall girl? Smart girl? I have all girls."

"What job do you do? How much money do you earn?"

If Tarun hadn't been a close friend, Jay would have turned around and walked back through the ivy-covered bower to the parking lot. No one would mark his absence. A sangeet was a celebration of food and dance, and a chance for the families to get to know each other before the formal wedding reception the next day. Jay usually put in an appearance for the meal and left when the dancing started. He had spent years cultivating the image of a successful CEO. He wasn't about to ruin it by burning up the dance floor with his *jalwas*.

"Stay on target, Dayal," he muttered as momentum propelled him forward across the manicured lawn and through the maze of matchmaking aunties. He spotted Tarun inside the restored open-front stone hacienda and changed course, biting back the feeling of doom.

Get a grip. They're just middle-aged ladies. They can't hurt—

"Who do we have here?" Three aunties accosted him only steps away from the door.

"He's Padma Dayal's son." The tallest of the three women checked her phone, without waiting for an introduction. She wore a bright blue sari edged in gold, her dark hair twisted in an elegant bun. "Age thirty-four, single, ex–air force, now CEO of a security company. His shoe size is twelve and he enjoys sports, race cars, and Italian food."

Jay startled at the accurate description. "Do I know you?"

"Mehar Patel." She gestured to her companions. "My cousin Bushra, and my sister Lakshmi."

"I saw him at a sports bar on the weekend," Bushra said, smoothing down her green and orange salwar suit. "I was in the neighborhood with the son of a friend and we thought we'd drop in on Zara."

"You made a match already?" Mehar gasped.

"He wasn't Zara's type." Bushra sighed. "No man is her type. I don't think we'll ever find her a match."

No surprise there. Zara had, after all, shot him with her paintball gun only shortly after they'd met. Still, he found it hard to believe that someone as vibrant and spirited as her was single. He filed that information away for later consideration.

Small and neat, and dressed in a yellow sari edged in silver ribbon, Lakshmi studied him intently. "There's a darkness around him."

"Don't mind her." Mehar patted his arm. "She's the family astrologer. She sees things. Very useful when we're trying to make a match. Not so useful if you're trying to decide what to eat for Sunday dinner."

"I told you not to get the fish at the market," Lakshmi muttered. "That bout of food poisoning was totally avoidable."

"You told me to be wary of fins," Mehar snapped. "I thought you meant people from Finland."

"If you'll excuse me . . ." Jay edged away as they continued to bicker.

"Jungle cats can see through the dark," Lakshmi called out to him. "Don't forget."

After making a quick escape, he joined Tarun, Maria, and Rishi at the bar. He ordered a scotch and soda to settle his nerves and shared the details of his close encounter with the aunties.

"I'm not going to miss those days." Tarun clinked glasses with Jay and Rishi. "I'm done being hunted as prey."

"Have you forgotten that Zara introduced us?" Maria gave him a nudge. "She's like a junior auntie-in-training. If not for her, you'd still be hiding behind potted plants."

Tarun's whole body stiffened. "It was just one time and I'd dropped something under the leaves."

Jay searched the crowd, only half listening as they told the story about how Zara had brought them together. She had to be here. He'd felt a ripple of excitement run through the crowd, a current of energy heading his way.

"Sorry. Oof. Was that your toe?" Zara's voice carried from the doorway, sending an unexpected thrill of anticipation shooting through Jay's veins. She didn't travel a straight path, but was constantly in motion, hugging one person, kissing the next, spinning around to greet some tall blond dude as she swiped a glass of champagne from a passing waiter. Vibrant. Alive. In a way he hadn't felt in years. Maybe ever.

As if sensing his presence, she looked up and caught his gaze just as the crowd parted. Her eyes moved slowly down his body, taking in his blue shirt, striped tie, and dark wool suit. It was just enough time for his brain to register her electric blue choli, cut to reveal her toned midriff and the gentle dip of her waist. Her matching skirt, embroidered with gold and pink designs, skimmed elegant shoes bright with gold sparkles, the same color as the glitter in her hair.

He didn't know whether to smile or scowl. But before he could do either, she gave a disinterested shrug and turned away.

Jay gaped, shocked to the bone. He'd never been given the cold shoulder by a woman before. He was a good-looking man, charming when he put in the effort, fit, and successful. For a moment he wished he'd worn something bold enough to hold Zara's attention—a patterned tie, a pinstriped shirt, maybe even a sweater vest. He had to give himself a mental kick when he realized he was still trying to find her in the crowd.

FOR the next half hour, Jay drank at the bar with Tarun's groomsmen and counted down the minutes until the dancing started so he could quietly slip away. Despite his attempts to put Zara out of his mind, he was hyperaware of her buzzing happily around the bar everywhere except near him.

He was brooding over the insult when Tarun introduced him to Salena Patel, a distant relation who had arranged all the flowers for the sangeet.

Jay didn't know anything about flowers. He and his mother had never had a garden. They'd lived in apartments in the most affordable areas of the city until he'd made enough money to buy her a house. His receptionist, Jessica, ordered flowers for his dates when special occasions arose, and his mother preferred practical gifts for special days.

"They're lovely," he offered.

"I did the flowers for Nasir and Priya, and I'm doing the flowers for the weddings of Layla and Sam and Daisy and Liam."

Jay didn't know any of the people she'd mentioned, although her expectant look suggested he should. Now that he'd exhausted his range of flower compliments, it was a struggle to know what to say. "Beautiful."

"Do you know who is beautiful?" She moved in closer. "My niece. She's a smart girl. Good salary. She has lots of energy. Not like those girls who just sit around all day staring at their phones. Very sociable. And a good heart."

"I'm not looking to get married right now." He shifted his weight, mentally calculating the distance from the bar to the door. If he had a clear path, he could get away in less than ten seconds.

Her forehead creased in a frown. "You have a girlfriend? Fiancée?"

"No."

She adjusted her glasses and stared him up and down. "Are you sick? Injured? Are you not earning? Why don't you want to get married?"

He searched for something to say. "It's not the right time."

"Always the young people say it's not the right time." With a sigh, she shook her head. "Always they think they need to have the perfect job and the perfect house and the perfect car. But no. These things are easier to achieve when you have someone by your side. Someone to support and help you." She turned and searched through the crowd. "Beta." She waved her hand. "Come. There's someone I want you to meet."

Jay cocked an eyebrow at Tarun in a silent plea for help, but his friend just laughed.

"I need to go and rehearse my dance for later tonight." Tarun dropped his voice to a low murmur. "I'm sure you can hold your own against Salena Auntie. She's half your size."

"Get ready," Salena said. "Here she comes."

OH God. Not Jay. Why wouldn't the aunties leave her alone?

Zara forced a smile for the man she had been trying to ignore all evening—a virtual impossibility given that he dominated the bar with the force of his presence alone. Tall and brooding, with a strong, sexy jawline, and the barest hint of a five-o'clock shadow, he was too attractive, too confident, too intense, and from the smirk on his face, clearly too aware of his charms.

"This is my niece Zara." Salena Auntie nudged her forward and launched into a quick summary of her attributes, which included being employed, helping the family, having good teeth, no mustache, and a very healthy appetite.

"This isn't 4-H, Auntie-ji," she murmured. "I'm not competing to win the blue ribbon for best in show."

"And she's funny, too," Salena said with a light laugh. "Just now she made a joke that I'm talking about her like she's a farm animal at the fair."

"Very amusing." Jay's flat tone suggested it was anything but.

Zara closed her eyes and willed the ground to swallow her up. "Jay and I have met. He was at the bachelor-bachelorette party."

"Even better." Salena patted Zara's hand. "Did you tell him your mother is a partner at a big-city law firm? And your dad . . ." She forced a wider smile. "Is an engineer."

"Auntie-ji . . ." Zara shook her head in warning. Her aunties always left out the most important part—the part that scared potential suitors away. "He isn't an engineer anymore. He's an artist and a musician. He'll be playing in the bhangra band tomorrow at the baraat." The traditional Punjabi music was now a feature of many Indian weddings, particularly at the groom's procession on the morning of the ceremony.

Salena clamped a hand around Jay's wrist as if she were worried he'd run away now that Zara's father's shame had been made public. The arts were low down on the list of desirable desi professions. Her father's career change was problematic for the aunties who were desperate to see her wed.

"Jay's mother runs the daycare where Taara Auntie takes her boys," Salena Auntie continued, seemingly unaware of the current of tension between them. "He was a captain in the air force, and now he is CEO of a security company. I didn't have time to find out more about him, but I'm sure he can tell you anything you need to know."

A wave of nausea crashed through Zara's gut when she recalled their conversation in the bar. *I'll bet he's one of those wannabe military types who spends his weekends playing paintball with his geek friends, pretending he's the real deal.* What had she been thinking? But that was the problem. She was always living in the moment, not thinking at all.

"Thank you for your service," she mumbled, her cheeks burning. She could only hope he'd been as drunk as she'd been and didn't remember the slight.

"Pleasure." The deep rumble of his voice made her toes curl. "I'm the real deal after all."

Oh God. She willed the floor to swallow her up. Where was a natural disaster when she needed one? "I'm sorry. I shouldn't have said what I said at the bar. I didn't know you were . . . you."

"I'll leave you two to talk." Salena Auntie clasped her hands together. "I have a good feeling about this. I think I'll be adding another match to my summer scorecard. Mehar won't know what hit her."

An awkward silence followed. Desperate for a distraction, Zara stopped a passing waiter and took a glass of champagne from his tray.

"Drink?" She offered the glass to Jay.

He was enjoying her discomfort, she realized when he smirked. "I thought you preferred beer, or does it hamper your powers of observation?"

"Take the drink," she snapped. "It might help."

"With what, exactly?"

"With your tendency to grumpiness and reluctance to smile." She knew she was being defensive but it was incredibly annoying to have her missteps called out, especially when being this close to him, breathing in his scent of pine and crisp ocean air, made her knees weak and her stomach twist in a knot.

"I smile," he retorted, not smiling.

"At what? A pleasing financial statement? A perfectly polished belt buckle? An employee who shouts *How high?* when you tell them to jump? A paintball team that obeys your every command?"

Jay arched an eyebrow, a superior gleam in his eyes. "We would still have won the game if we'd followed my strategy."

"You're probably right," she admitted with reluctance. "But would it have been fun? Why spend hours crawling through cold damp leaves covered with spiders when you can run through the forest dodging enemy bullets while your team cheers you on?"

He was silent for so long she wondered if she'd offended him. "We clearly have different ideas of what constitutes fun," he said finally.

She tipped her head to the side, considering. "You're still talking to me, so I don't know that we do." Most corporate types would have left by now. They didn't usually like to be teased or challenged and she'd really pushed the limits with Jay. But she couldn't help herself. There was something about him that made her want to take the risk, to dig deeper and see what lay beneath that stoic exterior. No matter the cost.

"When is the last time your heart pounded with excitement, Jay? When is the last time something took your breath away?"

She heard shouts and laughter behind her. Someone bumped into her from behind. She stumbled forward, hands flying up to brace against his chest. Too late she remembered the glass in her hand. And then she was enveloped in warmth.

WHEN Jay had started his weekly visits to his mom's daycare, he'd worn his suit. On the first Friday, one of the toddlers painted a happy face on his bespoke Italian wool jacket. The second week, a first grader cut off his tie. He sat on green paint on his third visit and was drawn into a water pistol fight—Adrian had started it—on his fourth. Given his experience with sartorial mishaps and the fact he always had a change of clothes in his car, a spilled glass of champagne was hardly a disaster.

At least not until his brain registered that Zara was in his arms.

"Watch where you're going." Jay scowled at the dude who had bumped into her, sending him scurrying back to his friends with a mumbled apology.

Willpower and an awkwardly placed champagne flute kept Jay from pulling her closer. She felt right in his arms, her soft curves fitting perfectly against his body. He drew in a breath and the scent of her perfume, sexy and bold, clouded his senses—as did the light brush of her hair against his cheek when she pulled away.

"I'm so sorry." Her breath hitched, long lashes fluttering over soft cheeks. "Let me clean you off." Before he could respond, she whipped off her dupatta and patted his chest.

Jay glanced up, wary of attracting attention. He went to great pains to avoid this type of humiliating situation. And yet he couldn't move. Couldn't breathe. Couldn't think of anything but her gentle hands on his body.

"You don't have to—" His words caught in his throat when her hands moved downward, a light pressure over the ridges of his abs and then across his belt. When the tail end of her long scarf brushed his fly, he silently cursed the salesman who had insisted that pleats were out and tight dress pants were in fashion.

"My dad has this same belt." She polished the buckle and the situation down below became critical. Could he distract her with conversation?

"You mentioned he plays in a bhangra band." His voice was so rough and hoarse he almost couldn't believe it was coming from him.

"Yes." She looked up, the scarf dangling from her fingers. "He almost lost his life in a car accident and had an epiphany. He gave up his career to pursue his passion for art and music."

Passion. Bad word. His body tensed as his blood rushed through his ears like a freight train. He tried to draw deep calming breaths through clenched teeth and made a hissing sound instead.

"It destroyed my parents' marriage." She sighed, balling the scarf in her hand. "It was one of the reasons I didn't pursue theater at college. That and the fact I would have been disowned. Now I have to get my fix by acting in community theater in my spare time and dancing and singing at weddings." She glanced toward the door and the courtyard beyond, where the festivities would take place. "Are you dancing with the groom's squad tonight?"

He steeled himself against regret. "I don't dance."

"Bad experience?" Her face creased with sympathy. "Did you try it one time? Mess up the steps? Were you stumbling around the stage not knowing what to do, and people were laughing, and you were utterly humiliated, so now you're afraid to do it again?"

Jay frowned. "No. That's not—"

"An old girlfriend, then?" She put a hand over her heart, and her dark eyes glistened. "Did you two dance beautifully together until she ran off with someone else and broke your heart? Did you vow you'd never dance again because every time you heard 'The Humma Song' you thought of her and it hurt too much?"

Jay's mouth opened and closed again. He was a practical person who lacked even a shred of imagination. How did she come up with these ideas so fast? "Absolutely not."

"So, you're just insecure," she said. "Otherwise, you'd be dancing tonight to support Tarun."

Bristling, Jay gave an indignant huff. "I'm not insecure."

"Well, then, let's see what you've got." She spun in a slow circle, humming a tune as she rocked her hips and undulated in front of him.

He couldn't take his eyes off her. Had to take his eyes off her. Had to do something because there wasn't enough slack in his pants to accommodate his rising desire.

"Have a little fun with it, Jay. How about some jazz hands?" She waved her hands in front of him.

"I'm not interested in public displays of any kind." He instantly regretted his abrupt tone when her smile faded.

"Of course not." Her voice sharpened. "What was I thinking? You must be desperate to get away." Without warning, she dropped to a crouch in front of him and dabbed her scarf against his thigh.

Pat. Pat. Pat.

His mouth went dry. "What are you—?"

"Just getting those last few drops. It spilled all the way to your knee."

Brain freeze. He couldn't keep up on the crazy road trip from insult to admonishment to sexy-woman-dancing to jazz hands to woman-on-her-knees-with-her-hands-on-his-thigh. Was she trying to seduce him? Confuse him? Tease him? Torture him? Or did she really not understand the effect her position might have on a man?

"Stop." He caught her slim wrist, drawing her up from the ground. "I'll take care of it myself."

"Are you sure? I'd hate to think of you walking around all evening in wet pants. I dated a male model a few years ago and every time I looked at him . . ." She shook her head and sighed. "Let's just say I know from experience how uncomfortable wet pants can be. Sometimes it's just better to go without."

Jay tried to push that mental image out of his head. Failed. The need to flee the scene became a pressing concern. If he'd thought the situation was bad when she was patting him down, it was nothing compared to the thought of all those sexy curves bare under her skirt.

"I don't need your help." He backed away when she lifted the scarf again. "You've done enough."

Zara's shoulders stiffened. "Then I won't take up any more of your time."

He instantly regretted both his words and his sharp tone. But before he could apologize, she turned and strode away.

Buttoning his suit jacket to hide the stain, he watched her work her way through the crowd. If he hadn't been so unsettled by her attempts to clean him up, he would have handled the situation better, he told himself. He had simply overreacted because of the public display.

It had absolutely nothing to do with the fact that she was the most captivating woman he'd ever met or that she made him feel things he shouldn't feel, want things he shouldn't want.

Nothing.

7

B<small>Y</small> the time she arrived at Tarun and Maria's wedding reception on Saturday night, Zara wished she'd made different clothing choices for the wedding events. She hadn't been able to move more than a few steps all day without being accosted by yet another auntie looking to make a match. The fun, flirty outfits she'd worn for the morning baraat and the afternoon ceremony had caused enough problems, but tonight her bright teal lehenga choli, heavily embroidered with gold thread, was attracting aunties like shoppers to a Black Friday sale.

"My nephew Akash is visiting from India. Big, strong boy and only one foot shorter than you."

"My cousin's sister's son just graduated with his Ph.D. in statistics. He reads dictionaries in his spare time. He eats only raw. Very healthy."

"My neighbor's boy is single and is looking for a nice girl to cook, clean, and bear his children."

Dodging and weaving through the crowd in the receiving area, she stopped to chat with uncles, cousins, and friends that she hadn't seen since the last wedding season. With upbeat bhangra music in the background and everyone dressed in their wedding best, it was impossible not to feel happy despite the constant harassment. Weddings were magic and the noisier, the better.

"Here she is. Here she is." Taara Auntie grabbed her cheeks and gave them a squeeze. "We hardly ever see you, beta. Layla and Daisy are around all the time. The boys miss seeing their cousin."

Zara suspected her aunt's school-age boys didn't give a damn about their grown-up cousin unless she was bringing them treats. Her aunt was infamous for her bad cooking, often offering her Indian American fusion creations to unsuspecting newcomers. Her children had quickly learned to scavenge for food wherever they went.

"I've been busy with work." She also made a point of staying away from large gatherings if she knew her mother was going to be there. Although most of the season's weddings were for friends and relatives from her father's side of the family, there were always one or two where her mom would be present. Luckily, this wasn't one of them.

"Come see your aunties." Taara Auntie released her cheeks. "They need a distraction. Lakshmi and Bushra were fighting because Bushra refused to walk in threes when we got here and then laughed at Lakshmi when she said it meant heads were going to roll. Now they aren't talking to each other . . ." She trailed off when Zara moved in the opposite direction.

"Don't you want to see your aunties? They have some nice boys for you to meet."

"Of course, Auntie-ji. But I promised to meet Parvati to check out the seating plan. I'll stop by later." She yanked a bundle of business cards from her purse. "These are for my new firm. Could you hand them out for me?"

"Of course, beta." Taara Auntie studied the picture on the front. "I like it. I'm sure Lakshmi will have a prophecy about the tiger. She read my tea leaves and said someone was watching me. Can you imagine?"

After making her escape, Zara met Parvati at the entrance to the banquet hall. Her friend had changed into a vibrant emerald green lehenga choli, heavily embroidered with silver thread. Ornate silver earrings and a matching choker set off her thick dark hair.

With a sigh, Parvati pointed to the nearest seating chart. "We're at one of the random singles tables."

"A-list with the cool relatives and fun friends?" Zara asked. "Or B-list with the people Tarun and Maria don't really like but had to invite? Not that it matters. I can work my matchmaking magic on anyone."

"Seriously?" Parvati lifted a brow. "I see it as another boring night where we watch everyone at the couples tables having fun and feeling sorry for us because we're stuck with the drunk cousins, divorced uncles, and horny college dudes trying to get lucky."

"You need to be more optimistic." Zara pulled a small makeup mirror from her bag and checked her lipstick. "I see it as an opportunity to match up a few lonely souls and bring a little joy into their hearts or some loving into their beds. I made six matches last wedding season. I want to beat my record."

"You're a rishta auntie in the making." Parvati rolled her eyes in mock disgust. "Why don't you join their pool?"

"I'm not ready for the big time." Joining the rishta auntie competition would be admitting that she truly had no intention of ever getting married, and there was a small part of her that couldn't take that final step.

"Kamal will be happy to hear that you're still available. He's at our table."

Zara bit back a groan. Kamal had been crushing on her since sixth grade when she'd made the ill-fated decision to give him a valentine because she'd heard through the family grapevine that he was struggling to make friends. "You'd better sit between us. He drank one watered-down shot of gin at the sangeet and told me I could feel free to 'take advantage of him.'" She punctuated the words with finger quotes. "Then he asked for 'hugsies' like his mom gives him at bedtime. I almost threw up all over his shoes. How unappealing is that? I can drink five shots of gin and still walk a straight line."

"I thought you were going to say that the part about his mom was what curdled your stomach," Parvati said.

"His mom is kinda hot, so I took that part as a compliment."

Parvati tapped the bottom of the list. "There's a last-minute addition to our table."

"Who?" Curious, she squinted at the list, but Parvati quickly covered the handwritten name.

"The one and only—drumroll, please—Jay Dayaaaaaal!"

Zara stared at her friend aghast. "No."

"Yes. I heard Stacy talking about it. Apparently, he usually sits with his mom, but she invited a plus-one at the last minute so he was banished to the singles table."

Could this night get any worse?

Zara looked around for one of the tuxedo-clad waiters she'd seen carrying trays of champagne. Copious amounts of alcohol were going to be required to get through dinner. "This is going to mess up my plan to match up everyone at the table." She heaved a sigh. "He's too gorgeous. He'll attract all the attention while he sits in smug silence thinking up ways not to have fun. The straight dudes are going to miss out."

"Does this fatal attraction also extend to you or does Kamal stll have a chance?" Parvati grabbed two glasses of champagne from one of the passing waiters and they walked into the ballroom.

"Are you kidding me?" Zara's face twisted in a scowl. "Kamal never stops talking. I can't be with someone who talks as much as me. It's stressful. Every time I open my mouth, I'm worried he's going to interrupt me before I finish what I have to say. And when he is talking, I wonder when it will be my turn to talk. It's different with quiet guys. I don't have to worry. They're good listeners because they only talk when they have something to say and not just for the sake of talking."

Parvati spent a full ten seconds saying nothing while she adjusted her lehenga with her free hand, tightening the waist, smoothing the skirt, and fluffing the ruffle around the hem.

"What is it?" Zara narrowed her eyes. "What's wrong? Your lehenga is perfect. You also know you look stunning. So all this adjusting means you've got something to say that you don't think I want to hear."

"Jay isn't a big talker." Parvati lifted a brow. "He's also hot with a capital *H-O-T . . .*"

"Don't be silly." Zara sipped her champagne, letting the sweet, fizzy liquid linger on her tongue. "He's the last man I would ever want to be with. We have absolutely nothing in common. In fact, he's my complete opposite." He also wasn't interested in her, as evidenced by his abrupt dismissal at the sangeet the other night. She hadn't appreciated his sharp tone when she was just trying to help, especially after the moment they'd shared when he'd held her in his arms. So strong and steady. Safe. For a blissful few moments she'd felt a sense of calm. She should have known it wouldn't last.

Mehar Auntie announced the imminent arrival of the bride and groom and Zara and Parvati joined the crowd near the entrance to the lavishly decorated ballroom. Salena Auntie had gone over the top with the decor. Enormous displays of pink and orange flowers hung from the ceiling over red-and-purple-covered tables and elaborate floral centerpieces. Two pillars bearing replica statues of the Greek goddess Aphrodite flanked the head table, and fairy lights and lanterns twinkled in every corner.

Zara pulled out her phone and snapped a few photos for her wedding folder. Not that she planned to get married, but one day Parvati would meet her special someone and she wanted to be prepared to be the best bridesmaid ever.

Always the bridesmaid. Never the bride. For some reason the words didn't sit as lightly on her heart as they usually did.

JAY pulled out his chair at the singles table and cursed every bhangra band that had ever existed.

If Tarun hadn't hired a bhangra band for his baraat that morning, Jay would have skipped the boisterous, colorful, music-filled groom's procession and put in a few hours of work at the office before the ceremony. But Jay's mother loved the upbeat rhythmic music and there was no way he could make her go to the celebration alone.

If not for that bhangra band Jay wouldn't have noticed that one of the musicians bore a striking resemblance to Zara. The trim, middle-aged man with thick dark hair and a wide smile had amped up the energy with his dhol beats, banging out a rhythm for the dancers in their matching red and purple outfits. He wouldn't have asked the man beside him if he knew the drummer. The man wouldn't have introduced himself as Ajay Singh and they wouldn't have struck up a conversation. Ajay wouldn't have mentioned he was a widower and had planned to skip the reception because he felt too old to be seated at the singles table. Jay's mother wouldn't have offered him Jay's seat beside her. And Jay wouldn't have had to take Ajay's place with the lonely singles.

It was definitely the band's fault.

A woman in a frilly pink dress initiated a round of introductions. A distant cousin with a pointed goatee. A college roommate who looked like he'd been at the bar since it opened. Tarun's colleague from work who had been separated from the rest of her work friends and couldn't sit still. He shook hands with Kamal before he took his seat. The dude had hunted him down at the bar after the paintball game to apologize for shooting him in the back and had bought Jay a shot of whiskey to make amends.

"Zara must be sitting in one of those seats," Kamal said, gesturing to the two empty chairs beside Jay. "I saw her name on the list for our table."

Jay's heart skipped a curious beat. Leaning to the side, he read the fancy script on the nearest card. ZARA. The fates had conspired; whether for or against him was yet to be determined.

Where was she? He searched the banquet hall and spotted her taking pictures of Tarun and Maria in front of the head table. She stood out, even in a room filled with color. It was her spirit, he decided as he watched her dashing back and forth to take pictures from different angles, a sparkle that made her shine.

With her free hand she waved Tarun and Maria into position in front of one of the pillars flanking the table. Tarun took one step back and then another. His back collided with the pillar, knocking the statue out of place. It rocked violently, teetering on one edge before toppling over and hitting the floor with a deafening crash. The statue's head separated from the body and rolled away with the momentum of the fall.

"I'll catch it." Zara's voice echoed in the stunned silence of the ballroom. Pushing past a frozen Tarun, she chased after the rolling head, her skirt hiked up to expose two long, shapely, tanned legs, silver stilettos pounding across the tile floor.

Jay couldn't tear his eyes away. This morning, he'd been dreading the evening. Now his heart pounded with the thrill of the chase, and he felt utterly and blissfully alive.

"Got it." She grabbed the head mid-roll and held it aloft with one hand to the cheers of the crowd.

It should have struck him as odd when she brought it to the table, but he was already expecting the unexpected when it came to Zara.

She introduced herself to their dining companions before placing the head beside Jay's water glass, its vacant pupil-less eyes staring into his soul.

"You again," she said without even the hint of a smile. "I shouldn't have cut my nails this morning."

"I beg your pardon?" Jay was a logical man. Conversations usually started with a greeting, followed by pleasantries and then the small talk he despised but had to learn in order to function as the CEO of a national business.

"Her aunt believes cutting nails on a Saturday brings bad luck." Parvati slipped into the seat beside Zara, nodding a brief greeting.

"You don't mind if I leave Aphrodite's head there." Zara's bracelets jingled softly when she patted the plaster hair. "I don't want anyone to trip on their way to the buffet."

"Was that a rhetorical question?" He shuddered under Aphrodite's sightless gaze. "Yes, I mind. Could you not find someone on staff to take it, or even reattach it to the body?"

"I could put it in your lap. Or would that be too exciting for you?"

Her sharp tone made him bristle. "Is this the part where we talk about how you're the fun one and I'm the stick-in-the-mud?"

Smirking, she stood. "This is the part where I leave you and Aphrodite to get acquainted, because she isn't going anywhere until after dinner."

Before he could respond, Zara was up and hugging a woman at the table beside them. Then she was at the next table, shaking a man's hand. A few moments later, she was twirling a little girl in a pink party dress, and after that she was talking to a woman in a wheelchair. She rejoined the table, launched into a story about her cat that had everyone in stitches, and followed it with a dissection of her ill-fated singles table dates from the last wedding season.

"Who else is wondering *Why me? How did I wind up here when all the cool people are at the couples table?* and *Why am I such a loser?*" Zara raised her hand, her gaze sweeping the table like she was a stand-up comedian onstage. "You don't have to worry. I enjoy matching people up, and with my track record of success, you won't be single for long. You'll also avoid any potentially embarrassing situations like doing the nasty in a supply closet with the supposedly single best man who isn't single, or kissing the groom's twin brother who is actually the groom."

"To be fair," Parvati interjected, "they were identical twins and she didn't know I'd taken the other twin home with me."

"Just be careful what you wish for," Zara continued. "I wound up playing naked chess in a hotel room with a chess grandmaster because I made the mistake of taking off my clothes and saying, *Let's play.* I like chess but after a night of drinking and dancing, *Rook to queen's pawn six* wasn't really the kind of fun I was after."

And then she was gone in a whirl of laughter, leaving Jay with a mind full of images that were not suitable for a family wedding.

"She's going to miss the buffet," Jay pointed out when their table was finally called.

Kamal gazed longingly across the room, where Zara was talking to three aunties in brightly colored saris. "She'll be back. Just make sure you don't stand beside her unless you have a change of clothes."

"As a matter of fact, I do." Jay prided himself on never making the same mistake twice. He'd brought an extra suit just in case he had another sartorial disaster.

"So, what's your poison, Jay?" Zara joined the buffet line a few minutes later. "Let me guess. Something dark and spicy that packs a lot of heat. Maybe a *rista*? Or a *naga* curry?" She studied him, shaking her head. "Hmmm. Not so exotic. I think you're more of a vindaloo. Rich and complicated with hidden depths. Every bite satiates your taste buds and leaves you craving more."

Unsettled by her seemingly casual yet unnervingly accurate assessment, he turned his attention to filling his plate from the lavish spread. Indian uncles used the buffet as their basis to judge whether or not a wedding was a success, commenting and critiquing on the type of food, the spiciness level, the timing of the meal, and the variety of dishes. As he made his way down the line, Jay couldn't imagine they would find cause for complaint. His disappointment came not from the quantity or variety of food but because he had to return to the table before he got to the end of the buffet, due to the insufficient size of the plate.

"My aunt and uncle catered the dinner." Zara joined him at the table, her plate piled high. "They own the Spice Mill. I don't get down to their restaurant in Sunnyvale very often, so this is a treat. Did you get a samosa? No one makes them the way Jana Auntie does."

"I have more than enough." He gestured to his mountain of food, the scents of cinnamon, cardamom, and cloves making his mouth water.

"If you had enough, you wouldn't be devouring my samosas with your eyes." She speared a small samosa with her fork and dipped it in one of the small pots of chutney that had been placed on the table while they were at the buffet. "Eat this. I have four more weddings to attend this summer. I need to pace myself."

"No, thank—"

She cut him off by shoving the samosa in his mouth. Jay had never had the desire to stuff his mouth so full he resembled a chipmunk. Etiquette demanded he not remove the offending food, so he attempted to chew and swallow the delicious potato-filled pastry without embarrassing himself.

"What do you think?" Zara asked.

Jay dabbed his lips with his napkin. "I think it was unnecessary to shove the samosa in my mouth."

"Was it not the best samosa you've ever tasted?"

He gave a begrudging shrug. "Yes."

"Then nothing else matters." She settled back in her chair. "Be glad I gave it to you because they'll be gone before you make it back to the buffet for seconds."

His gaze flicked to the head on the table. "Should I also be glad of our unwanted guest?"

"Unwanted?" Her eyes widened as her voice rose. "She's the goddess of love, fertility, beauty, and desire. Who could be more perfect for a wedding? Although . . ." She tapped her lush lips, considering. "She does have a bad side, but you can't blame her. Who wouldn't have issues if you'd been born from the sea foam created from Uranus's blood after his youngest son, Cronus, castrated him and threw his genitals into the sea?"

The woman in pink choked on her food. The man with the goatee barked a laugh. Jay crossed his legs, although his family jewels weren't under threat.

"She also had many adulterous affairs," Zara continued to her now rapt audience of singles. "Most notably with Ares. So maybe cutting off her head is a good thing." She lifted a forkful of biryani. "Did you know her name gave us the word *aphrodisiac*? Or that her Latin name, Venus, gave us the word *venereal* for venereal dis—"

Jay cut her off with a raised hand. "Not something I really wanted to think about over a meal."

"I think about things like this all the time," Zara said. "My brain never stops. Sometimes I wish it would slow down."

"Maybe if you just focused on your food," he suggested, not unkindly.

"Good idea. It's best when it's hot."

If he thought he'd bought himself enough time to eat in peace, he was gravely mistaken. He had managed only one bite of his meal before she began to talk again, keeping her voice low. "What do you know about the two people on the other side of the table? Do they seem compatible? They had a moment there when she choked."

"I know they're competent adults who can find their own partners."

"Jay." She sighed. "Do you always have to be such a grump?" She tore her naan in half. "I matched Tarun and Maria and many other happy couples. This wedding season, I intend to help a few more sad singles find their happily-ever-afters."

"Did you ask them if they want you meddling in their lives?" He bit into a tender piece of lamb. The korma was seasoned to perfection.

Her smile faded the tiniest bit. "I'm guiding, not meddling. What I do takes a lot of skill."

"There is no skill involved in saying *A, meet B*." He was not usually so disagreeable, but he enjoyed baiting her. Not just because she was always up to the challenge, but because it meant she wouldn't jump up to talk to other people. Although it made no sense, he wanted her all to himself.

"I'm not talking about introducing two random people like the aunties do to rack up their wedding rishta scores," she snapped, her temper rising. "I get to know the person so when their perfect match comes along . . ." She threw open her arms and Jay ducked from the blow he saw coming. "BOOM. It hits like lightning. True love."

"No such thing." He added a spoonful of mango chutney to his plate. "The romantic idea of love involves sacrificing the self with no expectation of reward. We live in a world where people are inherently selfish, which means true love cannot exist."

"Oh, Jay." She patted his arm. "To be so naive . . ."

"I'm a realist," he said. "People get together because of shared interests and not because of whimsical romantic ideals. There is no magic or chemistry. There is no such thing as true love."

His mother said she'd fallen in love with his father after seeing him across a crowded room, and look how that had turned out. If his mother hadn't entertained such romanticized ideas, she never would have married his father only to be abandoned nine months and one baby later.

Zara nibbled on a piece of naan. "I can sense your despair. Don't worry. I'll find someone for you, too."

He felt his stomach muscles twisting in a knot. "I have neither the time for nor the interest in a relationship."

"Finally, we have something in common." She held up her hand. "Give me a high five. Singles forever."

He felt a stab of guilt when he gently slapped her palm. He'd made a promise to his mother to make an effort to find a partner. But he couldn't take what he couldn't give, and he had nothing to offer after the devastating accident that had ended his time in service.

"What about you?" he countered. "A matchmaker who believes in true love but plans to stay single forever? I believe that's called an oxymoron."

"I believe in love and romance for everyone else." Zara

shrugged, her smile fading. "I have a serial-dating habit and poor judgment when it comes to men. The last guy I was with was secretly married and had a kid. Relationships just aren't for me. My life is already full with family, friends, and theater. I've also just started a new job at a law firm, and I need to stay focused so they'll keep me on as a permanent associate."

"You're a lawyer?" He supposed it made sense. There was a certain theatrical element to court, and Zara was outgoing, intelligent, and clearly not afraid to speak her mind.

"I'm with Cruz & Lovitt. We specialize in personal injury." Zara pulled a stack of cards from her purse and handed one to him before passing them around the table. Jay had never seen a professional card with a tiger on it before, but it suited her.

"I'll keep it on file." He tucked the card into his pocket.

"I wanted to be an entertainment lawyer." She gave a resigned smile. "It didn't work out. I did give my card to Chad Wandsworth last weekend and he said he liked the tiger. I'm hoping one of his celebrity friends gets seriously injured—purely for professional reasons—and he says, *Hey, you should call the tiger firm*, and then I'll have a celebrity client, which is one step closer to my dream."

"I work with celebrities all the time." He was having trouble concentrating on his words with her leaning so close. She smelled of honey and cinnamon and the sweet treats his mother used to bring home every Friday from work. "My company provides personal guarding services to foreign dignitaries, billionaires, politicians, sports teams, movie and Broadway stars—"

"Movie and Broadway stars?" Zara grabbed his tie and yanked him forward until they were almost nose to nose. "Names. Give me names. Who have you guarded? A-list? B-list? Anyone from *Hamilton*?" Her full attention was on him now and it was hard not to get pulled into the depths of her liquid brown eyes.

"Our client list is confidential."

"Did you work for Lin-Manuel Miranda?" She tipped her head back and gave the kind of groan he'd only ever heard from a woman between the sheets. "What was he like? Tell me. No. Don't tell me. We're in public and I can't be responsible for what might happen if you do."

His mouth opened but no words came out. He'd convinced himself there was no chemistry between them. But now, with her face only inches away, he was almost overwhelmed with the desire to taste the curve of her lips.

"C'mon, Jay." She leaned close, the gold flecks in her eyes sparkling, her voice a husky purr that he felt as a throb in his groin. Had he ever met a woman with eyelashes so long? He could swear that every time she blinked, they swept over her cheeks.

"Just one name," she pleaded. "One itty-bitty little name for me to fantasize about when I'm alone in bed tonight." She ran her tongue over her bottom lip, slow and sensual. "Or even better, an introduction. I'll make it worth your while."

Jay swallowed hard, loosened his collar. Need, tightly controlled, began to unravel. He knew he shouldn't ask, but the words came out just the same. "What do you mean *worth my while*?"

"What do you want, Jay?" Her breath whispered against his cheek. "What is your greatest desire? World domination? Ten glamor models in a limo? Your own island? An endless supply of samosas? Six blue silk ties? A perfectly balanced set of accounts? A night of hot sex, no strings attached . . . ?"

His mouth went dry. "Are you offering to sleep with me for an introduction?"

Shock chased horror across her face, putting an instant chill on his desire. "I didn't mean me." She gave a hollow laugh. "I'm not that desperate."

His jaw dropped. Was she serious? "You think only a woman who's desperate would sleep with me?"

"No," she said quickly, her lips flattening in a grimace. "I meant I'm not so desperate for a celebrity introduction that I would sleep with someone to get it." She tilted up her chin. "But I could find someone for you if that's what it takes . . . whatever the cost."

He stared at her aghast. "You're going to hire a hooker?"

"Jay." She heaved an exasperated sigh and fell back in her chair. "Why do you always think in extremes? I'm a matchmaker. I can find you a match."

"For a hookup?" His brain was still stuck on "hot sex" and wouldn't let go.

A slow smile spread across her face. "I can do better than that. I'm going to find your perfect match. It will be my ultimate challenge. I will save you from the time-consuming perils of the dating pool and a life of singles table loneliness, all for the low, low price of a simple celebrity introduction."

Jay didn't need a match. He didn't need a girlfriend or a wife or even a hookup. Work was all consuming. His goal was almost within reach. Loneliness was a small price to pay for success. But he'd made that promise to his mother, and now the woman who had shot him in the ass was offering him a way to fulfill it.

He couldn't deny she had piqued his curiosity. And it wasn't just about a match. She had touched something inside him. Something he had buried beneath the darkness that woke him night after night. He could feel when he was with Zara. She had crashed into his life like a hurricane, and after years of feeling numb inside, he was tempted to ride out the storm.

"Hello? Jay? Are you in there?" She rapped his head with her knuckles, and every nerve ending in his body fired at once. "Do we have a deal?"

Even as he hesitated, his betraying mouth was forming the word, "Yes."

"Yessssss!" She pumped her fist in the air. "This is going to be fun. I know that word isn't part of your vocabulary but by the time I'm done with you, it will be."

"That sounds like a threat." Why had he agreed to this? He didn't want "fun." He didn't even want a match. Maybe she'd put something in his wine.

"It's a promise." She bounced in her seat, her enthusiasm almost infectious. "I need to get to know you better so I can find your perfect match. Why not enjoy the time we spend together?"

"Can't I just fill in a form with my details and you find someone with similar interests?"

With a sigh, Zara shook her head. "Jay. Jay. Jay. My matchmaking inventory consists of people I know. I'm not going to hook up a friend or relative with some random dude I just met at the singles table."

"I'm not some random dude," he huffed. "We met at paintball and then again at the sangeet. We've been sitting here talking all evening. I'm a simple man. You've seen all there is to see."

"I've seen the surface. Now I need to see what lies underneath." She gave him a broad smile. "Don't look so worried. I won't take up much of your time. Maybe two or three interviews at most. How about Wednesday afternoon? I'm in settlement meetings Monday and Tuesday, superior court on Friday and Wednesday morning—"

"My lawyer will be in superior court on Wednesday morning," Jay said, interrupting. "We're trying to get a case against our company thrown out of court."

"Perfect. "I'll come to your office Wednesday afternoon and you can tell me about the kind of woman who rocks Jay Dayal's world."

Jay had no idea what kind of woman would rock his world, but the prospect of spending time with Zara alone was not unpleasant. Maybe there was a woman out there who could handle the darkness inside him.

After a quick number exchange, she stood and lifted Aphrodite's head. "I'd better go and turn this in. I told the manager I'd look after it until after dinner. Do you want to give her a kiss for luck?"

"No." He tipped his chair back, holding up one hand to ward her away.

"Just one kiss." She took a step closer and tripped over his foot, falling against him. With reflexes developed through years of military training, he caught Zara as momentum carried them crashing to the floor.

It was only seconds after they hit the ground that he saw a familiar face looking down from above.

"Hello, Mother."

"Jay." She lifted an eyebrow. "If I'd known you were going to have so much fun, I would have sent you to the singles table years ago."

8

THE problem with handing out business cards at big events was that sometimes people crawled out of the woodwork with the oddest stories.

"What was it this time?" Janice asked after Zara had seen her father's third cousin's husband's sister's niece out the door. The firm receptionist was adept at playing Candy Crush on her phone while pretending to work.

"An *Oops, I left it in the body cavity* medical malpractice case," Zara said. "That's the second one today. What's my next appointment?"

"Check the online calendar. I'm trying to finish the level here." Sixty years old, Janice had been fired from her last three law firms because her crude, salty personality and eclectic sense of style had offended the clients. Lean and ripped from intense daily workouts at her local gym, her long hair dyed golden blond, she wore a low-cut pink T-shirt that read, *Don't lick the pole*, from her days as a dancer at the Big Banana strip club on Broadway Street. With only a few years to go before retirement, Janice wasn't about change, but Tony and Lewis were all about giving people a second—or in her case, fourth—chance. Everyone at Cruz & Lovitt had been hired because they had nowhere else to go.

Zara glanced down the hallway. "Tony is coming."

Janice dropped the phone onto her lap, morphing from hard-nosed to helpful in a heartbeat. "How can I help you?"

"Next appointment."

"Taara Patel. I'm guessing she's another one of your relatives coming for"—she glanced over her shoulder at Tony and raised her voice—"free legal advice. What did you do? Set up a billboard somewhere?"

"I passed out hundreds of cards at a wedding over the weekend." She folded her arms. "Why do you always give me such a hard time?"

"Because nothing ever bothers you," Janice gritted out. "It's not normal. Bad shit happens and you just keep smiling. Someone needs to scratch that Teflon coating and show you the world isn't all sunshine and rainbows."

"I know exactly what the world is like," Zara said. "I'm a child of divorce. I've lived through multiple self-inflicted catastrophes, lost two jobs and multiple boyfriends. Just because I choose to stay positive, doesn't make me a bad person."

"Who's a bad person?" Tony asked, catching the tail end of their conversation.

Lifting a brow, Zara glared pointedly at the phone in Janice's lap.

"No one." Janice forced a smile. "We're all good here. Good people. Good times."

Zara briefed Tony on the case on her way back to her office, highlighting that costs might be an issue if the case went to trial. A contingency arrangement in which the firm would receive a percentage of any settlement or judgment at the end of the case was the only option.

"While I appreciate your strong family values," Tony said, "we are running a business here. We need clients who can pay." He pulled out his lightsaber and swished it through the air, filling the hallway with the light and sound.

"Are you threatening to hurt me with your toy lightsaber if I don't bring in paying clients?" Zara already knew he was going to let her take the case. The lightsaber came out only if he was in a good mood.

"It's not a toy," Tony said curtly. "It's a fully functioning replica. And of course I'm not threatening you. That would be illegal and a violation of the state bar's rules of professional conduct. I simply had a desire to get in some practice at the same time we were having a conversation about the importance of balancing paying and nonpaying clients." He flicked the lightsaber off and spun it around his thumb before holstering it like a gunslinging pro. "However, because I just won a bid on Han Solo's belt buckle from the original *Star Wars*, I'll let you take the case on a contingency basis."

"Thank you." Every new case was another step toward making her position permanent, and she was always grateful for a chance to help out family.

"Well done for bringing it in," he continued. "I always love a good *Oops, I left it inside* lawsuit. When the case is over, you can add the scissors to our trophy jars. We've got sponges, retractors, clips and clamps, suction tips, gauze, forks . . ."

"Forks? How would a fork get inside a body cavity?"

"Who knows? Maybe the surgeon got hungry in the middle of the operation. I know I always get a craving for steak tartare when I'm watching *Grey's Anatomy*."

Prepared to meet one aunt, Zara was surprised a short while later when Taara Auntie arrived with Lakshmi Auntie and Mehar Auntie in tow.

"I like your new office, beta." Mehar settled into the chair in front of Zara's desk. "And that man out front in the green hat."

Divorced at thirty-five and now a teacher and Bollywood dance instructor after a change in career, Mehar was always on the lookout for eligible single men. As usual, she was stylishly dressed, her makeup perfectly applied, and her hair cut to accentuate her heart-shaped face. By contrast, Taara looked tired and harried, no doubt from chasing after her two boys. Lakshmi, the family astrologer, wore layers of mismatched clothing, her long hair braided down her back.

"He's not good for you," Lakshmi said. "I had a bad kiwi for breakfast. It means men in green hats should be avoided."

"You just want him for yourself," Mehar huffed. "And the bad kiwi just means you don't know how to pick fruit."

"Stop fighting, you two." Taara Auntie settled in the seat beside Mehar and handed Zara a Tupperware container. "I made a special fusion dish for you. Curried Tex-Mex sauerkraut pickle sea bream surprise."

"It sounds delicious." Hand trembling, Zara took the container. Everyone in the family knew never to eat Taara's concoctions. Zara had heard a rumor that cousin Daisy's fiancé Liam had actually eaten a full portion of Taara's infamous shark stew, but she didn't believe it. "I'll have this for dinner. I was planning on working late so now I won't need to order in."

Taara beamed. "Such a good girl."

"I knew she was going to be a good girl when she was born on a full-moon night." Lakshmi Auntie tugged on her braid. "But her path is not an easy one. Many hills and valleys. Many dark shadows. I did see a goat in Potrero Hill the other day with one green eye and one blue and that means the undead will help lift Zara's burden. Also, kumquats."

"Or your vision means that one of the city's grazing companies has reintroduced the employment of goats to eat their way through the invasive vegetation," Mehar said dryly. "And possibly people are introducing exotic fruit into their diet."

Lakshmi bristled. "Goats are well-known purveyors of the future. The kumquats aren't connected. They have their own path."

"Okaaaay." Zara raised her voice to cut off the runaway conversation train that was heading in a direction she didn't want to go. "So, what can I do for you?"

"This." Taara held out a small black camera. "I was putting your cards on the tables at the wedding and I thought, why not see what you have to say about this problem? I bought a home-security camera to keep an eye on my boys when they're playing in the basement. This camera is the most popular one. I can watch the boys on my app and speak to them using the two-way audio feature. I liked it so much I recommended it to everyone I knew. It seemed to be working fine until the other day a man started speaking to the boys through the camera when they were playing, calling them a racial slur and telling them to engage in destructive behavior."

"To be fair," Mehar muttered, "no one really needs to tell your boys to engage in destructive behavior. I'm still trying to pay off the plate glass windows they broke from your last visit, and my cat's fur still hasn't grown back."

Zara had to agree. Taara's boys were known hell-raisers, quiet only when they were watching their favorite hockey team play. They wore Sharks jerseys, slept in Sharks bedding, and had full-size foam shark costumes to wear to home games. "What happened next?" she prompted to deflect Mehar's mumbled complaints.

"The boys called me, and I went downstairs and confronted him." Taara's voice raised in agitation. "He said he'd hacked our security system and I would have to pay a ransom in bitcoin to stop his cyberattack. I deactivated the camera and called the police. They said they couldn't do anything because they couldn't trace the hacker. So, then I contacted the manufacturer. They said it was my fault for using a weak password." She pulled out her phone and turned it around to show Zara a string of twelve random letters and symbols. "That's the password. There is nothing weak about it. The problem is with their system."

Zara paused in her note-taking. "Were they able to access any sensitive information—bank accounts . . ."

"My children!" Taara leaned forward. "He was watching my children, speaking to them, scaring them, invading our privacy. We felt exposed. And I'm not the only one who's been attacked—Mehar and Lakshmi also had dealings with this man. It's not right. The company shouldn't be allowed to sell these products. Families are at risk."

"Let me talk to the partners and look into it," Zara said, turning over possible causes of action in her mind. "Cases like this are difficult because it's hard to prove you suffered any damage aside from the privacy violation."

After she'd collected their information and completed all the documentation, she stood to show her aunts out but they seemed in no hurry to go.

"We brought you a surprise," Mehar said, grinning. "A big one."

"It's a man," Lakshmi added. "For you to marry."

"You weren't supposed to tell her," Mehar snapped. "That's the point of a surprise."

Zara's blood ran cold. She should have known they were up to something. Taara could have come in to discuss the case on her own.

"Deepa's cousin's sister's nephew was at Krishna Fashions when we went to collect our wedding clothes." Mehar gave her a dreamy smile. "Very handsome. Good to his family. And he is earning. He's waiting in reception. Taara will get him."

Zara glared at her aunts after Taara had gone. "You kidnapped him, didn't you?"

"Of course not," Mehar said. "He had a choice. Dinner at Taara's or a visit to see you."

Taara returned a few moments later, slightly out of breath. "He escaped. We have to track him down."

"Maybe you should take it as a sign that he's not interested," Zara pointed out as they moved to the door.

Lakshmi frowned over her shoulder. "Who wouldn't be interested in our Zara?"

"You'd be surprised. I'm a bit much for most guys." But not Jay. Despite the fact she'd shot him, spilled a drink on him, and knocked him out of his chair, he was still willing to let her find him a match. Nothing ruffled his feathers. He was so cool and collected; she felt she could breathe when he was near. Calm. Safe. It was unsettling. Dangerous. The sooner she found him a match, the better.

· 9 ·

"I CAN'T believe this." Jay opened the boardroom door for Lucia Sanchez, senior partner at Tillbert & Huttle and J-Tech's corporate attorney. She had stopped by after court to discuss their failed motion to have the hacker case dismissed. "First the judge refuses to throw the lawsuit out and now Triplogix refuses to settle."

"I'm not worried." Lucia swept past him and into the hallway of J-Tech's corporate office. Tall, slim, impeccably groomed, and dressed in a fitted black suit and white blouse, Lucia had a reputation as a shark in the courtroom. With J-Tech's chance for international expansion at risk, Jay needed her killer instincts to make the whole lawsuit go away. "You hired the best and that means we'll get rid of this lawsuit before it ever gets to trial."

"That's what you said before the hearing." He knew he was being unfair, but the future of his company—his dream—was at stake.

"I meant it. We're still a long way from trial. Nothing is written in stone."

He hoped that was the case, but the longer it dragged out, the less likely their chances of securing funding from Westwood Morgan. If not for the meeting he had set up with Zara later in the day, he would have locked himself in his office and tried to bury his frustration in paperwork.

"It sounds like someone's having a party," Lucia said as the sound of laughter and chatter drifted down the hallway.

"I'm sure that's not the case," he said firmly. And if it were, heads would roll. J-Tech had already been accused of unprofessional conduct in the Triplogix lawsuit. He didn't want Lucia to think the accusations might be true.

"I can't believe Jay fell out of his chair!" Jessica's voice rang out from reception. J-Tech's receptionist had a distinctive Australian accent and a tendency to speak at full volume.

"He caught me and Aphrodite's head. It was amazing."

He knew that voice. His pulse kicked up a notch as he rounded the corner to the reception area. Zara looked up from her perch on Jessica's desk and smiled.

"We were just talking about you."

Vibrant in an emerald green dress and a colorful scarf, she brightened the modern white and glass reception area, filling the small space with her energy alone.

Acutely conscious of Lucia beside him, he frowned at Jessica and the rest of the administrative staff crowded around her desk. "Why is no one working?"

"It's my fault," Zara said. "I wanted to get a feel for what kind of employer you were so I asked Jessica if I could talk to some of the staff. They had some great stories to share."

"What stories?" It had never occurred to him that his staff might gossip behind his back. Not that there was anything to tell. He arrived at work promptly every morning at seven and left every night at ten. Except for his lunchtime squash games with Elias and his evening workout, he rarely left the office.

"Don't worry about it." She held up a clipboard. "I've got all the notes right here. I'm kicking it old-school with the paper and pen because I can't take good notes on my phone."

Jay introduced Lucia and she shook Zara's hand. "It's nice to see you again. I enjoyed meeting you. I'm sorry it didn't work out."

"You know each other?" Jay asked.

"I interviewed at Lucia's firm," Zara said. "You're in good hands. She's the best when it comes to corporate litigation. What's the case about?"

Jay had no hesitation sharing the details. The case was a matter of public record. "One of our biggest clients suffered a data security breach. We provided physical security for the building. They've sued both J-Tech and their cybersecurity provider, alleging that someone broke into their office and downloaded the virus into their system. There's no way that happened. We've been through the security footage and my men are solid. Lucia was at court today trying to get the case against us dismissed but the judge wouldn't buy it."

"Maybe it was an inside job," Zara said offhandedly. "My roommate's ex-boyfriend Jimmy used to infiltrate companies to steal their confidential information and then sell it to the highest bidder. He's the reason I was so flustered at the interview."

"I did wonder," Lucia said. "You seemed a bit . . . distracted."

Pain flickered across Zara's face an instant before she smiled. "It was a bad day. My roommate, Parvati, had just broken up with Jimmy and had eaten herself into a food coma when he showed up at the door drunk. I had to act as a go-between until the police arrived."

"My goodness." Lucia raised a perfectly manicured brow.

"Jimmy was in the Mafia." Zara shrugged as if Parvati's Mafia ties were no big deal. "I didn't feel safe after he pointed at me through the window and did the *I see you* with his fingers and then drew a line across his throat. The whole horse-head-in-the-bed thing . . ." She shook her head. "I wasn't up for that. I had just bought new bedding and you know how hard it is to get horse blood out of sheets."

Lucia didn't miss a beat. "Actually, I don't."

"It's not easy," Zara said. "So I called my cousin Aamir. He works with the South San Francisco Police Department, and he and his partner came to deal with Jimmy."

Should he shut the conversation down? Surely she didn't want to share fabricated stories with the senior partner of one of the top firms in the city. But what if it wasn't fabricated? What if Parvati really did have a boyfriend in the mob and Zara was familiar with the difficulties of getting horse blood out of sheets? He had to know. "Then what happened?"

Zara heaved a sigh. "Jimmy's on the run now. I think he's living in Florida. He and Parvati sorted things before he left. If he hadn't cut off Aamir's partner's fingers, everything would have been fine. Anyway, by the time I'd cleaned up all the blood, it was late, and I had to rush to get to the interview, which is why I wasn't at my best . . ." She trailed off when Lucia grimaced. Jay took that as a cue to step in for the save.

"I'll just see Lucia out and then we can have our meeting." He moved toward the door but Lucia didn't follow.

"Where did you wind up after interviewing with us?" Lucia asked Zara.

"Cruz & Lovitt." Zara launched into a jingle with a jazz-hands finish. "Sound familiar?"

"Yes." Lucia's lips curved at the corners. "You have the tiger mascot."

"Everyone knows the tiger." Zara handed a business card to Lucia. "In case you ever need legal advice. We're the number one personal injury firm in the city."

"I'm not surprised. Tony Cruz was at the top of our class in law school." Lucia tucked the card away in her purse. "I always wondered where he landed. He was incredibly gifted but he didn't fit into the traditional mold. He had long hair, tattoos, and he refused to wear a tie."

"He still won't wear a tie," Zara laughed. "But he has had a few haircuts."

After Lucia had gone, Jay sent his staff back to work, making a mental note to find out what tea had been spilled about him and how he could prevent such office gossip in the future.

"You're early," he said to Zara. "I had blocked off two hours and forty-five minutes for our meeting, assuming it would start at three."

"I wanted to make sure I had enough time to talk to your staff." Zara shrugged. "I can come back later."

That was the last thing he wanted. She had already brightened up an otherwise bad day. "Lucia's visit was also unexpected, so I had to rearrange a few meetings. It's not a problem."

"I sometimes wonder if I should have accepted Lucia's offer," Zara mused as he led the way to his office. "Her firm has an entertainment law department. I would have met a few celebrities by now, maybe even been invited to the Academy Awards."

Had he misunderstood her conversation with Lucia? "I thought you just had an interview and it didn't go well."

"It didn't go well," she said. "My head wasn't in the game after all that nonsense. You try to do an interview after you've been mopping up blood and running around with an ice bucket collecting severed fingers. I'm still embarrassed by how badly it went."

He slowed his steps as they neared his office, turning to face her. "It couldn't have been that bad if she offered you the job."

"She offered me the job because I was at the top of my class and I'd never lost a case in my previous two firms. Unfortunately, my methods were too unorthodox for them, so we parted ways by mutual agreement. Lucia interviewed me as a favor to my mom when I was struggling to find a new position, and I guess she liked what she saw. But by then I knew I was never going to fit into a big-city firm, so I turned her down to take the job with Cruz & Lovitt."

His brain was still stuck on the severed fingers. "So your story about the Mafia boyfriend was all true?"

"I wasn't about to lie to the senior partner of one of the biggest firms in the city." She scribbled something on her clipboard.

"What did you write?" Curious, he tried to peer over her shoulder, and she turned away.

"I wrote down that you are lacking in business sense." She lifted an admonishing eyebrow. "There's no point burning bridges. I might want to work at Lucia's firm someday. Maybe she'll have a case to send my way, or vice versa. In any event, lies are bad. They come back to bite you in the ass. Remember that."

Jay was fairly certain he would remember every single moment of the last twenty minutes for the rest of his life. And they had another two hours and twenty-five minutes of their allotted appointment time to spend together. He felt a curious sensation in his chest. Something he hadn't felt since he was boy on Christmas Eve. It took him a moment to identify it as excitement.

"Would you like to come in and see my office?" He stepped to the side to allow her to pass.

"Actually, I'd like to see your restroom."

Puzzled, he frowned. "What could you possibly learn about me in the restroom?"

"I would find out whether or not you provide toilets for your guests who need to pee."

Mortified by his misstep, he directed her to the restroom and returned to his office. He had only just finished checking his e-mails when Zara walked in the door. "So, this is how the other half lives."

"I don't live here," he said. "I work here."

"Not according to your staff. They say you're here all hours of the day and night and also on the weekends. They also said that your couch has a pullout bed for quick naps, and that you have extra suits and ties in your wardrobe, and folded shirts in your desk drawer. No one mentioned boxers but I do hope you have a fresh supply so you don't have to reuse the same pair."

He gave an affronted sniff. "Certainly not."

Zara wrote on her clipboard and again his curiosity was piqued. "Now what are you writing?"

"You're very nosy. I'm going write that down after I finish making a note to find someone for you who doesn't require much time and attention. Recreation and social time are clearly not a priority in your life. The human equivalent of a succulent would be best."

Jay leaned back in his chair and folded his arms across his chest. "You want to match me up with a succulent?"

"A human succulent. Prickly. Resilient. Able to survive hot climates, cold temperaments, and emotional drought. Sprinkle a few e-mails on her, maybe buy her a lunch, and that should keep her going through the long cold months."

"You think I'm hot," he said, his voice smug. For some reason her opinion mattered to him, all the negativity aside.

"You know you are or you wouldn't be puffing out your chest." She made another note and looked up just as he opened his mouth. "Don't even ask."

"What's next?" Jay inquired. The time was going far too quickly. "What else do you need to see to get to know me?"

"Your apartment was on my list but now that I see your office with its minimalist vibe, your painfully tidy desk, and lack of personal items, I'll just ask: Is your apartment sparsely furnished with only the essentials—I'm talking couch, coffee table, maybe a chair, TV, bed, dresser, kitchen table, and chairs?"

"Yes."

"No paintings on the walls, decor, ornaments, books, throw pillows, blankets, pictures, statues, magazines, newspapers, signs of life, or anything that might reflect your personality, such as it is?"

Jay shifted uncomfortably in his seat. "No. I don't spend a lot of time there. It's just mainly to sleep."

"Good. Then we don't need to waste time visiting your place," she said. "I'm in your head, Jay. I'm walking all around in there. Another day or two and I'll know you as well as I know myself."

His stomach tightened at the thought of Zara breaching his walls and seeing what lay beneath. Would she still want to find him a match when she found out he was responsible for the deaths of twelve men? And what about the nightmares? There was a reason he never asked his hookups to spend the night.

"I think we should go for a stroll." She walked slowly around the room, inspecting the abstract pictures on the walls—he'd left the decor to the company's interior designer. "I'd like to see how you interact with the common people."

"They're just people. Same as me."

Zara pulled open his closet door and peered inside. "What are these?"

Jay shut down his computer and crossed the room to see what had caught her attention.

"Company uniform. Elias and I used to work every event, but after we expanded nationally, we hired a local team so we could focus on running the business."

"You get plus marks for that." Zara smiled. "Women love a man in uniform."

Did she love a man in uniform? The question sneaked into his brain like the paparazzi sneaked into the celebrity events J-Tech was hired to protect.

"Do you still have your uniform from when you were in service?" She closed the door and made another note on her clipboard. "I asked around about you at the wedding. Eight years in the air force. Multiple combat deployments in Iraq and Afghanistan. Decorated combat search-and-rescue pilot and—"

He could almost feel a steel door slam down in his mind. "That part of my life is over and not on the table for discussion."

"I'm so sorry. I shouldn't have asked." Her smile faded, and he immediately regretted his abrupt tone.

"Where would you like to go?" He straightened his tie and stepped away from her soft, agile body and her seductive floral scent.

"I don't like to make plans." Her smile returned, beating back the gray clouds that had rolled in when she'd brought up his past. "Let's see where the wind takes us, so long as it takes us to food."

"I DON'T usually eat at this time." Jay unwrapped his hot dog and settled on the grass beside Zara on the lawn in Yerba Buena Gardens. "I have also never come to this park and I don't usually sit on the grass."

"You're almost like an alien." Zara took a small bite of her hot dog, desperately trying not to get ketchup all over her mouth. Despite his uptight demeanor, Jay had been surprisingly willing to follow her through the city streets in search of the perfect hot dog, answering her questions about his work and the celebrity parties he'd guarded—no names disclosed, of course. She'd felt safe with Jay, free to talk without having to worry about everything around her. He ushered people out of her path with a wave of his arm. His gentle hand on her back steered her around fire hydrants, dogs, strollers, and small children and pulled her to a stop at traffic lights. He was like a watchful guardian angel.

And now here he was sitting on the grass on a sunny afternoon in his expensive wool suit, eating a hot dog like he'd never tasted anything better in his life.

"Slow down there, buddy," she teased. "You don't know what our Earth food might do to your system."

Jay finished his last bite and dabbed his lips with the paper napkin. "I now have the energy to continue my quest for world domination."

Zara's head jerked up and she gave him a steady look. "Did you just tell a joke?"

"No." His face froze with a guilty expression. "I don't tell jokes."

"That sounded suspiciously like an attempt to be funny. I'll write down that you have a nascent sense of humor but it's hidden beneath your cold, icy exterior."

"Very eloquent," he said dryly.

Zara looked up and grinned. "I learned all sorts of big words in law school. How about these? *Hobbies and activities.* Go."

Jay stretched his legs out in front of him. His face was softer now, his body less tense. She liked to think she'd helped him loosen up, because the more time she spent with him the more she suspected what he showed on the surface was only the tip of the Jay Dayal iceberg.

"Paintball with my business partner once or twice a month.

Lifting weights at the gym. The occasional early-morning run. Squash . . ."

Zara's pen flew over her clipboard. "Anything that does not involve physical activity? Not that I'm against physical activity. On occasion I have been known to go for a run or do a spin class at the gym. But just listening to you is exhausting."

"On a sunny day I'll take a pile of unread *Economist*s and sit on my balcony with a glass of wine—"

"Stop." She held up her hand. "I'm not writing that one down. The idea is to find you a match, not bore them to death. How about something fun?"

"That is fun."

Zara sighed. "Normal fun."

"I go to the San Francisco Auto Show every year," he offered.

"Now we're talking. I used to go to the show with my dad and older brother, Hari, until he moved to San Diego to get away from our dysfunctional family. Now I just go with my dad. We both love cars. He was horrified when I told him about a case I had the other week. I got to visit a movie set and watch a man jump out of a helicopter, set himself on fire, and then drive a car into a wall. It was amazing."

"The case or the burning man?" He leaned back on his elbows, one foot crossed over the other. A lion in repose. If he got any more chilled, he'd probably fall asleep. Not that it would be a bad thing. Then she could check him out properly instead of shooting surreptitious glances from beneath her eyelashes. He was the most gorgeous man she'd ever met. Perfect hair. Perfect body. Perfect face. All he needed to do was smile and she wouldn't have to find him a match; her friends would be begging her for an introduction. The thought didn't please her the way it should have. Perhaps she needed to spend more time with him, narrow the field to ensure she found the right woman instead of making the easy choice.

"The sports car," she said, tearing her gaze away before she started contemplating the likelihood that his perfection extended below the belt. "It was a Ford GT. It crumpled like a piece of tinfoil. I had planned to buy one when I won the lottery, but now I'll have to go for the Lamborghini Aventador S. It's a beast."

He lifted a brow. "You know your cars."

"It's important to know your dream car, especially if you win the lottery. People like details. It's so boring when lottery winners say they're going to take a vacation, or buy a new car, or build their dream home. Which car? Where is the new house going to be? How many bedrooms? Where are you going on vacation? Are you going to quit your job? They always say *no* but invariably they do."

She was talking too much. She had a tendency to run on when she was nervous, and Jay lying in the sun, jacket and tie off, made her feel uncharacteristically self-conscious. Usually she didn't care if there was a dab of lipstick on her cheek or if she overshared personal information, but he was so calm and in control, so solid and stable, she didn't want him to see the hot mess she usually was. "Would you quit your job if you won the lottery?" she asked to turn the focus of the conversation back on him.

"I built my company so I can hardly walk away." He lay back on the grass, hands now behind his head, his broad chest and hard pecs now fully on display. Drool became a bigger concern than ketchup and she held her napkin to her lips. She had a sudden urge to stretch out beside him and rest her head on his chest. He would curve one strong arm around her, lean down, and . . .

"Is something wrong? You're staring into space."

Zara shook herself out of her daydream. She really needed to get a grip. What kind of matchmaker fantasized about her own clients? She was done with relationships. Her breakup with her ex Javier had finally woken her to the fact that her parents' divorce had made her unable to form healthy attachments. Her new therapist, Catherine, thought she had a fear of abandonment. All Zara knew was that she never wanted to experience the loss and devastation she'd felt when her family had been ripped apart, when she'd learned the lesson that marriage wasn't forever and love could stop.

"So what are you looking for in the future Mrs. Dayal?" she asked.

"Whoa." Jay stiffened. "You said match, not wife. I'm down with meeting someone to accompany me to business events or the odd social evening when our schedules allow, but marriage requires the kind of commitment that I can't give right now."

"Good to know." She spoke as she wrote the words down. "Afraid of commitment."

Jay bristled. "I'm not afraid. I just don't have time."

"You might want to explore that with your therapist," she said. "Is it really an issue of time or is it avoidance? Take me, for example. Child of divorce. That right there will screw anyone up. I unconsciously sabotage relationships because I don't know how to receive or accept love, and I don't want to get hurt, blahblahblah. And then there's the whole mom issue . . ."

"I don't have a therapist," Jay said.

"It's the twenty-first century," she blurted out. "Who doesn't have a therapist? I've been through four or five in the last five years, and I have a psychology degree so really I could be saving money by treating myself."

Jay sat up suddenly, his face smoothing to an expressionless mask. "I don't need any help."

Zara didn't need a psychology degree to know she'd touched a nerve. She scrambled to find a topic that wouldn't trigger him. "How about family? Brothers, sisters, cousins, aunts, uncles . . ."

"It's just me and my mom." He stared up at the blue sky. "She had me when she was seventeen. Her parents were immigrants who were from the same village from India. They came to California together to work in IT and settled in San Diego. They disowned her when they found out she was pregnant. Even now, they refuse to acknowledge we exist, and the rest of the family followed suit." His hands fisted against his thighs. "My dad was in the country from London on a university exchange program. He left shortly after I was born. He didn't want anything to do with us, either. We don't know anything about his family, and I have no interest in ever finding them."

Zara gave herself a mental kick. Another bad topic. Was it possible to get more feet in her mouth? "I'm really sorry. It must have been so hard for your mom."

"She's the strongest person I know." Jay's voice filled with pride. "She worked three jobs to put food on the table and still found time to get her high school diploma. She finally found a permanent position at a daycare and studied at night to get her early-childcare degree. Now she's a part owner of the daycare with the woman who first gave her a chance."

Zara loved how proud he was of his mom, but what about him? Who had looked after him while his mom was working three jobs? Had he had a lonely childhood? She'd had eleven years in a happy family, and even after the divorce, she'd still had two parents and dozens of relatives to look after her. "I'd love to get to know her better. We didn't really have a chance to chat at Tarun's wedding because she was laughing so hard. Will she be at any of the weddings this summer?"

"She was at Tarun's wedding and I think she's been invited to a few more." He didn't seem to have any issue with Zara meeting his mom. She would have to find her at the next wedding. Not just to get more information about Jay, but because she was interested to meet a woman who had become such a success after a rough start in life.

"So what kind of woman are you looking for? Let me guess. Professional. Sophisticated. Classy. Intelligent. Basically, Lucia but younger, or do you like a little Mrs. Robinson between the sheets?" She took another bite of her hot dog. Was there any better food?

"My relationship with Lucia is strictly professional, but yes, I'd be interested in someone similar."

"So, you want a mini-me," she teased. "I mean a mini-you. Not me. Obviously. Lucia is pretty much the opposite of me, which is another reason I knew that job wouldn't work out."

"You have ketchup on your cheek." He took a napkin and gently dabbed it at the corner of her mouth.

Desire flooded her veins followed by a wave of desolation. She could easily fall for a man like Jay. Smart, handsome, ambitious, successful, and yet she sensed a longing in him, a secret Jay waiting to be free.

"Is it gone?" Her voice came out in a whisper.

He leaned in and studied her with a serious intensity that took her breath away. He was so close she could see the gentle dip in his chin, the dark stubble of his five-o'clock shadow even though it couldn't be much past four o'clock. His lips were firm and soft, his mouth the perfect size for kissing. She drew in his scent: pine and mountains and the rich, earthy scent of the soil she'd turned in the garden when her family was whole and she never had to wonder whose house she was in when she woke up in the morning.

But this wasn't the time to be thinking about being held in Jay's strong arms or what it would be like to kiss him, or how just being near him calmed all the wayward thoughts in her head. She was supposed to be concentrating on finding him a match and where she should get autographed when he made the promised celebrity introduction.

"We should go." She jumped up so abruptly her half-eaten hot dog fell to the grass. "I have to get back to the office, and I don't want to exceed your two-hour-and-forty-five-minute time limit."

Jay picked up the hot dog and carried it to the nearest bin. "When do you want to meet again?"

His question sent a curious thrill rocketing through her veins. She hadn't put him off with her rambling, or her quest for the perfect hot dog, or even the uncomfortable questions she'd asked as they lounged in the sun. She couldn't have been more excited if he'd asked her on a second date. Except he wasn't really interested in her that way, and she needed to keep that in mind. The last thing she wanted was to get into a Cyrano situation where she would be forced to help someone else win the heart of the man she loved. She made a mental note to rewatch the 1973 Broadway version of the play with its soaring ballads and rousing word- and swordplay as a reminder of the heartbreak that could result.

She pulled out her phone and pretended to study the screen to stop herself from saying something stupid like *How about tonight?* "Hmmm. I have a big settlement meeting on Friday so the rest of my week is shot. I'll have to let you know."

If he noticed her cool dismissal, he didn't react. Instead, he said the one thing that would ensure she wouldn't be able to sleep until she saw him again. "I'll be waiting."

WHAT the hell was he doing? Jay pulled open the door to court-room 62 and slid into the rearmost bench, grateful for the high school students and court watchers who had filled the remaining seats in front of him. Zara had sent him a message letting him know she would be free on Friday after court to meet him for a drink at a nearby restaurant, but he'd been beset by curiosity. How did a woman who shot people in the ass and knocked them out of their chairs try a legal case? He had to know. Instead of going over the latest financial statements from J-Tech's statewide branches, he'd asked Jessica to call an Uber to take him to court.

Plaintiff's counsel put his client on the stand. Dressed in a 49ers football jersey and jeans, the middle-aged man limped to the witness stand, leaning heavily on his cane. Through his testimony, Jay learned that Zara's client had allegedly gone through a red light and hit the plaintiff's vehicle in the middle of a left turn. Severely injured, the plaintiff claimed he could no longer play football with his son, nor could he work at his job as a painter because the injuries to his back and neck had left him with restricted mobility, limited use of his arms, and chronic pain.

Poor guy. One chance encounter and his entire life had changed forever.

The plaintiff was offered up for cross-examination. For the first painful two minutes, Zara searched through her files. The judge sighed loudly and urged her to hurry while opposing counsel snickered. Finally, she pulled out a piece of paper and approached the witness box.

Her cross-examination was sharp and focused. She started with questions about the witness's family life before drilling down into the details of the activities he claimed he could no longer do. The witness shifted uncomfortably in his seat. His lawyer objected but was overruled.

"You testified that your son was drafted for the NFL," Zara said, the tone of her voice changing from demanding to conversational. "Did he get his love of the sport from you?"

"I played in college," the witness said. "Wide receiver. I was a lock for a top-ten draft selection until I tore a ligament and that was the end for me."

"You must have caught some good ones in your time." Now her voice was all warmth and sympathy, tinged with awe.

The witness's eyes grew misty. "I miss those days."

Plaintiff's counsel objected on the basis of irrelevance, and the judge sustained. Zara walked back to her table and consulted her notes.

Was that it? He'd been expecting some theatrics, a smoking gun, or even a witness reduced to tears. Even without any legal training, he could see her cross-examination hadn't elicited any particularly useful information, and yet she didn't seem perturbed.

Zara bent down to grab something from her bag. "Hut!" She spun around and threw a foam football at the plaintiff, her shout echoing through the courtroom, freezing everyone in place.

The plaintiff shot out of his seat and took two steps to the side, hands in the air. "I got it. I got it." With a jump he grabbed the football and held it up, victorious. His smile faded as he stared at the stunned crowd, clearly realizing what he'd just done.

"Objection." Plaintiff's counsel glared at Zara. "What was that?"

"I believe it's called a Hail Mary pass." Zara smiled at the judge. "No further questions."

Jay's phone buzzed in his pocket and he slipped out of the courtroom. Damn shame. He could have watched her all day.

THREE Pesos was not the kind of place Jay usually went for quiet conversation. The upscale Mexican restaurant and saloon was a sensory overload of Mexican decor, music, conversation, and rich mouthwatering scents. Cacti and succulents, fake chili peppers, sombreros, baskets, and woven blankets were stuffed into every alcove and piled high on every shelf. A collage of Talavera plates juxtaposed with paintings of Mexico and faded prints of old Mexican films covered one yellow-stuccoed wall.

They joined the mix of suits, tourists, and casual diners in the booths. The focus at the bar was a vast lineup of mescals, but Zara had ordered a Mexican mai tai in a tall painted glass. She'd taken her hair down after settling her case and removed her suit jacket to reveal a sleeveless red top, the neckline dipping down to the crescents of her breasts. She wore a silver dragonfly necklace with a blue enamel center that sparkled in the overhead lights, and somewhere between the courthouse and the restaurant she had added a matching clip to her hair. If not for the fact she had brought her laptop to the restaurant, she could have been his date for the evening. The thought was not unpleasant.

"I watched your trial," he said when they were settled. "I was surprised the judge allowed such an unconventional strategy."

"I saw you lurking in the back." Zara grinned. "I wouldn't do that with any judge. Some of them are real sticklers for the rules and he rightly sustained opposing counsel's objection. My purpose wasn't to get his actions on the record. I wanted them to settle, which they did. They asked for an adjournment before the judge gave his judgment, and we got the offer we were hoping for."

"Congratulations." He appreciated the strategy behind the risk as much as the win.

"I'm in a celebratory mood. Be warned." She pulled out her laptop, raising her voice over Vicente Fernández's "Volver, Volver" playing over the tinny speakers.

Jay quickly whisked her glass out of the way, silently congratulating himself on averting a near disaster. In fact, he'd managed to keep her path clear all the way from the courthouse to the restaurant, walking slightly in front so that she could talk without having to worry about anything in her path. He felt a sense of pride at keeping her safe, like it was something he'd been born to do.

The waiter came by to take their orders. Zara chatted briefly with him, learning more about his life in a few minutes than Jay knew about most of the staff in his office. She made people smile, he realized, her genuine interest in people breaching walls he could never cross.

"I've put all my notes into my 'Find Jay a Match' document," she said, peering over her laptop. "I have a few more questions about the kind of woman you're looking for."

"Ask me anything." He sipped his drink, letting the bittersweet liquid linger on his tongue as he settled back in his seat.

"Active or not active? I'm guessing active since you're a sports nut and look at you. Muscles all over. Not an ounce of fat. You're a man who looks after yourself and I'd say you would like someone who values fitness, too."

"I guess—"

"Travel or no travel? I'd guess travel because you were in the air force. You don't take a job like that if you're a homebody, and if you travel, you'd want a partner who travels, too."

"Yes, but—"

"Working or stay-at-home?" She didn't even pause long enough to let him talk. "I'd guess working. You've had two careers and built your own business. I think you'd appreciate a woman who is independent, educated, and can contribute to the family finances . . ."

She trailed off when Jay shook his head. "You're forgetting that I'm just looking for something casual. My mother asked me to make an effort to find a partner and I'm curious about who you think would be a good match. But I don't want anyone to get the wrong idea. I'm not interested in anything long-term."

"Sorry. I got carried away." She grimaced. "I'll scratch the next question, which was about kids."

"I've never even thought about kids." But he had. As a boy, he had wanted what his friends had: the noise and chaos of a big family. Birthdays with so many people they spilled into the yard. Weddings so huge they needed a giant venue. Aunties and uncles and cousins who would be there no matter what. He loved his mother, respected her choices, and was deeply appreciative of everything she had done to give him a happy childhood. But sometimes he had felt painfully alone.

"I know this is probably premature because we're still in the fact-finding stage, but there is someone I think you should meet." Zara opened her purse and pulled out a card. "My father is an artist as well as a musician, and he's showing a new collection next Monday at the Indra Roy Gallery. I thought of Indra right away when we made our deal. She's smart, elegant, and sophisticated, and her gallery was just elected to membership in the prestigious

Art Dealers Association of America. She's everything a workaholic, *Economist*-reading CEO could want. You can drop by any time after seven. If she doesn't suit, it's no harm, no foul because she won't know that's why you're there."

Her fingertips brushed his skin when she handed him the card, sending a current of electricity sparking through his body. He didn't want to move his hand away.

"I'm impressed how you just interviewed yourself to talk me into meeting Indra."

"Ah." Her breath left her in a rush, and she was instantly contrite. "I get carried away sometimes."

"I noticed, but I would call it enthusiastic." He noticed a lot of things about her. The gentle curve of her neck, the glow of her skin, her easy laughter and sunny smile. What was it about Zara that fueled this scalding awareness? He tried to focus on their conversation and stop thinking about her lush lips and how soft they would feel if he kissed her. Had he ever had this type of reaction to a woman before? When she looked at him, he could almost see another world in the depths of her warm brown eyes. A world where drinks spilled, heads rolled, footballs flew across courtrooms, and the dark place inside him was banished by the sunshine of her smile.

"When I'm focused on something, it's to the exclusion of everything else," she continued. "It's one of the reasons why I don't get involved in any serious relationships. I'd be so focused on that person, the world could collapse around me and I'd never notice. No one wants that kind of attention."

Jay could think of worse things. As a boy whose father didn't want him and whose mother was working three jobs to keep a roof over their heads, he had been desperate for attention of any kind.

The food arrived, and with it a green margarita in an enormous glass, courtesy of the bartender with whom Zara had shared a two-minute conversation while they had waited to be seated.

"That's a lot of margarita," Jay pointed out.

"I'm a lot of woman."

Laughter escaped him—so rare and unexpected he almost didn't recognize the sound. What would it be like to laugh like this every day? To be in a relationship with someone who made him feel so alive?

Zara wrapped one hand around each glass. "You'll have to peel me out of the seat when it's time to leave."

"Tell him you don't need it. I'm sure he'll take it back."

"That's hilarious." Zara chuckled. "Send back a gigantic free margarita. You kill me, Jay. I knew you had a sense of humor."

She thought he was funny. Now she was smiling at him, licking the salt from her glass off her finger. What the hell was he supposed to do? Where was he supposed to look when her tongue was gliding over her plump lips and her eyes were dancing and her shirt had slid down to reveal the firm smooth crescents of her breasts?

Jay took a spoonful of his red pozole, distracting one sense with the other. The flavor, rich and robust from the addition of the homemade red chili sauce, smoked paprika, and masa harina, dazzled his tongue and gave him something to think about that didn't involve kissing or touching a beautiful, fun-loving attorney who was trying to find his match.

Zara managed two bites of her enchiladas before the soft strum of a guitar broke the silence. "A mariachi band! Let's request a cumbia and dance."

"How about we request something low-key and conducive to eating in our seats?" He could see where this was headed. There would be no casual conversation over a quiet dinner. She was already halfway out of her seat.

"Hey. Hey. Hey. Hey!" The five performers moved toward them as the first chords of the song echoed through the restaurant.

"El Mariachi Loco"!

And she was gone. Moments later she was dancing with the band, lifting her knees along with them in time to the music. A few more restaurant patrons jumped up to join her and they did the hand jive together.

"I see your foot tapping," she called out. "One dance."

Jay shook his head and forced his foot to still. The restaurant was in the middle of the financial district, where he might be seen by potential clients, or even the bankers he was trying to court as investors. He had worked too hard to risk his reputation, even if he'd been tempted to join her.

The lead singer put his sombrero on Zara's head and pulled her close, his hips moving in a way Jay didn't want to see another man's hips move when he was so close to the woman Jay had fantasized about kissing only moments ago.

As if he could hear Jay's internal dialogue, the singer caught his gaze. His lips spread in a smug smile and he slid his hand down Zara's back to the curve of her ass. Zara slapped his hand away but not before Jay felt a fierce and totally inexplicable wave of possessiveness wash over him.

Not my fight. But he was already out of the booth and across the floor. It was the disrespect the singer was showing toward her, he told himself, the danger he represented, and the gauntlet he'd thrown at Jay's feet. Nothing more.

"You came!" Zara flung herself into his arms before he could even open his mouth to give the singer a piece of his mind.

Jay gave a satisfied growl and wrapped his arms around her, acutely aware of her soft sexy body pressed up against him, her warmth seeping into his skin like a drug. Something loosened inside him and he bit back a sigh.

"Jay." She breathed his name and their eyes met, locked. The world fell away, the music fading beneath the pounding of his heart and the rush of blood in his ears. Raw need spiraled inside him, and in that moment he knew two things: he was going to kiss her, and it was going to happen now. He lowered his head, closing the distance between them, his thoughts centered on naked bodies, cool sheets, panted breaths, and the thudding of his headboard against the wall.

He was only seconds away from tasting her lips when she shattered the moment with the terrible words, "Let's dance!"

Before he could process the shock of his lips meeting only cool air, a firm hand clamped down on his shoulder. "Jay! I thought that was you."

Jay turned and tore his mind away from unrequited desire and the throb of his pulse in his groin. *Work. Business. Investor. Thomas.*

"Thomas." He squeezed the banker's hand. "Nice to see you." His gaze flicked over Thomas's shoulder to the octopus with the double-jointed hips, but Zara had positioned herself out of his reach.

"Don't tell me you were about to dance." Thomas chuckled. "I don't think the board would go for a CEO who breaks out the *zapateado* in the middle of negotiations."

"No. Of course not." He gave a dismissive laugh. "I was looking for the waiter so I can pay the bill and get back to the office."

"He might be over at our table. Brittany had some questions about the menu. She likes everything to be perfect for our clients."

Of course she did. But he would rather be here watching Zara dance in a battered sombrero than at another stuffy corporate dinner where he had to worry about everything from the fork he used to the placement of his napkin.

Thomas leaned in, raising his voice over the music. "Yours isn't the only company considering international expansion."

"I'm not afraid of a little competition," he said with a confidence he didn't feel in the least.

"How is that lawsuit going?" Thomas asked.

"We're still working on it." He couldn't lie but he also couldn't tell Thomas they'd just lost their chance to have the case thrown out of court. If he was here with another potential client, Jay wasn't about to hand him the knife to stab J-Tech in the back.

"Good man." Thomas clapped him on the shoulder. "I'll leave you to it. Keep in touch."

Jay returned to the table and sent a quick message to Elias to let him know that Thomas was exploring other investment opportunities. What the hell was he doing here? He had work piling up on his desk, and he still needed to figure out how to deal with the lawsuit before it destroyed his dream of taking J-Tech to the top. Instead, he was wasting time with a woman who was determined to find a match he didn't even want. Why had he jumped on her crazy bandwagon to a place he wasn't even ready to go? He flagged down the waiter and requested the bill. By the time Zara returned to the table, he had counted out the tip.

Her smile faded when she saw the receipt. "Are you leaving?"

"I was just being efficient. I need to get back to the office and this way we won't have to wait after we're done."

Zara sat across from him and two-fisted her giant margarita glass, her face disappearing when she took a big sip. "I know what happened. You saw me dancing with the mariachi band and you thought there was no way I could find you a serious match."

Her assessment hit a little too close to home. "Actually, I was thinking that I need the banker in the corner to finance the international expansion of my company and that's not going to happen if he sees me dancing around a restaurant like a fool."

Zara froze, the glass partway to her lips. "You think I looked foolish."

"No. Of course not." He backtracked quickly, giving himself a mental kick for his thoughtless words. He wasn't angry with her, but with himself. For a few seconds, he'd forgotten what mattered, imagined something that wasn't there. "I enjoyed watching you dance. I wish I could feel that free."

"You can." She smiled, but her eyes had lost their sparkle.

"I have to be this man," he said, patting his tie.

"You can be any man you want to be. It's up to you how you choose to live your life."

Bristling at the unspoken admonition, he snapped, "The way you chose to be a lawyer instead of pursuing your dream?"

Zara put down her drink, her brow creasing. "The way I chose to be *this* lawyer," she said. "I didn't fit in with the eighteen-hours-a-day, dress-in-black, stab-each-other-in-the-back-as-you-climb-to-the-top crowd but I kept trying because I wanted to make my family happy. I was mulling over Lucia's offer when I met Tony Cruz. He interviewed me wearing a Yoda hat while his partner Rollerbladed around the office because he thinks best on wheels. I knew right away they were my people because they made me want to take a risk. Do I still dream of being onstage? Yes. But I volunteer in community theater so I can get my musical fix while working for a firm that is committed to helping the little guy instead of lining the pockets of their corporate clients."

"I'm sorry," he said contritely. "I was out of line." What had gotten into him? He didn't think less of her or the firm she was with. Instead he admired Zara for her courage, for taking a risk, for knowing herself well enough to go looking for the firm that would suit her best.

"Yes, you were." She ate her meal in silence, watching the band now singing on the other side of the restaurant.

"If you don't want to go through with our arrangement, I understand," Jay said, desperate to get her talking again. Zara wasn't a quiet person and her silence just felt wrong. "I shouldn't have said what I did."

Zara made a circular gesture with her hand. "Keep going."

"You want me to leave?"

"I want you to keep groveling. You made a good start. Keep it up."

"I don't grovel," he huffed. "I apologize."

"Once is an apology." She took a sip of her margarita. "Three times takes you well into grovel territory. Maybe you should kiss my shoe."

"Seriously?" he spluttered. "I'm not going to . . ."

He trailed off when she laughed. "You're so easy to wind up. Your face . . ." She doubled over, her shoulders shaking.

Affronted, he leaned back and folded his arms across his chest. "I take it this means you don't want to end our arrangement."

"Are you kidding?" Zara tipped her glass toward him in a mock toast. "You need a woman to straighten you out. Now I'm even more committed to finding your match."

· 11 ·

Zara met Parvati a few blocks away from her father's gallery after miraculously finding a parking spot on her fifth drive around the Mission.

"I don't know why I let you talk me into these things. I don't know anything about art." Parvati brushed a hand down her slightly rumpled black dress. She kept it in the back of her car for last-minute dates, emergency drinks, and tonight, Zara's father's art exhibition.

"You don't need to know anything," Zara said. "You just need to be there to show support. He's been working on this collection for two years. It's so secret he wouldn't even show it to me."

"I'm a terrible liar," Parvati said. "If he asks what I think, I might just blurt out the truth."

"He'll be too busy to ask. I've invited dozens of people. Friends, relatives, everyone at my law firm, random people on the street . . . I didn't want him to open to an empty gallery."

"And I don't want to show up with low blood sugar." Parvati gestured to a nearby food truck. "I need food. I've only had a sand-wich and a chocolate bar since four A.M. this morning."

Zara followed Parvati across the street. "Bushra Auntie gave me a copy of the guest list for the wedding next Saturday. I think there are a few potential matches for Jay if he and Indra don't get along."

Parvati studied the menu on the side of the truck. "Are you serious? After what he said to you in the restaurant? Forget the stupid deal you have with him. You can find your own celebrity clients."

"I think I rattled him." Zara waved a dismissive hand. "People get defensive when you expose their pain. Besides, he apologized. In fact, he groveled, and very nicely, too. I'm totally over it."

Parvati knew her too well to believe the lie. "There's something else. What didn't you tell me?"

Zara toed the ground with her shoe. "There was a moment on the dance floor when I was hugging him . . ." She shrugged it off. "It was nothing." Another lie. She could still feel the raw heat of him, the muscles hard beneath her hands, the strong arms holding her tight, the warmth of his breath on her lips as he bent down to give her a—

"Obviously it wasn't nothing or you wouldn't have tried to hide it." Parvati's sharp voice pulled her out of the fantasy. "Spill."

"There was a . . . bump."

"A bump?"

Zara's cheeks heated. "You know . . . when a guy is . . . liking . . . to be hugged."

"An erection?" Parvati's lips quivered in amusement. "Is that what you're trying to say? I'm a doctor. I know what an erection is. What I don't understand is what it was doing there. I thought you two didn't get along, that you were complete opposites. Didn't you call him cold, arrogant, egotistical, and cocky?"

"Yes . . . but there's more to him than what's on the outside." What if she hadn't run scared? What if she'd closed the distance between them and tasted those lips? Or what if she'd imagined it, and he'd been leaning down to tell her that their food was getting cold?

Parvati ordered her sandwich, a side of fries, macaroni-and-cheese egg rolls, and a soda.

"How are you going to eat all this before we get to the gallery?" Zara helped by carrying the second tray of food.

"Resident trick. Eat fast or die. It's a known fact that anytime a resident sits down to eat, there's a code blue or some other dire emergency."

"I think the emergency is your total lack of nutrition. I don't know anybody who eats worse than you. And you're a doctor. What kind of message does that send to your patients?"

"They don't know all my secrets." Parvati grinned. "And they never will."

INDRA'S gallery was in a reclaimed brick building that had once been a garage. Plateglass windows had replaced the folding doors, and the concrete floor had been polished to a shine. Spotlights on the exposed ceiling were pointed at the sheet-covered paintings on the wall. It was her father's biggest exhibition. Zara counted at least twenty paintings around her, and that didn't include the over-flow that was hanging in the annex out back.

"I'm worried about the big reveal," Zara said as they walked into the gallery. "What if no one likes his new collection?" Her father's paintings were mostly abstract images, loud and angry and fierce with color. They jarred her insides and made her brain hurt. She preferred the calm of landscapes and gentle colors—an escape from the chaos of her life, an anchor in the stormy sea.

"Then he'll learn not to paint things like that for next time." Parvati finished her soda and tossed the can in the bin.

"Zara. Darling." Indra descended on them, all toned arms and twiglike legs, her dark hair twisted in a perfect chignon that made her look older than her thirty-two years. She wore an elegant, sleeveless, long black dress and a single strand of pearls. "Your father will be thrilled you came."

"I couldn't miss it for the world." She air-kissed Indra while Parvati snickered beside her.

"Why all the sheets?" Parvati asked Indra after Zara had introduced them.

"We're going for a feeling of total immersion, as if you jumped off a cliff into the ocean. The fear. The thrill. The take-your-breath-away moment when you are surrounded, absorbed, fearful, enraptured, and enthralled." Hand against her forehead as if shading her eyes from bright sunshine, Indra turned from side to side with quick, jerky movements. "You are falling, sinking, enveloped. You look around. Searching. Questing for the surface. But the images are everywhere. Enfolding." She extended her toned arms above her head. "You reach . . ." She kicked back, her dress moving to the side to expose a slim foot and a jewel-encrusted Manolo Blahnik stiletto. "Kick. Swim to the light." Her arms moved in a mock breaststroke. "Your eyes clear. You are buoyant, supported, loved. And now you understand."

"That makes absolutely no sense," Parvati muttered under her breath.

Zara jabbed her with an elbow. She was used to Indra's enthusiastic interpretations. "You want it to be a surprise," she translated for Parvati.

"Exactly, darling." Indra pressed her hands together, red-painted nails gleaming in the light. "I'll go let your dad know you're here."

"This is who you picked for Jay?" Parvati shook her head, watching her go. "Babe, you're losing your touch."

"I haven't seen her for a while. I forgot how excited she gets when there's a show. But she's got a master's in art, good connections, and I've never once seen her with a hair out of place." She looked around the bustling gallery for Jay. After their slightly awkward conversation at the restaurant, she wasn't sure if he would show up tonight.

"I wonder what she'd be like in a hospital gown," Parvati mused. "You'd be surprised how a person's true nature is revealed once you strip away all the trimmings."

"Not really interested in imagining anyone in a hospital gown, Parv."

"Really?" Parvati's voice rose in pitch. "That's the first thing I think about when I meet someone new. What's underneath? What are they trying to hide? How much ass is going to show through the crack that can't be closed?"

"My two favorite girls." Zara's father came up behind them and wrapped his arms around their shoulders. He had always been the most affectionate in their little family of four. "I can't believe how many people are here." He released them to say hello to a couple nearby.

"You're just such a perfect daughter," Parvati whispered in her ear. She was the black sheep of her academic family, disappointing her parents because she'd become a doctor instead of getting a Ph.D.

"Just don't tell him I invited everyone. I've never seen him this excited." Her father's shows were usually low-key affairs attended by family, critics, and a few of his loyal supporters. Although he sold enough to pay the bills, his work had never attracted the kind of attention Zara thought it deserved.

"I want to introduce you to the partners from my new law firm," Zara said when her father rejoined them. She had been pleasantly surprised when they'd expressed an interest in coming to the show.

After a brief chat with Tony and Lewis, they worked their way around the room chatting with all the guests while Parvati waited at the makeshift bar for drinks. It warmed her heart to see her dad so happy. She could never forget how utterly devastated she'd been the day her mother asked him to leave. Even now she still felt a niggle of fear that someone would tear him out of her life again. They were a family; then they weren't. Within days of his departure, every trace of her father had been removed from the house. His paintings stripped off the walls, cooking pots emptied from the cupboards, clothes ripped from their hangers. His outdoor studio disappeared one afternoon while she was at school, to be replaced by a garden box that never saw a single seed.

"Attention. Attention." Indra tapped her glass with a spoon as if they were at a wedding and it was time for the bride and groom to kiss. The white-coated waiters put down their trays, each taking up a place beside a painting. "We're ready for the big reveal. Someone dim the main lights. The switch is beside the door."

Zara looked over to make sure someone was covering the lights. Her heart skipped a beat when she saw Jay at the entrance with a friend. Tall and heavily muscled, the dude was Parvati's type right down to the beachcomber hair and the lack of a tie.

At a wave from Indra, Jay lowered the lights until the only illumination in the gallery came from the spotlights directed at the sheet-covered paintings.

"We now present to you a study in the female form. A decadent rendering of the essence of a woman. Prepare to amazed, astounded, challenged, absorbed." Indra raised an arm and the waiters pulled down the sheets. "I present . . . *Vulva Fruit*."

Oh. My. God.

Zara couldn't speak. Her breath was trapped in her lungs. She stared at the giant paintings of fruit cut in half and displayed as female genitalia. A papaya, dark seeds spilling from the center. A peach with soft pink flesh around a dark core. She would never be able to look at an orange again without thinking about the suggestive curve of juicy segments around a hollow center. And who would have thought a cantaloupe, a quarter sliced out to reveal the sweet and sticky center, could be so erotic? Worse were the fruits with fingers in them, gently resting on the lips of small openings, or thrust deeply into soft centers.

Bile rose in her throat. Her knees wobbled. She bent over heaving as her betraying lungs refused to let in any air.

"You're okay." Parvati rubbed her back. "It's going to be okay."

"My bosses . . ." She wheezed in a breath. "My bosses are here. My relatives. Friends. Even my hairdresser. I'm going to have to leave town. No one will ever speak to me again. I'll be fired and who will hire me when they find out about"—she waved a hand in the air—"this?"

"It's art." Parvati yanked her up by the collar. "Get a grip. People are watching. They're looking to you to see how to react. Pretend it's all good, that you knew what was coming. If you aren't surprised, they'll think it's okay."

Zara straightened, her vision immediately assailed by a six-foot painting of a pomegranate dripping with cream. "He's my dad," she moaned. "I can handle dad dances or dad jokes or even dad jeans. This is all the dad humiliations on Earth rolled into one."

"Isn't it incredible!" Indra joined them, her voice lowered to a whisper. "The silence in the room says everything. They are in that moment of total submersion when words fail them. The patriarchy has been challenged today. We have reclaimed ourselves, our femininity, our very essence . . ."

"My dad painted these," Zara pointed out. "He's a man."

"Your father understands women in a way few men do," Indra said. "It really is quite remarkable."

"Why does this always happen to me?" she asked Parvati after Indra breezed away to speak to someone who was examining the price tag beside the peach. "Why can't I have a nice normal life? Why is it always chaos and disaster and . . ." She waved vaguely at the walls. "Vulva fruits?"

"Because you're the kind of person who takes risks." Parvati turned slowly, taking in the room. "And because you have a big heart. A normal person wouldn't have invited everyone they knew to the gallery when they hadn't seen the paintings, especially with your father's history."

"You're talking about the shoes." Zara sighed. Her father had gone through many phases in his artistic career, from the landscapes and villages of his youth to loud angry abstract forms, and from animals in shoes to people with office supplies for heads.

"I'm talking about you putting yourself out there to support your dad and to help two people find their special someone."

A groan dropped from Zara's lips. "I invited Jay. What was I thinking? He's so uptight he'll probably have a heart attack."

"I don't think he's that worried about it," Parvati pointed out as Jay and his friend studied a picture of a papaya. "In fact, I'd say he's having a pretty good time."

· 12 ·

JAY couldn't remember when he'd had such an entertaining evening. When Zara had given him Indra's business card, he'd tucked it away without giving it a second thought. He usually spent his evenings working, and with the lawsuit still moving ahead, solving the mystery of the hack was of vital importance. But how many desi artists were there in San Francisco? Why did Zara think a gallery owner would be a good match for him? And what was going to happen next?

As it turned out, it was far more than he had expected.

"This is the best." Elias's grin spread ear to ear. "When you invited me to an art show, I was thinking of splattered paint on canvas or boring landscapes. I'm surprised the police aren't running in here to shut them down for public indecency."

"It's just fruit." Jay couldn't turn his gaze away. Everywhere he looked, another colorful, suggestive image assailed his senses. With no real experience of art shows to draw on, he tried to play it cool, but it was damn hard when every image made him think things he shouldn't be thinking in a room full of art connoisseurs.

"C'mon, man." Elias pointed to a split melon drizzled with cream. "That is not just a painting of fruit. And I would know. If there weren't a risk we'd get hit with a sexual harassment suit, I'd buy one for my office. Who is this dude? How do you know him?"

"He's the father of a woman I met at a wedding." He searched for Zara in the mostly silent crowd. "She offered to set me up in return for a few introductions to our celebrity clients."

"She must be something if she managed to get you out of the office." Elias chuckled. "This place is smokin'. The women are hot. There's free food and drinks. And I could look at these paintings all night."

"Has anything caught your eye?" A tall, slim woman in a long black dress joined them near the door. She introduced herself as Indra, the gallery director. Elias gave Jay a subtle nod of approval before excusing himself to talk to two women engrossed in a painting of a split avocado.

"Not yet," Jay said. "It's a lot to take in." Where was Zara? Wasn't she supposed to be here making the introductions and smoothing things along?

"Come," Indra said after a moment of awkward silence. "I'll show you the banana. It's more relatable for men."

Fifteen minutes with Indra, and Jay knew she wasn't the woman for him. Although on the outside she was everything he'd thought he wanted—cultured, sophisticated, poised, and elegant—he didn't feel even a flicker of attraction. There was only one woman he wanted to talk to tonight and she was on the other side of the room, drinking like there was no tomorrow.

He excused himself the moment they were interrupted and joined Zara and Parvati at the bar.

"Look who it is." Parvati blocked his path, glaring so fiercely he stopped in his tracks. "Where's Indra?"

"She's talking to someone who's interested in buying the strawberry."

"Maybe you should go and wait for her in the prickly fruit section," she snapped. "Or better yet, go check out the lemon."

"Parv. No. It's okay." Zara finished her drink in one gulp and gave Jay an uneasy smile. "So what do you think of her?"

He didn't get a chance to answer before Indra swooped out of nowhere and clamped a hand around his arm. "Darling, come. I want to introduce you to the artist and his muse."

"His muse?" Zara stared at Indra aghast. "Are you serious?"

"Oh yes." Indra beamed. "She inspired this celebration of womanhood."

A sound erupted from Zara's lips. Half groan. Half moan. "No," she said quietly. "No. No. No. No. No." Without any warning, she bolted across the gallery to the entrance and hit the glass door at a dead run.

HE found her in the alley, one hand on the brick wall, the other braced on her knees, body shuddering with every breath.

"Are you okay?" He reached for her hair and gently pulled it away from her face. The thick strands slid like silk across his palm. "You hit the door pretty hard. Parvati's trying to find some ice."

"I'm going to be sick."

"You might have a concussion . . ."

"A concussion?" She straightened and frowned. "Are you kidding? I've run into glass doors before. That was nothing. I've knocked myself out twice, and once I even broke my nose. I'm very hindbrain driven. Very primal. The barest hint of danger and I'm gone. My prefrontal cortex doesn't even have a chance. If there was a zombie apocalypse, I would definitely be a survivor."

"Are you sure you're okay?" He ran a hand gently over her head, feeling for a bump as she rambled about instinct and the psychology of fear and something about jumping out of a moving car when she was a child.

"Yes. I mean, it was humiliating, but not as humiliating as inviting everyone you know to your father's art exhibition only to discover it's . . ." She shivered, her face crumpling. "Vulva fruit."

He wasn't used to seeing her like this—raw, unguarded, vulnerable, real. And cold. There was a chill in the air and he kicked himself for not noticing the goose bumps on her arms right away. "It's not that bad. People seemed more intrigued than offended." Jay slid his jacket off his shoulders and wrapped it around her.

"This is the kind of thing you see in movies." Her face softened. "Old-school chivalry. I've never had a guy give me his jacket before."

"You just haven't met the right guy." His hands were still on the lapels. He meant to bring them together. Instead, he drew her closer, so close he could almost see the electricity arc between them in the dimly lit alley, feel her energy ripple over the fine hair on his arms.

"What are you doing?" Her husky voice sent a shiver of desire down his spine.

He gave in to his protective urge and wrapped his arms around her, pulling her against his body. "Keeping you warm."

With a sigh, she melted into his chest. "You give good hugs." She burrowed closer and all he could think about was how perfectly she fit against him, her head tucked under his chin, soft curves molded against his body.

"Not only do they have a warming effect," she mumbled against his shirt, "they also make everything seem less dire. So what that my dad painted vulva fruit? Or that he had a live muse who is wandering around the gallery right now eager to talk about her experience with my bosses, my postman, my local grocer, my friends, and my family? It's no big deal. Am I right?"

Warmth flooded through him. She loved her dad and he understood that love, the willingness to do anything for the parent who'd raised you. The gallery was full because of her. Indra couldn't say enough about Zara's efforts to support her father. And now that she was over the shock of finding out there was a muse—he still couldn't wrap his head around that one—she was planning to go back inside because it was the right thing to do.

"It's art," he said. "I'm sure everyone understands that. They certainly were . . . stimulating." He needed to put the brakes on any thoughts about the exhibit and the sensual suggestive displays that had served only to spark his desire.

"His paintings used to be very different." She rested her head against his chest. "Mostly they were of his village in India, people he knew, events from his past, things he missed. They were calm and soothing, and there was so much depth to them, so many layers." Her chest rose and fell with a sigh. "He doesn't paint like that anymore. Not since my parents got divorced. I was only eleven and it utterly destroyed me. I think it destroyed him, too. My mom tried to limit his access. She thought he was a bad influence, but it turns out we share the same 'impulsive hot mess' genes and no one is to blame."

"From what I've seen, neither of you qualifies as a hot mess," he said. "Indra hardly had a moment to talk because there were so many interested buyers clamoring for her attention. Elias even wants one for our office."

She looked up, her head tipped back in the perfect position for a kiss. He saw desire in her eyes that reflected the need in his. "You like them?"

"You might be surprised what I like." He was almost overwhelmed with the temptation to stroke her cheek and feel the softness of her skin. He wanted to kiss his way down her throat, feel the flutter of her pulse beneath his lips. Some secret part of him burned for her, wanted to capture her essence and drink her in. His heart pounded wildly. *Christ*. If he managed to leave this alley without kissing her, it would be a miracle. When had he last felt this rush of adrenaline? When had he last felt so utterly alive? So out of control?

He pulled away abruptly, breaking the connection between them. "Your dad will be wondering where you are. I'm sure Parvati has found some ice by now."

"Yes, you're right." She drew in a ragged breath, her voice high and faint.

"Ready to face the fruit?" He held out his hand, needing that small connection before they left the intimacy of the alley.

"I'm just holding your hand out of an abundance of caution." She slid her palm against his. "I don't want to crack my head twice in one night."

"Perfectly understandable." He liked holding her hand, but more than that he liked the idea that she was relying on him to keep her safe. Liked it a little too much, considering what had brought them together.

"You're smiling." She fiddled self-consciously with her hair, pushing back the gentle curls as they walked toward the main road.

"I'm just glad you're okay," he said. "Let me know if you feel unsteady or if you need to stop for another hug, since I am a master hugger."

"It was good," she said stiffly. "Not great. Don't get too cocky. I was, in fact, assessing your hug potential for future matches."

He barely managed to choke back his laughter. It was getting hard to remember this was the same woman who had stolen his paintball victory and shot him in the ass—the woman who had turned his life upside down in two short weeks. "Like a test drive?"

She shrugged and looked away, but not before he saw the faintest quiver of her lips.

"What else do you assess during these test drives?" He felt electric, every nerve in his body firing at once, this attraction raw and unexpected. "Tires?"

As one, they slowed a few feet before the sidewalk, stopping in the shadows as if neither of them wanted to step into the glare of the lights.

She turned to face him, her gaze dipping to his shoes. "They do seem to be in good working order."

"Suspension?" He took a step closer and heard her breath catch in her throat.

"A little bit stiff." She licked her lips. "I think we're in for a rough ride."

"Acceleration?" Jay shoved the warning voice out of his head and cupped her jaw, brushing his thumb over her soft cheek. Her gaze grew heavy and she sighed. Or was it a whimper? He could barely hear over the rush of blood through his ears.

"A little too fast," she whispered, leaning in. She pressed one palm against his chest, and in that moment he knew she wanted him, too. "Maybe I should test the handling."

Dropping his head, he brushed soft kisses along her jaw, feathering a path to the bow of her mouth as he slid one hand under her soft hair to cup her nape. He felt like he'd just trapped a butterfly. If he didn't hold on tight, she might fly away. "Or the navigation."

She moaned, the soft sound making him tense inside. His free hand slid over her curves to her hip and she ground up against him, a deliciously painful pressure on his already-hard shaft.

"Navigation it is." He breathed in the scent of her. Wildflowers. A thunderstorm. The rolling sea.

She turned her head before he reached her mouth. "I'm supposed to be finding your perfect match."

"Indra wasn't my type." He groaned when she pressed cool lips to the heated skin of his neck, teetering on the edge.

"Who is your—"

"Zara?" Parvati's voice echoed down the street. "I've got the ice."

With a gasp, she stiffened. His mouth left her skin before she stepped away.

Her soft, wet lips and the heat in her dark eyes stoked his hunger. He drew in a slow breath and tried to center himself. Of course she was right to stop this. They were totally wrong for each other. His perfect match was someone like him. Someone who didn't dance in restaurants or run into doors. Someone who wouldn't threaten his self-control with one simple touch.

"We're here," she called out.

"Are you okay?" Parvati joined them a few moments later, eyes narrowing on Jay's jacket, hanging on Zara's shoulders. "It took me forever to find a bag for the ice. Let me take a look."

"I'm good. Really."

Parvati squinted in the dim light. "Your pupils are dilated. That's not a good sign."

Zara coughed, choked, shot a panicked glance in Jay's direction. "It's just the light, Parv. I'm fine." She shrugged off the jacket and handed it to Jay without meeting his gaze. "Thanks. I've warmed up now. Nothing like an exhibition of vulva fruit to freeze the blood in a person's veins."

Jay folded the jacket neatly over his arm. "Anytime."

"I'd better get in there and congratulate my dad." Her smile didn't reach her eyes and he had a sudden fear he'd broken something between them.

"Indra is proclaiming it a huge success." Parvati turned Zara's head from side to side, inspecting her face.

"I hope he doesn't move on to breasts as bread loaves next." Zara gave a hollow laugh. "I don't think I could take dual pumpernickel with almonds on top."

Parvati snorted as they walked away. "He could do desserts. Plum pudding would work nicely. Or gulab jamun."

"You're going to ruin desserts for me forever." Looking over her shoulder, Zara called out to Jay, "Aren't you coming?"

"I have to get back to the office." He was in no condition to go back into the gallery, much less wander through an exhibition of erotic art. What he really needed to do was go home, take a cold shower, and try to clear his mind of soft lips and warm hands and heavy gazes filled with lust.

Her shoulders slumped the tiniest bit. "I'm sorry things didn't work out with Indra."

"It was for the best."

Still, she didn't move. "Jay?"

"Yes?" He couldn't leave until she left. Couldn't move in case she came running back to him. Couldn't breathe because desire still had him in its grip.

"Excellent brakes."

ZARA'S head had only just hit her pillow when her phone buzzed with a text. Marmalade, annoyed at the interruption, put a furry paw on her cheek as if to hold her in place. The ginger cat had squeezed in an open window one afternoon when she and Parvati were at work and had made their apartment his permanent home.

"I need to get that. Don't steal my pillow." She rolled over to grab her phone and Marmalade swiftly moved into position.

"I can put you out," she warned him as he made himself comfortable in the center of her pillow. "You'll have to sleep all alone on the couch. How would you like that?"

Marmalade twitched his tail and closed his eyes. He knew she didn't have the heart to move him.

JAY: Did you get home safely?

ZARA: Yes. Parvati had the strange idea that we were being followed, but I told her she watched too many crime shows.

JAY: Head okay?

ZARA: Fine. Dr. Parvati put me to bed with an ice pack and two aspirin and told me to wake her in the morning.

JAY: What happened in the alley . . .

ZARA: Stays in the alley. It won't happen again.

It couldn't happen again. She could still feel his hands on her body, his lips brushing her cheek, the firm grip of his hand on her neck, the raw heat of him. If Parvati hadn't found them at that exact moment, Zara might have gone too far. He was too damn hot, too sexy, too irresistible. Too utterly wrong for her. Jay Dayal was a dangerous man.

JAY: I owe you a celebrity introduction. We've been hired to provide security for a movie wrap party on Tuesday for a zombie film. I can get you in if you'd like to meet the star, Bob Smith. The movie is called "Day of the Night of the Evening of the Revenge of the Bride of the Son of the Terror of the Return of the Attack of the Alien, Mutant, Evil, Hellbound, Flesh-Eating, Rotting Corpse Living Dead Part 6: In Shocking 4-D."

ZARA: Did you just put "zombie," "movie," and "celebrity" in the same sentence? The answer is YES!

JAY: I'll send details.

"PARVATI! Wake up!" Zara flicked on Parvati's bedroom light, startling her friend awake.

Instantly alert, Parvati rolled over. "What is it? Fire? Break-in? Do you have a headache? Dizziness?"

"Jay invited me to a wrap party. I'm going to meet the stars of *Day of the Night of the Evening of the Revenge of the Bride of the Son of the Terror of the Return of the Attack of the Alien, Mutant, Evil, Hellbound, Flesh-Eating, Rotting Corpse Living Dead Part 6: In Shocking 4-D* next Tuesday. What am I going to wear?"

Parvati groaned and pulled her pillow over her head. "Maybe we could discuss it when it's not midnight and I have to get up in five hours for my shift."

Zara paced around Parvati's room, stepping over clothes, pizza boxes, and piles of medical books. "I need to borrow your black dress. I saw Lucia Sanchez at Jay's office and she looked very chic in all black. That's going to be me. Conservative and professional. I'll introduce myself, hand out a few cards, and leave. No booze. No food. No dancing. No fangirling. No asking for autographs except maybe one on my arm. No trips, falls, accidents, or chaos . . ." She trailed off when Parvati pulled off the pillow to shake her head.

"You're not a black-on-black person. You're a bright-colors-and-sparkles person. Just be yourself."

"I can't be myself." She leaned against the dresser piled high with plushies that Parvati had received as gifts from the many men she'd dated and dumped. "Myself will trip on the stairs, spill champagne, or set someone's hair on fire. Myself will set off the sprinklers or fall through a drum kit." She swallowed hard. "Myself almost kissed Jay in the alley and now I can't stop thinking about it."

Her hand went to her cheek where the memory of his lips made her heart thud and her toes curl. If she hadn't turned her head, she could have had those lips. She could have kissed him until every breath had left her lungs. She could have given in to the tidal wave of desire that had roared and crashed through her veins.

"Don't worry." She held up a hand when Parvati opened her mouth, no doubt to remind her of her first impression of Jay. "I told him it wouldn't happen again."

"I am worried." Parvati tucked the pillow behind her head. "You seem to be in denial about the fact you're hot for him despite his considerable list of flaws."

Zara joined Parvati on the bed. "You're right. He's exactly the kind of emotionally unavailable guy I'm attracted to. And then it's all, *Surprise! I've got two kids and a wife*. And then I'm hitting him in the face with a passion fruit pavlova I had ordered from a bakery an hour away, and his kid is saying, *Daddy, who is that mean lady?* I don't need that kind of drama in my life."

"So, what's the problem? You're supposed to be finding his match."

Zara tipped her head back and groaned. "He's irritatingly thoughtful. He came to rescue me in the bar when he thought the singer was being a little too handsy, and tonight he came out to the alley to make sure I was okay. He wrapped his jacket around me because I was cold, and then he gave me a hug. He's got a sense of humor when he lets his guard down. And he's so sexy, Parv. The way he looks, the way he walks . . . the confidence . . . that ass . . . When he almost kissed me, he looked at me like I was the only person in the world."

"If he's got all that going for him, why does he need a matchmaker?" Parvati fiddled with the blue ribbon around the neck of one of her plush bears. Over the years, they'd increased in size, each lover trying to outdo the rest.

"Maybe he's lonely. He mentioned his mom wanting him to find someone. I don't think he's really taking it that seriously. He keeps saying he isn't interested in anything long-term. We have that much in common."

"So, sleep with him. Scratch your itch and move on." Parvati tossed the bear to Zara and she caught it in her arms.

"I don't even know if he's interested. Maybe he was just messing around. And what if he's my kryptonite, Parv? What if I really fall for him and it kills me?"

"I think you're being overly dramatic, but fortunately your best friend is a medical professional. I'll be here to make sure that doesn't happen. Now can I go to sleep?" She lay down and pulled the duvet over her head.

Zara squeezed the bear to her chest. "Parv?"

"Mmmhmm?"

"Am I too much?"

Parvati pushed back the cover. "What do you mean?"

"Do I talk too much? Am I . . ." She hesitated. "Do I put too much of me out there?"

Parvati's jaw tightened. "Did Jay say that to you?"

"No. Of course not. I was just wondering . . ."

"You are perfect," Parvati said firmly. "Exactly the way you are. Your colorful clothes. Your sparkle. The way you light up a room. Your long train-of-thought sentences when you're excited. I love everything about you and so do your friends and your family. Anyone who thinks otherwise is a loser and not worth your time."

Zara swallowed past the lump in her throat. "Maybe I won't wear the black dress."

"Damn right. You should wear the red one that you wore to your uncle Nadal's sangeet. I will never forget how he ripped a tablecloth off one of the tables and wrapped you up like a mummy until one of the aunties found a long coat to cover you up."

"I do look fabulous in that dress," she mused.

Parvati pulled the covers back over her head. "Wear it. Go to the party and be yourself. Forget about Jay and meet lots of celebrities and have a fabulous time. I'm on the night shift on Tuesday. If you have to call an ambulance, tell them to go to Bay 5. I'll be waiting."

· 13 ·

ELIAS was in his element. Thirty minutes into the wrap party and he had already thrown out a trespasser, called the police to pick up a drug dealer, and stopped a zombie attack on the complimentary buffet. Jay hadn't seen him this happy in years.

"Damn. I missed this." Elias held a hand up to stop a group of clearly underage zombies at the door. "We should do this more often. Keep up our skills."

"It does have its appeal." Jay pulled two zombies apart and confiscated the fake leg they'd been fighting over. After J-Tech's national expansion, they'd put together a solid team of ex-military specialists to deal with the on-site guarding work so they could focus on running the business. But Jay had to admit—as he rescued a zombie hooker from slipping on a pool of fake blood—that he missed being part of the action.

He checked the door again for Zara. He'd moved too fast in the alley, assumed too much. Hopefully, they could go back to being . . . what? Friends? He didn't want to kiss his friends. He didn't fantasize about them in the shower at home until his blood ran hot and the water ran cold.

About to walk away, he spotted Zara by the cloakroom having a heated discussion with a zombie bride who was checking coats. His breath caught when the bride stepped to the side, giving him a glimpse of Zara in a curve-hugging red dress that left her back bare but for the crisscross of thin red straps. She looked beautiful, sexy, and the sight of her made his pulse kick up a notch.

Shut it down. He put the brakes on the runaway train of lust. They'd agreed what happened in the alley was a mistake. With the international expansion so close he could almost taste it, Zara was a distraction that he couldn't afford. Even this deal to find him a match was time he would never recover. And for what? Someone to accompany him to business dinners or to occasionally warm his bed at night? He didn't need a partner, and she deserved someone who shared her energy and passion, someone as vibrant and alive, someone who could be there for her in the way he could never be.

Steeling himself against temptation, he made his way to the cloakroom, only to take a step back when Zara scowled.

"Is something wrong?"

"I look—"

"Beautiful."

"Ridiculous." She fisted the skirt of her red dress, tightening it around her curves in a way that made his mouth water.

"Why didn't you tell me it was a zombie costume party?" she demanded. "I wouldn't have come dressed like this."

He drew her away from the zombie bride, who had a line of customers waiting to check their coats. "I thought you were here for professional reasons. It didn't even occur to me that you would want to dress up."

"This is me we're talking about." She pressed a hand to her chest between her breasts, drawing Jay's attention to an area that was best not thought about in public. "I never pass up an opportunity to dress up. Never. And zombies? Are you kidding me? I have everything I need at home. I was a zombie for the Christmas party at my second law firm. I had rotting-flesh patches, teeth hanging out of my mouth, shredded clothes . . . I was going to bring a spare leg from the morgue, but Parvati said she'd get into trouble."

"Indeed." He didn't want to ask why the morgue had a spare leg or why they didn't come in pairs.

"I would have killed it tonight, Jay." Her hands found her hips. "Killed it. No one does zombies like me . . ."

He held up his hands, palms forward. "My bad."

She sighed, her shoulders slumping. "Now what am I going to do?"

"Work with what you've got?" He couldn't imagine anyone who wouldn't be interested in hearing her pitch when just the sight of her took his breath away. And after seeing her in court, unorthodox though her methods were, he would be happy to give his whole-hearted recommendation as to her professional skill.

She lifted her skirt, studying the hem of her dress. "Good idea. Do you have a pair of scissors?"

He stared at her, aghast. "You don't need to destroy your clothes."

She gave him a soothing pat, every press of her palm sending a zing of heat through his chest. "Zombies don't dress in nice clothes. I'll need to tear up my dress. Oh, and I'll break off one of my heels to get the zombie lurch. I can shred my stockings, muss my hair, a little makeup . . ." Her face brightened. "I'll let you get back to work. The next time you see me, I'll look amazing."

She looked amazing now, blazing as hot and wild as a forest fire. It seemed almost criminal that she would hide all that beauty under zombie rags and makeup.

He caught Elias checking her out and his eyes narrowed. Maybe a zombie costume wasn't such a bad idea after all.

• • •

ZOMBIE fever had swept through the party. Jay couldn't tell the good zombies from the bad—or maybe that was a tribute to the acting skills of the guests. He'd set up a perimeter fence around the buffet table, forcing the zombies to stand in a civilized line for their food instead of mobbing the table in a feeding frenzy. He'd stepped on so much fake blood he was certain his leather shoes would never be the same. Zara had been missing for well over an hour, and he couldn't spot her in the crowd.

"Party's getting out of hand," Elias said. "You want me to shut things down?"

"We can handle them. I've got a line of cabs standing by outside. First sign of trouble, and we'll start hustling people out the door."

"You want me to start with that one?" He pointed to a woman wrapped in bloodstained rags, a crown of skewered meat on her tangled hair, eyes dark circles in a mottled gray face. Balanced on a table, she cheered on the zombie doing shooters at the bar.

Relief flooded through his veins. Even if he hadn't recognized her face, he would have known Zara from the energy that pulsed around her. "No. I'll deal with her."

"Jay!" Zara lurched toward him when he reached her table. "How did you know it was me?"

"Your shoe."

She lifted her foot to look at her heel and lost her balance. He was there to catch her fall. Arms wrapped around her, he lowered her to the ground, her soft, curvy body, wrapped in nothing more than a tablecloth, sliding against his chest.

"Oh." She let out a soft sigh, her breasts crushed between them, hands holding his shoulders tight. "Good catch."

"It's my job." He looked down at her blacked-out eyes, cheeks smeared with gray makeup, lush lips painted a garish red. There was no reason to keep holding her, but he couldn't let go. Only when she flashed him a rotted-teeth smile did he finally release her.

"Where did you get all . . ." He waved his hand vaguely over her outfit. "This."

"I couldn't bear to cut up my dress, so I grabbed a tablecloth and asked around if people had any extra accessories. One guy had these extra teeth." She gave him another grin. "Someone had makeup and baby powder. I picked up the rotting-flesh patches off the floor, and I made the crown from the meat section at the buffet. It's nothing like my zombie costume at home, but I fit right in."

"I've been waiting to introduce you to Bob. Are you okay to meet him like this? Zombie princess in a ham kebab crown doesn't scream professional."

She brushed off his jacket, now covered in makeup and powder. "I already met Bob. I challenged him to a beer funnel contest. Guess who won?"

"Not Bob."

"Of course not Bob." Zara laughed. "He was a good sport about it. Afterward, we had a chat and he said he'd never met a more relatable attorney. He autographed my arm and I gave him my card. He even asked for extra cards to give to his friends."

"Well, that was . . . lucky." He didn't want to think about the good-looking celebrity drinking with Zara and touching her arm. Jay had planned to be there for the introduction. Celebrities were a horny bunch and it was his job to keep Zara safe.

"Luck had nothing to do with it. My beer funnel skills are unmatched." She leaned up to press a kiss to his cheek. "Thanks for the invitation."

He felt that kiss like a brand on his skin. How was he supposed to stay focused on his goal when she did things like that? How was he supposed to work when she looked so sexy in her bloodstained tablecloth? This wasn't his path. She wasn't his woman. Even if she didn't find him a match, he'd upheld his part of the bargain and he could easily end this arrangement and move on with his life. "I have to get back to work," he said abruptly.

"There's lipstick on your cheek." She rubbed his skin with a gentle brush of her thumb and pleasure spilled over him, freezing him in place.

"Is it gone?"

"No." She bit the soft flesh of her lower lip and gave him a sultry smile. "Maybe I should kiss the other side and make it even."

He jerked away, hands flying up in a warding gesture. If she came too close, if she touched him again, he would kiss her, powdered hair, greasy makeup, kebab crown and all.

"C'mon, Jay." She gave him a rotted-teeth smile, lurching toward him on one red shoe. "I don't bite."

He took another step back, desperate to get away from her addictive warmth, her sunny smile, her sexy body, and her wicked laugh. His heel caught on something and he went down. The last thing he heard before he blacked out was a zombie scream.

PARVATI answered the phone with a breathless, "Hello?"

"If somebody falls and bangs his head on a cauldron full of Jell-O brains and loses consciousness for about five seconds, does he need to come to the hospital?" Zara glanced over at Jay, who was back at his post near the door. He didn't seem to be affected by his minor accident other than it had made him more grumpy than usual. He'd barked at her to get away and then stormed off to the restroom to clean his suit. Five minutes later he was kicking zombies out of the party with a vengeance.

"Oh, it's you." Parvati breathed a sigh. "I didn't recognize the number."

"Phones aren't allowed at the party because they don't want people taking pictures and selling them to the press," Zara explained. "I'm using the bartender's landline. It's so cute. I didn't know they made landlines anymore."

"I'm assuming we're not talking about you being injured."

"It's Jay." She waved to the bartender to refill her zombie punch. Her last cup had been all eyes—lychees with blueberry pupils. After the recent disaster, she needed all the alcohol she could get.

"I accidentally caused him to fall over backward and bang his head on a cauldron full of fake zombie brains. I was pretty sure he lost consciousness for a few seconds, although he may have been closing his eyes at the sheer irony of it all."

"How are his pupils?" Parvati's voice turned serious. "Is he dizzy? Nauseous?"

"He's fine, I think." She turned in her chair to make sure he was still standing. "Every time he looks at me, his eyes narrow so it's kind of hard to tell. But he is stomping around, and he can lift two zombies at once and toss them into a cab. The ladies seem to love it."

Stunning in his dark blue uniform and security vest, he clearly didn't have to work at attracting attention. Women were drawn to him even when he was just standing still. It would have been incredibly annoying except for the fact that he barely looked at them. Every offer was brushed off with a bland expression or a firm, curt gesture.

Except for the zombie bride.

While Parvati rattled off a list of possible symptoms, Zara watched the zombie bride make her second approach. Earlier in the evening the bride had broken through Jay's defenses by pretending to hurt her foot. Jay had carried her to a chair, slipped off her sparkly stiletto, and examined her foot right down to her perfectly manicured toes. If Zara hadn't been about to do shooters with Bob and his zombie lieutenant, she would have pointed out that there was nothing wrong with the bride's foot, and only five minutes prior she'd been dancing up a storm.

This time, the zombie bride had washed the makeup off her face and combed her hair, revealing honey gold curls beneath the tangles. Her sleeveless bridal dress hugged her slim figure, the bodice loosely laced as if it could barely contain her generous breasts.

"Zara?" Parvati raised her voice. "Are you still there?"

"Yes." Zara watched the bride snake her way across the room, hips swaying, tongue flickering as she licked her lush lips to a shine. A predator stalking its prey. "What should I do about Jay? He said he doesn't do hospitals. The party is basically over."

"Just keep an eye on him. If he gets a headache, blurred vision, slurred speech, or unusual fatigue then take him to the nearest hospital. If he comes here, I can take a look at him."

She ended the call just seconds before the zombie bride went in for the kill. Hair toss. Giggle. Simper. Flutter the lashes. Hand on the arm. *Pathetic.* Zara knew all her tricks. She waited in breathless anticipation for Jay to brush her off—a step away, a fake call, or a shake of the head—but no. Jay moved closer. He murmured something in her ear, his face soft and gentle. And was that . . . a smile? Elated, the zombie bride leaned up on tiptoe and kissed his neck. Zara's stomach clenched. What the hell was he doing with that piece of zombie trash?

"How's my little zombie lawyer princess doing?" Bob put an arm around her waist and twirled her onto the dance floor.

"Good." She forced a smile. As far as celebrities went, Bob was

D-list who thought he was C-list, and pretended he was B-list. He'd wiped off his zombie makeup after the beer funnel fiasco to reveal a large forehead, deep-set eyes, and a narrow jaw. His face was distinctive, if not odd, and it was clear he was destined to be a character actor if he made it out of the land of zombie films.

"I've got a suite in the hotel across the street." Bob leaned down to nuzzle her neck. He smelled slightly off, like he'd just finished the plate of zombie brain blue cheese liver pâté. "We're heading over there for the after-party. I've got so much zombie dust you'll be able to roll naked in it on the bed."

"Tempting." She looked around the club, but Jay and his zombie bride had disappeared. "Tell me more."

"It's just me, a couple of guys from the crew, and—"

"Should I call your cab?" Jay's dark menacing shadow swallowed Zara's view.

"Excuse me. We're dancing." Her anger rose when she noticed he'd brought along the zombie bride. "And then we're going to party in a bed of zombie dust in Bob's hotel suite."

"I don't think so," Jay said firmly. "You're going home."

She wrapped her arms around Bob and glared at Jay. "Get over your bossy self. How I choose to spend my evening is none of your concern."

"Maybe we could go, too." The zombie bride curled her talons around Jay's arm. "The party's almost over."

"The more, the merrier." Bob slid an arm around Zara's waist. "Let's get the party started."

Zara had a settlement meeting on Thursday morning. She needed tomorrow to prep, but damned if she was going to leave the party alone after Jay had hooked up with the wrong kind of bride right in front of her. "Just give me a minute to change out of this tablecloth."

"Why bother?" Bob asked. "You're just going to take it off anyway."

Jay growled. At least she thought it was a growl. But then he rubbed his head and she became more concerned about a possible concussion than the way that sound rumbled through her body.

"Do you have a headache? Dizziness? Blurred vision?" She shook off Bob's arm. "I talked to Parvati and she said I should keep an eye on you in case you have a head injury." Her gaze fell on the simpering bride. "Of course, if you've got someone else to look after you tonight, I'll be free to continue my super fun evening with Bob." She held her breath, silently wishing he did have a headache—just a little one. Bob's zombie dust party was the last place she wanted to be.

"Now that you mention it . . ." His hand went to his head, his brow creasing in a frown.

"Oh my God. I'm calling an Uber right now." She gave Bob's arm a squeeze. "Don't you worry about a thing. I'll handle this. I'm so sorry I'll have to miss the after-party. I've always wanted to roll naked on a bed of zombie dust in a room filled with strange men, but I'd better get Jay to the hospital. I'm pretty sure the cauldron was unstable, and the fake blood on the floor was a definite slip-and-fall hazard. You don't want a lawsuit on your hands."

"Lawsuit?" Bob's eyes widened. "I don't want any negative publicity."

"Don't worry." She put an arm around Jay's waist as if he was about to collapse and she'd actually be able to stop his fall. "I'll take care of everything."

"AROUND the back to Bay 5." Zara leaned over the seat to talk to the Uber driver. "It's the last one on the left."

"That's for ambulances," Jay pointed out.

"It's also for people who have a friend who is an ER doctor and is giving them special treatment. I come here all the time. It's not a problem."

"What do you mean you come here all the time?" Jay rubbed his head. He suspected the headache was more at the thought of Zara going to a slimy D-list actor's zombie dust party than any injury he'd suffered from the fall. Or maybe it was because he associated hospitals with the worst times in his life: his mother's illness and the aftermath of the crash that still gave him nightmares. Those first few days in the field hospital, still suffering the effects of a parachute drop too close to the ground, he'd had to watch soldiers bring in the bodies of the men he couldn't save.

But no one was dying today. He didn't even know why he had come except that Zara had threatened to put herself in a dangerous situation and he didn't want to let her out of his sight. And maybe someone could give him a couple of pills to make the damn headache go away.

"My overzealous nature lends itself to the occasional injury," Zara said. "It's no big deal. No one has been seriously hurt or killed.

At one point I contemplated having my dates sign a waiver before we went out, but then I figured that was just asking for trouble. People aren't as careful when there's a waiver in place. They take unnecessary risks. I didn't want that to happen."

Zara hadn't been kidding about being in the hospital before. Jay felt like royalty when they were greeted warmly and then whisked through admissions at super speed. By the time Parvati joined them in the small curtained cubicle, he realized the whirlwind process had numbed the anxiety he usually felt when he visited hospitals or accompanied his mother for medical procedures.

"So . . ." Parvati smirked. "I understand that you fell backward and hit your head on a cauldron full of zombie brains. If I wasn't a professional, I would ask if it helped."

"Parv . . ." Zara shot her a warning look.

"There are just so many things I want to say." Parvati chuckled. "So, so many things. But instead, I'll just give you this . . ." She held out a folded pink square of cloth. "It ties in the back."

Jay frowned. "I beg your pardon?"

"Change into the gown," she said. "It's hospital policy."

His stomach clenched. This was getting out of control. It was one thing to keep Zara away from Bob. Another to subject himself to such humiliation. If he'd really been concerned about the fall, he could have contacted J-Tech's staff doctor, who would have been happy to stop by his place and check him out. "I thought you were just going to assess my injury and look into my eyes with a bright light. That sort of thing."

Her lips twitched at the corners. "You have insurance. I think we'd better be thorough. I've ordered a CT scan and for that"—she opened the gown with a flourish—"you'll need to put this on. And don't worry. I've seen it all."

"I'm suddenly feeling better." There was no way he would suffer the indignity of a hospital gown.

Zara sat on the bed beside him and put a gentle hand on his arm. "I thought you lost consciousness for a few seconds. I know you were up right away and tossing bad zombies around like there was no tomorrow, but I really think you should get checked out to be sure."

Her touch, her warmth, her soothing presence. Jay had been looking out for himself since he was ten years old, taking on the responsibility of shopping and meals so his mother could work extra hours. As a captain, he'd been responsible for his men. As a son, he'd looked after his mother when she was ill. He was the protector, not the other way around. But in that moment, he would have done anything she asked. Giving Parvati a brief nod, he said, "I'll stay."

"I'll send a nurse to get you set up when you're done."

Zara followed Parvati outside the cubicle. Her voice dropped to a low murmur and he focused on getting changed and trying to tie the stupid gown so his ass wasn't hanging out the back. By the time she pulled back the curtains, he was on the bed, a blanket over his legs, his body swathed in thin cotton.

"You look very fetching in pink." Zara's lips quivered with a smile.

"I blame you for this."

Zara shrugged. "How was I to know you were so frightened of zombies you'd back away and fall into a cauldron?"

Their conversation drifted to his security work. Zara pressed him for details of the celebrity parties he'd attended until a nurse whisked him away for the CT. When he returned half an hour later, she showed him pictures of the movie stars she had deduced were his clients. He couldn't tell her that she had guessed them all.

"You don't have to wait," he said after a nurse stopped by to let him know the results might take a few hours.

Zara heaved an exasperated sigh. "Don't be ridiculous. I'm not leaving you alone. If you hadn't agreed to come, I would have called you every hour to make sure you were okay. This way at least one of us can get some sleep." She wandered over to the medical equipment on the back wall and absently flicked a switch.

"I thought you were going to Bob's party." Jay settled back on the bed. He couldn't remember the last time he'd been in a bed for anything other than sleep or sex. Relaxation was not part of the success equation.

"Are you kidding?" She pressed a button, then another. "Did you seriously think I was going to a hotel room with a bunch of random drunk dudes to roll around in a bed covered in enough illegal substance to put us all away for life? I'm a lawyer. I like being a lawyer. I'm not going to throw it all away for a chance to represent D-list celebrity Bob Smith. And what kind of celebrity name is that? I told him he should get a stage name if he plans to make it big. Something cool. Vin Diesel's real name is Mark Sinclair and Cary Grant used to be Archibald Leach. I'm sure we could jazz up *Bob Smith*."

After watching her in court, he should have known better. Nothing got past Zara even if her attention seemed to be focused elsewhere. He wouldn't make that mistake again. Especially if it meant he'd wind up in a hospital bed for a slight headache that could have been cured with a good night's sleep. The only way this situation could get worse was if . . .

"Jay? What the hell are you doing here?" Thomas walked over to the bed. "Brittany is a few cubicles down getting treated for an allergic reaction. People don't seem to understand that *allergy to nuts* means she can die if she eats them. Fortunately we had her EpiPen with us and we got here in time so she'll be fine."

Jay made the introductions. He shook Thomas's hand so hard the other man winced.

"Well . . ." Thomas wiggled his fingers by his side. "You certainly don't seem ill."

"I'm not," Jay said, his voice firm and loud. "Not at all. I was just about to head back to the office. This was just a . . ." What the heck was he supposed to say? He couldn't tell Thomas the truth. Taking a deep breath, he shot Zara a quick, desperate glance, praying she wouldn't talk about cauldrons. She caught his gaze and gave him the barest of nods.

"He's trying to be modest," Zara said quickly. "And stoic. J-Tech was providing on-site security work at a celebrity party where I was a guest. You know how crazy celebrities can get."

Thomas nodded. "We have several entertainment clients."

"Well, then, you know how quickly things can get out of hand," Zara said. "Jay and his team had it under control in no time, but in all the craziness he took a blow to the head. He said he was fine, but as a personal injury lawyer, I recommended that he get it checked out. You can't be too careful for both legal and medical reasons when it comes to head injuries even if the injury would not in any way affect the ability of an individual to perform at a hundred ten percent efficiency as Jay always does."

"Good to know it's nothing serious." Thomas moved away. "I'd better get back to Brittany."

"Thanks for the save." Jay relaxed back on the bed after Thomas had gone. "That was the investor who's hopefully going to fund our international expansion."

"I remembered him from the Mexican restaurant." She perched

on the end of his bed. "I thought you'd want to assure him you would be back to work tomorrow and ready to dominate the world of security services." She stretched her arms over her head and yawned. "Good thing he didn't want to stay and chat. I'm beginning to crash and I don't have any gummies in my purse for an extra boost." She shrugged when he lifted a quizzical brow. "It's a weird energy thing. My dad is the same. We can push past our limits but then we just run out of energy and BAM. We're out."

"Why don't you lie on the bed beside me?" He turned on his side and shifted to leave a space on the bed, although there wasn't much room to move.

"It wouldn't be . . . appropriate." The longing in her eyes when she looked at the space he'd made for her belied her words.

"If you're worried that you're supposed to be finding my perfect match, I promise not to let her know we shared a bed." He edged farther to the side, grateful for the railing that kept him from falling. "I have no ulterior motives, especially with all these people running around, and I don't think there are any rules against it. The couple across the way are lying together and no one has said anything to them."

"Since you put it that way . . ." She squeezed into the tiny space beside him, resting on her side. Three seconds later, she pushed herself up on one elbow. "As much as I appreciate the offer, this bed isn't big enough for both of us."

Jay eased onto his back, wrapped one arm around her and settled her head on his chest. "How about this?"

Zara snuggled beside him. "Acceptable."

It was more than acceptable. Despite being so uncomfortably out of his element, and in a place that usually sent his pulse skyrocketing, he felt curiously calm.

"I used to play with the hospital equipment when my mom was going through her cancer treatment." Jay's lips brushed Zara's hair. "I couldn't just sit there and worry. I needed to do something with my hands."

"Is she okay now?" Zara looked up, her forehead creased with worry.

"She had her five-year check and everything was good." He hesitated, wanting to share his concerns with someone, but not sure if he could. "I was worried about her when she asked me to promise to try and find a partner so I wasn't alone. It was an odd request. She knows how important my work is to me, what I want to achieve. I thought maybe the cancer had come back and she didn't want to tell me. I'm still not sure."

"You'll have to ask her. Things like that are too important to go through alone."

She was right. The discussion was long overdue. He'd been avoiding asking the question because he was afraid of the answer. But it wasn't about him and his fear of losing his mom. It was about her and giving her support even if she said she didn't want it. Much as Zara had just done for him.

Zara toyed with the edging on his gown. "My entire family takes things to the next level. They don't ask for promises. They force-feed me men. I'm surprised one of my aunties hasn't popped up here saying she was just in the neighborhood and look who is with her—a hapless eligible bachelor who let himself be dragged across the city by an auntie he barely knows because he's that desperate for a wife."

"Why don't you tell them to stop?" Her hair was soft on his cheek, the floral scent partially masked by baby powder and ham kebab. She had changed out of her costume and washed off her makeup before calling the Uber, but her hair still carried the telltale scents.

"Same reason you made that promise to your mom." She smiled, her dark eyes warming. "I love them. They're my family."

A tidal wave of emotion flooded through his veins. "I want to kiss you right now," he murmured softly.

She tipped her head back and looked up at him through long, silky lashes. "That could be the head injury talking. I had the same feeling in the alley after I ran into the door at the art show."

"Maybe it wasn't the head injury." He brushed his lips against her forehead, delighted when she softened in his arms.

"What kind of matchmaker would I be if I sampled the goods?"

"A thorough one."

"I can't do this, Jay." Her breath whispered over his lips. "My life is one disaster after another. If you're not already hiding something—wife, kids, criminal past, cat allergy, weird fetish, cult membership, double life—then I'll unconsciously sabotage our relationship and you'll never want to speak to me again."

"I'm not asking for a relationship," he said. "Just a kiss." He traced the curve of her jaw, a feather-light touch over soft skin.

"One kiss." She bit her lip, her eyes dark with desire. "No one has ever asked to kiss me. It usually just happens. We're talking on the couch or lying on the bed and then our faces move closer and I know we're going to kiss. My heart starts to pound in anticipation and I hold my breath and . . ."

"Shhhh." He slid his hand around her neck and pushed himself up so he could clearly see her face.

"Is it now?" she whispered.

"Yes. It's now." He kissed her gently, softly, pressing his lips against the soft bow of her mouth. Everything stilled, the sounds of the emergency room fading away beneath the pounding of his heart and the rush of blood in his ears. With a sigh, she opened to him, stealing his breath with the slow sweep of her tongue. Abandoning himself to the sweetness of her mouth, he pulled her on top of him, palms skimming her lush curves, fingers sinking into the silk of her hair. Her scent, the soft moans and panting breaths, the tremble of her body, the white-hot heat that blazed between them. It was too much and not enough. He understood now why his mother had asked for the promise. A lifetime of these kisses was far better than being alone.

"Blood work." An amused voice froze the blood in his veins.

Zara stiffened and slid to the side, burying her face in his shoulder. Somewhere in his lust-soaked brain he remembered that they were in a hospital and that he'd come here for a reason, although he couldn't recall exactly what that was.

"Well, that was fun." Zara pushed herself up after the nurse had taken another vial of blood. Mercifully, she hadn't said anything about their lapse of judgment. "I feel like I've just been caught making out with the high school quarterback in my parents' basement."

Jay tightened his arm around her when she moved to leave. "Where are you going?"

"I think it might be better if I sit chastely on a chair at the other side of your cubicle because if we keep doing what we were doing things might not end well for either of us."

His chest puffed with pride. "I am an exceptionally good kisser."

"I give you a B-plus."

"Are you kidding me?" His voice rose in pitch.

"I can't give you an A." She lay back beside him, her head on his chest. "You'd have nothing to strive for."

"Maybe I should try again right now." He touched her face, cupped her jaw in his palm.

"One kiss." She gently moved his hand away.

"One kiss." Jay smoothed back her hair, listening to the rhythm of her breaths. He couldn't remember the last time he'd felt so relaxed. Content. So damn right.

"Jay?"

"Yes?"

"The day we met on the paintball field, would you ever have imagined we'd be here?"

He chuckled, amused. "In a hospital because I fell trying to get away from you? It wouldn't have been out of the realm of possibility."

She pushed herself up on one arm and glared. "That's not what I meant. Would you have imagined we would ever kiss?"

"No," he said honestly. "I thought you were the most irritating woman I'd ever met. Also, you shot me in the ass. It didn't scream romance."

"I thought the same about you." She lay down again, her palm resting on his chest. "Yet here we are."

"Indeed." She'd crashed into his life like a hurricane and damned if he could let her go.

He heard his name in the distance. A murmured conversation. The thud of boots and the squeak of leather.

"Jay." His mother walked into the cubicle dressed in head-to-toe black leather, a motorcycle helmet in her hand. "What happened? Are you okay? Rick and I were out for a midnight ride when I got a call from the hospital because I'm listed as your emergency contact. He's just parking the bike."

Zara jerked up and rolled off the bed, landing in a squat on the floor. She pulled herself up and straightened, a stiff smile on her face.

"I'm fine," he said. "I had a fall at work and I came as a precaution."

"I'm Zara." She held out her hand. "I don't know if you remember me, but we met at Tarun's wedding. I was on the floor. With the head . . ."

Jay's mother shot him a sideways glance, her lips tipping at the corners. "I do remember you. It's not every day I see my Jay rolling around on the floor during a wedding."

"We weren't rolling around, Mom," he gritted out. "We fell."

"I brought Jay to the hospital," Zara said quickly as if sensing the rising tension. "He didn't want to come, but he hit his head pretty hard on a cauldron, so I thought he should get it checked out."

"A cauldron?"

"Zara is a matchmaker. She's helping me find someone to fulfill my promise to you. In return, I offered to introduce her to a few celebrities. We were at a movie wrap party tonight so she could meet one of the actors."

"Zombies." Zara held out her arms and lurched forward. "It was the bomb."

His mother gave a snort of laughter, her eyes glistening with amusement. "It sounds like fun."

"It was work," Jay snapped, inexplicably irritated that his mother and Zara had bonded over his humiliating accident. "There was nothing fun about it."

He could see he'd been too harsh when Zara froze mid-lurch, a pained expression on her face.

"It looks like you're in good hands, so I'd better get going." She grabbed her bag and gave his mom a half smile. "It was nice to see you again."

Before he could apologize, she pushed aside the curtain and walked away. Mouth agape, Jay could only stare at her departing form.

"I really like her," his mother said.

Jay liked her, too. So why had he pushed her away?

· 15 ·

It wasn't easy to find potential matches for Jay in a hotel ballroom that held over five hundred guests, but after four days of radio silence, and having convinced herself that a kiss was just a kiss, Zara was up to the task.

"His name is Jay Dayal." Zara crouched beside Mara Bedi and her mother and flashed a picture of Jay that she'd scraped off his website. "He was a captain in the air force and now he's the CEO of a successful security company. He's tall, very fit, intelligent, and well educated. He owns a condo and a car. No pets. No siblings. No family but—"

"No family?" Mara's mother shook her head.

"It's just him and his mom." A mom she'd barely had a chance to meet because she'd been so spooked by her sudden arrival. What had she been thinking? She was supposed to be finding Jay a match, not seducing him when he was lying injured and vulnerable in a hospital bed. His mother must have been appalled by her behavior, and Zara couldn't blame her. At least she'd been able to put some distance between them and get her head back in the matchmaking game. But despite her best efforts, things weren't going to plan.

"I'm sure he's a nice boy, but marriage is about family," Mrs. Bedi said. "Without family he's not—"

"Of course. I understand." Zara stood quickly, trying to fight yet another inexplicable surge of relief. Three attempts. Three failures. Her matchmaking mojo was off. No matter how hard she tried to deny it, something had changed after their kiss, and it was making it almost impossible for her to hold up her end of the deal.

She walked away, her legs stiff beneath her soft net ivory lehenga. She'd decided to go full scandal by wearing a long, white, layered chiffon skirt and a sleeveless red embroidered choli with spaghetti straps and a plunging neckline, baring an auntie-gasping expanse of middle. An arm full of bangles, giant silver and red earrings, and a thick matching choker completed the look along with a sparkly pair of red stilettos.

"Beta!" Her father stopped her on her way to the bar. Parvati had just texted to say she was waiting with two mojitos and some gossip she was desperate to share. "You haven't come to visit since the show. I was getting worried." He gave her a warm hug and a peck on the cheek.

"Just busy with work." She swallowed her guilt. How was she supposed to visit him after seeing that display? She needed more time to process it. Maybe in another few weeks she'd be able to get over her fear of what he planned to paint next.

"My show was a tremendous success." He beamed. "I sold most of the paintings and I have commissions to do ten more. And Indra said when your friend Jay stopped by the gallery this week—"

"Wait. What?" Her heart leaped in her throat. "Jay went to see Indra?"

"Yes. She said they had a nice dinner and talked about art long into the evening."

His words hit her like a blow to the chest. Jay and Indra. She hadn't seen that one coming. But what did she expect? She'd made it clear when she left the hospital that their kiss was just a kiss. Was it really so surprising that he'd be interested in someone Zara had chosen? She was an excellent matchmaker and it looked like her 100 percent success rate was going to remain untarnished this year.

Her father's brow creased in a frown. "Is something wrong?"

"No." She tried to shake off the strange feeling in her stomach. She'd made her decision, so why did she feel a flare of panic at the thought of Jay and Indra together? "I'm happy for you."

"You look sad, beta. Do you want to come and sit with your old dad and your uncles?"

"Uh-uh. Nope." She held up a hand. "I'm good with the singles table."

"Do you know who else will be at the singles table?" He made a waving gesture and a short, round man with a goatee stepped out of the shadows. With his dark hair, thick black beard, and chestnut sherwani he had been almost completely hidden.

"This is Rohit Sharma." Her father patted Rohit on the back. "He's the son of a friend from my university days. He is a nice boy. Two degrees in computers and math. He builds model cars and he likes cats. What do you think? Do you want this one? Should I ask when this venue is free?"

Zara groaned inwardly and shot an apologetic look at poor Rohit, who looked as horrified and embarrassed as she felt. "I thought you said it would be subtle," she muttered under her breath to her father.

"It was. You didn't see him hiding until I told him to come out."

"It was lovely to meet you, Rohit." She plastered a smile on her face. "I'm actually just on my way to meet my friend. She's a bridesmaid and only has a few minutes to chat. I'm sure I'll see you again at the table." She turned to her dad, dropping her voice so only he could hear. "I'll see you on the dance floor and we're going to have words."

Twenty minutes, two mojitos, and some not-very-interesting gossip from Parvati later, she told her about Indra and Jay.

"Big deal," Parvati said. "I thought that was the point of matching them up." She fiddled with the folds in her skirt. The bride, Rucha, had bought pale pink saris for the bridesmaids to wear and Parvati couldn't get hers to fit properly. She'd never been a sari girl.

"It is. It was. It's . . ." Words failed her.

"What's the problem?"

"The kiss." Zara dropped her head to her hands. "It messed everything up. All I can think about is that kiss and how I want more kisses."

Parvati tipped her head back and groaned. "I am so done with hearing about that kiss, and not just from you. The entire department has been talking about it all week. If Jay ever winds up in the ER again, he'll be treated like a king."

"I've never been kissed like that." Zara's fingers went to her lips. Even now she could feel the softness of his mouth, the slow, gentle sweep of his tongue. She could hear the rasp of his breath, see the fire in his eyes, and feel his hot, hard body beneath her.

"If you want more of those kisses, you'd better do something before Indra runs away with your man or Rucha's cousin Binita gets her claws into him. Rucha put her beside Jay at your table. She thought they would hit it off."

"He's not my man." Zara sipped her drink. "He had a head injury when he kissed me. He wasn't thinking straight. He probably regrets it and that's why I haven't heard from him all week. I sent him some dating profiles and he didn't respond. He wasn't even at the sangeet last night. And who doesn't think a zombie party is fun? We have nothing in common."

"Maybe you scared him away. I've seen some of those dating profiles. If I was a guy, I'd run away as fast as I could."

"You're not helping, Parv." She swallowed the last of her mojito, warm and sickly sweet. "If he and Indra are together, then I'm happy for them. Really. I am."

"That's great." Parvati said absently, staring at Vivek Kapoor, the wedding's celebrity guest and a minor Bollywood star. A distant cousin of the bride, he had moved to the Bay Area with big dreams of switching from Bollywood to Hollywood. So far he'd played the funny desi sidekick in several action and rom-com films, but had been unable to land a leading role.

Zara's eyes narrowed as Vivek posed for yet another selfie with a fan. "Seriously? He's all flash, no substance."

"All that flash is going to be at the singles table with you," Parvati said. "Look how he moves his hips. It's like they're not even part of his body." She groaned in frustration. "Of all the times to be stuck in the bridal party. I'll be at the front of the room and he'll be at the back."

"I think that's a good thing. He's not worthy of you."

"I don't want worthy. I want hot. I want a man who knows how to move his body beneath the sheets." She finished her drink in one gulp. "I need you to be my wingwoman tonight. If ever you needed to use your matchmaking chops for a good cause, tonight is the night."

Zara shook her head even though they both knew she couldn't deny her best friend. "I need to take a matchmaking break. I feel burned out."

"I neeeeed Vivek." Parvati grabbed her shoulders and gave her a gentle shake. "Be a good bestie and sit beside him at the table so no one else steals him from me. Tell him you have a fabulous friend who is desperate to meet him."

Zara surveyed the room, charting a path between her present

location and the table. Rishta aunties were lurking everywhere, trying to appear innocent while they searched for their prey.

"I'll do my best." Taking a deep breath, she focused on her goal, walking as fast as she could to build up momentum so she couldn't be stopped.

"*I have someone for you to meet. Very robust. Forties are the new twenties . . .*"

"*. . . doctor says the rash isn't contagious.*"

"*Look who is here. So nice. Ten cats . . .*"

"*. . . just out of prison but it was a false charge . . .*"

"*He sings soprano in the choir . . .*"

"*. . . all men have flatulence. It's no big deal.*"

Zara made it to the table unscathed and quickly checked the name cards. She put herself between Vivek and some dude named Clive, leaving Jay and Rohit on the other side of the table. She had only just finished rearranging the seating when people started to arrive, introducing themselves as they sat down.

The dude beside Rohit was the groom's college buddy who was clearly hungover from the night before and didn't seem inclined to talk. Beads of sweat clung to his clammy forehead, and his hand shook when he reached for the bread rolls. Beside him, Binita, a pretty woman with a sleek black bob, was busy taking selfies from every angle while Kamal tried to photobomb her every shot. The bride's work friend, Clive, a Jason Momoa miniature with an extra helping of beard, gave Zara an exaggerated wink when he took the seat beside her, clearly thinking he was getting lucky tonight. Desperate to escape her fate, a woman in a white dress kept leaving her seat every two seconds to talk to people at a couples table nearby.

Vivek arrived and spent a few moments basking in adulation. It wasn't going to be easy to sell Parvati when she wasn't around, es-

pecially when the woman in white spotted him and raced back to
the table at double speed.

Jay was the last to arrive. Zara hadn't seen him since the night
of the party. He wore a black suit, cut perfectly to fit his magnificent body, his strong jaw was shaved, his hair neatly combed. Why
did he have to look so devastatingly gorgeous? It was only a wedding. Why couldn't he have come in jeans?

His gaze flicked from Vivek on her left to Clive on her right.
His jaw tightened almost imperceptibly, but he took his seat beside
Binita without saying a word.

Silence descended on the table.

"I guess we're not the in-crowd." Zara forced a smile when the
table nearest them erupted into laughter. "They're probably all
watching us, expecting us to pair off by the end of the evening as
if we came here desperate for a hookup." She wasn't feeling her
usual cheerful matchmaking self with Jay glaring at her from across
the table. What was that all about? He was the one who hadn't returned her messages.

"Maybe tonight is your lucky night." Clive waggled a bushy
brow. One did the work of two because they were joined in the
middle. "The man of your dreams might be right in front of you."

"Wedding hookups are fun, but they never lead to long-term
love." She looked around the table, deliberately avoiding Jay's gaze.
"How many of us have woken up in a strange bed the night after a
wedding and gotten the hell out of there as fast as possible?" She
raised her hand, her smile fading when no one followed suit. "Okay.
Just me."

Stop. Please. Just. Stop.

But she couldn't stop. It was too awkward. No one was talking,
and Binita was besotted with Jay, and the woman in white was all
over Vivek, and Kamal was doing magic tricks, and Clive's eyebrow

wouldn't stop wiggling, and there was only one man at the table worth the morning walk of shame and he'd had dinner with Indra.

"How about a drinking game?" Zara suggested. "That might loosen things up. I went to a destination winter wedding in Colorado a few years ago. I think we polished off six bottles of red wine. Or was it white? After a couple of rounds of wine pong, they all taste the same. Chitchat became flirting became crazy dancing and then we all wound up naked in the lake. As you do." She looked around expectantly, hoping that others might share their own stories about skinny-dipping in a freezing lake while drunk, but everyone just stared. "That night didn't go so well," she continued. "I hooked up with one of the groomsmen but he couldn't warm up, if you know what I mean."

The college dude choked on his beer. Clive licked his lips—at least that's what she thought he was doing under all that hair. Binita stared at her with wide-open eyes. But Zara was on a roll and couldn't stop.

"Anyway, as it turned out, it wasn't a performance issue. He had hypothermia and they had to take him away in an ambulance."

Still nothing. Tough crowd.

"Would anyone like some wine?" As if someone had finally taken pity on her, the server appeared at the table.

"Me." Zara held up her glass. "Fill it right up. Can you leave a bottle or twelve?"

After the glasses were filled, she decided to focus on Vivek. Parvati had already sent her four texts asking about her progress, and the woman in white had finally left him alone to powder her nose with a friend.

"We're so delighted you could be here," Zara said. "I've seen all your Bollywood films. What's your next project?"

"I just got a role in a new zombie film." He puffed out his chest.

"It's called *Night of the Living Hell Reincarnated Mutant Corpse Son of the Father of the Grandfather Evil Terror Grain-Fed Free-Range Bone-Sucking Undead Part 4: In IMAX 3-D*."

"Zombies?" Her eyes widened and she squeezed his arm. "I love zombies. I was just at a wrap party for *Day of the Night of the Evening of the Revenge of the Bride of the Son of the Terror of the Return of the Attack of the Alien, Mutant, Evil, Hellbound, Flesh-Eating, Rotting Corpse Living Dead Part 6: In Shocking 4-D* last week. I met Bob Smith." She looked over at Jay to share in her excitement only to find him scowling at her. What the hell was going on? He was all soft smiles and gentle whispers when he talked to the simpering Binita.

"Bob was supposed to play the commander," Vivek said. "But he's been caught up in some kind of scandal and I heard they're considering replacing him. I hope not because it would be an honor to work with such an artistic genius. He's a method actor. Did you know he lives as a zombie for three full months before filming, to get into the role?"

She tried to pay attention as he talked about filming, but now Binita was touching Jay's palm. What was that all about? Two-timing bastard. What about Indra? Why couldn't he just pick one woman? And why did she have the overwhelming desire to claw out Binita's eyes?

Gritting her teeth, she turned her attention back to Vivek, who was back on the topic of zombies. The college dude interrupted with questions about zombie sexy times and whether all the important body parts were operational in the undead. Clive snickered like a teenager. Zara wanted to tell him he wasn't getting lucky tonight but she couldn't get a word in because he wouldn't stop talking about how being between jobs had encouraged him to focus on himself and now he only ate raw.

The woman in the white dress returned and went balls to the wall to get Vivek's attention back on her. She twirled a lock of her silky, dark hair around her finger. Batted her long eyelashes. Laughed at everything Vivek said, including his sad story about the death of his childhood pet and his plastic surgery failures. Not wanting to disappoint Parvati, Zara made a last-ditch, desperate attempt to talk up her friend.

"My friend Parvati has a collection of kites." Zara edged her chair closer to Vivek. "It's amazing. When she's not at the hospital, where she works as an emergency room physician, or doing volunteer work for inner-city kids, or modeling for desi magazines, or watching another zombie movie marathon, she's out on the beach . . . flying them . . . in the sky."

"You're lucky to have found someone," Vivek said. "I'm still single." He gave the woman in the white dress a smoldering look. "And available."

What had happened to her matchmaking chops? Parvati was going to kill her. "We're not together," Zara blurted out. "We live together but we're not *together* together. She likes men. Well, she also likes women. But not me. She does like me, of course. We're friends. But I like men. Just men."

"I'm a man," Clive said. "All man."

She mustered a cold smile. "Thank you for clearing that up."

Turning back to Vivek, she gestured to the dance floor, where Rucha and Rishi were having their first dance. "Parvati will be dancing next. If she wasn't a doctor, she would have been a pole dancer."

"I can pole dance." Clive put his arm around her chair. "I learned when I was tree planting in the Canadian wilderness."

Zara put up a hand, warding him off. "Please don't tell me . . ."

"I was surrounded by beavers. Brown, black, brown and black . . ."

"Single ladies!" The MC's voice rang through the hall. "Time for the bride to throw the bouquet and then you can hit the dance floor."

Rucha stepped into position, ready to toss her bouquet to the baying, slavering mob of excited women crowding the dance floor. Zara hunched in her seat, trying to hide. Aside from the singles table, the bouquet toss and single ladies' dance were the most humiliating wedding rituals for single people.

"She's single!" Clive grabbed Zara's hand and held it high, ensuring he wasn't getting lucky tonight.

One of the bridesmaids screamed in delight and dragged Zara to the dance floor, placing her squarely in front of the melee. Zara glared at Parvati, who mouthed an apology before slinking into the crowd.

The giggles. The countdown. The good-natured shoving that would momentarily turn into a no-holds-barred brawl. Dozens of hands outstretched, bangles clinking, rings glittering, long nails sharpened to claws.

And it was off. The bouquet soared over her head. All hell broke loose. Lehenga were hiked up thighs, sharpened stilettos pounded across the tiled floor. There was a bump. A set. A scrum. A scream. Zara tried to push her way through the frenzy. She made it to the edge of the dance floor only to see the bouquet heading her way.

Heart pounding, she jumped and spiked the flowers away. Too late she realized her high school volleyball skills were a little bit rusty. Instead of heading into the seething mass of desperate singles, the bouquet flew straight at the back of Rucha's head.

A blur of black. An elegant hand. Jay caught the bouquet midflight and tossed it into the crowd.

"Quickly." He grabbed Zara's hand and pulled her off the dance floor. "Let's get you out of here."

Zara was more than happy to follow Jay off the dance floor. He led her through the expansive hallways and out onto a secluded balcony overlooking a manicured garden.

"I'll have to remember to give you a call the next time my friends set up a volleyball game on the beach," he said, barely winded.

Zara bent over, wheezing out a breath. "I didn't mean to spike it at her head." She stood and gripped the railing, cursing herself yet again for her impulsiveness. Why couldn't she be more like her mother? Always cool. Always calm. Always poised no matter what the occasion. "I guess you're the next one who's going to get married since you actually caught it."

He gave her an affronted stare. "You caught it first."

"Technically, it wasn't a catch because I didn't hold it. I simply redirected its path." She looked out over the gardens, where Vivek stood near a fountain, his expectant gaze on the patio where people had spilled out to dance.

"Is he waiting for you?" Jay's voice was tight, strained.

"What?" She frowned. "Me and Vivek?"

"You spent most of the dinner talking to him." His hand fisted on the balcony. "He'd probably think a zombie party was the most fun he'd ever had."

Zara felt a flutter of excitement in her belly. Was he jealous? Not that jealousy was a good thing, but glaring was caring. "Can you imagine a bigger disaster? He's like me—reckless, impulsive, accident-prone—he just hides it better. He told me he had to hire an assistant to follow him around and move things out of his way because when he's in character and focused on his lines, he forgets where he is. He fell into the ocean on his last set."

"So, he understands you."

"I don't even understand me," she said dryly. "I can't imagine the guy I was trying to prime for Parvati would have better insight."

"Parvati wants him?"

"She's hot for him, but because she had to sit with the bridal party, she asked me to be her wingwoman. I was supposed to talk her up and keep all the competition away. Honestly, between helping out Parvati, keeping the hirsute pole dancer away, checking in on you and Binita, and trying to get people talking, the evening has been utterly exhausting."

His lips twitched, but his voice was even. "Why would you be checking in on me and Binita?"

"In case she was the one, and I could add a match to my season scorecard." She tossed her hair, trying to show him it didn't matter that he'd been all careless whispers and touchy palms with a stranger he barely knew. "Or . . . is it Indra? I heard you two got together."

Part of her hoped he would say yes. They'd had their kiss and it was great, but he'd found someone else. But another part, the deep secret part of her that felt so calm and safe when he was near, hoped for a different answer, even though it scared her.

"I'm not interested in either one of them."

Her heart skipped a beat then pounded in her chest. "Why? What's wrong with them?"

"Not my type."

"I thought you and Indra had dinner and talked long into the night." She shivered from the intensity of his stare.

"I wanted to buy some artwork. Indra ordered dinner so I could take my time looking through the portfolio."

"Oh." Her breath left her in a rush. "Of course you did. That's what I thought. You're not really the type who would be into selfietakers with palm fetishes or gallery owners who show suggestive fruits."

"You were jealous." Lips quivering in a smug smile, he closed the distance between them, backing her up against the brick wall.

"Don't be silly. I just wanted to get my facts straight so I would know when to add your match to my wedding season scorecard. When I heard about your visit . . ."

He lifted an eyebrow. "How did you hear about it?"

"There are no secrets in the Patel family. Everybody knows everything. Gossip is an Olympic sport. It's only surprising that it took two days instead of two minutes."

"I have a secret nobody knows." He braced one arm on the wall beside her head and she mentally engaged in unhealthy booze-fueled speculation.

They'd agreed on one kiss. What if he wanted more?

· 16 ·

Zara wasn't listening.

Jay knew it for a fact because her eyes were slightly glazed. When she was listening, or talking, Zara stared directly at him, giving him all her focus and attention. The only time she hadn't focused was when he'd kissed her, and since it was all he'd been thinking about since the last time he saw her, he was pretty sure she was thinking about it, too.

"What secret?" She pulled her bottom lip between her teeth and damned if he couldn't take his eyes away.

"I'm good at hugs." He traced the thin strap of her choli with his finger, and she drew in a sharp breath.

"I know."

"I'm also good at kisses." He followed the embroidery, his finger skimming over the crescent of her breast. It was her passion that drew him, he decided, that and her ability to make the best of every situation even if it meant putting herself out there and suffering as a result.

Constrained by a fierce desire to succeed, to prove himself to a father who didn't want him, he had sought that same freedom in the air force, where he could lose himself to the adrenaline rush and the endless blue sky.

"Is your secret a supreme self-confidence and an ego so big I have to step around it?" She put one hand on his chest. For a moment he thought she'd push him away but when she didn't move, he felt an overwhelming sense of relief. He'd wondered all week if he'd scared her away with that kiss. It had been hell giving her space, but he couldn't take any chances. Slowly but surely Zara was working her way under his skin.

"I don't give my secrets away for free." He slid one hand around her waist, pulling her close.

Zara melted against him, hands sliding up and over his shoulders. "Will you tell me for a kiss?"

"Possibly." He drew his finger down, following the edge of her top where it dipped low between her breasts. Her skin was soft, her perfume so lush and sensual it clouded his senses.

She leaned up, feathered kisses along his jaw. "Can it be now?"

He meant to give her a soft kiss, a gentle kiss, testing the waters to see if she truly wanted to come on this ride with him. But the moment their lips met, something snapped inside him. Four days of longing and fantasies. A lifetime of loneliness. A need so fierce, he twisted his hand in her hair and claimed her mouth in a fury of passion and desire.

Zara groaned and melted against him. He could feel the rapid beat of her heart, taste the sweetness of chocolate in her mouth. Never comfortable with public displays of affection, he didn't care if the entire world saw them so long as she kept kissing him and never stopped.

"Jay." She drew back, breaking the spell. "What's the secret? Tell me or I won't kiss you like that again."

Laughter warmed him. "The secret is . . ." That he wanted her. Needed her. Was willing to do whatever it took to convince her that he was nothing like the lovers who had hurt her in the past. But he couldn't tell her. Not yet. Not if he wanted to keep her in his life. "I want to put a pause on our deal."

"What does that mean? You don't want me to find you a match?"

"I think you need to get to know me better," he said, nuzzling the slim column of her throat. "Then you'll know my perfect match when you see her."

"Mmmm." She tipped her head to the side, giving him better access. "Good idea. I really shouldn't have jumped into this without doing the proper research. Usually I know the people I'm matching, but you are still a bit of a mystery."

A smile spread across his face. "I am open to being unraveled."

He was only vaguely aware of their trip to her house. There was a company limo—he didn't know who ordered it, maybe him?—and Zara straddling his lap, grinding against him until he was so hard he could barely see. Eyes watching in the rearview mirror. Someone—the driver?—mentioned something about a privacy screen. And then they were alone behind a smoky glass shield, and his fingers were buried in the softness of her hair, and he was devouring her mouth like he hadn't kissed a woman in years.

There were groans—his—and moans—hers—and cool hands under his shirt, nails scraping his skin, zings of electricity along his nerves, clothes tearing . . .

"Not here." Her words. Because if he had his way, she'd already be naked and the limo driver would have been handsomely paid to take a coffee break somewhere far away.

He had a vision of himself pushing her onto the seat, flipping up that pretty skirt, and hammering into her until they both shattered in ecstasy and she screamed his name. Had he spoken those words out loud?

"Law . . . Indecent exposure . . ." Words he didn't understand except they meant more waiting when he ached to get his hands on her, strip her naked, and make all his fantasies come true.

Insatiable, he tore open her top and flicked the catch on her bra, freeing her breasts from their restraint. Beautiful. Round and firm. Nipples hardened to deliciously dark peaks. He drew one into his mouth, licked and sucked until she cried out. Her hand tightened in his hair until pain merged with pleasure, and he couldn't think beyond doing it again.

"This is probably a mistake."

Definitely not his words, and belied by her laughter, her frenzied pawing at his shirt, and the scatter of buttons across the limo floor. *Wild.* He had captured her wild and it would set him free.

Nails scraping down his chest, yanking on his belt. His cock hard and pulsing in anticipation.

"How much longer?" Fingers stroking. Hand in his boxers. The mind-numbing pleasure of her palm on his shaft.

Time didn't matter. The need to have her was fierce and intense, demanding instant satisfaction. He wanted her. Here. Now. Hidden by blacked-out windows in the dead of the night.

With rough hands, he shoved her skirt over her hips. Red silk panties. Teasing. Tantalizing.

"Tear them off." Her urgency pleased him, called to the animal frenzy of his lust.

"Law? Indecent exposure?"

"Fuck it."

Her panties rendered with a soft whimper, fluttered to the floor. Soft and dark her secrets beckoned. He parted her folds and sank a thick finger deep inside her wet center. She gasped, arched against him. He gave her another finger, his free hand in her hair, holding her still, baring her neck for the heated slide of his lips.

A third finger. Gentle strokes. Hungry kisses. His thumb stroked over her swollen nub. A guttural groan and she came, her inner walls tightening around him.

Dazed, languid, she collapsed forward against his chest. He hissed in a breath when the down between her legs brushed against his cock.

"Does your fancy limo come with condoms?" Her breath was hot against his skin.

"Of course." They kept their clients well supplied.

She moved back to accommodate him as he rolled on a condom. Then she stroked and squeezed until rational thought was a distant memory and all that was left were need and want, lust and desire. He dragged her up, claiming her mouth as he thrust inside her. Pleasure so exquisite, he closed his eyes and tried to take a mental snapshot of the moment.

Bracing herself on his shoulders she rode him, levering her hips as she brought him closer and closer to his peak.

Control. He needed it. In one swift motion he shifted, carrying her down so she lay beneath him, clothes half off, hair tangled, lips swollen from his kisses, wanton and free.

Lifting her legs to his hips, he thrust into her. Slick walls tightened, made his eyes water. His hips pistoned, driving deep until pleasure peaked and they both found release.

Skin slicked with sweat, heart pounding, he leaned over to feather kisses over her nose, her cheeks, her jaw, memorizing the moment. Drifted away.

"Jay?" The sound of his name on her lips shocked him back to a reality he wasn't ready to face.

"Hmm." He could stay here forever with her soft warm body

beneath him, the taste of her on his tongue, the heady scent of sex and perfume lingering in the air around them.

"Is that all you've got?"

Zara dreamed of a drowning man.

She was back on China Beach, walking hand in hand with the head lifeguard, Clayton Heales. Zara had crushed on Clayton since she'd obtained her lifeguard certification at the age of twenty-one, but Clayton wasn't interested. He'd called her crazy. Fun to have at a party but not to have in his bed. But now here he was, buff and tan, his blond hair glistening in the sun. It would have been perfect except for the man in the ocean.

His shouts became urgent, pulling her partway out of the dream. She buried her head, desperate not to let the moment go.

A storm rolled in, turning the calm, shallow water into a raging sea. The man disappeared and then resurfaced, panicked and splashing, unable to see how close he was to shore. With one last longing look at Clayton, she grabbed her board and ran to save him, paddling with strong strokes as the waves tossed and the rain fell. She could almost taste the man's terror, feel his heart pound. She reached for him. Too late. He was gone.

She woke with a start. For a moment, she was still in the ocean, the shouts of the drowning man ringing in her ears. Then her mind cleared. She was alone in her bed.

"Jay?" She turned on her bedside lamp and saw Jay pulling on his boxers near the door.

"I have to get going." His cold, hard voice and the sheen of sweat on his body told her the shouts she'd heard had not been a dream.

She glanced over at the clock. "It's three in the morning."

"I couldn't sleep."

"Because of the nightmares." She knew she'd called it right when he froze.

His jaw tightened and he turned away. "I'm sorry if I woke you. I'll be out of here in a few minutes."

She couldn't let him go home in the dark to an empty apartment when he was so obviously distraught. Acting on impulse, she slid out of bed and walked toward him. His gaze dropped to her naked body, and he drew in a ragged breath.

"Zara . . ." His voice caught. "I never stay overnight for this very reason."

"That's fine. I had no expectations beyond a fun night together. This was just temporary anyway until I found your match or we got tired of playing this game." It wasn't fine, but it would have to be. After their night together, she couldn't go back to pretending she didn't want him, but she couldn't risk getting too involved.

When he didn't move, didn't reach for the rest of his clothing, she walked right up to him and wrapped him in a hug. Skin to skin. Soothing his pain away.

He stiffened but she didn't let go. After a few minutes, she felt the tension ease from his body. His arms came around her, and he rested his cheek on her head.

"Do you want to talk about it?" she murmured against his chest.

"No."

"Do you want to have some hot sex instead of getting into a cold cab and driving away?" She looked up and grinned. "I'm awake. You're awake. We've only gone three rounds. Why not make it an even four? I'm already undressed." She took his hand and drew it down between her legs. "You don't even have to waste time with foreplay. This is what you do to me. I'm all ready to go."

"I shouldn't . . ."

"Don't tell me you don't want to." She ground her hips against his cock, now rock hard beneath his boxers. "I simply won't believe you."

Jay groaned. "I do, but . . ."

"But what?" She dropped to her knees in front of him and drew his boxers down to his ankles. His cock, thick and hard, bounced gently in her direction. "You don't like soft wet lips, firm hands, and skills honed by years of beer funnels." She flicked her tongue over the swollen head of his shaft. "Say yes. Say you'll stay long enough for me to chase your demons away."

His hand dropped to her head and he swallowed hard. "Yes, but I'll do the chasing."

Moments later, she was back on the bed, her brain still trying to process how quickly he had moved and what kind of man would turn down what she'd just offered. And then she wasn't thinking because his fingers were deep inside her and his face was above her, his gaze fixed on hers as she drowned in sensation.

"I think someone has control issues." She arched her back when he drew his fingers away. "Lucky for you, I can handle that sort of thing."

He gave her a slow, sensual smile and released her long enough to grab a condom and sheathe himself. "Open for me, sweetheart." His voice deepened, husky and low, with a delicious hint of rough.

She did as he asked, anticipation curling in her belly. Jay knew what he was doing in bed and she liked him taking the lead. Instead of wondering what came next and where she should touch and what he might like, she could just let go. Feel instead of think. Calm the frenetic activity in her mind.

He kissed his way down her body, his heated breath sending ripples of electricity over her skin. His hand touched between her thighs and he spread her moisture, gently teasing. When his finger brushed over her clitoris, the spark of sensation sent a flush of heat through her veins. She lifted her hips in invitation, but Jay pushed himself up and straddled her body instead.

"Not yet."

"That's very unkind." She mocked a frown. "I have been very hospitable. The least you could do is give me some loving."

With a chuckle, he leaned over and drew her nipple into his warm, wet mouth, licking and sucking until every tug tightened her core. When she thought she couldn't take any more, he turned his attention to her other breast and then feathered his lips up her throat and teased open her lips.

He kissed her deeply, thoroughly, sweeping inside her mouth to touch, to taste, to own every part of her. His hand slid down between her legs, finger stroking her clit. Demanding and teasing. Together the dual sensations left her blazing with need. Relentless, his fingers spread her moisture, circling around and around the place she desperately wanted them to go, until her muscles were tense and quivering and she was shaking with desire.

When she thought she couldn't take any more, he pushed back, shoving her legs apart, and positioned himself at her entrance. "Are you ready for me, sweetheart?"

"Yes." She liked to be his sweetheart. Even if it was just for the night. But talk was cheap and her body was hot and aching. She'd been ready for him since the moment she'd jerked awake.

Bracing himself on her headboard, he thrust inside her. Stilled. Shuddered. Only then did she realize how badly he needed this, needed her.

She opened her mouth to speak, but he pushed deeper, filling her completely. His muscles quivered with every thrust. Faster. Harder. Her mind calmed and she gave herself over to the frenzy of passion, meeting his every stroke with a rock of her hips, riding the tidal wave of sensation until it swept her up and carried her away.

He followed her with a guttural groan and then collapsed beside her on the bed.

"Do you still want to go?" she whispered.

Jay rolled to his back and pulled her over his chest, settling her against him. "Not yet."

"WELL, look what the cat dragged out." Zara looked up from her coffee when Jay walked out of the bedroom with Marmalade in his arms. He had stayed in the shower after they'd made use of the soap and the warm water and the fact he was strong enough to hold her up against his hips.

"We've come to an understanding." He sat at the kitchen counter and took the coffee she offered. "I'm the alpha of the bedroom and he can be alpha everywhere else."

"Very sensible." She pulled out a bag of bagels and offered it to him, unsure what to do. Now that they were both dressed, everything seemed too civilized. She still couldn't believe he'd stayed the rest of the night, sleeping deeply and peacefully until she'd woken him in the morning. "I'm not much of a breakfast person. I usually pick something up on the way to work."

"I can cook," Jay said. "I have excellent breakfast-making skills."

"I have excellent breakfast-eating skills, but I have a rehearsal for a community theater production of *The Pirates of Penzance* in an hour and I can't be late." Although tempted, she didn't know what this was and she didn't want him to get any ideas. A night of sexy times was one thing. Morning breakfast was something else entirely, and she was suddenly desperate to be alone.

"I would be a formidable pirate," he said, musing. "I have a gift with swords, as you well know."

Laughter bubbled up in her chest, easing her tension. "I think someone is overly pleased with himself this morning."

"You're still here. I take that as a marker of my success." He added cream and two sugars from the tray she'd left on the counter. Clearly, he wasn't in a hurry to go.

"It's my apartment, Jay. Even if your performance was subpar, it's not like I could go anywhere."

"Subpar?" He choked on his coffee. "That word and my name should never be used in the same sentence."

"Are you some kind of cat whisperer?" she asked when Marmalade purred, rubbing his head against Jay's chest. "He doesn't like strangers."

"I'm hardly a stranger. I've been here all night." He sipped his coffee with his free hand. "Cats love me. I made friends with a stray cat at a base in Afghanistan. He followed me everywhere. I said goodbye when we had to leave but he stowed away on our cargo plane. He came with me on every mission after that." His face softened. "I named him Storm because there was a storm the night I found him."

Marmalade purred so loudly Zara had to laugh. "You have tamed the savage Marmalade beast. I'd say that definitely makes you a cat person. Do you still have Storm?"

Jay's face smoothed to an expressionless mask, and he shook his head. Sensing the loss had been difficult, she scrambled for a neutral topic to lighten the mood.

"Did you learn anything about me while you were alone in my room?" She didn't know if he'd been poking around, and she didn't care. Zara had nothing to hide.

His face lightened in an instant. "I did see some interesting lingerie on your dresser. Why wasn't it worn for me?"

Amused by his look of righteous indignation, Zara laughed. "You didn't seem interested in seeing me in any clothes."

He shot her a pointed look. "Next time."

Next time? Was there going to be a next time? Was this, as she'd told the singles table last night, just a wedding hookup that would end when he walked out the door? Or was it something more? Something she'd promised herself never to do again.

Sweat beaded her brow. She tugged open the kitchen window to let in some air, making a mental note to tell Parvati that she wanted a bigger kitchen the next time they moved. Restless, she tidied up the kitchen, washed the dishes, and put the coffee and bagels away, all while Jay sipped his coffee and stroked her betraying feline. When there was nothing left to do, she grabbed her purse from the counter, hoping Jay would take the hint.

"My theater is on the way to your office. Do you need a lift?" After riding in his limo last night, she didn't know what he would think of her blue Chevy Spark.

"I'll call an Uber. I got a message from Lucia this morning. She might have found a way to get the lawsuit against our company dismissed. Elias and I are meeting her at the office in a few hours."

"On a Sunday?" Tony and Lewis didn't expect their associates to work on weekends unless absolutely necessary.

"Lucia and I both work weekends. Elias won't be happy, but he'll be there. She said you gave her the idea to investigate former employees when you suggested it could be an inside job and they've found a likely suspect. I'm just glad it'll be over. We can't afford a lawsuit on our books. It would destroy any chance we have of getting funding for our international expansion. My dream almost slipped through my fingers."

She smiled, pleased that she'd been able to help, and even more pleased that they both had somewhere they had to be. "I would have invited you to watch the rehearsal but maybe another time." It was easy to make the offer knowing he couldn't come.

"I'll have to wait for opening night." He sipped his coffee like he had all the time in the world, like she wasn't standing in the kitchen holding her bag all ready to go.

Marmalade jumped off Jay's lap and rubbed against her legs, reminding her that she'd forgotten the most important male in the house.

"It's not for another three months." Her pulse kicked up a notch for no discernible reason. "We probably won't . . . I don't even know . . ." She yanked open a drawer, looking for a can opener. "You won't even remember me by then. Wedding season will be over. We'll be back to our normal lives . . ."

Jay froze, the coffee cup partway to his lips. She tensed, heart thudding in anticipation of his reaction to her subtle hint. He would agree and their night would be just that—one night. Or, he would protest and she'd have to tell him that she couldn't get involved but she was still committed to finding his perfect someone. Either way she was going to be disappointed.

"I'd better call that Uber." He put down his cup. "I'll need to swing by my apartment to change before I meet Lucia."

Zara let out the breath she didn't realize she'd been holding. She hadn't considered a third option: Jay wouldn't take the bait.

17

"WHERE were you last night?" Rick looked up from the couch when Jay walked into his apartment. "Did you get lucky?"

It took Jay a moment to come down from the high of his night with Zara to form three coherent thoughts: 1. This was his apartment; 2. He was a grown man who hadn't had to account to anyone for his whereabouts for almost twenty years; and 3. Rick had made himself comfortable on Jay's Italian leather couch with his boots on the glass coffee table, a carton of chicken wings on his lap, and *Days of Our Lives* blasting on Jay's big-screen TV.

"I have a kitchen," Jay pointed out. He and Rick had moved past the pleasantries and into bare tolerance after their first dinner together at the food truck. "It has a table."

"Yeah, got that." Rick took another wing from the box. "Problem is, your mom's busy cooking and there's no room to eat. She enjoyed looking after you a little too much after your head injury. Now she's convinced you're gonna starve if she doesn't fill your freezer." His lips quirked in a smile. "How's the head?"

"Fine."

Rick snickered. "Christ. When I told my buddies you got a minor concussion after banging your head on a cauldron full of zombie brains—"

"Mom?" Jay made a hasty retreat and followed the delicious

scents of cinnamon, cardamom, and cloves to the kitchen, determined to convince his mother to dump Rick and find someone with a slightly less biting sense of humor.

"Have a seat." She pointed to the table with her wooden spoon. "I was just about to grate some coconut on the *rava upma*. You can eat it while it's hot."

Jay wasn't about to turn down a home-cooked breakfast even if the table was so full there was barely space to eat. The South Indian delicacy made with fresh vegetables, spices, lentils, aromatic nuts, and curry leaves had been a childhood favorite.

"I've made enough food to last you a few days." She spooned the rava upma into a bowl. "You won't go hungry."

Jay surveyed the foil-covered dishes on the counter. "You've made enough food for a month."

"Rick and I are going for a drive this afternoon so I brought you a little something for Sunday dinner." She handed him the bowl. "When I saw your empty fridge, I went home to pick up my cooking supplies. I didn't want you to starve."

Jay's dislike for Rick increased another notch. Even when his mom had been going through her cancer treatment, they never missed spending Sunday evening together.

"I thought maybe you could share all this food with someone . . ." She wiped her hands on her apron, a seemingly casual gesture that was anything but. Jay knew that move—the inquisition was about to begin. "Maybe your friend from the hospital?"

Jay stirred the steaming dish. "We have an arrangement. Nothing more. She's still trying to find me a match. I introduced her to a minor celebrity. It's all going as planned. I'd made that promise to you, and our most promising investor hinted that community and family ties were important to the bank, so it seemed like a good idea at the time."

"And now?" She took a seat across from him, clearing a space for her elbows on his glass-and-steel table. He'd picked all his furniture in one afternoon, making his choices with functionality rather than aesthetics in mind.

"Now things are complicated," he admitted.

His mother lifted a basket from the counter and handed him a fluffy *pav*. "I saw your face at the hospital. It's not complicated at all."

"Whatever it is, I don't have time for it." He tore the soft roll in two. "We're about to settle a big lawsuit so it will be full steam ahead for the international expansion once we secure our funding. My focus needs to be on the business right now."

"Love doesn't come when it's convenient," his mother said. "It crashes into your life when you least expect it, when your guard is down and you're looking the other way. Love slips through the cracks and into the corners of your heart. By the time you realize it's found you, there is no escape."

"I don't know anything about love." He bit into the pav, savoring the soft texture and delicate flavor. "I do know that Zara can be impulsive and stubborn and she calls things as she sees them. She follows her own path and refuses to compromise even if it means turning down a job at the biggest law firm in the city, or losing a paintball game. I've never met anyone who takes so many risks or embraces life so fully. She's loud and colorful and passionate and utterly unapologetic about who she is. But she's also warm and kind and devoted to her friends and her family. She has no hesitation putting herself out there, and when things go wrong, she just bounces back."

His mother chuckled. "I knew l liked her when we met. Now I like her even more."

"She's the opposite of me," he grumbled. "We couldn't be more different."

"Are you sure about that?" She poured two cups of coffee. "Before you left home, you had that passion, that love of life. You came back to me in a dark place, and it hurt my heart that I couldn't do anything to bring that Jay back. It didn't help that you had to leave your career to deal with me."

"I didn't have to *deal* with you, Mom." Emotion welled up in his throat. "It was a privilege to be there for you the way you were always there for me."

"Hey, babe," Rick shouted. "You gotta get in here. This is the season where everyone gets drugged and kidnapped, and they all go around stabbing each other in the back. It's a fucking soap opera."

"It is, literally, a soap opera," Jay muttered under his breath.

"You got any more of that Chablis?" Rick called out. "Goes great with the wings. And some of those sweets you made last night? The yellow ones with the nuts on top."

"I thought he was a biker," Jay said. "The whole Chablis and *Days of Our Lives* thing is throwing me off. And he'd better not be taking you out on his bike after he's been drinking."

"Don't be hard on him." She covered the rolls and turned off the stove. "He's a good man. We're going in my car. I have to pick up some supplies for the daycare, and he offered to come with me and make a day of it. It's a big thing for him, traveling in a *cage*."

Jay leaned forward and lowered his voice. "What about that guy at the wedding? The one you invited to take my seat? He seemed . . . normal."

"And boring." His mother patted his shoulder. "But I asked him to sit with me because I wanted you to meet people and have some fun. After I saw you on the floor with Zara, I knew I'd made the right decision. And then when I saw you together in the hospital . . ." She put her hand to her chest, her eyes growing soft.

"Mom. She's gone through a lot. Bad relationships, her parents' divorce . . . She's not big on getting serious. And even if she was, there are things about me . . . stuff that happened. I don't want that darkness to touch her."

"That's her decision to make, not yours." She pushed back her chair and crossed the kitchen to the refrigerator. "From what you've told me, it sounds like she's strong enough to deal with whatever you throw her way and maybe bring some joy into your life."

Jay counted five casserole dishes and numerous small bowls in his once-empty fridge. His mother hadn't wasted any time.

"When I just mentioned seeing her again, she almost ran out of her own apartment." He'd picked up on her anxiety when he walked into the kitchen and she'd shoved the bag of bagels at him. He'd never been on the wrong side of a hookup. Usually he was the one running away.

"I've never known you to back away from a challenge." She took out a small container of milk *peda* and added a few to a plate. "Maybe you should invite her over for dinner. I've made all your favorite dishes."

Jay shrugged. "I don't know if I want—"

"Babe! He's got the gun. What a moron. His prints are gonna be all over it. I would have worn gloves. And it's fucking daylight. He's not real Mafia. You would never see them coming."

"I'd better go before he finishes all the wings." She picked up the plate of sweets, her lips tipping up with a smile. "Sometimes we find happiness where we least expect it."

Z ARA ran across the stage with the members of the chorus, straining to reach the high notes of "Climbing over Rocky Mountain." The set designers had created a beach scene using Styrofoam rocks and a poorly painted backdrop of the sky. With limited funds, the producer had decided to spend money on costumes instead of sets. She couldn't fault his choice. Her yellow ruffled dress and bloomers were a delight to wear, and she got to carry a parasol.

"Smile," David called out. "You're supposed to be having fun." The assistant director had joined the creative team at the last minute after his predecessor had been asked to direct a play on Broadway.

Zara danced and twirled with the rest of the chorus before helping to spread a blanket on the ground for their pretend picnic. Hopefully the musical would be a big success for the theater. Steeped in history and smelling strongly of old furniture and faintly of cigarettes, the cozy, intimate playhouse had retained much of its original woodwork and crown moldings. Stained-glass lights, thick curtains, and red plush seats gave it an art deco feel that was unmatched by any of the other community theaters she'd performed at over the years.

David nodded from the front row of the mostly empty theater as they rehearsed. Performers were allowed to invite friends and family to watch, but on a sunny day like today few people had shown up. She recognized the fiancé of a member of the chorus and the mother of the Pirate King, but not the man now leaning against the wall at the back of the theater. Squinting through the bright stage lights, she was just able to make out his face.

Jay.

A thrill of excitement shot down her spine. Never in a million years would she have expected to see him here, especially when he'd told her he planned to spend the day at the office. Her heart pounded even harder than it had the day Antoine Vaillancourt, star of her high school drama club, had accepted her invitation to come for a free large fries at Big Joe's Burgers, where she'd worked as a cashier during her sophomore year.

She twirled her parasol, belting out the words to the song with such enthusiasm that the performers next to her shot her curious glances. Heart racing, her smile stretching her cheeks to the max, she spun faster, kicked higher, jumped farther, threw out her arms, and accidentally slapped the woman beside her on the back of her head.

"I'm so sorry."

"Don't stop," David shouted.

Zara joined the rest of the chorus as they played ball with a red balloon. She felt hyperaware of Jay watching, and curiously self-conscious. The balloon drifted toward her and she batted it away so hard, it hit Julia—a lackluster Kate—in the face, throwing her off the beat.

"Stop the music." David jumped up from his seat. "Julia, you'll have to start over."

"It's not my fault," Julia snapped. "Zara attacked the balloon like she was trying to score an Olympic gold in beach volleyball."

"I think that's a bit of an exaggeration." Zara's cheeks heated. "It was just overinflated."

"You're going to have to deal with the unexpected every time we perform," David said. "The show must go on. You can't get distracted." He checked his watch. "I think we're done for the day. Let's all get out and enjoy the sunshine."

Zara left with the rest of the cast to change her clothes and have a quick word with the prop master about balloon alternatives for the picnic scene. By the time she was done, the playhouse had cleared out. She found Jay waiting for her beside the stage.

"I can't believe you came." She threw her arms around him and gave him a hug.

His arms tightened around her. "You said you would have invited me if I'd been free. I didn't want to miss the chance to see you, so I asked Elias to handle the meeting with Lucia."

"I never imagined you'd be interested after I threw you out of my apartment." She released him when he gave an indignant huff.

"You didn't throw me out. I left of my own volition."

"It was a metaphorical throw." She sat on the edge of the stage, and he eased himself up beside her.

"That's the problem with lawyers," he said. "You're too good with words. Simple guys like me don't have a chance."

"You're hardly simple. A little uptight, perhaps. Definitely a workaholic. Inflexible. Controlling. Maybe a bit broody—"

"I'll stop you right there before my ego gets too big to contain." His lips twitched at the corners. With his shirt open and his suit jacket folded neatly in his lap, he looked more relaxed than she'd ever seen him during the day.

"What did you think of the rehearsal?"

"It was very entertaining," he said. "I wish I could dance like that. I have two left feet and no sense of rhythm. Avi doesn't know what he's in for when I show up for his groom squad dance rehearsals. I'm probably unteachable."

Zara jumped up on the stage and held out her hand. "I'll show you a few moves."

Jay hesitated, searching the empty theater. He was always so concerned about his image and reputation, and yet when they were alone together, he was a different man.

"Everyone is gone," she assured him, pulling up the "Dhinka Chika" remix on her phone. "It's just us. You can screw up as badly as you want and no one will see you."

Jay jumped up on the stage and carefully placed his folded jacket over a Styrofoam rock.

"Hands in your pockets and move them from side to side." She demonstrated the move, swaying in time to the music.

Jay gave her a horrified look. "I might be morally corrupted if I spend too much time with you."

"After last night, I'm pretty sure it would be the other way around." She rocked her hips back and forth. "Keep your hands in your pockets and do this, or are you not familiar with the pelvic thrust?"

"I think you know the answer to that question," he said, his voice smug.

Watching him now, it was hard to believe this was the same man she'd met on the paintball field. Beneath the walls and the shadows, he had an almost playful sense of humor.

"I am at once delighted and horrified to know that you excel at that move." She danced beside him, keeping him to the beat.

"'Horrified' is not a word commonly associated with my bedroom skills," he said dryly.

"Jay Dayal." Her hands found her rolling hips. "Are you cracking jokes?"

"Not about things that matter."

He was suddenly serious and Zara's skin prickled in warning. She liked what they had. A little sex. A little fun. Maybe even a little friendship. Why mess it up with "things that matter"?

"At least now I know how to motivate you to stay on the beat." She held her hands in front of her, palms forward, fingers slightly curved, wrists rotating back and forth. "Keep thrusting and add this movement."

"I am shocked by your filthy mind."

She slapped a hand to her chest. "In my innocence I cannot imagine what you find offensive about turning two doorknobs at once, but I suspect you'll prove a master of this move, too."

Jay proved adept at turning doorknobs while doing a pelvic thrust so she motioned for him to stop. "I have one more for you. It's very easy. You don't need to move your feet. Just your hands."

"Am I turning on or off light switches?" He lifted an inquisitive brow. "Jackhammering concrete? Painting a fence or waxing a car?"

"I'm opening your belt."

He jerked back when she reached for his buckle. "I don't think—"

Zara cut him off with a sigh. "I'm not intending to ravish you onstage, if that's what you're thinking. I'm planning to show you the belt step made famous by Salman Khan in the movie *Dabangg.*"

18

"OF course. That's exactly what I thought." Jay let out a long, slow breath. "The belt step."

This was a bad idea. He was already aroused from the hands-in-the-pants, pelvic thrusting, and the turning of doorknobs. Things were going to get out of control if she put her hands on his . . .

Chiefs. Buccaneers. Patriots. Steelers. Packers. Cowboys. Eagles . . . He focused on mentally listing every football team in the NFL so the part of him warmed up by all the sexually suggestive moves didn't get the wrong idea.

"Hold one end of the belt in each hand and pull your hips with alternating hands."

Taking a step back to put a safe distance between them, Jay yanked one side and then the other, forcing his hips to jerk in either direction with little thought to the beat of the music playing in the background, and a lot of thoughts about football.

Texans. Bills. Raiders. Bears . . . "Is that it?"

"You're getting it." Her furrowed brow belied her encouraging tone.

"I'm just not made to dance." He released the belt with a defeated sigh. "I should focus on what I'm good at. I can organize one hell of a bachelor party, order the booze, keep people in line . . ."

"Let me." She took the ends of his belt in her hands and gently tugged his hips back and forth, seemingly oblivious to the torture of her casual closeness and the scent of her floral perfume. "You're too hard on yourself, Jay. You don't need to do everything perfectly the first time. You don't need do it perfectly at all. No one is going to judge you if you're up there having fun."

He could feel the music now, flowing as she moved his hips.

"See?" She looked up and smiled, warm brown eyes drawing him in. "When you stop overthinking and just let everything go, you can belt dance with the best of them."

Jaguars. Giants. ColtsSaintsCardinalsPanthersRavensRams . . . No. Not Rams.

One minute they were dancing. The next, their mouths were crashing together and she was in his arms. He lifted her to his hips and her legs wrapped around his waist. Shudders racked his body. He spotted a giant boulder with a flat surface and carried her across the stage, his mouth fused to hers, tongues tangling, her hands raking through his hair as if she couldn't get enough. Catapulted by a desire so fierce it clouded his senses, he lay her gently on the surface and pushed up her clothing to bare her beautiful breasts. He sucked and licked, stroked and squeezed until she reached for him, tearing at his jeans with frantic fingers.

Driven by an insatiable hunger, he placed one hand beside her to take his weight so he could free his shaft and ease the tension that had been coiling in his belly since he'd walked out her door.

Except the rock wasn't a rock. Two people were heavier than one. With a high-pitched groan the rock gave way, and they fell to the ground in a sea of Styrofoam, canvas, and wire.

"What the hell is going on here?" An angry voice echoed through the theater.

Jay's protective instinct overrode his reserve. Yanking up his clothes with one hand, he hovered over Zara, keeping her covered until she'd straightened her clothing. When she gave him a nod, he pulled her up with him and spun to face the intruder.

"Can I help you?" He kept his voice calm and even despite the wreckage of the stage prop behind them.

"What are you doing to the set? I'm going to call the police." Tall and slim, with a face made of chiseled marble, the dude had the looks but not the muscle. If it came down to it, Jay could take him with one hand tied behind his back.

"It's okay. I'm in the show." Zara stepped out from behind him. "David said we could stay behind and rehearse. I tripped when we were dancing and we fell onto the rock."

It was a good story. Zara was always quick on her feet. Still, the dude didn't look convinced.

"I don't think I should let you go without talking to someone . . ." He pulled out his phone.

"You want me to throw him out?" Jay tipped his neck from side to side, making it crack. He didn't tolerate threats, especially when they were directed at someone under his protection.

"Um. No." She gave his forearm a warning squeeze. "But I do think we should go. He's probably here to rehearse for a different production."

Jay considered doing it anyway, just to wipe the supercilious sneer off the dude's face. But Zara was already off the stage and walking to the door. He shoulder-bumped the guy on his way past, just to let him know he'd been in the wrong and because he'd ruined what would have been his first chance to have sex onstage.

"I've seen all these musicals." Zara spun around when they reached the lobby, gesturing at the framed posters on the walls. "My dad always took me to the theater on our weekends together. I even saw a few of them on Broadway when I visited New York."

"What about your mom? Is she a fan, too?"

Zara rarely talked about her mother and he was curious to know more about her. He wanted to know everything about Zara and what made her tick.

She turned away, stared at the poster in front of her. "She can't stand musicals and she doesn't care for the theater. I'm seeing her this week for her birthday dinner and I have to remember not to talk about my extracurricular activities. Her life is all about her work, and she takes a dim view of things she considers frivolous."

"This isn't frivolous." He swept her hair over her shoulder and pressed a kiss to her nape. "Not if so many people enjoy it."

"Exactly." She looked over her shoulder, and the smile that spread across her face took his breath away. "Musicals capture emotion and make it bigger than life." She pointed to each framed poster in turn. "'I'll Cover You' from *Rent*? Destroyed me. 'Memory' from *Cats*? Focus on the pain and it will ruin you. 'Last Night of the World' from *Miss Saigon*? It's a love song, but oh my God . . ."

"So, they're all sad," he said. "No wonder your mother doesn't like them."

"Are you kidding? That's only one side of the coin." She twirled around the lobby. "You can't get much happier than 'Singin' in the Rain' or 'I Could Have Danced All Night' or 'Ding-Dong! The Witch Is Dead.'"

Jay didn't think he could get much happier than watching Zara dance around the lobby humming the tunes from the musicals she loved so much. When he was with her, he almost believed she could light up his darkness and set him free.

"If this is your dream, why didn't you pursue it?" He leaned against the wooden wainscoting beneath a framed poster of *Hairspray*.

"My family expected me to have a profession—even my dad. I took psychology at college because it was a science, which made them happy, and I thought it would help me become a better performer.

At college I got a chance to work with a law professor who brought creatives to campus. I realized I could put my dreams and a professional career together as an entertainment lawyer helping diverse artists in the industry."

"It sounds perfect."

"I thought so and my mom agreed." She ran her hand along the dusty edge of a picture frame. "She helped me get a start at a big-city firm with an entertainment practice, but it didn't work out. After two jobs and the interview with Lucia, I realized I could never be happy working at a place that stifled my creativity. I still love the world of entertainment. I scream when I see my favorite celebrities. I ask them for autographs. I'm on an alumni committee that promotes diverse artists, and one day I hope we'll see greater representation in the industry. But I love my new job. I love helping people who have been hurt and can't advocate for themselves. Dreams can change and it's not a bad thing. They can be what you make them, or you can live them a different way."

"My dream is to be successful." He folded his arms across his chest, watching the dust motes dance on the sunbeams shining through the window. "I want financial security so my mom and I never have to worry about having enough to eat or where we're going to sleep at night." His hand tightened into a fist, words he had never shared spilling from the dark secret part of him in a harsh, bitter tone. "Part of me also dreams about sticking it to my old man, who left when I was a baby. If he ever comes looking for me, I want him to see that I made it to the top. That I didn't need him. I want him to regret that he walked away."

"I can't imagine how hard that must have been." Zara slid her arms over his shoulders and pressed a soft kiss to his mouth. "But your mom must be very proud because she raised a strong son."

Jay held her tight, soaking up the warmth of her body. "She

came by this morning to drop off a meal for Sunday dinner because she's going away on a day trip, and decided to stay and prepare enough food for a family of ten: paneer tikka, *dahi bhalla chaat*, *rajma masala*, dal makhani, vegetable korma, chicken karahi, two types of biryani, mango cheesecake . . ." He trailed off when Zara laughed.

"I guess you won't be ordering in for a while."

"She was hoping I would have a guest." He hesitated, not wanting to scare her away, but also not wanting to let her go. "Are you free tonight?"

"You had me at 'enough food for a family of ten' but I would have been knocking on your door for a slice of mango cheesecake. Too bad your mom can't join us. I would love to steal her recipe."

"She might have come back early from her trip. I'll give her a call." Jay swept Zara up in a kiss. "There's only one thing you should know. Her boyfriend is a biker."

EXCEPT for the odd night when Avi and Rishi came over to watch a game, or Elias crashed after a long night out, Jay didn't socialize at his apartment. That meant Jay didn't know how to throw a dinner party for four guests. Luckily his mom was on the job.

"You've got everything in here," Zara said, unpacking one of his mother's sturdy plastic containers. "Napkins, wineglasses, a tablecloth, candles . . ."

"Mom, we didn't need all this." Jay took out a saltshaker and four silver spoons. "It's not like I have nothing."

"Actually, you do have nothing." Zara looked out over the breakfast bar to the living room. "You weren't kidding that day when you told me you only had the bare essentials. It looks like a showroom in here."

"They usually have some decor in showrooms," Rick called out from his seat on the couch. "Fancy pots, pictures of flowers, magazines so it looks like someone lives there. I used to work for a staging company, so I know all the tricks. We had eyeglasses that we put in every room, so it looked like someone had just been there all cozied up with a good book. We chose a different color palette for each house. You gotta stick to neutral earth tones or warm shades of white for flow then add a pop of color with the accents."

"I thought you said he was a biker," Zara whispered.

"It's a second career."

Zara and his mother chatted in the kitchen as they set the table. Zara was always friendly and outgoing, but listening to them together, he liked to think they had a special bond. He hadn't seen his mother laugh as much in years, and it turned out she had a love of musicals that she had never shared with him.

After the food was heated and ready to serve, they sat at Jay's small dining table and toasted the meal with a red wine from the Napa Valley his mother had picked up on her day trip.

"It's so lovely to finally meet you," Zara said to Rick. "Jay mentioned you were a biker but he didn't tell me you were a fan of the greatest soap opera of all time."

Jay froze, a roll in his hand. "Don't tell me you watch it, too."

"Oh yeah, baby." Rick held up his hand and Zara gave him a high five.

"I like all entertainment." She patted Jay's hand. "If it's on, I'll watch it."

Jay cocked a brow. "What about sports?"

"Not sports."

"But sports are entertaining." He couldn't help but enjoy watching her squirm.

She pushed her food around her plate. "Not my kind of entertaining."

"Documentaries?"

Zara rolled her eyes. "Are you trying to bore me to death?"

"You kids make a cute couple." Rick shoveled a forkful of biryani into his mouth.

"They aren't a couple," Jay's mom said evenly. "They have an arrangement. Zara finds Jay a girlfriend and he introduces her to some celebrities. It's how they do things today."

"Actually, we've put the deal on—"

"Seriously?" Rick interrupted with a bark of disapproval. "Jay, you gotta man up. You're missing out on a great thing. She's the real deal. How many women like *Days of Our Lives* and musicals and are smart enough to be a lawyer? I'll tell you from experience, there aren't many out there."

Zara gave a light laugh. "It's a mutual decision. We're having a good time just hanging out and enjoying each other's company but it doesn't mean anything. Isn't that right, Jay?"

No, it wasn't right. But clearly he'd misinterpreted the pause in their arrangement. Zara just wanted a good time. He'd been hoping it was something more.

"Yes," he said firmly. "That's right. Neither of us has time right now to get involved in anything serious." He sipped his wine but didn't taste it, looking everywhere except at his mother. He didn't think he could stand seeing the sympathy in her eyes. She knew him too well.

"Maybe Padma should start telling stories about when Jay was young," Rick suggested. "Or pull out an old photo album to really embarrass him."

Jay's mother laughed. "I've never had a chance to do that before. Next time I'll come prepared."

Next time. He looked around the table, at his mother and Zara laughing together, at Rick looking up *Days of Our Lives* facts on his phone, at the way they had filled his apartment with warmth and light and the delicious scents of his mother's cooking. He wanted a next time so desperately an ache bloomed in his chest. A next time with Zara sitting by his side, smiling at his mom, and squeezing his leg under the table every time Rick threw out a little nugget about his pre-biker days.

Jay couldn't deny it. He had feelings for Zara. Feelings so strong they threatened to crack the walls he'd built to keep himself safe. He hadn't had feelings for a woman in—never. But they were feelings she didn't share.

· 19 ·

INSTEAD of going directly to the table for her mother's birthday dinner, Zara went to the restaurant restroom. She had five minutes before her mother was expecting her, and she needed to get everything under control. There could be no accidents tonight. No falls, spills, breaks, or burns. She couldn't jump up from the table if she saw someone, or wave, shout, smile, or gesture. Even though it was an Indian restaurant, she would have to use her fork and knife instead of tearing her naan to scoop up her dal, and crunchy pappadams were out of the question.

She couldn't imagine a greater contrast to the dinner she'd shared with Jay's mom only two nights ago. So much laughter. So much warmth. They'd talked musicals and soap operas, swapped recipes, and shared stories. She'd been able to relax and be herself without worrying about what to say or how to act or what disaster was going to happen next. Drinks spilled and they cleaned them up. Rick overturned a dish of biryani and no one batted an eye. If not for the awkward moment when she told them she and Jay weren't really together, she could have stayed there all night. She was falling for him and nothing had ever scared her more.

Taking a deep breath, she smoothed her hair in the mirror. Parvati had helped her straighten out the wayward waves and curls and now her hair hung in a smooth, glossy curtain around her shoulders. To complete the business-professional look, she'd worn a shell pink blouse over black jeans and her favorite black boots. Parvati had lent her an authentic Gucci bag and she'd accessorized with a pearl necklace and a pink watch. No bursts of color. No fancy scarves or intriguing patterns. And not a sparkle in sight. Except for the boots, she was as close to corporate perfection as she could get. Hopefully it would be enough.

Forcing her lips into a smile, she pushed open the restroom door. Breathing in the familiar scents of sweet cinnamon, pungent turmeric, and smoky cumin, she made her way past the abstract paintings, gold metallic walls, and saffron-colored booths to the table where her mother waited with her longtime partner, Peter Roberts.

She greeted her mother with a kiss to the cheek and gave Peter a nod before sitting down. Her mother couldn't fault her appearance tonight, and yet looking at her with her dark hair pinned up in her signature twist and an elegant scarf draped over her chic black dress, Zara still felt awkward and unkempt.

"What a lovely surprise. You made it on time." Her mother glanced over at Peter and lifted her eyebrows as if she'd told him to expect Zara to be late. A lean man with a weathered face and graying hair, Peter was an anesthetist at the hospital where Parvati worked. He was easygoing and generally a nice guy who was happiest spending an evening at home cooking and watching detective shows on TV. To his credit, he never got involved in Zara's spats with her mother. Instead, he would excuse himself and return when the dust had settled.

Zara kept her hands in her lap so as not to accidentally knock over a glass, drop a fork, or drum her fingers on the table. After they ordered their food, she smiled politely as her mother told her about her new cases, the firm's planned expansion, the birthday breakfast Peter had prepared, and the cake her colleagues had brought to her office.

"It's too bad Hari can't be here," her mother said after the food had arrived. "He said his flight was delayed by bad weather at the airport."

Zara suspected the delay was less about weather and more about the fact that Hari hated the annual birthday dinner and had finally decided to give up even the pretense of wanting to be part of the family. Even so, he was her mother's favorite and usually provided a buffer on social occasions.

"I might have my first class action lawsuit," Zara said quickly when she saw her mother's lips thin. Hari's absence was just the kind of thing that could set off a chain reaction that would start with her perfect older brother and end with the disaster of her career. "I handed out my business cards at Tarun's wedding and some aunties came to see me."

Between bites of flavorful spinach *poriyal*, chicken masala, and *podi dosa*, she told them about the case without divulging which aunties were involved.

"What does it have to do with entertainment law?" Her mother dabbed her lips with a napkin. She was a master of subtle criticism.

"I've moved on from that dream." She spoke deliberately, meeting her mother's gaze as an equal even though she trembled inside. She'd said these words to Jay. Why shouldn't she say them to the person who needed to hear them most? "I'm happy where I am. I can make a real difference at Cruz & Lovitt helping real people instead of big companies. I'm hoping that this case will be so big they'll have no choice but to make my one-year contract permanent."

"Your potential causes of action aren't very strong," her mother said dismissively. "How do you quantify the damages? Someone spoke unkindly to your clients. They turned off the camera and returned it to the store. How did they suffer?"

"A stranger talked to my client's kids." Zara's voice rose in frustration. "He made racial slurs and told them to do terrible things. She didn't feel safe in her own home. And as for causes of action, what about negligence, breach of the implied warranty of merchantability, breach of implied contract, unjust enrichment, and violation of the Unfair Competition Law? It's a good case and Tony is letting me run with it. I thought you'd be proud of me."

"It sounds very interesting," Peter said quietly. "I have lots of friends who have installed security cameras in their homes. I'm sure they would be appalled to hear about this."

"She needs to be realistic." Her mother shot Peter a withering look. "If she wants to get back into a big-city firm, she can't get involved in something that's certain to fail. If she wants to do entertainment law she needs industry clients."

"Weren't you listening to me?" Zara threw her napkin on the table. "I don't want to get back into a big-city firm. I want to stay at Cruz & Lovitt."

"Darling . . ." Her mother sighed. "They advertise with a tiger. That does not scream professional."

"Maybe I don't want to be that kind of professional," Zara shot back. "We have name recognition. We have loyal and happy clients who refer their friends and family to us. And we have a great track record of success. We're the number one personal injury firm in the Bay Area."

"Are you sure they're going to make your position permanent?" Her mother shared a look with Peter. "I've heard they're struggling to bring in clients and their profits are down fifty percent. They haven't had a big settlement in over two years. You can't run a law firm on slips and falls. There is a lot more competition in the personal injury market than there was even five years ago."

A sudden coldness hit at Zara's core. "How do you know all that?"

"The legal world isn't that big, and I like to know what is going on with my daughter's firm. I also know that you bumped into Lucia the other day. She said her offer to join her corporate litigation department is still open. I know you prefer a more relaxed atmosphere, but beggars can't be choosers."

Zara's mouth went dry. Why hadn't Tony told her the firm was in trouble? Why hadn't he given her a heads-up that they might not be able to keep her on? "It might not be true," she said, more to reassure herself than to challenge her mother. "I'll talk to Tony tomorrow."

"Tony is not going to tell you anything different." Her mother sipped her wine. "You have a problem accepting that bad things sometimes happen, darling. When we told you about the divorce, you stood on the side of the road for hours screaming for your dad to come back, and then for weeks you pretended he was just away at a conference. I had to pack up all his things and repurpose the studio just so you would understand that we had to move on. When he finally got his own place, you pretended he was house-sitting for a friend. It went on and on. Really, it became rather tedious."

"It sounds to me like she was in a lot of pain," Peter said gently. "She was only what? Ten or eleven? That's a hard age to have your life upended."

"It was hard for everyone but we all got over it," her mother snapped. "I expected her to do the same."

Except she hadn't gotten over it. She still expected every fight to end a relationship and every relationship to end. Her deepest fear was losing the people she loved. It was the same kind of worry, the same fear that Jay had shared with her. That one day the person she cared about most would be gone.

"I have to get going." She couldn't stay here any longer, couldn't listen to her mother coldly dissect one of the worst nights of her life. She wished Jay had been here with his strong arms, warm hugs, and quiet understanding. Jay didn't judge. He liked her for who she was. So why had she told Rick they weren't together? Her words had hurt him. She'd seen it in his face, in the way his hand had tightened around his glass, in the speed with which he'd called her a cab when the night was done. And she'd felt it. Because when he'd agreed with her, she'd hurt, too.

"LET'S have a toast to a long and fruitful business partnership."

Jay and Elias clinked glasses with Thomas and Brittany in the upscale French restaurant Thomas had booked for their celebration. With the Triplogix lawsuit out of the way, Thomas had assured them that board approval of their international financing was all but guaranteed.

"That was the best call I've had all week," Thomas said. "To be honest, I was worried you wouldn't be able to get the lawsuit dismissed. The optics were pretty bad, given you are a security firm."

"We've put new procedures in place to ensure our clients are fully protected from disgruntled employees in the digital space," Elias said. "It's actually opened up a possible new area of business for us. Digital security is the next big thing."

"Delighted to hear it," Thomas said. "Brittany has a particular interest in digital security."

"I wrote a paper on it while I was doing my MBA." She smiled at Jay. She had been doing a lot of smiling at him across the table and he was picking up an uncomfortable vibe.

"It will give you two a lot to talk about when you're traveling," Thomas said. "Once we've got all the approvals, I'm planning to send Brittany with you when you open each of the international offices. We need eyes on the ground for our investment."

"We'll be spending a lot of time together." Brittany's smile widened. "I'm looking forward to it."

Jay felt something brush his pant leg. *Christ.* Was she seriously playing footsie under the table with her father right there? And what about Elias, who had been staring at her for the entire dinner? The dude was totally smitten, but Brittany didn't seem to know he existed.

"Excuse me." Jay got up and walked to the restroom to get away from Brittany and her under-the-table activities. How was he going to get out of this situation? One wrong step and he could blow the whole deal.

Five minutes later he exited the restroom only to find Brittany waiting in the hall. He should have known "Daddy's girl" wouldn't be denied.

"Fancy bumping into you here." She took a step closer, smoothing down her fitted black dress. "I was thinking we should get to know each other better since we'll be spending a lot of time traveling to the new offices. Maybe dinner at my place on Friday?"

Six weeks ago, he would have accepted her offer. She was in a position to make sure the deal happened, to bring him closer to his goal. But there was only one woman he wanted even if she didn't feel the same way about him. "I'm flattered, Brittany, but I'm seeing someone." He didn't want to lie. He hated lying. But Brittany wasn't the kind of woman who was easily put off, and a girlfriend was the simplest option.

"Elias said you were single."

"It's recent."

She gave him a calculating smile that made the hair on the back of his neck stand on end. "I would love to meet her. Maybe you both could join us next weekend at a celebrity charity event. The bank is the sponsor."

"I'll see if she's available." He felt like the hallway was closing in on him and had to fight the desperate, urgent need to escape.

"If not, you must still come." She put a hand on his arm, the seemingly casual touch making his stomach clench. "I'll send over some tickets for you."

"And Elias." No way was he going into the lion's den alone.

"Yes, of course. Elias." She tossed her hair and laughed. "I almost forgot about him."

Jay was damn sure she hadn't forgotten about Elias at all. "I should get back to the table." He moved to leave but she blocked his way.

"I'm so glad we'll be working closely together," she said, fingering his tie. "Daddy thinks the world of you."

"I respect his work." Sweat beaded on his forehead and his nerves went into overdrive.

"We're very close," she said. "If I'm unhappy, he's unhappy."

Jesus Christ. Was she threatening him? Even after he'd told her he was with someone? Elias needed to get his head in the game. "We'll do our best to keep you happy, Brittany."

Her smiled widened until he could see every one of her pearly white teeth. "I'm so glad to hear it."

ZARA tried to take in everything at once when she walked into the office after a long day of negotiations. She was half an hour late to meet Parvati for their shopping trip. But what she hadn't expected was that the more eccentric members of the firm would come out in force to keep her friend entertained.

"Sorry I'm late." She gave Parvati a quick peck on the cheek as she dodged Tony's lightsaber. "I was negotiating a contract for a stuntman who was afraid of heights, high speeds, loud noises, flying, water, fire, smoke, spiders, and scorpions and camels. It took forever."

"No problem," Parvati said. "Faroz and Tony have been educating me in proper fencing technique."

"It's all in the wrist." Tony's lightsaber made a sweeping arc, stopping only a few inches from Parvati's neck. To her credit, Parvati didn't move.

"Impressive," muttered Faroz, perched on the edge of Janice's desk. "You didn't even flinch."

"He's wearing a Yoda hat and swinging a toy sword," Parvati said dryly. "I didn't think he was a real threat."

"This isn't a toy." Tony stared at her aghast. "It's a custom-crafted fully functioning piece of art. Michael Murphy created this lightsaber from the same vintage Graflex camera flashes used to create the real prop, complete with a sophisticated sound board, advanced motion tracking, custom chassis, and crystal chamber that hews to the official source material."

Parvati yawned. "Can it kill me?"

Faroz pushed away from the desk. "Hit someone over the head hard enough with any solid material and you can do some serious damage. I saw a man killed with a plastic toy pail at the beach when I was in Guam."

"What were you doing in Guam?" Parvati studied him with interest. Zara made a mental note to pick up some earplugs on the drive home. No doubt Faroz would be spending the night.

"If I tell you, I'll have to kill you."

Parvati snorted. "You wouldn't be killing me with a plastic toy pail. It's not physically possible."

"It was full of rocks."

"Then he was killed by the rocks and not the pail."

"The pail held them together." Faroz grabbed a few decorative stones from the plant display along the wall and dropped them into his paper cup by way of demonstration. "He wouldn't have died if someone had thrown the rocks at him one at a time. So, therefore, he was killed by the pail."

"If you throw one of those rocks at me, I'll show you ways to die you never even imagined," Parvati warned.

Faroz's face brightened. "I thought I knew them all."

"Did you know about death by lightsaber?" Tony asked. "Many people think it's the same as a laser beam but lightsabers consist of a plasma blade powered by a kyber crystal. It makes for a cleaner cut."

"Either way, it's a shit way to die," Faroz muttered. "When it's my time, I want to go out fucking."

"You can't swear in a law office," Tony warned. "Decorum."

Faroz chuckled. "I heard you negotiating a settlement with the Hammer this morning. I'd say the bar is pretty low."

"Is it always like this?" Parvati whispered to Zara.

"Yes."

"Then you'd definitely better start rustling up some clients because this is where you belong."

Zara dropped her files off in her office and ten minutes later they climbed into Parvati's car, a black BMW convertible that she'd bought at auction.

"I gave my number to Faroz," Parvati said. "Is there anything I should know before I bring him home?"

"He doesn't talk about his personal life except to throw out little nuggets like *When I was in Guam . . .* or *Did you know a man can still talk when you cut out his tongue?* or *Poison is always your best bet for an assassination*, or my favorite, *I'd tell you but I would have to kill you.* I heard a rumor he was in the CIA but I don't believe it. Why would a CIA agent take a job as a private investigator for a law firm?"

"Maybe he needed a cover," Parvati said absently. "I don't really care what he does for a living. He's hot. He has an amazing body. He oozes sex. And I've always wanted to sleep with an older man."

"How about we don't talk about him anymore because I'll have to pick up the pieces when you use him and throw him away." She braced herself when Parvati blasted out of the parking lot, tires screeching when she rounded the corner.

"In a hurry?" Zara had always been a fast driver until she'd started working at Cruz & Lovitt and had seen firsthand the damage that could be done from reckless driving.

"I feel like I was just in the twilight zone. I need to calm down." Parvati slowed to the speed limit. "After our shopping trip, I want to order Chinese food and stream an old episode of Autopsy on HBO for a little relaxation."

"Normal people don't watch autopsies to relax."

"I don't watch it for the autopsy." Parvati stopped at a red light and checked out the hot guy in the red Porsche beside them. "My favorite part is guessing the cause of death. Was it a heart attack? Did he have a hidden cancer? Was there an amoeba in his brain? It's so exciting."

"You need to get out more. You're spending too long in the hospital. What about a hookup with someone I don't work with?" The guy in the Porsche was too busy admiring himself in the rearview to notice he had a sure thing right beside him.

"I hook up every day." Her grin flashed. "I see a good-looking resident or intern. Five minutes later we're doing it in the storage closet. Ten minutes later I'm back on the floor—seven if they paid attention in gynecology. I don't even ask for a name." She hit the accelerator and Zara's head slammed into the seat.

"Maybe you could introduce me to one the next time I'm in the hospital."

"Are you kidding me?" Parvati snorted. "You just had dinner with Jay's mom. A guy doesn't invite you to have dinner with his mom unless it's serious. And a woman doesn't go to dinner with a guy's mom unless she likes the guy. A lot. I'm not going to help you sabotage your relationship by introducing you to a meaningless hookup when you've got a man who is still the talk of the ER."

Zara's stomach twisted in a knot. "It's not a relationship. It was an arrangement that we put on a temporary pause. But this morning Tony told me that the firm is struggling financially. My job is at risk unless I find new clients. I need the arrangement to be on again. Jay has access to clients who, if injured and suffer a significant loss of earnings, could secure my future at the firm."

"You just want to meet celebrities." Parvati slammed on the brakes at a red light and grabbed her lipstick from the cupholder.

Zara gave an affronted sniff. "I want to meet people who may or may not work in the entertainment industry and whose lives may get destroyed by a freak accident that renders them unable to realize their earnings potential."

"Are you reading the small print from one of your ads?" Sarcasm laced Parvati's tone. "Don't try to change the topic. It won't work with me. You have feelings for Jay and now you're running scared."

"Definitely not." Zara folded her arms across her chest. "I promised to find him a match and that's what I'm going to do."

Parvati ran the lipstick around her lips, turning them from pink into a bright glossy red. "Does that mean you aren't going to sleep with him again?"

"It wasn't a big deal," Zara protested. "It was casual. We're casual. We had a fun night together, and that's all it was. Neither of us has time to get involved. He said so himself in front of his mom, which is why I really need to get busy finding his special someone."

"Never seen you run this hard, babe." Parvati rounded a corner with a screech.

Ridiculous. When had she ever become emotionally attached to a man after one night together? Usually she hustled them out the door before dawn, and by the time the sun came up she'd forgotten they'd ever been in her bed. Granted, she and Jay had spent a lot of time together, but that didn't mean anything when she was getting to know him for the sole purpose of handing him over to somebody else.

So what that he was the first person she'd thought of after the emotionally distressing dinner with her mom? He was especially good at hugs, so it was only natural she'd want to find comfort in his arms.

Still, something had to be done. In some silly, secret part of her heart, she wanted Jay to care about her as much as she cared about him, which was far too much for a woman who was simply not girlfriend material. Jay was calm and steady. He needed a woman who didn't attract chaos wherever she went. Someone who wouldn't be expecting the relationship to fail because she'd learned at a young age that love stops and marriages don't last forever.

It was time to get back to business. She had to find Jay a match.

· 20 ·

"ARE you planning to spend your entire evening working?"

Jay looked up when Elias walked into his office, a set of golf clubs slung across his back. "I get the most work done in the evening. No phones. No meetings. No distractions." No one to interrupt when his thoughts drifted to a beautiful lawyer with a sunny smile and an infectious laugh.

"No fun." Elias put the clubs down in front of him. "We need a fourth for our twilight game at the Ocean Course at Half Moon Bay."

"I can't," Jay said. "Thomas just sent over the final package for the board review. I want to get a start on it. We're almost there. I don't want to mess it up now."

Elias put down his clubs. "You're making me feel guilty."

"Just promise to keep Brittany entertained at the charity event tomorrow. She has a lot of pull with Thomas. I don't want her to feel left out. I'm planning to bring Zara if she's free so I won't be able to give them my full attention." He hadn't told Elias about the hallway incident. Better if he hooked up with Brittany thinking he was the one she wanted all along.

"I'm not even going to pretend I'm looking forward to it." Elias heaved a sigh. "You know I'm not good at high-society events. I'm a beer-and-hamburger kind of guy. She's going to take one look at me waddling around in a penguin suit and run in the other direction."

"It's not that fancy," he assured his friend. "You'll be fine. Zara is great at putting people at ease. I'm going to call her after I'm done to see if she can make it." He was counting on her love of celebrities to override any reticence to spend the evening with him at a social function. They hadn't talked about their relationship since the awkward dinner with his mom. He'd sensed she needed some space, and although it had killed him, he'd left her alone.

Elias had been gone only half an hour when Jay heard the rattle of a door, the creak of a hinge, a slam, and then footsteps. Had Elias left something behind? "You're going to miss your tee time," Jay called out. "What did you forget that's so important?"

"He forgot to lock the door." Zara walked into his office wearing one of her brightly colored dresses, this one with a blue skirt that swayed gently around her hips.

Words failed him. Not just because he'd missed her, but also because she had somehow managed to get into the office of a security company that had built its reputation on keeping buildings secure.

"How did you get in here?" he asked when he could finally formulate a sentence.

"I told the guard at the door that I was your attorney. I gave him my card to show I was legit. It isn't wholly untrue. I am an attorney and in a way I'm yours because we have an arrangement."

"Spoken like a true lawyer."

Zara gave him a curtsy. "At your service."

"Looks like I'm going to have to have a word with the guard at the desk."

"It's not his fault," Zara said quickly. "I distracted him. I noticed he had a picture of his kids on his desk. They were wearing pirate costumes so I told him about the musical and offered to leave some tickets at the box office for his family—"

"You bribed him." He stared at her, incredulous.

"I did no such thing." Her hands found her hips. "It was a genuine offer. He had already decided to let me come up and see you."

Jay made a mental note to thank the guard downstairs. If the dude hadn't been so easily distracted, Jay might not have had the chance to see Zara tonight.

"So, to what do I owe this pleasure?" He leaned back in his chair, folding his arms behind his head.

Zara put her bag on the chair across from his desk and pulled out a file folder. "Since our arrangement is back on, I've got some possible matches for you to consider."

"I thought we agreed to put our deal on pause." He'd been so surprised by her sudden appearance that he hadn't been paying attention. But now that she was closer, he could see something was wrong. Her eyes had lost their sparkle and lines of worry creased her forehead.

"We unpaused it." She stared at the floor, long lashes fluttering over soft cheeks. "I thought that's what was going on when we had dinner with your mom and Rick."

"You told Rick we weren't together. I was just following your lead." He knew he should be concerned about his unbridled attraction for a woman who might not want him. Instead, he was contemplating the best way to pleasure her once he got her on his desk, pretty skirt hiked up her thighs, stiletto heels over his shoulders.

"I'm not really into labels." She shrugged. "Together. Not together. What does it really mean? We have an arrangement and I just want to uphold my end of the bargain."

"So what was Saturday night?" His heart thudded a frantic beat.

"It was . . . fun," she said. "But now that we have it out of our systems, it's best if we get back to business."

Jay felt her words like a stab in the gut. Instinct told him they'd shared more than just physical intimacy during the night they'd spent together. They'd connected on another level, one so deep he couldn't believe she'd come to his office just to push him away. Something had upset her. He'd seen it when she walked in the door, and he could see it now in the way she avoided his gaze. If she wasn't going to be forthcoming, he would have to play the game. And Jay played to win.

"Take a seat and tell me what you've got."

She startled, like she hadn't expected him to capitulate, but recovered quickly. "Okay." She settled in the chair across from him and picked up the file. "First we have Vidya Reddy. She's an accountant with a multinational firm. She runs for fitness, enjoys classical music, and likes to garden. She's organized, focused, detail-oriented, and professional."

"Hmmm." He rocked in his chair. "Can she sing 'Climbing over Rocky Mountain,' create a zombie costume out of nothing, and give a man a wake-up surprise he'll never forget?"

She pressed her lips together and glared. "No. I don't believe so."

"Pass. Who's next?" He stood and walked around the desk, turning her chair so he could kneel in front of her.

"What are you doing?"

"Keep going. I can barely contain my excitement. What other lovely ladies have you chosen to warm my bed?" He gently removed one of her high-heeled shoes and pressed a kiss to her instep.

"Devika Malini." Her voice hitched and she hissed in a breath. "She's a software engineer from a well-connected family and CEO of a fitness clothing start-up—"

"Would she fill a room with people just to support her father without even knowing he planned to show a collection of vulva fruit art? Can she find the best hot dog in San Francisco? And is she flexible enough to do yoga poses in bed?" He licked his lips. "I found a new one for you to try, by the way. It's called leg behind head pose." Holding her leg with one hand, he kissed his way along her calf, pausing to nip gently behind her knee.

She swallowed hard, hands braced on the arms of the chair. "You aren't taking this seriously."

"I am taking it very seriously," Jay said. "But you've set a high bar and so far no one can measure up. I'm assuming the answer to all my questions is no for poor Devika. Who else is on your list?" Taking advantage of her easy-access skirt, he pushed it up so he could continue his kissing journey along the inside of one thigh.

"Jay . . ." Her voice caught, broke. "I'm trying to—"

"Find me a match. I know. I'm listening." He grabbed her hips and pulled her to the edge of the seat. "If you want me to stop, just say the word, but I do my best thinking when I'm distracted."

"Shobana Agarwal." She started to tremble when he ran a finger along the edge of her panties. "She had agreed to an arranged marriage but ran away the night before the ceremony and took their honeymoon flight down to Jamaica . . ."

Jay pressed a kiss to the soft cotton over her entrance. "Your panties are wet," he said softly. "I believe you once told me that you preferred going without in this type of situation. Let me assist." He slid his hands into the elastic of her panties and ever so slowly tugged them down. Zara lifted her hips and within moments she was bare.

"Tell me more about Shobana." He pushed her skirt up to her waist and pressed his lips against her glistening curls.

Zara groaned, crushing the paper in her hand. "She stayed

there two years working as a bartender, backpacked around the world, and worked as an elephant trainer in Thailand . . ."

He swept his tongue over her clit, teased at the hood. Her legs fell apart on a groan and he slid one finger into her slick, wet entrance. "Keep going. What did she do after the elephants?"

Her breath came in short pants. He added a second finger, shifting his position to accommodate the press of his hard cock against his fly. He had never been so aroused, his need for release almost painful. But this was about her. He teased her labia with his tongue, added a third finger. *So wet. So hot.*

"She . . . She got a job on a cruise ship as an acrobat with the entertainment team. She fell off the flying trapeze and got injured so she came home."

Jay froze, jerked his head up. "Did you say trapeze?"

Zara scowled and pushed his head back down with her free hand. "Forget about her. She's not your type."

"Trapeze artists are at the top of most male fantasy lists."

"She's not going to be on yours." She tore the paper in half and tossed it away.

"Anyone else?" He licked around her clit, fingers thrusting deep inside her, encouraged by her sharp gasp.

"A . . . A zookeeper in San Diego. She can wrestle lions, tame tigers, speak to rhinos, and she spent two years at an animal sanctuary in South Africa."

He moved his fingers fast, alternated between licking and talking. "Can she shoot a man in the ass at ten paces? Can she dance to Bollywood, mariachi, and musicals? Can she drink most men under the table?"

"No, but her hair is pink, she has a nose ring, and she rides a motor . . ." Her voice trailed off and her inner walls clamped around his fingers, her body going rigid in the chair as she hit her peak. Christ, he loved watching her come.

"Do you know what you get to ride?" He stood and swept his desk clear, spilling papers, pens, pencils, and his coffee cup onto the floor.

Languid in the chair, she licked her lips when he yanked open his belt. "Do I get three guesses?"

"You get one." He shoved down his pants and boxers. "A big one."

After he rolled on the condom from his pocket, he lifted her from the chair. Zara wrapped her legs around his waist, and he fit himself to her entrance. "Any other ladies you want to set me up with?"

She ground against him, testing his self-control. "Not at the moment."

"I didn't think so. How could you possibly give me away when you could have all this to yourself?"

"I don't have a choice." She let out a shuddering breath when he lowered her to the desk. "I have one month to bring in some new clients or my firm won't make my position permanent. The market is down and they can't afford to keep me. I'm beating every bush, trying to think of every angle. You have access to celebrity clients. Some of them might do their own stunts and get injured. I thought maybe you could introduce me to a few of your high-profile clients and I could spread some tiger love around."

Jay gritted his teeth against the urge to bury himself deep inside her. "Here's how these things work. Instead of tossing me aside like yesterday's news or hooking me up with trapeze artists and lion tamers, you could just say, *Jay, do you have any events coming up involving celebrities?* I would then check our schedule and let you know. I might even call a few friends in other security firms because we're all friendly in this business. In short, I would do anything and everything I could to help you."

Zara grimaced. "I was in a panic."

"So I guessed when you marched in here and demanded I hook up with some randos from your matchmaking pile." He tried to sound annoyed, but it was impossible with Zara laid out on his desk, all wet and ready for him. "I'm here for you. However you need me. I'm not going anywhere."

"Even if I can't give you more than I'm giving you now?" She bit her bottom lip, watching him intently.

"I'll take you any way I can get you," he said. "We don't need a label. Whatever you have to offer, just so long as you're in my life."

Now her eyes glistened. "You shouldn't say things like that when I'm half-naked on your desk."

"I can't think of a better time to be open. I'm not the kind of man who easily shares his feelings."

She reached for him, pulled him down for a kiss. "I feel calm when I'm with you," she whispered against his mouth. "You quiet the voices in my head. You make me feel safe. You were the first person I wanted to call when I found out I might lose my job, but I was afraid you'd think it meant something it didn't. I'm not relationship material and I don't think I ever will be."

"It would have meant you needed me and I would have liked to be needed. Promise me next time you'll call. My help never comes with strings."

"I promise," she said softly. "And I'm sorry."

He grunted his approval. "You grovel very nicely."

She tipped her head to the side, gave him a sensual smile. "Now, do I get that ride?"

. . .

HE waited until after. When they'd made use of the desk, and then the window and the wall. When the light had gone and the darkness flooded his office and the streetlights twinkled below them. When they lay naked on his couch, wrapped in a soft blanket Elias had ordered as swag when they'd attended a conference a few years back. When she was his again and not trying to set him up with rhino whisperers. When her head was on his chest and she lay languid in his arms.

"The banker who'll hopefully be financing our international expansion has invited Elias and me to a celebrity charity event on Friday night at the City Club." He pressed a kiss to her forehead. "They've invited quite a few big stars. I thought you might like to come."

"Seriously?" She pushed herself up but instead of a smile he got a scowl. "You're just telling me about this now?"

"You didn't give me a chance earlier," he protested in mock innocence. "You marched into my office and told me the deal was back on and then proceeded to bombard me with details about women who would never interest me because they aren't you. I didn't know what was going on."

"I told you right before . . ." She cleared her throat, her gaze dropping to their clothes scattered across the floor.

"Before you rode the big one." He gave her a self-satisfied smile. "The first time."

Zara threw off the blanket and left him to walk across the room. He would have enjoyed watching her if she hadn't been walking in the wrong direction.

"Where are you going?"

"I'm checking it out." She pulled out her phone and stabbed at the screen.

Silence.

And then a scream. "Oh my God! Lin-Manuel Miranda is going to be there! Jay! Ohmygodohmygodohmygod."

She ran toward him. Naked. It was everything he had hoped for and more. He held out his arms and she threw herself on him.

Too late, he realized he was utterly exposed.

· 21 ·

ZARA knew she'd made a mistake before she stepped out of the cab in front of the City Club. She should have worn the teal and blue dress with the crisscross front and the fluttery skirt. Instead, she'd put on the petal pink Chanel suit her mother had bought for her birthday a few years back. With its tiny bolero-style jacket and narrow pencil skirt, it had been uncomfortably tight on her curvy frame. Now, three years' worth of biryani, ice cream, and samosas later, it had been almost impossible to get on.

But this was Jay's event. He was meeting his most important investors, and they had the power to make his dreams come true. The pink suit was elegant and sophisticated, corporate but also classy. She'd accented it with chunky gold jewelry, pink stilettos, and a knockoff Chanel bag. With her hair straightened, her nails painted, and her makeup done to perfection, she was everything the future CEO of an international company could want in a party plus-one.

At least that had been the plan.

"Do you need a hand getting out?" The cab driver looked over his shoulder as Zara struggled to move. Something had happened in the last thirty-five minutes that had turned a slightly tight outfit into a torture device. Unable to contain the volume of her thighs, her skirt was straining at the seams, and damned if she couldn't move her arms in the extra skinny three-quarter-length sleeves. Even the shoes were now too tight, her flesh puffing up around the toes like she'd shoved two brown fluffy pavs beneath the delicate diamante straps instead of feet.

"I'm good, thanks." She drew in enough breath to finish the sentence, wondering if it was possible for a waistband to saw a person through the middle.

By the time she'd made it out of the cab, sweat had beaded on her brow and trickled between her breasts, staining the white silk sheath she'd worn beneath the jacket. She fastened the buttons to hide the evidence and looked for Jay.

Another problem emerged when she spotted him near the entrance. Extra-tight pencil skirts and extra-high stilettos were not a good combination. She shuffled along at a snail's pace as seniors with walkers raced past her to the door.

Jay strode over to greet her, all cool and calm and perfectly mobile in his dark fitted suit and flat shoes. Why had she thought the Chanel suit was a good idea? Why was the sun shining when she was already drenched in sweat? Why hadn't she listened to Parvati, who had warned her more wasn't better when it came to heels?

"You look beautiful." He pressed a kiss to her moist cheek.

"I was going for sophisticated, classy, elegant, and professional all at the same time." She tiny-stepped a spin for him, keeping her arms by her sides, praying he didn't spot the muffin top that had emerged from her skirt during the ride. This was why she didn't wear suits with short jackets. There was little room to hide.

"Objective achieved, but I like you in anything you wear." He leaned in to whisper in her ear, his hand sliding down to squeeze her ass. "Also, I like you when you wear nothing. That's probably my favorite look."

"Naughty." She lightly slapped his hand away. "This is a classy event. I looked it up online. They've booked three floors of the club for cocktails and mixing and mingling with the stars. Fifty of the five hundred guests are big-time celebrities, but you know who I want to meet most."

"The man whose picture dominates your bedroom and whose dulcet tones grace your speakers." He took her hand, leading her into the venue, seemingly oblivious to her slow shuffle walk. "If I wasn't brimming with self-confidence, I might feel threatened by your obsession with the musical star. Fortunately, I am secure in my masculinity and I have much nicer hair."

After checking in at the door of the former Stock Exchange Tower, they took the elevator to the tenth floor. The entrance to the club featured one of the most striking art deco interiors Zara had ever seen. With a thirty-foot-high Diego Rivera fresco painted on the stairwell, a ceiling covered with burnished gold leaf squares, and black marble and silver and brass accents everywhere she looked, it was sophisticated with the right amount of glitz.

"I love this place," she said, taking it all in. "It's very . . ."

"You."

She looked up at him and grinned. "Yes, it is. Very me. And the only thing that could make it better is to find my celebrity crush."

"We'll need to say hello to Thomas and his daughter, Brittany, first," Jay said. "I saw them at one of the standing tables when we walked in. Elias is already with them." He placed a firm hand against Zara's lower back. "This way."

"I know this event is important to you," she said as they wound their way through the crowd. "You don't have to worry. I'm keeping it low-key tonight. No breaks or spills. No rolling heads. No chaos or drama."

"You don't have to be anything other than yourself." Jay pressed a soft kiss to her temple. "I want you to have a good time, meet your crush, hand out some cards, and find a few clients."

Thomas waved them over to a standing table. Zara recognized him from the bar and hospital, and they shared a few pleasantries before he introduced his daughter. Brittany, wearing an elegant black dress and a strand of pearls, studied Zara with interest.

"What firm did you say you were with?"

"Cruz & Lovitt. We specialize in personal injury." She handed Brittany her card. Something about the banker's daughter set her teeth on edge.

Brittany studied the card, her lips quivering at the corners. "Oh. You're the *tiger* firm."

Zara drew in a deep breath, buttons straining on her jacket. Somehow her breasts seemed to have expanded on the ride over as well and seemed to be increasing in size by the minute. "We're a boutique firm." Zara forced a smile. "We won the largest plaintiff settlement in the state for a young client who was crushed by a falling telephone pole while riding his bike in a national park."

"It's not real law, though, is it?" Brittany said. "Those personal injury cases always settle. They rarely get to court."

"Zara was in court just the other week." Jay slid an arm around her waist. "I got to watch her trial. She was amazing."

"How lovely." Brittany reached for her glass, her hand brushing lightly over Jay's sleeve. "Jay mentioned you two just got together."

Zara's focus sharpened on the banker's daughter. Brittany wanted her man and was making no effort to hide it. Zara couldn't decide if she was insulted or impressed. Not that it mattered. Jay was hers and Brittany needed to get that message.

"When you know, you know." She leaned into Jay and nuzzled his neck. "Isn't that right, hon?"

"Yes, that's right . . ." Jay stiffened, cleared his throat. "Hon."

"So . . . Brittany." Zara sipped her wine again for the liquid courage it offered and to keep her hands away from Brittany's throat. "What do you do at the bank?"

Brittany launched into a rambling explanation of bank structures, financing groups, and her long list of credentials. Zara could only partially focus on her words because every two sentences or so Brittany's hand would fall gently on Jay's arm. "MBA blah blah blah. Isn't that right, Jay? Global markets blah blah blah. Jay knows all about that . . ." The sheer audacity of the woman astounded her, but not as much as the overwhelming rush of emotion she felt at the thought of Jay and Brittany together. It didn't make sense. Only a few weeks ago, she'd been trying to match Jay up with someone exactly like Brittany. Only the other night she'd told Jay's mom there was nothing between them.

"What's going on?" Jay murmured when Thomas drew Brittany away to introduce her to a colleague.

"Nothing." Jealousy wasn't an emotion she'd ever had before when it came to boyfriends. She'd never allowed anyone to get that close.

He put an arm around her shoulders. "Are you sure? You're scowling, and you've got that tiny crinkle in your forehead that you only get when something is really bothering you."

"She's after you," Zara blurted out, putting to one side for later consideration the fact he knew her so well. "You probably don't even realize it because you don't speak bitch."

Jay's voice took on a deep, steady warmth that made Zara's knees weak. "There's only one woman I want."

"I hope it's me or someone's getting a four-inch stiletto through the throat," she muttered under her breath.

Jay responded by leaning down to nuzzle her neck. "Your jealousy is turning me on. If you keep that up I might think you actually like me."

Why did he say things like that? Why did he have to call her beautiful when she felt like she was about to explode out of her suit like the Pillsbury Doughboy? Why did he tell her he would always be there for her? That his help came with no strings? That he wanted her any way that he could have her?

He wants me.

She'd tried to pretend she hadn't heard it but she had. Just like she'd tried to pretend she hadn't seen the hurt on his face the night she told Rick they weren't together. It was so frustrating. Why couldn't they have just enjoyed the pause in their deal, have a little fun sex, and move on? Neither of them wanted a relationship. So why was it beginning to feel like they had one?

The situation deteriorated over the course of the evening. Jay filled her glass and brought her snacks. When she shivered, he offered her his jacket. He boasted about her ingenuity in court and encouraged people to buy a ticket to her show. She most certainly did not sing like a nightingale and brighten up the stage. His disturbing pride in her accomplishments put a downer on what should have been a delightful evening. He seemed to have conveniently forgotten that she was a magnet for disaster and that he was supposed to be an arrogant officious jerk.

She was contemplating an early escape when a disturbance at the door caught her attention. News reporters and photographers backed into the room, shouting and waving. A murmur rippled through the crowd, a buzz of anticipation. Zara stood on tiptoe to see what was going on. And then Lin-Manuel Miranda walked through the door.

Acutely aware of Thomas and Brittany standing beside her,

Zara slapped a hand over her mouth to stifle her scream. Where should she get her autograph? She'd been so busy being annoyed by Jay's goodness that she hadn't even made a plan.

She needed to calm down. No. First she needed to ditch the jacket so Lin-Manuel could sign her arm. Her Wandsworth autograph had already faded despite the fact she hadn't washed that arm in weeks. He could choose left or right. Maybe she could get him to autograph both.

"I'll take it." Jay held out his hand even though she hadn't said a word. She shrugged off his jacket, wondering if this was what it was like for normal couples. Anticipating each other's needs. Understanding the compulsion to gush all over your favorite Broadway star. She supposed it was handy when said Broadway star was fifty yards away, and you had a limited window of time to get the autograph you'd been dreaming about for the last five years.

She had taken only a few shuffling steps forward when Lin-Manuel moved back toward the door. Her heart leaped into her throat. No. This couldn't be happening. She couldn't get this close to her celebrity dream only to be held back by firmly stitched pink Chanel and four-inch heels.

Strong hands gripped her hips, holding her in place. She looked over her shoulder and saw Jay kneeling down behind her.

"Shoes," he said.

"What?" Her voice wavered, the disappointment of missing her chance almost too much to bear.

"Your shoes. Quickly. Take them off. You'll be able to catch him in bare feet."

Hope flared in her chest and then faded. "But . . . my skirt. It's too tight to run."

Jay gripped the material on either side of the back slit and pulled it apart, rending the skirt a few extra inches at the seam.

"Jay . . ." Her voice caught when he slipped off her shoes, holding up his hand to help her balance. "I don't want to embarrass you. I promised myself I'd keep things low-key."

"You could never embarrass me." He gestured to the door. "Now run, sweetheart. Lin-Manuel Miranda is in the house."

It was stupidly romantic.

It was everything.

She had never been so irritated in her life.

· 22 ·

THE knock, when it came, startled her. Curled up on the couch watching *Annie*, with a carton of ice cream, a glass of red wine, and Marmalade purring on her lap, Zara was busy wallowing in self-pity and not inclined to answer the door.

How badly had she messed things up for Jay when she'd run barefoot across the City Club? Had it been enough to dissuade him from being so damn . . . nice? Where was the arrogant, officious, bossy Jay from the paintball field? She wanted him back.

Bang. Bang. Bang.

"Who is it?" The building had a buzzer downstairs and the other tenants on the floor kept to themselves. Parvati was out on a date for the evening and had her own key.

"Security." She didn't recognize the muffled voice, so she checked through the peephole and saw Jay's stern face partially covered in dark glasses.

"Jay?"

"J-Tech Security, ma'am. There was a theft at the City Club last night. Apparently, the thief fled in bare feet. We followed the trail to this address."

Zara swallowed hard. Time for the reckoning. She'd been too embarrassed to return to the table after her celebrity encounter so she'd called an Uber to take her home. She hadn't even said good-bye.

She opened the door a few inches. Jay was in full uniform: dark glasses, black hat, blue shirt, safety vest, black pants, heavy boots, and a utility belt that held a flashlight, baton, handcuffs, and a walkie-talkie. He was her fantasy come to life, but opening that door would mean dealing with the desperate, aching feelings she'd been trying so hard to ignore.

"There are no thieves here. You must have the wrong address."

"You have bare feet." He pointed to the floor, where her freshly polished nails gleamed in the light. Self-loathing didn't include missing her Saturday morning pedicure.

"So do a lot of people."

"Do those feet fit in these shoes?" He held up her pink stilettos.

"Are you Prince Charming?" Unable to resist, she opened the door wider. "If my foot fits, will you carry me away to your castle to be your princess forever?"

"I'll arrest you for leaving the scene of a crime."

Laughter bubbled up in her chest. This was so absurd. So utterly unlike Jay. He'd done this for her. Dressed up for her. And this game—this role play—was something he must have known she would love. A thick warm rush of feelings swirled through her, cloaking her in warmth. Before she had even made the conscious decision, she had fully opened the door.

"That's not very romantic." She moved to the side to let him in. "I suppose you can check the place out if you must, but you won't find any stolen property here. It's just me and my cat. My roommate is out on a hot date"

"We'll see about that." Jay stepped into the apartment, his uniformed presence filling the room. She was suddenly and acutely aware that beneath her robe she wore only an old T-shirt and plain white cotton pants.

Marmalade padded over and rubbed himself against Jay's

legs to say hello. Jay broke character to give Marmalade a good pet before crossing his arms over his massive chest. "Let's get started."

"I need to freshen up. I wasn't expecting visitors. You can check out the kitchen." She turned and raced for her bedroom, giving him a suggestive wiggle. Behind her, Jay gave a soft grumble of approval.

Closing the door, she put on the lingerie he had liked so much. Deep red with lace edging, the balconette bra and barely there panties had been an extravagance, considering she had sworn off relationships for life. She had just belted her robe when he slammed open the door.

"Kitchen is clear."

"There isn't much to check in here. Just the closet. Feel free to have a look." She sat on the bed and leaned back on her hands, letting the robe fall open just enough to give him the smallest peek.

Jay didn't even glance in her direction. Instead, he pulled open the closet door and rummaged inside.

"What's this?" Jay held up an unused personal vibrator, still in its box.

Zara's cheeks flamed. "That's not mine. Someone must have put it in there."

"Very suspicious." He placed the box on the dresser. "I'll leave it out for further inspection."

After he finished with her closet, he opened the dresser drawers one by one, giving her a lovely view of his perfect ass. "Nothing here. Time for the personal search."

His hard, searching gaze sent a thrill of arousal down her spine. She bit back a moan, her skin flushing with heat.

"Something wrong?" He took a step closer, loomed over the bed. In the dim light, his body seemed larger, menacing, his muscles tight and hard. He was so believable in his officious confident arrogance that it was almost too easy for her to get lost in her role as the thief who'd been tracked down to her lair. "You seem nervous. Are you hiding something from me?"

Zara licked her lips and scooted back on the bed. "No. Of course not."

Without warning, Jay reached over and grabbed her belt. With a hard yank, he pulled her toward him. Her robe slid up her thighs and Zara licked her lips in shameless hunger. Did he know how wet she was? How her breasts ached? How desperately she wanted him?

Jay gave a satisfied growl, holding her in place. "The law requires your consent for a search." He pulled her closer, his gaze hot and roaming. "I have to warn you. I am very thorough."

"I have nothing to hide." She was burning. Liquid fire rushed through her veins, pooling between her legs. It was like Jay had plucked her deepest darkest fantasies from her mind and was making them all come true.

He gave a small, calculating smile. "I don't leave anything untouched, sweetheart."

"I'm not your sweetheart."

"You will be when I'm done with you." He devoured her with his gaze, his eyes so dark they were almost black. "Robe off. I need to assess the search area."

She slid the robe over her arms and lay back on the bed. "How's this?"

He inhaled sharply, his gaze raking over her body, and then again more slowly in blatant sexual appraisal. "I see you've decided to make things difficult, but I can't be distracted."

"I'm not afraid of you." She arched her back, parted her legs just enough to tease. Did he think he was the one in control?

"You should be." His voice dropped to a husky growl. "Hands over your head. If you don't think you can keep them there and out of my way, I'll make sure you do." He yanked the belt from her robe and dangled it in front of her.

Zara understood right away what he was asking, but she was up for anything tonight. Anything to avoid the elephant in the room. His unspoken question. Her unknown answer.

"I'm afraid I won't be able to stay still. Who knows what could happen if my hands were free? I might get into all sorts of trouble."

He tied her hands together above her head with the soft terry belt. "Problem solved. Now let's get to the search." Standing at the foot of the bed, he removed his sunglasses and then unfastened his utility belt.

"What are those for?" Her eyes flicked to the handcuffs, then up to his face.

"You get those if your hands don't stay above your head." He straddled her thighs, the soft wool of his trousers an erotic burn against her skin. Without lifting his gaze, he ran the tips of his fingers over her nipple hard beneath her bra, sending a bolt of pure need straight through her body.

"I thought you were conducting a search," she gasped.

He grinned at her, his mouth now hovering over her breast. With one deft move he slid his hand behind her back to flick the catch of her bra then shoved it out of the way. "I am." The rasp of his tongue over her nipple tore a strangled cry from her throat. She writhed on the bed, but his body weight kept her lower half still and the belt kept her hands from moving.

"The first part involves lowering your defenses," he continued. "How am I doing?"

"Well, since I can't move and I can't think because my brain is fuzzed with lust, I'd say pretty well."

"Excellent." He licked his lips. "Let's continue."

She shivered as he circled one breast, and the other, dragging his hot, wet tongue over her nipples until they peaked. When she didn't think she could take any more, his palms engulfed her breasts and he squeezed and stroked until need coiled tight in her belly. She was ready. So ready. Her hips tilted up slightly, inviting.

Jay sat back, leaving her bereft. "All clear."

"Isn't there somewhere else you want to search?" She hated the desperate, pleading tone in her voice. But seriously? Was he going to leave her like this?

"All in good time." He gave a smug smile before leaning down to feather kisses over her heated skin. As promised, he left no inch of her body untouched. He brushed his lips over her forehead, the curve of her ear, her neck and shoulder, working his way down to her throat. Arms and elbows. Each of her fingers one by one. Breasts, hips, and belly. Thighs and calves. Feet and toes. Still, he wouldn't kiss her lips, or the place she wanted his kisses the most.

"I think . . ." She panted her breaths when he pushed to his knees and undid the buttons on his shirt. "You might have forgotten something."

"I haven't forgotten." He unfastened his pants and shrugged off his shirt, baring his beautiful chest, the ripple of his abs, and the soft trail of hair leading below. "I was saving the best for last." He ground his palm over his erection.

"Tease." She couldn't tear her eyes away. "Take it all off."

"You're not in a position to make demands." But he didn't make her wait. Instead he lowered his zipper and pulled out his cock. Thick and hard, he was more than ready for her.

"Do you want this, sweetheart?"

She wasn't complaining about the term of endearment now. "Very much."

He gave a casual shrug that belied the evidence of his desire. "Maybe when I've finished my search."

"What else . . ." Her voice trailed off when he lay between her legs, slid off her panties, and placed her feet on his shoulders.

"The best things are found in the most secret places." He lowered his head. His tongue did the most wicked things that had her arching and twisting on the bed.

"Jay . . ." It was a plea. It was a demand.

"That's Mr. Dayal to you." Without warning, he slid two fingers deep inside her, his firm steady strokes making all her nerve endings fire at once. His tongue found her sensitive clit and her inner walls tightened around his fingers. She soared and peaked, her orgasm crashing through her body in a tidal wave of sensation.

Dazed, languid on the bed, she watched him shrug off his trousers and roll on a condom. "Did you find what you were looking for?"

"Not yet." He lifted her legs, spread them wide, opening her for him as he positioned himself between her thighs.

"You're very good at your job." Now that her body was sated, she was generous with her praise.

"And you are a beautiful, sexy temptress who is about to be fucked by a man who wants her so desperately he's willing to do anything to have her."

She looked up, caught his gaze. Without his sunglasses or his gear, he wasn't a security guard. He was Jay. Her Jay, making her feel the truth of his words. She didn't want to pretend anymore. She wanted this part to be real.

"Kiss me."

His face softened and he leaned down and covered her mouth with his. Dark and dirty, hot and horny, sweet and utterly seductive. Damn, the man could kiss.

"I want you inside me." She swallowed hard. "I want . . . you."

"You have me—all of me." He pushed deep, filling her, stretching her, making her feel every inch of him. His smoldering eyes watched her intently, sending a current of need arrowing straight to her core. When she moaned, he moved his hips in just the right way to hit her most sensitive spot. Pleasure licked through her body and she surged toward the peak.

"Don't stop."

"No chance of that." His gaze didn't leave hers as he pulled out and thrust again, his hips moving hard and fast, arms braced on either side of her. The world fell away until there was only Jay, his scent, his heat, his muscles tightening and releasing, and his eyes locked on her like she truly was the most beautiful woman in the world. Heart-squeezing tenderness and wild heat.

She came in a roll of pleasure, a soul-deep release as she let herself go. Jay followed her with a quiet shudder that ripped the tension out of his muscular body with a groan.

"Fuck." He fell forward, his body covering hers, taking his weight on his elbows beside her. Small kisses to her lips made her feel seen and not forgotten.

"We just did." She looked up to her hands and he released them with one tug.

"Touch me, sweetheart. I want to feel your hands on me."

She held him close for what seemed like forever, breathing in his scent of sex and sweat and the lingering hint of his cologne. "Thank you."

"For what?"

"You made one of my fantasies come true."

"Anytime." He kissed her neck, her jaw, her cheeks and eyelids, branding her with his heat.

"Do you have a fantasy?" She ran her hands over his shoulders and down his back, loving the feel of his rock-hard muscles beneath her palms.

He reached for his utility belt. "What we just did. But with handcuffs."

Zara grinned. "This time I'm wearing the uniform."

HOURS later, after they'd exhausted every combination of uniforms and handcuffs, they lay together in Zara's bed, her head on his chest, his warm hand stroking down her back.

"I'm sorry I left the event," she said quietly, needing to address the unspoken tension between them. "I appreciated what you did, but I didn't think you would want me hanging around after that." Her hand fisted on his chest. "You were trying to impress your investors and I was trying to help you, but everything went wrong from the moment I put on that suit. It just wasn't me and I could see things were going to continue to go downhill after I took off my shoes. I'm no Brittany, and I don't want to be, but she's the kind of woman you told me you were looking for when we agreed I would find you a match."

"That was my decision, not yours." He twirled a lock of her hair around his finger. "And don't pretend this is about Brittany. You are much too self-assured to put yourself down that way. You know she has nothing on you. The real issue is that you like me too much."

"Seriously?" Zara pushed herself up. "I like you too much? Is it possible to be more arrogant?"

"I can't speak for anyone but myself, but you know it's true." Jay grinned. "You were going to stab your heel through her throat."

She pressed her lips together and glared. "I was speaking metaphorically."

"And I'm speaking plainly." His face grew serious. "I'm not interested in Brittany or any other woman like her." His deep voice rumbled through her body. "I thought I did, but what I really want is to be with a woman who takes risks, embraces life, and lives it on her own terms. Someone who brings joy and light and laughter when she walks into a room."

Zara gave a begrudging huff. "She sounds not too bad."

Jay laughed. "Her jealous streak is a huge turn-on. I think it's her most endearing quality."

"She also ruined your evening," Zara pointed out. "Don't forget that. You seem to only remember the good stuff and not the bad."

"You got your autograph." He ran his hand along the name scrawled on her upper arm in black Sharpie.

"Yes, and I also got a selfie with Lin-Manuel Miranda. And I got to tell him how amazing he is. It was awesome."

"That's all I wanted," he said.

She tipped her head back to look at him. "I thought you wanted to impress Thomas and Brittany."

"I want them to fund my international expansion. If they turn us down because you ran in bare feet to see your favorite musical star, then they aren't the kind of investors we want handling our project. Now that the lawsuit is gone, we have other options." He nuzzled her hair. "I just wish you'd waited for me. I wanted to see your face when you met him. I'd been looking forward to it all day."

"I'm sorry." Now that she understood him better, she regretted even more her hasty decision to leave. But what was she supposed to do with all his irritatingly attractive qualities? How was she supposed to keep him at arm's length when he refused to be chased away?

He grunted, pulled her tighter against him. "Not much of a grovel but I'll take what I can get."

Did he mean what he'd said? Would he take what he could get, even if that was only casual? She couldn't offer him any more, not when the thought of an actual relationship sent a wave of panic flooding through her veins. "What about our arrangement?"

"Let's put it on hold for now," Jay said. "I can't risk any poor woman turning up in the morgue with a pink stiletto in her throat."

"Don't get too cocky."

He took her hand and drew it down to his shaft, thick and hard between his legs. "Too late."

Zara rolled on top of him, seating his cock at the juncture of her thighs. "Does the hold mean no more celebrity introductions?"

"I'll still uphold my end of the bargain." He traced the line of her jaw with a gentle finger. "In fact, we just got a gig for Chris Moskovitz's birthday party. Are you interested?"

Zara sucked in a sharp breath and pushed up to a straddle. "THE Chris Moskovitz? One of Hollywood's famous Chrises? Star of *Lost Legend*, *Missing Mountain*, *Senseless Sea*, and *Dirty Desert*? The number one Chris on everyone's Chris list? The best Chris?"

A smile spread across his face. "That's the one."

"Oh my God." Unable to contain her excitement, she jumped up and paced the room. "When is it? Not that it matters. I'll be there."

"Two weeks." He rolled to his side and propped his head in his hand. "You'll be going as a trainee guard. It was the only way to get you in. You'll need to go through a safety briefing and wear a uniform. After tonight, I assume that won't be a problem. You wore it well."

She shivered under the heightened weight of his gaze. "Do I get a gun?"

"After what you did on the paintball field, definitely no gun." His lips quivered, amused. "I told his agent you're an attorney and you needed some on-the-job practical experience in a high-security environment for one of your cases."

"True but not entirely accurate." She grinned. "You'd make a good lawyer."

"And you made a good security guard, although you never figured out what was stolen from the City Club."

She tipped her head to the side, frowning. "What was stolen?"

"My heart."

· 23 ·

"WAKE up, sunshine."

Jay ripped the warm covers off Zara's body, exposing her skin to the cold morning air. A firm-but-gentle slap landed on her bare ass.

"Ow. No waking up. Sleep. Or sex. Anything just so long as we can stay in bed. It's Sunday morning. That's what Sundays are for. That's why Sunday begins with *S*."

"This Sunday is beginning with an *H*." Jay put her unused hiking boots on the floor beside the bed. "*H* for hike. I saw these in your closet last night, and I realized I couldn't even remember the last time I went for a hike. It's a beautiful day and I want to share one of my favorite things with you."

"What about your other favorite things?" Zara groaned. "Do any of them involve being horizontal? Or food? Or both at the same time?" She still hadn't had time to process his admission that she'd stolen his heart. What was she supposed to do with that? Did he think it would change things between them? Did he think it would change her?

"I'll make it worth your while." He used her own words back at her.

She rolled over and blinked, her eyes adjusting to the bright light. He was already dressed, his eyes sparkling, a grin spread across his face. Did he remember the nightmares he'd had last night? The moaning and thrashing? Shouts so loud Parvati had knocked on the wall. She'd shaken him gently, wrapped her arms around him, and spooned him from behind. After a few minutes, his tension had eased, and he'd fallen into a peaceful sleep.

"I'm going home to shower and change and get my gear," Jay said. "I'll be back in an hour. Be ready to rumble."

She had never seen him this happy, so she pushed her concerns to the side. "I'm not a hiker, Jay. You may have noticed those boots are barely used."

"Now they can be more used." He bent down beside the bed and gave her a soft kiss. "I want to show you the world from the top of a mountain. It's one of my favorite places."

Zara groaned and flopped onto her back. There was no resisting Jay when he looked at her like that with his puppy-dog eyes and his wide smile. And how could she say no when a man who usually spent Sunday in his office wanted to blow off the day to show her something he loved?

"Fine." She heaved a sigh. "I'll come. But you'd better make it up to me when we get back. I'll need pizza, ice cream, and lots of massages." She frowned when she caught the naughty gleam in his eyes. "Not that kind of massage. The kind where you rub my back for at least an hour and feed me chocolate and alcoholic beverages."

"I am a master of massage." He tipped his neck from side to side, making it crack. "Prepare to be amazed."

One hour later, Jay returned, wearing a pair of army fatigues and a khaki T-shirt that looked like it had been poured on his muscular body. Parvati's mystery date had turned out to be Faroz. They'd taken over the couch to watch *Spy Kids*. Zara still couldn't get her head around the pairing.

"All ready to go?" Instead of closing the door, Jay grabbed the top of the doorframe and did five easy pull-ups that made his biceps pop. "I've picked an easy seven-point-one-mile loop in Mount Tamalpais State Park. Anyone want to join us? The more the merrier."

Faroz got up and sauntered over to Parvati's bedroom door. "Nice day for a hike." He grabbed Parvati's doorframe and did ten pull-ups in quick succession then did a spin-turn jump to face Jay. "What do you say, Parv?"

With a sideways glance at Faroz, Jay grabbed the doorframe and repeated his set of five, this time with one arm. He dropped down with a grunt of satisfaction and the gleam of challenge in his eyes.

Parvati turned off the television and pushed to stand. "I say we'd better get out of here before all the testosterone in the air makes Zara and me want to do pull-ups on the kitchen cupboards and then we'll have nowhere to store our treats."

"Thank God," Zara whispered as she followed Parvati to her room. "I was worried I was going to slow him down. He'd be wondering why he brought me, and I'd be wishing I were home in a nice warm bath or lying in a park somewhere catching some sun. We would have a terrible time and he'd never invite me on a hike again, which wouldn't really be that bad, but also not good because he's kind of growing on me and—"

"Take a breath." Parvati pushed open her door. "It'll be fine. He said it's rated easy. How hard can it be?"

"KEEP your eyes on the road." Zara gave Jay's leg a gentle slap when she caught him glaring at Parvati and Faroz, who had been making out in the back seat since the start of the trip. "Honestly, you're worse than Parvati. Do you know how many accidents are caused by distracted driving?"

"We should be talking strategy, studying the flora and fauna and visualizing the trail," he grumbled. "You don't just walk into a hike blind. I don't understand why no one wants to look at the topographical map or download the bird-identification app."

"I looked at the map." Zara patted the knee she'd just tapped. "And I downloaded the app. I didn't know you were interested in birds."

"When I was young, my mom used to take me to the park and we'd try to identify the birds. I took it up again to pass the time when I was deployed. Some days we were just sitting around waiting for orders."

"I had pigeon pie when I was undercover in Morocco," Faroz said from the back seat. "It was like chicken potpie but with more flavor. If we see some pigeons, I can catch them with a snare and cook 'em up for dinner."

"He wants to identify them, not eat them," Zara snapped.

"Is there a difference?"

Jay turned into the parking area on Panoramic Highway and they piled out of the vehicle. He'd brought along a massive pack that he slipped over his broad shoulders. "I've got everything we need right here," he said proudly. "Tent, binoculars, grappling hooks, multi-tool, first-aid kit, altimeter watch, locator beacon, gaiters, flashlight, shovel, flint, ropes, solar blanket, flares, knife, SPF-rated lip balm, sunscreen, hand sanitizer . . . Pretty much everything you can think of. We'll be safe from blizzards, storms, avalanches, wild-animal attacks . . ."

"What if we're attacked by a murder of crows?" Parvati asked. "Like in that movie *The Birds*."

"I'm carrying." Faroz opened his jacket to reveal a weapon holstered across his chest. "We'll have a lot of pies."

Zara stared at him aghast. "Who brings a gun on a hike?"

"Someone hungry."

For the first part of the hike Zara half ran, half jogged beside Jay as he pointed out verdant canyons and shrubby meadows with sweeping views of the ocean. His enthusiasm was infectious, and she was able to ignore the wheeze in her lungs and the burn in her legs to share in his delight. Their adventure took a downturn when they hit Steep Ravine Trail and the walk turned into a climb.

"What is this?" Zara panted. "You said it was easy. I came for waterfalls, babbling brooks, fields of flowers, and selfies of my glowing face as I pose on flat forest paths."

"It was all right there on the topographical map." Jay frowned. "I thought you looked at it."

"I didn't understand it. Geography was my worst mark in high school." Her legs shook with each step. Unlike the stair climber at the gym, there was no off switch, no TV to distract her, no juice bar to replenish her energy, and no shower to cool her down.

"Do you need a rest?"

"Maybe just a breather." Shirt soaked with sweat, she bent over and heaved in a breath while Jay ran up the trail to see what was ahead. Faroz followed after him, their hike turning into a testosterone-laced sprint as they raced for the top. Parvati sat on a log beside Zara and offered her some water.

"Did you mention to Jay that your workouts usually consist of watching reruns of *Castle* while you pedal the stationary bike on level one? Or running from the couch to the fridge and back before the end of a commercial?"

"I walk," Zara said indignantly. "I'm not out of shape. Look how far I've come and I'm still standing."

"We are half an hour into a four-hour hike and your shirt is so wet you'll need to wring it out the next time we stop."

"But he's so happy," she said. "I've never seen him so happy. He's like a kid. Look at him bouncing around, running up and down the hill, doing pull-ups on the branches. I wouldn't be surprised if he starts climbing trees."

"Just watch your energy," Parvati warned. "He won't be so excited if you crash and he has to carry you down the mountain."

"He made me eat an energy bar and fill my bottle with Gatorade. I've also stuffed my pockets with gummy bears and trail mix. I'm good to go."

After Faroz and Jay returned, they followed Webb Creek and stopped to check out waterfalls and cascades before ascending a canyon nestled in a flourishing redwood forest. When Jay finally called a break, Zara collapsed in a soft bed of pine needles and tried not to sob.

"You're doing good." Jay bit into an energy bar. "We're almost halfway. There's a fixed ladder to help on a particularly steep section."

"It's so steep we need a ladder?" Her voice rose in pitch. "I can't believe I agreed to this."

"I can." Jay stretched out beside her. "You're doing it because you are a kind and generous person and because you like me."

Zara's gaze slid over to him, noting the smug expression. "You're okay."

"I'm more than okay or you wouldn't be here." He rolled to one side, propping up his head on his hand. "People with barely used hiking boots don't go on hikes with people they just think are 'okay.'"

"Fine." She heaved a sigh. "I like you."

"You more than like me." He scooted over until he was only inches away, his voice darkly teasing.

"Are you attempting to cross-examine something out of me?"

She pushed herself up on her elbows. "Because I am a cross-examination master and I can see through your tricks."

"Is it a trick to admit a truth?" he asked softly. "I more than like you."

Zara's pulse kicked up a notch and she jumped to her feet. "Break time is over. Let's get some more miles under our boots. The peak is waiting!"

"That's what Sven Helfenstein said when we were climbing Everest." Faroz caught up to them, his arm around a suspiciously disheveled Parvati. "Poor bastard didn't make it to the top. I don't use that phrase anymore because it's a bad omen."

"I don't believe half the things you say," Zara snapped, irritated that Jay had to make an already-challenging day worse by saying nice things and sharing his feelings.

"That hurts," Faroz said. "Just because you choose not to see what's in front of you doesn't mean it isn't real."

"I liked you better when you were sleeping on my couch in the office." She stomped away. "You didn't talk as much."

An hour later they reached the peak. Zara stood in the open grass, taking in the stunning view of the ocean and surrounding hillside. With the sun warm on her shoulders, a gentle ocean breeze cooling her sweat-soaked skin, and the subtle spicy-and-earthy scent of redwood in the air, she felt her pain and anger fade away.

"This is beautiful." She turned a full circle, taking it all in. "You do feel like you're at the top of the world. I take back all the mean things I said, as well as the swear words, curses, grumbles, moans, and a few unkind thoughts."

"I finally have service." Parvati held up her phone. "Good thing I wasn't on call today."

Jay put his arms around Zara, hugging her from behind. "The climb isn't always easy, but it's worth it in the end."

Zara leaned against him. So solid. So strong. So safe. She couldn't imagine not having him in her life. Maybe she did more than like him. What would happen if she said the words out loud?

"Jay?"

"Just a second." He released her and pulled out his phone. "I'm getting a lot of messages. It must be an emergency."

His face paled when he looked at the screen. He stalked over to the edge of the cliff to make a call and was back a few minutes later. "There was a motor-vehicle accident. Mom and Rick are in the hospital. They've been badly hurt."

Jay was barely aware of the hike down the mountain or the trip out of the park in his SUV. With Faroz at the wheel—Zara had refused to let Jay drive—and Parvati on the phone with her contacts trying to get more information about the accident, there was little he could do but worry. The accident hadn't happened on Rick's bike, as he'd initially feared, but in his mother's car at an intersection that she passed through every day. A pickup truck had blown through a red light, T-boning her car and sending it into a spin. Both she and Rick were in surgery, but their status was unknown.

Zara sat beside him and held his hand. He was grateful for her comfort, grateful for her friends who were there to support him, grateful that she had taken charge of the situation so he could focus on getting a handle on his emotions. He couldn't lose his mother. She was all the family he had.

Forty-five minutes later, Faroz dropped them off outside the ER. Jay had everything under control until he reached the hospital door. A cold chill swept through his body. Fear froze him in place.

"Jay?" Zara tugged his hand. "Come on. Let's get inside."

His heart pounded so hard he thought it would break a rib. Flashes of noises and images burst into his mind, stealing his breath away. A deafening crack. Flames. Twisted metal. Blood and falling bodies. Nausea gripped his belly and the world shifted beneath his feet.

"Jay!" Zara's voice was further away but sharp with concern.

Sweat beaded on his forehead and his stomach clenched with a violent pain that took his breath away. He braced himself with a shaking hand on the brick wall and tried not to give in to the black haze creeping in the sides of his vision. Terror. Panic. Screaming— God, the screaming.

"Jay? Talk to me. What's wrong?" Gentle hands cupped his face, cool and soothing, but she couldn't take his pain away.

He felt like he was choking, had to force out the words. "Just. Need. A. Minute."

"Parvati!" Zara's shout echoed around them, bouncing off the wall, the awning, the pavement under his feet. "Something's wrong with Jay."

Hands on his arms. Fingers on the pulse of his neck, his wrist. Dark eyes blinking up at him. A hazy face.

"Looks like a panic attack." Calm voice. Cool tone. Confident. "You said he was in the air force. It might be PTSD. Help him to the bench."

Panic? He didn't panic. He had been trained not to panic. He had banished the panic along with the memories of the helicopter going down.

Taking a deep breath, he forced himself to stand tall, pushed the fear back inside, back to the land of nightmares. His mother was in there and she needed him. He was no use to her standing outside. "I'm good." He shrugged off the hands, resisted the pull of the bench and the oblivion that waited if he didn't get a handle on this right now. Closing his eyes, he locked it down using the sheer power of his will.

"I think you should sit down." Zara tugged his hand.

"I said I'm fine," he barked. "You don't need to be here. Just go." Civility was a luxury he couldn't afford when it was taking all his effort to stay in control, to fight the horror of the past and the fear of losing his mom, of being finally and utterly alone. Body and mind on the edge, he couldn't handle emotion right now, especially not the complicated emotional tangle that was Zara Patel.

"I want to be with you," she said. "I want to be here for you."

"I can't." He ripped his hand out of her grasp. "I can't handle this right now. Zara, please just go."

THE nightmare woke him. It was always the same. One moment he was trading jokes with JD. The next moment JD was gone, and the world was smoke and fire and twisted metal and a hole where the controls were supposed to be. And then he was falling, spinning, the wind whistling through the shattered window, men screaming . . . Storm. Where was Storm? So much loss. So many souls. His heart breaking. The ground rushed up to greet him and he braced for the impact. This time he would do it right. This time he would go with them. This time he would be free.

"Jay. Wake up."

Heart racing, Jay jerked awake, his body drenched in sweat, his stomach roiling. Half in and half out of the nightmare, he shook his head, tried to clear the cobwebs from his brain. It had been worse this time, so much worse. So real. He could still smell the fuel, still feel the ache in his chest from the harness, the burn on his hand when he'd reached for a yoke and found flames instead.

"Jay."

A woman's voice. Low. Urgent. A waver of fear. Still, he didn't understand. Still, he heard the screams, felt terror wrap icy fingers around his heart.

"It's me. Zara."

He blinked, vision clearing as he pulled himself out of the nightmare. Zara stood at the foot of his bed, one hand over her eye. "What are you doing here?"

"I came to check on you. When you didn't answer the door, I asked your super to let me in. He knew me from the last time I was here. He was picking crab apples, and I gave him my aunt's recipe for crab apple jelly . . ." She trailed off, shaking her head. "It doesn't matter. You were having another nightmare. Worse than the other ones. I shook you and . . ." She dropped her hand. "I shouldn't have touched you."

He stared at her in horror. "I hurt you."

"I'm okay," she said lightly. "No damage. I just need some ice."

He pushed himself up, jaw clenched at the raw sting of being so brutally exposed. "You shouldn't be here."

"I was worried about you. When I found out your mom was out of surgery, I called but you didn't answer. A nurse at the hospital said a doctor had checked you out and insisted you go home. Did he give you something to help you sleep? I can ask Parvati . . ."

"No. I don't need anything." He was barely hanging on, his emotions raw and bare, the dark silent part of him still caught in the threads of the nightmare. He'd lost everyone—JD, his men, Storm. Tonight he'd almost lost his mom. And now Zara was here, seeing him weak when he was supposed to be strong, suffering because he'd lost control of his demons. He was no good for anyone. He'd been a fool to think he was. "Go home, Zara. Leave me alone."

"I'm not going anywhere," she said firmly. "If this were my family and my dad was in the hospital, I wouldn't be alone for a minute. My apartment would be filled with aunties and uncles, the counters would be heaving with food, and someone would have rented a room in the hospital so people could be there for him when he woke up. We are not meant to go through life's challenges alone. We don't have to shoulder all the burdens. That's what family is for, and since your family is in the hospital, you get me. I don't have to sleep with you. The couch is fine. But if you need to talk, or you need a hug, or you just need to turn on the television and have a warm body beside you, I'm here. I'm not a great cook like my aunties, but I've brought some groceries and I stopped at an Indian restaurant to bring some takeout so you're not going to starve." She turned away. "I'll be in the living room if you need me."

Something cracked inside him, spilling emotions all over the place. He waited until he heard banging in the kitchen and then he slammed the door.

· 24 ·

"DON'T even think about it." Jay's mother lifted a warning eyebrow when he walked into the hospital room she shared with Rick. After three days of heavy sedation following her surgery, she was finally lucid and aware. By contrast, after waking every morning to find Zara on his couch and his kitchen full of food, Jay was still angry and confused. Why wouldn't she just sleep at home? Why did she come over every evening just to sit alone on his couch? Couldn't she see from his closed door that he didn't want her there? Apparently she couldn't take a hint because every night she showed up to do it all again. What the hell was she trying to prove?

"What are you talking about?" He put a potted plant on the windowsill beside an enormous bouquet of roses, and dozens of colorful cards from the kids at her daycare. "Can't a son visit his mother in the hospital after she's been in a serious accident?"

"I know you." She gave him an admonishing look. "You're planning to ground me. Well, I will not be driven around in a fancy limo like I'm some big-shot celebrity. As soon as I get the all clear from the doctor, I'm buying a new car."

"I told her a Hummer H2 is the way to go." Rick gave him a nod when he pulled up a chair beside his mother's bed. "That thing is built like a tank. No one's gonna hurt her in three quarters of a ton of solid steel."

"For once, I agree with you." His mother had escaped with a concussion, a broken arm, internal injuries, and two broken ribs. Rick had taken the brunt of the impact, suffering a broken leg, a shattered collarbone, a punctured spleen, and more. The airbags had saved their lives but had left their faces a mass of bruises.

"I'm not driving a Hummer around San Francisco." She winced when she sank back in the bed.

Jay jumped up from his seat. "You want me to get the nurse? Do you need something for the pain?"

"I'm fine." She waved him back down.

"I'm not fine," Rick said. "The food here is shit. I sent one of my buddies out for some pizza and wings. He's getting your mom a couple of fish tacos and some of that healthy green juice that tastes like grass."

"Are you allowed to eat outside food?" He couldn't believe they could even chew with their faces so swollen and bruised.

"Nothing wrong with the stomach." Rick slapped his belly with his unbroken hand. "It's the padding. If I looked like you, I'd probably be dead. You've got no body fat. Go eat a couple of burgers, drink a few milkshakes, maybe get something deep fried. Calories save lives. I should put that on a T-shirt." He looked over at Jay's mom. "Hey, babe. What do you think? We could get his 'n' hers to wear under our jackets on our trip."

"We're taking Rick's bike down the coast when we're better," his mother said when Jay lifted a brow in inquiry. "We were planning to do it this fall, but we'll have to wait."

Jay held up his hands, palms forward. "You're going to ride on a motorcycle? After this? Seriously?" He shook his head. "I can't even . . ."

"Dude, you gotta chill," Rick called out. "These things happen. We were in a Volvo driving in a school zone, for fuck's sake. You can't get safer than that."

"You're angry because you're afraid." Jay's mom reached out her hand and he clasped it in his own.

"Of course I'm afraid," he gritted out. "I thought I'd lost you. Again. It was too much." His voice rose, raw and ragged. "What would I do? You're all I have." He squeezed her hand, trying to get a handle on the emotions that were still dangerously close to the surface. He hadn't slept more than a few hours since her accident, hadn't been to work or even the gym. He hoped that she wouldn't smell the alcohol on his breath, because it was the only way he could function without going insane.

"What about Zara?" Worried eyes studied his face.

He stood to pour her a glass of water. "I'm no good for her. Not like this. She deserves better. I'm a fucking mess, Mom. I almost couldn't walk into the hospital and when I did, they admitted me and had a shrink come and talk to me. She gave me some pills and insisted I go home until you were out of surgery. She said I was a liability risk and it wouldn't do you any good to see me that way."

"Zara didn't mention that you'd seen a psychiatrist."

Jay froze, his hand on the pitcher. "Zara was here? When did you see her?"

"I saw her this morning, but the nurses told me she's been here every day." She nodded at the windowsill. "Those roses are from her. She brought her doctor friend Parvati to meet me, and some of her aunts and uncles, and a cousin or two. It was like a party in here. We were never alone."

"They all knew *Days of Our Lives*," Rick called out. "One of her uncles downloaded the new season to my tablet for me. I've watched it three times already. More kidnappings. And everyone's running around with chloroform drugging everyone else. Where do they get it? That's what I'd like to know. It sure as heck isn't sitting on the shelf in my local Walmart."

"I'll tell her tonight not to bother you anymore." What the hell was Zara doing? This was his mom. He didn't need any help looking after her. He'd been with her through her cancer treatment and he'd be here through this.

Was Zara trying to torture him with kindness? He had too much to deal with to handle the emotions he felt when he was with her—emotions she didn't share. She'd said she wasn't interested in a relationship, and why would she choose a man so damaged, he'd hurt her in his sleep? He still felt sick to his stomach when he remembered her standing at the foot of his bed with her hand over her eye.

"You're going to see her tonight?" His mother's face perked up.

"She comes every night." He sank into his chair. "She sleeps on my couch, cooks breakfast before she goes to work, brings dinner every evening, and even leaves me a packed lunch to bring to the hospital. She sings to herself and she dances around the apartment. Yesterday, she decided to redecorate and now there are cushions and plants and knickknacks everywhere. My place is a disaster. There are clothes and shoes and handbags all over the floor. I can barely close the fridge because there is so much food. She even comes into my room to check on me when I'm sleeping." It wasn't the creak of the door or the soft tread of slippers on carpet, or even the sliver of light that told him he wasn't alone. It was her scent—wildflowers and cinnamon and a soft summer breeze.

Tears glittered in his mother's eyes. "She's taking care of my boy."

Jay bristled. "I don't need anyone to take care of me. Taking care of people is my job."

"Not now. Not like this." His mother patted his hand. "Talk to her, Jay. Or talk to someone. You have the number for the VA clinic. Maybe this is a wake-up call and it's time you finally got some help."

"Jay? Do you want some poison? Taara Auntie came by with some food." Zara settled on Jay's couch with her laptop to get some work done. She didn't expect him to answer. After five days of sleeping on Jay's couch, their little standoff had become a contest of wills. He wanted her here but he couldn't admit it. She knew as much because otherwise he would have locked his front door.

"It's a new fusion dish," she called out. "It looks like a gray blob with something swimming on top."

Moments later, the bedroom door slammed open. Jay walked past her to the kitchen and filled a glass of water. She could see his reflection in the TV. He was watching her, just as she was watching him.

"Since it's Friday, I was planning to watch something on TV after I check my e-mails. Do you want to join me?" She picked up the remote and flicked rapidly through the channels until she came to a baking show.

She heard a humph behind her and kept flipping. Footsteps. A looming presence behind the couch. *Military show*. Bad idea. *Medical drama*. Worse. He grunted his disapproval of reality TV, documentaries, and *Seinfeld* reruns. She stopped at a crime show and he walked around to sit at the far end of the couch. *Progress.* Ditching the idea of working when he'd finally decided to join her, she closed her laptop and settled back to watch the show.

Two episodes later, he finally spoke. The first words he'd said to her in five days. "Why don't you leave?"

"Hmmm." She stroked her chin as if considering. "Let me think. Maybe because your mother was in a serious accident. It triggered your PTSD and you had a full-blown panic attack at the hospital. Your nightmares have gotten worse. You aren't going to work or the gym and you're not taking calls from Elias or any of your friends. You aren't getting any help, and you are all alone. How is that for a start?"

His face smoothed to an expressionless mask. "So, you feel sorry for me."

"I feel compassion, not pity. And I'm worried about you. I don't abandon my friends. I'm here for you, Jay. Any way you need me."

With a huff, he walked back to his bedroom and closed the door.

A few hours later, she woke to Jay's strong hands lifting her off the couch. He carried her to his room and placed her gently in the bed. Climbing up behind her, he tucked her against his body, his arms wrapped tight around her like he was afraid to let her go.

"I was piloting a helicopter south of Kabul on my last deployment," he said quietly. "My copilot JD was making plans for all the things he was going to do when we got back home, and we were joking about some girl he said he was going to marry. We were bringing eleven marines as reinforcements to one of the bases. It was a perfect day. Sunny. Clear sky. We were about ten minutes from our landing site. Storm was in the helicopter with us. He was being a goofball, making everybody laugh. The shot came out of nowhere. One second things were all good, and the next we were going down. Controls were shot. JD was just . . . gone. Men were screaming. There was nothing I could do. I watched the ground rush up to meet us, figured I'd die with my men. Instead, I woke up in a field hospital with just a couple of broken bones." His arm tightened around her. "I don't know why I didn't die with the rest of them. I should have died with them. It wasn't right."

"It's no wonder this has been so hard for you." Zara turned in his arms. "What can I do to help?"

He let out a shuddering breath. "You can go find yourself a guy who's not all messed up."

"I kinda like this guy." She leaned up to kiss his cheek. "If you hadn't noticed, messed up is my specialty."

His hand slid under her nightshirt and he stroked the curve of her hip. "I need you."

"I was hoping you'd say that." She drew his hand down to her lace-covered rear. "I've been wearing special panties every night in case you did."

SHE woke with a start to bright sunshine and the sound of breaking glass. Shaking off sleep, she made her way to the kitchen, where she found Jay cleaning glass off the floor.

"I wanted to make breakfast," he said by way of explanation.

"It's all made. All you had to do was heat it up."

Ten minutes later they sat across from each other at Jay's small table. Zara had warmed up some *sali par eedu* for a carb-protein combo that could conquer the day, along with some *rava pongal* and rich dark coffee for the perfect morning meal.

"This is better than toast and eggs." Jay dug into his meal with gusto.

"Mehar Auntie made it. I took her to see your mom because she's always great company. She also goes a little cooking crazy when anyone she knows is in the hospital. You should see our fridge."

"I'll bring the leftovers to Mom and Rick," Jay said between bites. "They need to eat something healthy. They've become junk-food addicts. Their room is like a frat house with all the burger wrappers and pizza boxes, and the TV blaring all day long." He scraped his hand through his hair. "Rick won't stop talking about the accident, so I have to live it over and over and over again. I'm going to ask Avi to put us at a different table for his wedding if Mom and Rick are still planning to attend."

"Us?"

"You and me." Jay sipped his coffee. "We're a couple. We can sit at the couples table now."

Zara put down her fork and carefully chose her words. "Jay, I was here for you because you needed me. I won't deny we have chemistry in bed, and I enjoy spending time with you. I love your sense of humor, and your protectiveness, and how you always make me feel safe. But mostly I love how you accept me for who I am. I don't have to pretend with you. I can laugh and dance and run barefoot through a party to meet my celebrity crush, and I know you'll still be there when I get back."

Jay stilled, the coffee cup still steaming in his hands. "That's how things are supposed to be when couples get together."

"But we're not a couple," she insisted. "In the big scheme of things, nothing has changed. I've always been up front with you about my limitations in the relationship department, and I thought you understood and accepted that. I can't take that extra step where we open our hearts and pour out our souls, because I'm the kind of person who would just keep pouring until everything was gone." She took another bite of her meal, but it turned to sawdust on her tongue. "I was devastated as a child when my dad drove away. I didn't understand what was happening. One day we were eating ice cream and playing ball in the park and the next he was gone. I didn't know that conflict leads to permanent separation. I didn't know love wasn't forever."

"We're not them," he said abruptly. "I know all that about you and I love you just as you are." He reached for her hand. "I love you, Zara."

Zara's heart squeezed in her chest. He loved her. He loved her and now she'd have to walk away. She'd made a terrible mistake coming here. Why hadn't she considered that in his vulnerable emotional state he might mistake her gesture of support as something else entirely?

"I have to go." She jumped up from the table, upsetting the little dishes of dip she'd put out for their meal. Where were her damn clothes? Why had she brought so much stuff with her? How was she going to get it all out to her car?

"I didn't mean to scare you." He followed her through the living room. "I just meant I accept you with your limitations. We can take it as slow as you want. Whatever makes you comfortable."

Zara stripped off her pajamas and yanked on her jeans, hopping across the clothes-strewn floor. She found an orange shirt that was only slightly stained and pulled it on, desperate to get dressed before he touched her and she fell under his spell again.

"Jay, you're going through a hard time." She stuffed her clothes in the nearest bag, heedless of the inevitable creases. "I came here because I was worried about you, because we're friends. It's what I would do for anyone I care about. If I've led you to think it meant something else, I am so sorry."

"Don't go," he said. "You don't need to run from me. We can talk about it."

"I don't want to hurt you any more than you're already hurting." She grabbed her bag and shoved the last of her things inside.

"Zara . . ."

"I'm sorry, Jay. I made a mistake. I can't do this anymore."

· 25 ·

BLEARY-EYED after spending the last twenty-four hours watching soul-destroying musicals, Zara had just put on *Les Misérables* for the second time when Parvati walked in the door after finishing her shift. "Not that again. Honestly. Aren't there other sad musicals you can watch as you wallow in self-pity?"

"I watched them. And when I ran out of sad ones, I watched the sad scenes of the happy ones. I've seen *West Side Story* three times, so I can remind myself how ill-fated relationships are supposed to end. But *Les Mis* is the best. It reflects my inner angst."

"I thought you said you and Jay didn't have a relationship." Parvati pulled a tub of ice cream from her shopping bag and tossed it to Zara.

"Spoon?"

"I thought your heart was broken and not your legs." She headed for the kitchen. Parvati talked tough but she was a softie inside.

"I can't get up when I'm in the depths of despair." Zara collapsed back on the couch. "Why would he say that to me, Parvati? Why?"

"Because he loves you, I guess. That's what people say when they fall in love."

"But he can't love me. I made it very clear that I was unlovable and that I couldn't love him back. Everyone else has followed the rules. Why couldn't he?"

"Hmmm." Parvati tapped a spoon to her lips. "Could it be . . . ? Perhaps it's because . . . I think . . ."

"He loves me," Zara said with a dejected sigh.

"Bingo." Parvati joined her on the couch and handed her the spoon. "It's not something people can control."

"But why?" she moaned. "I was looking for his perfect match. And then we got a bit distracted by our sexual chemistry. But we both understood that it wasn't going to last forever. Nothing lasts forever. He would have gotten tired of having sexy times in all sorts of different places, and I would have gotten bored of having multiple orgasms, and we would have gone our separate ways."

"Except it wasn't just about sex." Parvati pulled the lid off a second ice cream container. "You had fun together. He went to see you rehearse because it's what you love to do. He took you to the City Club knowing that you'd go crazy when you saw Lin-Manuel Miranda. You—and I still can't believe this—went on a hike because it made him happy. That give-and-take is called . . . wait for it . . . a relationship."

"It's a disaster." Zara popped open her container. "He's emotionally vulnerable. His mom is in the hospital. He has PTSD. This is not the right time for him to fall in love." Her breath caught when an idea occurred to her. "Maybe he isn't really in love. It's just his illness talking. He thinks he loves me because he needs a connection, but now that I'm gone, he'll realize it wasn't real and we can go back to things the way they were. I should probably start looking for matches for him. I did promise to find him someone by the end of the season."

"I'm pretty sure that despite the fact he's not in a good place right now, his feelings for you are real," Parvati said. "His eyes light up when he sees you. When we were hiking, all he cared about was showing you the waterfalls and the flowers and the damn birds and plants. If Faroz hadn't kept pulling me into bushes and behind trees for hot forest sex, I would have been bored out of my mind. Jay wanted to share his joy with you. He wanted you to be happy. Do you know what Faroz said?"

"If you tell me, will you have to kill me?"

Parvati laughed. "He told me a long story about some CIA spies who met at Quantico but could never be together because they were always sent to different parts of the world. But every time they crossed paths, they realized their feelings hadn't changed. Finally, they quit the agency and got married. Of course, it ended badly as all Faroz's stories do. Some Russian agent found them and slit their throats while they were sleeping. But they died together. That's the point."

Zara glared at her. "That's the worst story I've ever heard. Was that supposed to cheer me up? Are you telling me that if I hook up with Jay, some Russian agent is going to come and slit our throats, but it's okay if we're dead because that's true love?"

Parvati sighed. "The point was they were meant to be together."

"I'm not meant to be with anyone. That's what I told him. I thought he understood that. I thought we were having a good time. And then . . ." She opened and closed her fist in the air. "Bombshell. I love you. Way to ruin a good thing."

"You do realize that you've never done this after any other breakup." Parvati licked her spoon. "There has never been any sobbing through *Les Misérables* while stuffing your face with ice cream. What do you think that means?"

Zara shrugged. "No one else ever said *I love you*."

"You never gave anyone else a chance." She put her feet up on the table and grabbed the remote. Usually Zara found something else to do when Parvati started flipping through crime shows and autopsy cases, but tonight they suited her mood.

She ate a spoonful of ice cream, but didn't register the taste. "So, you're saying it was opportunistic? If I'd given anyone else a chance, they would have fallen in love with me, too?"

Parvati paused at a true crime show. "I'm saying you let him in for a reason. You gave him that chance for a reason. Some part of you knew you could trust him with your heart. Now you're hurting because that's what happens when you love someone, and you can't be with them anymore."

When you love someone . . .

"Oh God." Her heart skipped a beat, stuttered in her chest. She knew this feeling. The sickening devastation of loss. The terror of the unknown. The uncertainty about a future in which love wasn't forever—it stopped.

At least she had thought it stopped.

But if it stopped, she wouldn't be here on the couch eating too much ice cream and preparing herself to weep uncontrollably from the start of Valjean's soliloquy to the moment he walked into the beautiful candlelight. Instead, she would be at her father's loft celebrating that one of her cousins got a B-plus on a test—her father used any excuse for a party so he could play his drums and dance.

"Parvati . . ."

"Took you a while." She scooped some more ice cream from her container.

"It hurts but it's not destroying me." She made a quick silent assessment of her body. No pain. No bruises. No restricted mobility. No weak joints or trembling hands. Yes, her heart ached, and yes, she felt sad. But with a little ice cream and some sorrowful singing, she had a feeling she'd be okay.

"That's because you're not eleven years old." Parvati settled on a rerun of *Autopsy: Confessions of a Medical Examiner* and relaxed back on the couch. "You are in control of your life. You can make your own choices. You can write your own story—or musical, since it's you we're talking about. You can give this one a happy ending."

"What am I supposed to do?" Her voice rose in agitation. "I crushed him, Parv. He said he loved me and I ran out of there like *Hamilton* tickets were on sale."

Parvati tore her gaze away from the chainsaw-wielding medical examiner. "I hope you didn't break anything on your way out."

Zara put the lid on her ice cream and returned it to the freezer. "I don't know how to do this. I don't know how to love someone. I don't know how to be loved in a romantic way. And why me? Why would he fall for me? I'm a disaster waiting to happen."

"Maybe he likes disasters," Parvati said. "Maybe he's wound up so tight he looks at you and sees a path to happiness. Maybe he sees what we all see. That you are utterly and completely worthy of love."

Emotion welled up in Zara's throat. She was saved from an embarrassing flood of tears when the ME on TV started his chainsaw and sliced into the body on the table. "I need to visit my dad. I want to ask him about the divorce. We never really talked about it, and I think before I make any decisions, I need to understand what really happened."

"Does that mean I can eat your ice cream?" Parvati held up her empty container.

Zara twisted her lips to the side, considering. "I'm not sure. I don't know how to walk this path. I think you'd better leave it for me. Just in case."

• • •

NESTLED in the middle of the Dogpatch, Zara's father's live/work space was the quintessential artist's loft. Built over three levels, it boasted high ceilings and an open floor plan, large warehouse windows and skylights, white walls awash with prints, and a polished concrete floor coated in paint splatters.

She greeted her relatives as she made her way to the kitchen, where aunties and uncles were gathered around a long table piled high with food.

"Beta! We were wondering when you would get here." Taara Auntie gave her a quick hug. "I made something special for the party. It's in the plastic container. Do you want me to put some on a plate? It's chimichanga samosa trout surprise."

Zara bit back a grimace. "Maybe later, Auntie-ji. I need to talk to my dad."

"He's in the studio warming up. Wait one moment before you go." She waved over Mehar and Lakshmi Aunties, who had positioned themselves at the far end of the table, away from Taara's containers.

"We were wondering how the security camera case is going," Taara said. "Have you filed any papers with the court?"

"It's not going very well," Zara admitted. "The partners don't think we have enough plaintiffs to make it worth the risk for the firm. I'm afraid we won't be able to run with it."

Taara Auntie frowned. "Not enough Patels? I told everybody about the cameras."

"When she says 'everybody,'" Mehar said, "she means everybody. Not just locally but across the country. Your auntie has a big mouth."

"Not as big as yours." Taara Auntie turned on her with a

scowl. "You told everybody about that incident with Lakshmi's eyebrows."

"It was you?" Lakshmi's voice rose. "No wonder my kiwi tasted sour this morning and I couldn't find my other sock."

"Maybe you shouldn't have shaved them off in the first place," Mehar retorted. "I don't know who told you that you always looked surprised, but you didn't look any different without them."

Taara shut them down with a warning shake of her head. "We need to think less about eyebrows and more about Zara and her case. What can we do to help?"

Zara shrugged. "To be honest, I don't even know if I'll be at the firm much longer. Things aren't looking good financially, and unless I bring in some clients, they might not be able to keep me."

"How many clients do you need?" Mehar pulled out her phone. "Ten? One hundred? Five hundred? One thousand? You tell your aunties and we'll get them for you."

"These are people we're talking about, not a few dollars to buy myself a treat."

"They are Patels." Taara Auntie's voice was firm. "And they have security cameras because I spread the word on my social media channels. We'll find them all and bring them to you so no other families have to be afraid in their houses and our Zara can have her job."

"It's a nice thought but . . ."

Lakshmi patted her hand. "It will all be good. Trust your aunties. Also, wear flat shoes. You'll never get where you want to go if you have to run in heels."

After leaving her aunties, she climbed the stairs and found her father in his studio, practicing his beats. He wore a long plain white kurta that went down to his knees and loose pants that gave him room to move when he was playing his dhol.

"I'm giving a show for the family to celebrate Darpan's good grade," he said. "I need some practice before I perform at Avi's wedding next week. I hear I'll be sitting alone at dinner."

"Who told you that?" Like she had to ask. The Patel gossip mill never stopped.

He grinned as he pounded softly on the drum. "You know how the family is. Everyone saw you with that nice boy at Rishi's wedding, the one who was at the gallery until you ran into the door. And then I heard you asked Mehar to look in on his mom at the hospital after she was in an accident. Once your aunties were involved . . ." He pounded out a drumroll. "It was all over for keeping it secret after that."

Zara bristled. "There is nothing to keep secret. We're not together."

"Why would you ask Mehar to visit his mom in the hospital?"

Zara shrugged. "I didn't want her to be alone. And I only mentioned it to Mehar Auntie. She was visiting a friend in the hospital and I saw her in the hallway. I told her about Padma and how she didn't have family and the next day Padma's room was full."

"Exactly." He punctuated the word with a loud bang on his drum.

"We were friends, Dad. We had a . . . thing."

"A thing?" He raised a brow. "Sounds serious."

"It wasn't. I mean it was, but it wasn't. The idea of getting that close to someone gives me hives. I don't want to spend my whole life just waiting for the day it's going to end."

"I married your mother believing it was forever," he said. "I loved her. I still do."

This was her chance. She'd never had the courage to ask him about the divorce, assuming it was a memory too painful to discuss. "What happened?"

With a sigh, he put down his sticks. "Your mom and I had much in common when we got together," he said. "We were both professionals, both first-generation immigrants, both focused on our goals and being the best we could be. My art was just a hobby then and something I planned to pursue when I retired." He removed his shoulder strap and put his drum on its stand. "Then I was in the car crash and my entire world changed. I lay in my hospital bed thinking that if I had died, I would have had only one regret—that I didn't pursue my dream. So after I recovered, I quit my job, built the studio, and started to paint." He paused to take a sip of water. "Your mother thought it was just a phase, but I had changed after the accident and she had stayed the same. She resented me for it. She said I'd emotionally abandoned her. She couldn't see what I'd seen—that life is short and you have to live your truth, embrace your joy, and pursue your dreams." He gave a wistful smile. "I wish I could have brought her on this journey with me."

"How did it end?" She'd known about her father's epiphany but not how her mother had felt betrayed.

"We were living an illusion because we couldn't face the reality that we had lost each other and didn't know how to find each other again. And then one day she decided it had gone on too long. I don't know why it was that day or why it was so sudden. She came home from work, walked into my studio, and told me it was over and it was time for me to go."

"I'm so sorry, Dad," she said softly. "I can't imagine how that would have felt."

He was silent for a long moment, staring down at his empty hands. "I only wish we could have given you and Hari some warning, let you get used to the idea, but I was in shock. I couldn't think. I loved your mother. She is a strong, intelligent, beautiful woman who used to sing like an angel and give Mehar a run for her money on the dance floor. But she lost herself in work and forgot what is important in life. If I could turn back time, I would still choose to marry her." His expression was almost wistful. "We had some good times together."

"But you would lose her again," Zara protested. "You would get hurt again."

"But I would have experienced love," he said. "And love is worth the pain."

· 26 ·

JAY was dreaming of being lost in the forest when someone shook him awake.

"How long have you been sleeping in the office?" Elias pulled the blinds, flooding the office with light.

"A couple of days." He sat up on the couch, rubbed his eyes. Truth was, he was afraid to fall asleep in his apartment without Zara there to keep the nightmares away. He'd come to the office on Saturday after visiting his mom and worked until he was so exhausted, he couldn't keep his eyes open. Rinse. Repeat.

"How's your mom?"

"Improving. She should be going home in a week or so. How are things going with Westwood Morgan?"

"Everything is in order." Elias pulled the last blind. "The board is meeting this week. Brittany says at this stage it's basically a rubber stamp of approval. She's looking forward to traveling around the world with you, opening up all those new offices. Kinda wish our board had picked me to be the CEO instead of the CFO. I used to hate the travel when I was deployed, but now that I've had my feet on the ground for so long, I kinda miss it."

"I'm sure we can work something out," Jay said. "If my mom isn't fully recovered when we start the international openings, I'll need to be here. No way I'm leaving her alone with Rick."

"You look like shit, by the way." Elias never pulled his punches.

"I'll hit the showers in the downstairs gym and change before the rest of the staff arrive. I've got extra suits in the closet."

Elias leaned against the credenza, thick arms folded, his words heavily weighted. "That's not what I mean."

Jay got the message. Elias had encouraged him to seek treatment before, but he hadn't had time for illness—mental or physical—when he had a company to build. He'd managed the nightmares like he managed everything else. With tight control, strict rules, and willpower. But this time it wasn't just about him. This time he had a reason to get well.

Jay dropped his head to his hands, elbows resting on his thighs. "I almost lost my mom. Again. Kinda threw me for a loop."

Not an easy admission, but then he'd made an even bigger admission to Zara. Anything else paled in comparison. He hadn't meant to tell her he loved her. Hell, he hadn't even realized it himself until he'd said it out loud. But he'd had a few days to think about it, and he acknowledged the truth of the words. She was the light in his life, the sun to his shadows. She was smart, warm, loyal, sexy, and funny and it was impossible to resist her sweet exuberance. Life was interesting and exciting when she was around. She made his heart pound just being near her, and he was damn sure he made her heart pound, too. But he needed to sort out his shit. He wanted to be the best man he could be. For her. For his mom. For Elias. And for himself.

"I've been there," Elias said. "Sand used to do it for me. We were in the desert when I was shot. After I came home, I couldn't go to the beach. I'd start shaking and break out in a sweat. It didn't make sense. There was no danger. It was all kids and beach umbrellas and ice cream and hot dogs. But that's the thing about PTSD.

You don't know when you're going to hit a trigger. And when you do, you need the tools to work your way through it."

"You were seeing a guy . . ." Jay drew in a ragged breath. Admitting he needed help wasn't as easy as he thought.

"Dave Richards. He's a psychologist at the VA clinic. He really helped me out. I'll give you his number." Elias grinned. "Tell him I went to the beach the other day and stayed there so long I got a fucking tan."

JANICE was playing Candy Crush when Zara walked into the office. She'd clearly just come in from a smoke and her clothes reeked of tobacco. "You've got a new-client meeting this afternoon. I've put it in your schedule. He says he's an actor." All this without lifting her head. But today, Zara didn't care.

"A celebrity client? Are you serious?"

"I said he's an actor." Her three-pack-a-day habit had given her voice a gravelly rasp that wasn't out of place in a firm with a tiger for a mascot. "I didn't say he's a celebrity. At least he wasn't until he got caught snorting coke off some skanky bitch's ass at a party. I looked him up online after he called. If that's the kind of law you're planning to practice, I'm going to have a word with Tony. I won't work in that kind of environment. I have standards."

"We just filmed a commercial where we're all roaring in a jungle of cartoon tigers," Zara pointed out. "Right now, Tony is contemplating whether we should wear tiger suits for the next one. Finances are so tight Faroz just chased an ambulance all the way to the hospital. The bar can't get much lower."

Janice gave an indignant huff. "Yeah, well, I won't be asking for his autograph."

"What's his name?"

"Bob Smith."

"I NEVER thought I'd be pulling out your card so soon after we met." Bob settled in the seat across from Zara. He looked like he hadn't slept for days. Lines of strain were etched into his brow, and his jaw was rough and unshaven. Dark circles under his eyes made them seem more prominent, and his skin was pale and blotchy. He wore a baseball cap and a puffy jacket, even though it was seventy-five degrees outside.

He looked better as a zombie.

"I saw you at the City Club party the other night," he said. "I remembered you were the tiger lawyer from the ads on TV."

"I'm glad they made an impression." She made a mental note to tell Tony the tiger should stay.

"I wanted to talk to you but you looked like you were in a hurry to leave." He removed his cap and ran his hand through his thick, dark hair. "I shouldn't have even been there. My agent thought it might help my image, but as you can imagine, everyone just wanted to talk about the pictures."

"What pictures?"

Bob pushed his phone across the table. "I'm sure it's all over the world by now. You know how the press gets when there's a celebrity scandal."

Celebrity scandal? Zara's heart drummed in her chest. This was it. Her first entertainment case with a client she'd brought in herself. Clearly nothing said *professional competence* like doing beer funnels while dressed as a zombie.

She studied the pictures on Bob's phone. "Is this . . . ?" She looked closer. Yes. It was the zombie bride who had tried to hook up with

Jay. Zara almost felt sorry for her. She could have had a wild night of sex in a limo. Instead, she'd wound up half-naked on a restroom floor with Bob Smith sniffing lines of white powder off her ass.

"It's in the news, the gossip columns, the blogs . . . everywhere. The utter destruction of my career is online for the world to see." He spat the words out, thin hands shaking as he pointed to the screen. Method actor. Definitely. If he managed to pull himself out of zombie hell he might actually make it to the B-list.

"That's me high on zombie dust in the restroom with the gal who was checking coats. She said she wanted to give me a special surprise before we went to the hotel for the after-party. I got a surprise all right. When the producers saw those pictures, they terminated my contracts for *Day of the Night of the Evening of the Revenge of the Bride of the Son of the Terror of the Return of the Attack of the Alien, Mutant, Evil, Hellbound, Flesh-Eating, Rotting Corpse Living Dead Parts 7 and 8: In Shocking 4-D.* They are even talking about cutting me out altogether and replacing me with a digital zombie. They said it's a family franchise and they don't want their lead star to be associated with sex and drugs." He toyed with his hat. "The whole thing is crazy. I'm a celebrity. What celebrity doesn't do drugs?"

Zara knew many celebrities who didn't do drugs, but this wasn't the time to share. She handed the phone back to Bob. "I'm sorry this happened but—"

"But nothing." Bob turned his furious gaze on Zara. "I hired J-Tech to take care of security and part of that was making sure no one got into the venue with a phone or recording device. They were supposed to check everybody and make sure all electronic devices were left at the door."

Jay's fault? She couldn't imagine he would make such a serious mistake. He was so careful about everything.

"I went through their screening," she said. "They were very thorough."

"Then explain this." Bob flipped the phone around to show her yet another unflattering picture, this one of him and the zombie bride doing the nasty over the sink. "I'm surprised it wasn't all over the BBC and other world news. Or maybe it was. I just can't read any other languages."

Zara doubted that a D-list celebrity with only a few credits to his name—one of them a failed kids' TV pilot about a superhero who had opened a microwave too soon and thereafter could transform himself into a bowl of soup—would be of interest to the BBC, but she wasn't as plugged into the celebrity world as Bob.

"My career is ruined," Bob spat out. "*Day of the Night of the Evening*—that's what we call the film because frankly the title is a mouthful—was going to be as big as the Marvel Universe. There could have been sequels and spin-offs and spin-offs of the spin-offs. And what about merchandising? My character could have been on everything from T-shirts to fuzzy blankets to those cute slippers that squeak when kids walk. I could have been immortalized in plastic. Maybe even wax. I should have just paid the blackmail money."

Zara's heart almost stopped in her chest. "Jay blackmailed you?"

"The dude who took the pictures got my e-mail address and tried to blackmail me for five hundred thousand dollars. I don't know who it is, but he clearly knows nothing about show business or how little we get paid. It was so ridiculous, my agent thought he was bluffing so we told him to take a hike, and look what happened. I called the police and they said there was little chance of finding him because everything was online."

"We have a good investigator," Zara said. "We'll do our best to find him and bring him to justice so he doesn't do this to anyone else."

"Justice?" Bob snorted. "I don't give a damn about justice. This business is all about reputation and now I've got none. Zilch. My name is dirt in the zombie world. I can't even be a children's entertainer. No one will hire me now." His snort became a snarl. "I need to make up that lost income. I've gotten used to living a certain lifestyle, and I'm not gonna give it up just because I was having a little fun. I definitely want to go after the blackmailer, but since the police were so sure I'd never find him, I was thinking I should go after J-Tech. After all, it's their fault. If they hadn't let the dude in with his phone, I wouldn't be in this mess. They're a national company. I'm sure they have deep pockets. I want to sue them for everything they've got. I could have made millions, maybe even billions if zombie toys became the next big thing."

Zara felt sick to her stomach. It was just her luck that her very first entertainment law case with a real-life celebrity had to be against the man who had introduced her to the client in the first place—the man who claimed he loved her. How could she betray Jay by turning that kindness back on him? And how could she act against J-Tech knowing that the company couldn't afford to get involved in a lawsuit? It would be the end of Jay's dream.

On the other hand, a high-profile lawsuit would secure her future in the firm and give her a foot in the door to the entertainment industry.

"How do you know Jay?" she asked, stalling for time. "I thought you two were friends."

"Our moms went through cancer treatment at the same time at the same hospital." He put his hat back on, tucking a few rogue curls under the band. "You get to know the people supporting the people when you're there all the time. He told me if I ever needed security for an event, I should give him a call. So that's what I did. After the filming was done, I offered to host the wrap party because I heard Keanu Reeves does that kind of thing and I fucking love Keanu."

She nodded in agreement. "Who doesn't?"

"I called in that favor from Jay and he set it up. I said no phones, cameras, or recording equipment. The A-listers always have that rule, and since I'm going to be A-list one day, I try to live my life like an A-lister would."

"That makes sense."

Bob's puffy jacket rustled as he sat back in his chair, one skinny ankle crossed over his knee. "He wouldn't have let a camera slip through if I was A-list. His reputation would be ruined just like mine has been ruined." He slammed his fist on the arm of his chair. "Well, fuck him. And fuck his company. And fuck whoever took those pictures. I'm going to sue them all and you're going to help me because you're fierce like a tiger." He roared so loudly Zara jumped in her chair.

Moments later Janice flung the door open. "What the hell?"

"Everything is fine." Zara took a breath to calm her racing pulse. "Mr. Smith is just enthusiastic about our firm mascot."

"Whew." She gave a sarcastic smirk and wiped a hand over her brow. "I thought there was an animal in here."

"I'm a method actor," Bob said, puffing out his chest. "It's understandable how you got confused. I spent a few hours this morning watching tiger shows and practicing the roar before I came here so I could understand your firm better."

"That's true dedication to the craft." Janice's voice dripped sarcasm, and Zara could sense more coming.

"We're all good here," she said firmly. "You can go."

"Does he do lions? Can he pounce?"

"Thank you, Janice. Close the door, please, on your way out."

"So how do we start?" Bob asked. "Do you want me to sign things? Do you need a retainer or something like that? I'm gonna make sure it hits the press the minute we file. If I'm going down, I'm taking J-Tech with me. This is going to be a big case for you. Huge. You're lucky I saw you at the City Club the other day, or another lawyer would have gotten the case."

Something niggled at the back of her mind. "I might have a conflict of interest," she said, thinking quickly. Maybe she wouldn't have to make the decision. Maybe it had already been made for her thanks to the Rules of Professional Conduct. "I can't represent you if there's any appearance of impropriety, and Jay and I—"

"Are you guys together?"

"Well . . . no." Because he'd told her he loved her and she'd run out the door. Because she'd realized she loved him and had no idea what to do with that. Or how to fix what she'd broken.

"So, what's the problem?"

Zara shifted in her seat. "We were . . . sort of . . . involved. For a short time. It wasn't serious . . ."

At least not to me.

"Ah. Bad breakup. I get it." Bob grinned. "So this is perfect. It's the ultimate revenge. He introduced you to me and now you're going to sue his ass."

She gave him a tight smile. Regardless of how badly she wanted this case, she didn't think she could betray Jay by taking Bob on as a client and turning around and *suing his ass.*

"I definitely came to the right place." Bob rubbed his hands together. "The tiger says it all. Fierce. Predatory. Powerful. Prince of the jungle. The other firms I visited were boring. All dark suits and solemn faces. None of them would dress up for a zombie party.

They don't understand the industry like you do. They don't understand this." He pointed to a framed picture of a tiger on the wall. "The killer instinct."

The other firms. He'd interviewed other lawyers before he had come here. If she turned him down, he'd just find someone else to take the case. And what if Jay's team hadn't been negligent? Would another firm conduct a thorough investigation or would they just start the lawsuit and leave it up to J-Tech to prove it wasn't their fault and in the process lose their key investor?

"I'll need to run this past one of the partners," she said. "I'll be back in a minute. I'll send Janice in with some coffee."

"Does she have any raw meat?" he called out. "I'm still in character."

She found Tony in his office and explained the situation.

"If you're not together then there are no professional-conduct issues," he said. "But you can't talk to Jay about the case or the client until the matter is resolved, and a relationship is out of the question. In fact, it would be best if you blocked his calls and messages until this is sorted. If you're wrong and J-Tech was negligent, that could mean years, or it would mean dropping the case and dealing with the financial repercussions."

"I was there," she said. "They were very thorough. They had all sorts of metal-detecting gadgets and four guards at the door checking bags. And something doesn't feel right about the pictures. How could Bob not see someone standing in the restroom with a camera? It wasn't very big."

"That's a lot of faith you're putting in your gut." Tony pulled out his lightsaber and gave it a swing. "If you clear J-Tech, and you don't find the person who took the pictures, you'll have put a lot of time into a case that goes nowhere. It would be better for your billables to sue J-Tech and make them prove they weren't liable.

Given our financial situation and your tenuous position in the firm, do you really want to take the risk?"

"Yes." She didn't even need to think about it. There was no way she was going years keeping Jay at arm's length. She loved him, trusted him, had faith in him. And she needed him to know it.

She just hoped he didn't find out that she was planning to *sue his ass* to save him.

JAY studied the e-mail from Chris Moskovitz's assistant with disbelief. *Contract canceled*. Because of a lawsuit against his company? He'd been staring at his screen for the last fifteen minutes but so far, the words hadn't changed.

"I got here as fast as I could." Elias burst into his office. "Jessica and I went for a lunchtime run in the park. She beat me again, but I'm doing sprints in the mornings so . . ." He trailed off. "What's wrong? What's the big emergency?"

"Were we served with notice of any legal proceedings?"

"Not that I know of."

"I called Lucia because she's our solicitor of record and she didn't receive anything, either. She's going to look into it and call me back."

Elias threw himself into the chair across from Jay's desk. His hair was still wet from his shower, his shirt clinging to his damp shoulders. "So, who's suing us?"

"Bob Smith. Apparently, someone got a phone into the zombie party venue and took some compromising pictures of him that he alleges have ruined his career. Chris heard about it and had his assistant cancel our contract. I called her up and she said he's just landed the role of a lifetime and he can't take any risks. They need a security company that can make sure no cameras or paparazzi get into their events."

"There's no way anyone got into the zombie party with a camera." Elias straightened in his chair. "We had four people on the door, and we were using a high-sensitivity metal detector—it can detect a phone inside any body cavity."

"Not an image I wanted in my head."

"Just saying. No. Fucking. Way."

Jay handed Elias his phone opened to the app where Bob's party pictures were splashed out on the front page. "The evidence speaks for itself."

Elias ran a hand through his hair, scattering droplets of water across the carpet. "How the hell did that happen?"

Jay had been wondering that himself. He trusted the members of his team implicitly. They were serious, professional, and conscientious. In all the years they had worked for him, they had never slipped up. That meant the mistake was on him.

"It had to be me. Zara was there. I was distracted . . ."

"No." Elias shook his head. "Not a chance. That's not you."

"Maybe it is. I don't know who the hell I am anymore." He'd had two sessions with the VA clinic psychologist, and they'd made a start unraveling his pain and guilt about the crash. It was going to be a long, slow process, but he'd taken the biggest step and he was committed to seeing it through to the end.

Elias studied the pictures. "Why is it such a big deal? I see pictures of celebrities like this all the time. It blows over quickly and for some it's good PR."

"The zombie movies are family films. Snorting coke off a naked woman's ass on a restroom floor isn't good for the image."

"What about our funding?" Elias said. "We still don't have

board approval. We're obligated to disclose any litigation pending against the company."

"I know." Jay sighed. "Just when everything was looking up, it all goes to shit again."

His phone rang and he took the call, motioning for Elias to stay when he heard Lucia's voice on the other end. He put the phone on speaker and they leaned in to hear what she had to say.

"It's bad news, I'm afraid. Though I did have an interesting conversation with Moskovitz's attorney. He was present when Bob told Chris about the security breach at the party. Apparently, Bob said he'd hired the best lawyers in the Bay Area to sue J-Tech. He called them the apex predators of the city."

"No." Jay was barely aware of the word coming out of his mouth. All he could feel was the chill of the blood in his veins, the slow pumping of a battered heart, and the soul-destroying crush of defeat. If Zara had wanted to send a message that it was truly over between them, she couldn't have done a better job.

"Yes," Lucia said. "Cruz & Lovitt."

After the call ended, Elias leaned forward, his face creased in disbelief. "Zara's representing Bob? Against us?"

"She knows what this lawsuit will do to our chances of getting our funding." Bile rose in Jay's throat, the sense of betrayal almost overwhelming. "I pushed too hard and she ran. I never imagined she would do something like this."

Elias stood, rubbing his temples with one hand. "What did you do to piss her off so bad?"

"I told her I loved her." He still loved her. Even though his heart was hurting, that was never going to change.

"Those aren't the kinds of words that make people turn around and stab you in the back," Elias said. "There's got to be more."

"Her job is on the line." His chest was so tight he could barely breathe. "She needs clients and entertainment law was her dream. It's why I introduced her to Bob and why I was going to take her to Moskovitz's birthday party. What haven't we sacrificed for this dream?"

"We haven't thrown anyone we cared about under the bus," Elias retorted. "I just can't believe it. Zara wears her feelings on her sleeve. It's all out there for everyone to see. She's not the kind of person to pull an underhanded move like this."

"Why are you defending her?" Jay snapped. "You hardly know her."

"Because you do know her, and you know something isn't right. I can see it in your face. I can hear it in your voice. Send her a message or call her. Find out what's going on. I'm sure it isn't what it seems."

Jay grabbed his phone and sent Zara a quick text asking her to call. He studied the screen and then showed it to Elias. "No delivery notification. I've been blocked."

"Maybe she's not staring at her phone," Elias said. "Try her office."

Jay called her office and the receptionist informed him that she'd been instructed not to put through any of his calls. "It's over," he said to Elias, his shoulders slumping in defeat. "Everything is over. The international expansion. The dream . . ."

And Zara. He'd pushed too hard and she was never coming back.

"YOU'RE staring at that seating plan like you want to destroy it." Dressed in an elegant green and gold salwar suit, Parvati leaned against the wall outside the dance hall where Avi and Soroya's sangeet was about to begin.

"Jay was supposed to be at my table but someone crossed out his name." She tapped the handwritten scribble. "I don't know how I feel about it. On one hand, it would have been awkward if he knew about the lawsuit. How would I have let him know I accepted the case solely to save him from an unscrupulous firm that wouldn't care enough to make sure they were suing the right company? On the other hand, what if he hadn't found out and he wanted to talk? I could hardly ignore him if we were sitting at the same table. And we do need to clear the air."

"Why are you worrying about it?" Parvati grabbed her and pulled her into a small alcove just as a group of aunties paraded by. "He's not going to be at your table. In fact, I don't see his name on any of the singles tables, so maybe he isn't coming."

Zara's breath caught in her throat. "What if he's at a couples table, Parv? What if I hurt him so badly that he decided I wasn't worth the effort anymore, and he found someone new? Oh my God! What if I have to see him with another woman? And then what if they hit the dance floor and he has incredible moves and it's all because of me? I'll be kicking myself for taking his love and throwing it in his face because I'm such a coward." She staggered back to the nearest wall. "I can't handle it. I can't be here if he's with someone else. It might even be too late. His mother wouldn't see me at the hospital the last time I went to visit. I think she knows what I did to her son."

"Get a grip." Exasperation showed on Parvati's face. "You'd better go to your table. I have to find Faroz and get to ours. He said he has to keep a low profile at big events because people from his past might try to kill him. I think he's been hiding in the restroom."

"'Ours'?" Zara checked the seating list. "We're not at the same table?"

"I decided at the last minute to bring Faroz as a plus-one, so I'm at the couples table tonight."

Zara sucked in a breath, her stomach twisting in a knot. "But we're singles. We don't belong at the couples table, Parv. You can't do this to me. You can't leave me alone."

"You won't be alone." Parvati's voice dropped to a soothing tone. "You can always come over and talk to me and see what it's like on the other side. I'm sitting two tables away. This isn't the reception. No one is really here for the food. We'll be at the table an hour at most and then we'll be dancing the night away."

"Beta! Look who is here!"

Zara's punishment for not moving fast enough to her table was Bushra Auntie and a skinny dude with a thin mustache and thick glasses who didn't look a day over eighteen.

"Bajaj is my cousin's husband's brother's uncle's boy here from New York. Thirty-two and already the CEO of a successful juice company." Bushra clapped her hands in excitement. "They have all juices: mango, apple, orange, pineapple, grape, carrot, cucumber, beet, cantaloupe, celery, cherry, clam, spinach, strawberry—"

"I've got it, Auntie-ji."

". . . wheatgrass, watercress, vegetable, plum, lychee, turnip, guava, tomato, and prune—I do like a nice glass of prune juice in the morning. Keeps things regular."

Zara cringed inside. Unlike most of her family who delighted in having long-winded discussions about body ailments, Zara liked to keep her personal troubles to herself. "That's . . . um . . . good to know."

"It's our best seller," Bajaj said. "We don't dilute it. One glass is the equivalent of eating thirty pitted prunes. You see immediate results."

Was it possible to be a worse salesman? Zara didn't think so. "Not something I've ever really wanted to try, but I'll make a note of that for middle age."

"Take this." He handed her his card, white with a picture of two wrinkled prunes in the background. "If you're ever in New York and need juice, just give me a call."

"Thank you." She tucked the card into her purse. "That's very kind. I do get thirsty from all that pollution."

"I've got some free juice samples in my car . . ." He smoothed his mustache and gave her an exaggerated wink. "Maybe we could sample them later." He said *sample* with a little roll of his shoulders and a shake of his oversize head.

Where was Parvati? Was the dude seriously trying to get it on with her in front of her aunt by luring her to his car with free juice? Parvati would have been in hysterics by now.

"Gosh. Thanks. I'm actually all juiced out for the day. And I'm . . . with someone." At least she would be if she could get the damn lawsuit out of the way and then find a way to fix things with Jay.

She would fix things. She was smart and capable and a damn good catch and she still had Lin-Manuel Miranda's name on her arm. If that wasn't lucky, she didn't know what else was.

PICKINGS were slim at the singles table. A barely legal cousin of the bride who claimed to be a famous influencer. Avi's work friend who was sweaty from his golf game and hungover as hell. A divorced aunt and a widowed uncle who had clearly been put together in the hopes that they'd keep each other entertained. Kamal on her right. A woman who looked like she'd walked off the set of an A-list film. And a dude in an expensive suit who looked incredibly bored.

After introducing themselves, they all sat in silence.

Kamal nudged Zara with his elbow. "Say something," he whispered. "Getting the conversation going is your thing."

"I'm not up for it today." She drained her third—or was it her fourth?—gin and tonic and looked around for a waiter to open the bottles of wine on the table. If it took any longer, she was going to crack them open with her teeth. Jay wasn't here and it was entirely her fault. He'd given her a gift, and she'd thrown it in his face. She needed a little something to numb the pain.

"Don't worry." Kamal patted her hand. "I'll handle it."

"Handle what?"

"So . . ." Kamal raised his voice loud enough for everyone at the table to hear. "Here we are at the singles table. They're probably expecting us all to hook up. Am I right? Who wants to get down and nasty? Pick someone and get it on."

"What are you doing?" Zara hissed under her breath. "You sound like you're doing bad stand-up comedy in a dive bar."

"I'm doing your job to help you out." Kamal smiled warmly. "I'll keep us all entertained so you can wallow in your self-pity. I heard you broke up with your boyfriend."

"I didn't have a . . ." The response was almost automatic but she caught herself again. She'd been afraid to say it, just as she'd been afraid to admit she'd fallen in love. "It's a temporary break. We have some things to work through."

"Did anyone go to a wedding in a cold place and jump into a lake naked and then not be able to have sex because the guy was too cold?" Kamal looked around expectantly and held up Zara's hand. "Only Zara?"

With a groan, Zara dropped her forehead to the table. "Please stop," she whispered under her breath. "I appreciate what you're doing but . . ."

"Zara!" Lakshmi Auntie hurried over to her chair with Bushra and Mehar Aunties behind her. "I saw a three-eyed crow!"

Bushra caught Zara's gaze and held up her hand, making the motion of bringing a bottle to her lips.

"She hasn't been drinking, Bushra," Mehar spat out. "Really. That's very unkind. She was watching *Game of Thrones*."

"I don't need to watch TV," Lakshmi protested. "My visions keep me entertained, and one them was of a crow with three eyes. It's a portent of doom."

"These are my aunts," Zara said to the fascinated table guests. "Don't mind them. Maybe Kamal can tell my story about shooting a dude in the ass at a bachelor party and watching him try to sit through the wedding dinner without wincing, and how I felt good about it because the dude was so officious and arrogant, but I didn't know at the time that he would turn out to be the best thing in my life and I threw it away because I'm a hot mess who is afraid of commitment."

"Is it your story or my story?" Kamal asked, frowning. "Maybe I should tell more about the skinny-dipping."

"And maybe Lakshmi can tell us more about doom," Bushra said dryly. "Whose doom are we talking about here? My doom? Zara's doom? Or are you just sharing helpings of doom all around?"

"Crow means flight," Lakshmi said to Zara. "Three eyes is—"

"Doom." Bushra shook her head. "Doom for everyone. This crow really is a downer."

"Lakshmi reads tea leaves, palms, faces, and horoscopes for a small fee," Mehar advised everyone at the table. "If anyone is interested, we'll be in the lobby after dinner. She also does weddings, henna parties, and bar mitzvahs."

"When did you start pimping out Lakshmi Auntie?" Zara asked Mehar. "I thought she only did that kind of stuff for family."

"She wanted to share her gifts," Mehar said. "I thought why not make money at the same time? You wouldn't believe how many people hear the doom speech and are motivated to turn their lives around."

"Sure. I get it." She heaved a sigh. "Who doesn't need a little doom in their life?"

"Are you single?" the uncle at the table asked Lakshmi.

"She's a gifted astrologer and life coach," an indignant Mehar sniffed. "And she makes soaps. She didn't come here looking for a good time."

"Yes, I did." Lakshmi smiled at the man. "I'm single. Do you like kumquats?"

Mehar and Bushra shared a glance. They were used to having their pick of eligible wedding bachelors of a certain age. Zara didn't think they'd ever lost out to quiet Lakshmi, who had always seemed content to watch the world go by.

"Save me a dance." The uncle pointed at her and then the dance floor while making a clicking sound with his tongue.

"Even Lakshmi Auntie can find a man," Bushra mumbled as she turned away to follow her sisters.

"Don't be so hard on yourself," Zara called out. "She probably saw it coming."

"This red wine reminds me of the story of how Cronus castrated Uranus—how is that possible? Ha ha ha—and threw his man parts into the sea, making lots of blood." Kamal was on a roll. "How about that red foam?"

"What god did I offend to be made to suffer through this?" she whispered to the man in the suit seated beside her.

He lifted his glass in a mock toast. "Welcome to the singles table. It looks like you're here to stay."

· 28 ·

"ARE you sure you're going to be okay?" Jay settled his mother on the couch in her living room.

"It's just a few breaks and bruises, and Rick will be here with me. I have lots of friends, Jay. They're doing a dinner train. We'll have more than enough to eat."

"Rick isn't in much better shape."

"We'll look after each other," she assured him. "You won't have to worry when you're away."

Jay adjusted her pillows. "I'm still not sure if I'm going. We reported the possibility of a lawsuit to our investors, and they've put off the board approval meeting until we find out if it's going ahead or not."

Part of him was relieved at the delay. It meant more time with the psychologist at the VA clinic, more time to work through his pain, more time to learn to accept the things he could not change and more time to evaluate his priorities. Zara had taught him that there was so much more to life than sitting behind a desk. He would never have imagined a world of vulva fruits, zombie parties, pirate musicals, footballs in courtrooms, celebrity galas, and role play without her. He would never have been tempted to dance in a Mexican restaurant or seduce a woman in his office. He never would have laughed as much, smiled as much, or felt as connected with someone as he had with her. Now that his life was just about work again, he realized how empty it had been.

Jay's mother settled back in her chair. "I still can't believe Zara would take a case against you. She came to the hospital every day I was there. I didn't know what I would say to her after you told me about the lawsuit, so I asked the nurse to tell her I was tired, but that just felt wrong. I know that girl in my heart, Jay. You have to talk to her."

"She won't take my calls or answer my messages. There isn't anything I can do."

"You could have gone to the sangeet last night."

He balked at the admonition in her tone. "Who would have brought you home?" He'd called Avi to let him know he wouldn't be able to make it because he had to look after his mom, but the truth was he couldn't face Zara. He'd never opened himself up the way he had with her, never imagined he would be so spectacularly shot down, or that she would turn around and make absolutely sure they couldn't be together. He'd given her space, but she hadn't come back, and their time apart had simply heightened his desire. He loved her. And only if she couldn't love him back would he be able to let her go.

"Jay," Rick called out. "Where's the remote? I started watching *The Great British Baking Show* when I was in the hospital and I wanna see the end of season two. The British are so fucking polite. Cakes fall, cookies burn, and barely a whimper. They smile on the outside, but inside you know they're shitting themselves. I want to see one of them break. A swear word or a shout. Maybe slam a spoon on the counter. Real drama. And while you're up, can you bring me some of those pastry things with the cream in them that Zara brought to the hospital? There's a couple of them left."

"She brought them every day," his mother said when Jay's jaw tightened. "And every day, all she talked about was you."

ZARA teetered on the windowsill when Faroz and Tony walked into her office, startling her. With one hand on the flimsy curtain rod and the other on her phone, she was precariously positioned. One wrong step and she would tumble to the ground.

"I told you she was one of us," Faroz said.

Tony nodded. "I knew it when she came to the interview with only one shoe."

"I got stuck in a grate." Zara stretched, trying to get her phone as high as possible. "How about some help here?"

"You seem to be handling it all just fine," Tony said. "What exactly are you doing?"

"I'm trying to take a picture of the crash test dummy lying on the floor in the corner." She pointed to the dummy they used in personal injury cases to show how a body moved or didn't move on impact. He had a sculpted head with two black button eyes and a movable torso and joints. Janice had dressed him in a low-cut POLE BITCH shirt and a pair of tiny jean shorts.

"Might I suggest a change of vantage point to someplace more secure?" Tony suggested. "Not that I want to interfere with your creative process but I don't think our insurance covers injuries that result from deliberately putting yourself in danger because you have a kinky crash test dummy fetish."

"I need this shot." She leaned forward and the curtain rod bowed and swayed. "It'll help me solve the case."

"Detectives solve cases," Tony pointed out. "Lawyers litigate them. If we solved all our cases we would have no way to make money."

"This one needs to be solved." She snapped a quick picture seconds before the rod broke. Zara lost her balance and fell but managed a save and landed on her feet.

"Nine-point-one for the roundoff finish." Tony clapped. "The Europeans voted as a bloc so your score is lower than expected."

She sent them both a look of disapproval. "It would have been a ten if I'd had a little help."

"I believe in people learning lessons the hard way," Faroz said. "That's how I learned not to stick my head in an oven."

"Really?" Tony gave him a curious look. "I didn't have to learn that lesson. It was one of those things I just knew. Like don't run into traffic or drink turpentine."

"Wish someone woulda told me about the turpentine," Faroz muttered. "Kept thinking I had indigestion."

Zara checked her shots and motioned for them to join her at her laptop. She clicked to the pictures of Bob and the zombie bride on the restroom floor.

"What do you see?"

"I see that you're into porn." Tony made a *tsk tsk* sound with his tongue. "To be honest, I would never have thought that about you. But to each her own. However, as managing partner, I feel it necessary to remind you that porn is not permitted in the office."

Zara tipped her head back and groaned. "This is our client Bob Smith and a woman from the zombie party. The pictures are his proof that someone got a camera into the party past J-Tech's security." She held up her phone. "Now, what do you see?"

"I see your dummy is positioned wrong," Faroz said. "He should be naked, on his front with his head on her—"

"Not that." Zara shook her head impatiently. "The angle. Where would the person who took the picture have to be standing?" She pulled out a 3-D scale drawing of her office. "I was in the restroom at the party venue a few times. It's slightly larger than my office. But to get a picture of the dummy from that angle, I would need to be at ceiling height." She flipped to another screen with pictures of the dummy taken from different angles.

Faroz studied the picture intently. "Maybe he had the camera on a selfie stick. Or he could have blown the pictures up."

"First of all, 'he' would have to be a 'she' because they didn't have gender-neutral restrooms and anyway I'm pretty sure someone would have noticed a nine-foot man standing in the corner. Second"—she flipped back to her pictures—"you can see where I blew these up. The angle still isn't right."

"Is this why you haven't filed a petition yet?" Tony asked. "You don't think the pictures are real?"

"I do think they're real, but something doesn't make sense. I need to visit the venue. It's all about perspective."

ZARA didn't waste time. Her first order of business when she arrived at the club was to make Faroz pretend to stand in line.

"Jay was here." She pointed to a spot beside the door. "And Elias was on the other side. They had the metal detector between them, and two guys inside at a table going through purses and bags. Every hour they would switch, and four different guys would take the door."

Faroz appeared less than impressed. "And I'm standing here . . . why?"

"I want to do a full walk-through as if you were someone trying to sneak in a phone from the line right through the security check."

Faroz sighed. "I'm no actor. I'll do the walk, but I won't talk the talk."

They inspected every inch of the building, searching for mail slots or places where a person could sneak in a phone. When they'd exhausted every option, they went to the restroom where the picture had been taken.

"Don't even think of asking me to lie on the floor and pretend to be Bob Smith," Faroz growled. "It's filthier than the swamp I had to hide in for three days in Vietnam." He held out his hand. "I'll take the pictures. You lie on the floor."

Zara lay down in Bob's approximate position while Faroz took pictures from various angles.

"Nope." He studied the pictures on the phone. "Whoever took the pictures was taller than me."

"How tall?" She glanced up, past Faroz's head, and spotted a camera in the corner of the room and gestured for him to look up. "That tall?"

"Yeah." He nodded. "Something like that."

With the manager's assistance, they got the unit down. She recognized the brand right away. "This is the same camera my aunties had." She looked over at the manager. "Is this the only one?"

"I've got them all over the bar and outside, too. I can watch the whole venue through my phone. We're a national chain with a hundred fifty clubs throughout the U.S. and I'm pretty sure they all use the same cameras. Never heard of any problems with them."

"Well, you've got a problem now." She handed the camera back to him. "A hacker took control of the camera and posted pictures of what was going on in this restroom online. You could be at risk of a lawsuit, and you may wish to pursue action against the manufacturers of the camera or the hackers when we find them." She handed him her card. "If you're interested in joining our class action, just give me a call. And please send my details to your head office if they want more information."

Almost giddy with excitement, she threw her arms around Faroz as soon as they were outside and gave him a hug. "Do you think you can find the hacker and find out who posted those pictures online?"

"I've got a contact in the FBI. Pretty sure he'll be able to help me out."

"You know what this means, Faroz?"

"No, but I'm sure you're gonna tell me." He gently loosened her grip and stepped away, putting a few feet between them.

"It means J-Tech wasn't negligent. It means I could have another client for my class action against the manufacturer of the cameras. It means justice for Bob." She clapped her hands together. "It couldn't be more perfect. Jay will never know there was a lawsuit pending against his company. Now I just have to figure out how to make things right when I see him at the wedding tomorrow."

"What does that mean, 'make things right'?" Faroz lifted an inquisitive brow.

"It means . . ." She twisted her hands together, considering. She'd been so focused on getting rid of the lawsuit, she hadn't thought through exactly how she would fix things with Jay. "I want things to go back to the way they were."

"That's the problem with the past." Faroz shrugged. "You can't go back. You have to move forward."

"I don't know how to do that. I liked what we had and then he ruined it by telling me he loved me. I thought if I apologized, we could pick up where we left off."

"Except now all the shit that's gone down between you is still out there." He shoved his hands in his pockets. "It can never be the same, but it can be something new. You just have to be brave enough to embrace it."

• • •

As far as baraats went—and Jay had attended dozens of them over the years—Avi's groom's procession put all others to shame. Tarun had hired a cable car to transport him to his ceremony. Rishi had arrived in a horse-drawn carriage. But Avi drove up to the wedding venue in a 2016 McLaren 650S Spider.

Jay had never thought about his wedding before, but if he ever did marry, the Spider was definitely the way to go.

With his focus on his duties as part of the wedding party, he wasn't tempted to look for Zara but part of him was still hyperaware of the slightest disturbance in the colorful crowd. Was that her spinning around a pole in a blur of blue and red? Or over by the entrance in a splash of teal and gold?

"Let's get a beat!" Tarun jumped on a low wall to amp up the crowd and a musician started a rhythm on his dhol drum.

"I thought you'd be the first one dancing," Tarun said, coming up beside him. "I heard you got your funding for your international expansion. Congratulations!"

Jay nodded his thanks. He still couldn't believe that the lawsuit had vanished as quickly as it had appeared—Lucia had phoned with the good news—and that Thomas had pushed through the funding. He hadn't been prepared for the bank to move so quickly, nor to have them insist that someone accompany Brittany to London the very next day to start making arrangements for the opening of their first international office.

They followed the crowd to the ceremony, and then returned to keep an eye on the Spider until the rental company came to collect it.

"Kinda wish I'd gone for something like this instead of the cable car." Tarun ran his hand over the gleaming red hood. "I don't know what I was thinking."

Jay laughed. "You were thinking quirky. Nothing wrong with that."

"If you and Zara got hitched, what would you have for your baraat? It better not be something like this. I won't be able to handle the jealousy."

"I don't know what's happening between us," he admitted. "I've got some stuff I need to work out and I guess she does, too. She's better off with someone else."

"Sorry, man." Tarun clapped him on the back. "After I saw you two together at Rishi's wedding I thought you had something that was going to last."

"So did I." The lawsuit was gone, and with it the sense of betrayal. Elias was right. Backstabbing wasn't Zara's style, and he couldn't believe she'd resort to something like that simply because he'd told her he loved her.

"She would love this car." He opened the door and peered inside at the sleek black leather interior. He could imagine Zara in the driver's seat, windows down, hair blowing in the wind, pedal to the floor. Just the thought brought a smile to his lips. He missed her. He missed her laughter and her energy. He missed her crazy stories and her impulsiveness. His life wasn't the same without her in it.

He checked his watch and gave Tarun a nod. "I'm heading to the airport. Let Avi know I've gone."

THE entire day had been a disaster.

First, Parvati had forgotten to tell Zara that she'd been called into work. Since it was her job to wake Zara in time to get ready for the baraat, Zara didn't wake until the baraat was over. And that meant she'd missed a chance to see Jay. By the time she got to the scenic golf club where the wedding was taking place, the ceremony had already started and she had to stay in her seat, which made it almost impossible to find him among a crowd of hundreds. In the hours that followed, she'd wandered through the garden hilltop, and in and out of the golf club restaurant, wondering if he had come to the wedding at all.

"Beta!" Taara Auntie waved her over to the parking lot, where a group of aunties were gathered around a silver minivan. "I have something to show you."

"Is it drugs? You all look very suspicious. Are you dealing out here?"

"It's better." She opened the hatch. "Here you go," she said, pointing to boxes filled with security cameras. "You said you needed more plaintiffs. These are just from local people. Bushra has a spreadsheet of names from all over the country. One thousand of them."

Speechless, Zara picked up one of the cameras—the same brand of camera she'd found in the club. "You collected all these?"

"After I told people what had happened to me, they didn't want them, so I sent some of the young people to pick them all up. Each one has the name and address of the purchaser on it, and I've told our family in other states to send them to your firm and do the same. Is this enough to save your job, beta? And to start the case?"

"It's more than enough." She threw her arms around Taara Auntie. "I don't know what to say. Thank you."

"Don't thank me," Taara Auntie said. "I was the one who told them to buy the cameras in the first place. Once I spread the word on social media about the hacker, everyone wanted to help."

"Has anyone seen Jay?" she asked. "I've been looking for him everywhere. I need to tell him about this and talk to him. There are things I need to say."

"Tarun's unloading equipment just over there." Bushra pointed him out. "He might know."

Zara chatted briefly with Tarun about Maria and his honeymoon and his life as a newlywed before she lost her patience and cut to the chase. "I'm looking for Jay."

Tarun leaned against the door. "He said you were suing his company. Is that right?"

Her heart skipped a beat. How had Jay found out? "Yes. No. It's complicated. We're not suing his company anymore. But, oh no, Tarun. If he thinks I am . . . I didn't think he would find out. I need to find him right away."

"He's at the airport," Tarun said.

"Oh my God!" Her hand flew to her mouth. "Lakshmi Auntie was right. The three-eyed crow." She pulled out her phone and sent Jay a flurry of messages all while running back to the van where her aunties were packing away the cameras. "I need to get to the airport. Whose van is this?"

"Mine," Bushra Auntie said, pulling open the door. "What's going on?"

"Jay is leaving the country. I have to catch him. I have to tell him I didn't mean to sue his company. I need to tell him I'm sorry, that I was scared of commitment because of the divorce, that I didn't think I believed in love, and I'm an idiot, and I love him."

"Those are all good reasons for a high-speed chase." Mehar pulled open the door and the aunties piled inside.

Bushra took the wheel, and Zara slid in beside her.

"Let's rock and roll." Bushra started the car. "If we're fast we can have our adventure and make it back in time for dinner."

Zara looked over her shoulder. "Does anyone have flat-soled shoes?"

THE first time Jay was paged he thought the airport was looking for a different Jay Dayal. His name wasn't that uncommon and it was an international airport. The second time they called his name, he noted they weren't calling Jay Dayal for a flight, but to report to customer service. The third time, since the plane was delayed and he had nothing to do, he decided he might as well check to make sure it wasn't him they were after.

He made his way down to the customer service desk and his breath caught in his chest. The last person he'd ever expected, and the only person he wanted to see, stood by the counter.

"Jay!" Dressed in a red and gold skirt with a matching top that left her midriff bare, her feet tucked into a pair of thick white running shoes, Zara raced toward him, heedless of the people in her way. She knocked over a paperback book stand, tipped a pile of luggage, and startled a man into dropping his ice cream cone. And still she came.

"Jay! Don't go!"

Go? There was no going. His feet were firmly planted on the floor, his eyes locked on Zara as she flew through the airport toward him, dark hair streaming down her back. Had he ever seen a more beautiful sight?

For a moment, he thought she'd slow to a stop. They would look at each other, and she would say what she'd come to say, and he would have to respond that he was broken inside but on the mend, and he wanted her but only if she wanted him. But this was Zara. And she didn't stop until she was in his arms.

It would have been romantic if her momentum hadn't carried them back. He stumbled, hit a cart, and they went down in a pile of luggage and red silk.

"Are you okay?" Somehow, he had managed to keep her safe, holding her tight as he took the fall.

"Yes." Still wrapped in his arms, she looked up. Her lips were close enough to kiss and he was tempted, so tempted to taste her once more. Was he a fool to want her even after she'd so brutally pushed him away?

After they'd stood and straightened their clothes, Jay drew Zara over to a quiet corner under the stairs.

"Why are you here?"

"You can't go," she said. "You can't leave. Not until I explain."

Hope flared in his chest and he crossed his arms to keep it in check. "I know about the lawsuit."

"I know. That's why I had to come. Client confidentiality meant I couldn't even tell you Bob had come to see me. I took the case because I knew you weren't negligent, and if I didn't take it, Bob would have gone to someone else who wouldn't care that there might be another culprit when there was a defendant with deep pockets right in front of them. I knew that would mean the end of your funding, the end of your dream. So I took the case to make it go away."

His brain was struggling to keep up, but he got the key message. She'd been trying to help him.

"I figured it out," she said. "There was a security camera in the restroom and it was hacked. It was an inside job. You're in the clear."

Her words took one layer of hurt away, but not the other. "That's good to hear, but—"

"I did it for you, Jay." She cut him off, her voice urgent. "I did it because I love you."

I love you. Maybe he hadn't heard her right, or maybe she was acting, or maybe she was just telling him what she knew he wanted to hear.

"I know I hurt you," she said. "You made me feel things I'd never felt before. I didn't know what to do with them. I was so wrapped up in the fact love could end, I didn't realize when it was beginning." She was hugging herself now, hands wrapped around her middle, shifting her weight on her enormous white shoes like she was expecting to be rejected all over again.

So he closed the distance between them and took her in his arms. She was as soft and warm as he remembered and she smelled of wildflowers and fresh ocean air.

"I wanted to be loved," she murmured against his chest. "But the closer people got to me, the more terrified I was of getting hurt. I pushed people away because I didn't know how to be loved. I didn't think I could love you the way you deserved. But you just kept coming back." She looked up, her eyes deep, dark, and dangerously intense. "I didn't believe that anything could be forever, but this feeling, this love, I can't imagine it ever going away."

She loved him. She loved him and she wanted it to last. He wrapped one arm around her waist and cupped her nape with his other hand. He kissed her softly, gently, taking his time because he wasn't worried he would lose her. This love wouldn't end.

"Say it again." He nuzzled her neck.

She knew exactly what he wanted. "I love you. I might still get scared sometimes and push you away, but—"

"I'll still be here," he said. "I'm not going anywhere."

"Well, you are." She looked around. "When is your flight?"

"It's not my flight. I'm picking up Avi's uncle. He's flying in from Delhi and his plane was delayed."

She shuddered in his arms. "You're not leaving?"

"I already made arrangements for Elias to do most of the international travel. He and Brittany have hit it off. I just couldn't leave my mom and I couldn't stop hoping that we could work things out. I'm also seeing someone about my PTSD and I'm committed to seeing it through to the end. I want to be the best man I can be. The best Jay."

"You are the best man. You're my man."

"And you're my heart." He jerked his head to the side. "We have an audience. Do they belong to you too?"

"My aunties. They saved the day. Bushra Auntie even gave me her shoes." Her smile softened. "We should get back to the wedding."

"I'll be there as soon as Avi's uncle arrives." He gave her one last kiss. "Maybe you can find some seats for us at the couples table."

WRAPPED up in Jay's arms for the last dance of the evening, Zara snuggled against his chest listening to Ben E. King sing "Stand By Me." "This is hands down the best wedding season I've ever had."

"Because of me," Jay said, his voice smug.

"Mostly because of you."

He stiffened. "Why not all because of me?"

"Well, for starters, we wouldn't be here if Tarun and Maria hadn't gotten engaged and decided to have a paintball party. And if you hadn't been so arrogant and officious, I wouldn't have shot you in the ass and you wouldn't have noticed me. I would have been just another scantily clad woman prancing through the forest."

He nuzzled her neck. "I noticed you the second you ran onto the field screaming, *I'm heeeeeere.* I thought to myself, *That's my kind of woman.*"

"You did not."

He brushed a kiss over her forehead. "Maybe I had a few different thoughts, but I couldn't take my eyes off you."

"Except when I was crawling behind you in the forest, staring at your ass."

Another smug smile. "She likes my ass."

She reached down to give him a squeeze. "It's a nice ass, as you are very well aware."

He rocked her from side to side to the music, his arms tightening around her. "What other things do you like about me?"

"I like how you fish for compliments when your ego is already so big I have to step around it."

"That's not the only big thing I have," he whispered in her ear.

"Jay." She mocked a frown. "You're ruining our dance with your filthy sex talking."

"You like my filthy sex talking." His voice dropped to a low rumble. "You like everything about me. You came running through the airport in giant-size auntie shoes to stop me from getting on a plane. If that's not worthy of a musical number, then I don't know what is."

She tightened her arms around him. "I thought I was going to lose you. I had no choice. You're my Jay and I had to find you."

"You never lost me." He pressed a soft kiss to her forehead. "I love you and this love won't end."

"Even when you thought I was trying to destroy your company?"

"That was slightly disconcerting . . ."

Zara made a mental image of this moment: the soft music, Jay's strong arms around her, the scent of his cologne, the way his eyes never left her as if he could watch her forever. "Does this mean I'm free of the singles table?"

"I can promise as long as you're with me you will never have to share your naked chess and skinny-dipping stories again."

"Jay?"

"Yes, sweetheart?"

"I didn't find you a match."

"You found someone better," he said. "She brought light to my darkness and joy to my soul. She gave me love and laughter and happiness. She's perfect. And she's mine."

· EPILOGUE ·

ONE YEAR LATER

STEPPING down as CEO of J-Tech was the best decision he had ever made, Jay mused as he zipped up his camo coveralls.

First, it meant he could keep his boots on the ground in the city and continue his treatment at the VA clinic. Coming to terms with his past meant no more nightmares. No more nightmares meant more sexy times in bed. More sexy times in bed meant a shortage of condoms. A shortage of condoms meant an unexpected surprise. And that meant a proposal at the place where they had first met so they could have a shotgun wedding.

Zara had worn camo—no more stained dresses for her. She'd bought her own weapon—a Tippmann Alpha Black Elite—so she could join him and Elias at their monthly game. She had no idea that he planned to propose that sunny Saturday afternoon. In retrospect, he should have given her warning. She'd pulled the trigger in shock and shot him in the chest. But it had all worked out in the end. Six months later the bruise had healed, and they had a small wedding at the Conservatory of Flowers with seven hundred of Zara's closest friends and relatives, Jay's mom, Rick, and a handful of Jay's friends. They bought a house in Richmond, close to his mother and Rick. Marmalade stayed with Parvati, her new housemate/bedmate Faroz, and a collection of vulva fruit paintings that

Faroz thought were better than the lost Picassos he'd uncovered in a Moroccan art sting.

Second, inspired by Zara's work on her class action lawsuit and the clear need for digital security to protect the software that had been hacked by a seventeen-year-old boy in his mother's basement, stepping down as CEO meant Jay could work on expanding J-Tech into cybersecurity, ensuring they would be able to ride the new technology wave. But only on weekdays. Weekends were for family.

Third, his reduced hours meant he had more time to look after little Zayn so his mother could focus on being the best lawyer and community theater star she could be. She was trying out for Maria in *West Side Story*, and going by the beautiful lullabies she sang every night, he was sure she'd get the part.

He looked down at his son sleeping in the baby carrier against his chest. Almost four months old, he was too heavy for his mom, so now baby carrier outings were Jay's responsibility. Not that he found it a chore. He would have carried Zayn around all day if Zara would have let him, but their house was constantly full of relatives desperate to hold him. Little Zayn had even brought Zara and her mother together and they'd all spent many evenings and weekends talking through the issues that had driven them apart.

Finally, giving up his CEO duties meant Jay could be on the paintball field for another of Zara's cousins' bachelor-bachelorette parties, and this time he was out for revenge.

"I'm heeeeeeere." Zara came running through the field to the practice range. Dressed in camo, her hair tied back in a ponytail, she was even more beautiful now than the first day they'd met.

"The cake is in the fridge. Food platters are ready. I got a job offer from Lucia and I turned her down. There's extra milk in the car for Zayn—"

"Whoa. Back up." Jay held up a warning hand. "What do you mean you got a job offer from Lucia?"

"She heard that my class action suit settled and saw my interviews in the news. She said I was still the kind of lawyer she was looking for. She offered me a good salary and access to her celebrity clients. She said she could make me an entertainment-law star."

"It's what you always dreamed about."

She pressed a kiss to his cheek and one to Zayn's head. "I have everything I need right here. And I'm not planning to leave Cruz & Lovitt anytime soon. They're my people. They gave me a chance. They believed in me. And they're quirkier than I am. They're also willing to listen to my ideas to expand the firm and make it a little less . . . tiger." She gave a little roar and mocked a scratching claw.

"Method acting?"

"I learned from the best." She grinned. "Bob was so happy with the settlement, he gave me a few lessons. He was rehired for *Day of the Night of the Evening of the Revenge of the Bride of the Son of the Terror of the Return of the Attack of the Alien, Mutant, Evil, Hellbound, Flesh-Eating, Rotting Corpse Living Dead Parts 7 and 8: In Shocking 4-D* and he got a part in *Zombies in Paradise 6: Return of the Day of the Night of the Living Undead Dancing Mutant Zombie Chicken-Loving Strippers: In Glorious 4-D*. He's huge now, and he's referred all sorts of celebrities to me. And this morning . . ." She bounced up and down in excitement. "I got a call from Chad Wandsworth! He still had my card from the day I spilled a milkshake all over my boobs. Can you believe that?"

Jay could indeed believe it, and he didn't like the idea of the Man of the Year staring at a card and thinking about his wife's breasts. "I hope you told him to get lost."

"Darling, your possessive side is showing, and I have to say it turns me on."

"Not in front of the baby." He put his hands over Zayn's ears to shield him from Zara's naughty talking.

They walked over to the practice range and Zara zipped up her coveralls. "Why are you wearing camo?" she asked.

"You didn't think I'd come to a paintball field and not play? I asked to be put on your team."

"Not with a baby, you're not."

Jay laughed. "Your mom is just parking the car. She's going to take him for the afternoon. I couldn't give up a chance to get my revenge for the last time we played at a bachelor-bachelorette party. Someone is getting shot in the ass today and it isn't going to be me."

Zara leaned up to kiss him. "That was a fun time."

"It was the best time." He pulled her close so he had his entire family in his arms. "It was the day I met you."

Acknowledgments

Writing this book during a global pandemic was a challenge. Some days it was hard to be funny. You can only watch so many videos of cats and cucumbers before your laughter becomes a snicker becomes a sigh. If not for all the people in my life who supported me and bought me treats, I might still be watching those videos today.

My mom, dad, and siblings, who encouraged me to tell endless stories on long car trips as a source of free entertainment. Gee, thanks.

Sarah B. and Alice, my childhood friends who are always the first to like my social media posts no matter how self-aggrandizing they are. You guys rock!

Anne, my rock and good friend, who makes me run up mountains both physical and metaphorical without a GPS.

My editor, Kristine Swartz, for her insight, wisdom, and constant inspiration in the department of delicious baked treats. And the entire team at Berkley—Brittanie, Jessica, Lindsey, Randie, and many more—who designed such a beautiful cover, helped me polish the story, and launched it into the world with all the fanfare an author could want.

My agent, Laura Bradford, who excels at soothing savage beasts, aka authors in a panic, and telling them all the nice things they want to hear.

My husband and children, who have learned how to forage for food and clean clothes and how to entertain themselves because MOMMY IS WORKING. All very useful skills in the event of a zombie apocalypse.

And to the cucumber-hating cats: I still think you're funny.

Photo copyright Linda Mackie Photography

Sara Desai has been a lawyer, radio DJ, marathon runner, historian, bouncer, and librarian. She lives on Vancouver Island with her husband, kids, and an assortment of forest creatures who think they are pets. Sara writes sexy romantic comedy and contemporary romance with a multicultural twist. When not laughing at her own jokes, Sara can be found eating nachos.

CONNECT ONLINE

SaraDesai.com

Ready to find
your next great read?

Let us help.

Visit prh.com/nextread

Penguin
Random
House